THE WINE OF DREAMS

Even when they had all contrived to clamber up from the boats that had brought them, the newcomers were no more than six in number, sent against a company of defenders that still numbered nearly a hundred, but these were monsters of a far more extravagant kind than any the defenders had seen before.

They were six-limbed, their hindquarters being reptilian save for the fact that they had massive stings like scorpions. Their forequarters had the merest hint of humanity about the articulations of their arms, but these were clawed like those of the horned beastmen. Their heads were insectile, with large compound eyes, but their mouths were like circular sphincters from which huge tentacular tongues extended like writhing snakes. They were huge, longer and taller than horses.

These enemies, unlike their predecessors, were silent – which allowed Matthias Vaedecker the opportunity to be heard again.

'Blademen fall back!' he was screaming. 'Bowmen, shoot! Flood the fiends with arrows! Now! Now!'

Also from the Black Library

GOTREK & FELIX: TROLLSLAYER
by William King

GOTREK & FELIX: SKAVENSLAYER
by William King

GOTREK & FELIX: DAEMONSLAYER
by William King

GOTREK & FELIX: DRAGONSLAYER
by William King

SPACE WOLF
by William King

SPACE WOLF: RAGNAR'S CLAW
by William King

GAUNT'S GHOSTS: FIRST & ONLY
by Dan Abnett

GAUNT'S GHOSTS: GHOSTMAKER
by Dan Abnett

HAMMERS OF ULRIC
by Dan Abnett, Nik Vincent & James Wallis

EYE OF TERROR
by Barrington J. Bayley

INTO THE MAELSTROM
edited by Marc Gascoigne & Andy Jones

REALM OF CHAOS
edited by Marc Gascoigne & Andy Jones

STATUS: DEADZONE
edited by Marc Gascoigne & Andy Jones

A WARHAMMER NOVEL

THE WINE OF DREAMS

Brian Craig

A BLACK LIBRARY PUBLICATION

Games Workshop Publishing
Willow Road, Lenton,
Nottingham, NG7 2WS, UK

First US edition, December 2000

10 9 8 7 6 5 4 3 2 1

Distributed by Simon & Schuster
1230 Avenue of the Americas
New York, NY 10020

Cover illustration by Adrian Smith

ISBN 0-7434-1158-7

Set in ITC Giovanni

Printed and bound in Great Britain by
Omnia Books Ltd, Glasgow, UK

See the Black Library on the Internet at
www.blacklibrary.co.uk

Find out more about Games Workshop
and the world of Warhammer 40,000 at
www.games-workshop.com

Chapter One

One of the first things Reinmar Wieland had learned after assuming his adult duties was that the early afternoon was always a quiet time in a wine merchant's. Eilhart was a town dominated by convention, and convention dictated that the housewives of the town did their shopping early, while the milk and meat were still fresh and the best vegetable produce was still to be found on the stalls in the market square.

Wine did not, of course, need to be bought while it was fresh. Quite the contrary, in fact; the very first of the many slogans that his father Gottfried was attempting to drum into Reinmar's head held that 'good wine matures well'. Like all the other slogans it was subject to all kinds of exceptions, the value of an individual flask depending on its source as well as its age, but that did not prevent Gottfried Wieland from intoning the words as if they were holy writ. Nor did it inhibit the housewives of Eilhart from shopping for their measures of Reikish hock at the same time as they shopped for all the day's goods, in the early morning.

The consequence of that habit, for Reinmar, was that he had to rise at six and take his station at the counter before the bell in the tower of the corn exchange chimed seven. This would not have been so terrible had he been able to bolt the door of the shop when the market stallholders packed up their goods and trestle tables and set off home, which they invariably did before four in the afternoon. Unfortunately, the wine shop always had a second busy period at dusk, when labourers, journeymen and apprentices would begin to wend their way home from their various kinds of work. This was the time when all those among them who fared for themselves – the unwed and widowed who were inconveniently boarded – would provision themselves for the evening.

Wine was twice as necessary to customers of the second kind as it was to the members of larger and more careful households, because they had to eat the worst meat and the most worm-ridden vegetables. A swig of wine between mouthfuls of food lent great assistance to their palatability.

In the Empire's great cities, Reinmar's father had informed him, all manner of spices were available to disguise the rottenness of poor meat, but such luxuries were much harder to come by in Eilhart than in Altdorf or Marienburg. 'For which you and I should be profoundly grateful,' Gottfried Wieland had added, 'for it increases demand for our product, and hence its value. You will doubtless hear other traders wondering aloud why the Wielands have never attempted to extend the scope of our business further north than Holthusen, but the towns further down the Schilder are easily reached by the riverboats that ply their trade along the Reik – and lie, therefore, on the fringe of a much bigger and much more competitive marketplace. Whenever you hear our own boatmen cursing the difficulty and tedium of steering barges through the locks between Eilhart and Holthusen – and you will, when you learn that aspect of the trade – you ought to give thanks, for that is what secures our virtual monopoly of local business, and keeps at bay the spices that would reduce demand.'

It was, alas, hard for Reinmar to be grateful when the chief effect of this second wave of daily custom was to delay closing the shop until he was sorely tired. It was not so bad in the depths of winter, when dusk fell before the market bell chimed five, but in summer the light lasted for a full three-quarters of the day and outdoor labourers were kept so hard to their work that they would still be staggering through the door – invariably carrying a fearsome thirst – at three hours to midnight.

Reinmar had, of course, suggested to his father that the shop could be closed for a few hours early on summer afternoons without any noticeable loss of profit, but Gottfried Wieland was not the kind of man to take such suggestions well.

'Close the shop!' he had exclaimed, as if the notion were the rankest heresy. 'No noticeable loss of profit! What kind of tradesmen would we be if we were not available to our customers at any hour at which they cared to call? This is the Empire, my boy, not Estalia or Tilea. We are civilised folk, and industrious too. Can you possibly think that life is difficult because you must sometimes stand at a counter for fifteen hours in a day? What of the folk who toil in the fields and the forges? What of the men who load and unload the barges, or the men who go up to the forests to cut wood and burn charcoal? Our life, Reinmar, is extraordinarily good and easy by comparison with the great majority of men, and it is honest toil that has made it so. We are not aristocrats, to be sure, but there is a dignity and purpose in trade which cannot be valued too highly. Carpenters make chairs, cobblers make boots and tanners make saddles, but tradesmen make money. There are men abroad in the world who resent tradesmen and affect to despise them as usurers in disguise, but it is our great fortune to live in Eilhart, where even the common folk recognise that no finer thing can be said of any man than: *he makes money*. And of all the wares in which a man might trade, there is none finer than wine. Cheap wine makes life tolerable to the poor, and good wine is the best of all the pleasures available to the comfortably off.'

Gottfried Wieland always emphasised the first word whenever he pronounced the phrase 'good wine'. He was so besotted with his merchandise that he seemed to consider its finest fraction to be virtue in liquid form. The local constables and the town magistrate had been known to take a different view of the poorer fraction favoured by the town's admittedly tiny criminal element, but their low opinion did not impress Gottfried in the least. 'Drunkards will drink no matter what,' he would say, waspishly. 'Better they should intoxicate themselves with honest wine than anything worse.'

Reinmar did not know exactly what the words 'anything worse' were supposed to signify, but he knew that the Wieland shops did not stock schnapps, and that Gottfried always pronounced the words 'Bretonnian brandy' as if he were spitting acid. To Reinmar, Bretonnia was a fabulous place – the substance of travellers' tales. Its boundaries lay no more than forty leagues to the south, as the eagle flew, but one had to be an eagle to get there because the Grey Mountains were virtually impassable hereabouts; there was no convenient pass nearer than the Axe Bite, which lay forty leagues to the east.

One day, Reinmar knew, he might go downriver as far as the Schilder's confluence with the Reik – but no further than that, if he were content to be a dutiful son. In the daydreams with which he whiled away the slow afternoons, however, he often toyed with the notion that once he had gone so far from home it would be easy enough to take a westbound boat to Marienburg or an eastbound one to Altdorf. Perhaps he would never see Bretonnia, but he would see civilisation at its finest: a world in which a free man might make the most of his freedom.

In his daydreams, Reinmar longed to be free. In his daydreams, he yearned for a better world than one in which achievement was measured in honest toil and virtue in good wine.

The hope of one day being able to defy his father's sterner advice was what carried Reinmar through every lonely hour that he had to spend standing by a counter in an empty shop, and that hope increased with every year that went by as his fourteenth, fifteenth and sixteenth birthdays passed. As he grew older, his duties were further extended, and so was the intensity of his frustration. 'It's always the way,' his grandfather would say, when he took leave to complain. Even his grandfather, who seemed to be perpetually at odds with Reinmar's father, had become grudging with his sympathy of late – but he was an old and sick man, who regularly demanded far more sympathy than he was prepared to offer. Reinmar's nearest neighbour and closest childhood friend, Marguerite, was infinitely more generous but had lately become far less imaginative.

'But it is always the way,' she told him. 'That's what life is like.'

Reinmar's seventeenth year was the first in which manning the shop had become a full-time occupation with no allowance for any part of his education. Even his training in the arts of self-defence, which he had always enjoyed, was now considered to be complete. From now on, if Gottfried Wieland had his way, Reinmar's work would be Reinmar's life. Sometimes he wondered whether he might not do better to take his skills to the city and become a soldier in the Reiksguard. Reinmar had, of course, always known that the family business would become his work, but while he still had opportunities to play he had not anticipated the crushing weight with which responsibility now seemed to bear down upon him. As the days of his seventeenth year lengthened from winter to spring and from spring to summer the shop was transformed in his imagination into his prison, and he began to fear that once he was fully committed to it he would never be released.

Apart from his daydreams, however, there was one prospect to which he could look forward and whose anticipation saved him from despair. When the crops had ripened in the summer sun and the harvest was gathered in he would go up into the hills with Godrich, his father's steward, taking sole responsibility for the very first time for the purchase of this year's vintages.

The time soon came when he began to count down the days to this expedition, and the countdown in question inevitably came to seem exceedingly slow, but Reinmar could not help thinking of it as the countdown to a moment of decision: the moment when he would have to settle his own mind once and for all as to whether he would accept the life that his father had designed for him, or whether he would hazard everything in following one or other of his speculative dreams.

He always assumed, as he mulled this matter over, that the choice was his alone and that it would be freely made – but he had known no life other than the everyday life of the townsfolk of Eilhart, and he had innocently taken it for granted that a life of that kind was an unchanging and unchangeable ritual, safe from all disruption.

That assumption was, of course, quite false.

The afternoon on which Reinmar's countdown reached single figures for the first time was a particularly vexatious one. The weather was exceedingly warm and sultry, and the atmosphere in the shop seemed as thick as soup. The morning rush had ended early because the town's housewives had not wanted to linger too long outside on such a day.

To make matters worse, Reinmar had offended Marguerite two days before. He had charged her with 'pestering him with trivia', and he knew from long experience that unless some powerful motive intervened she would avoid him for at least three days. Although he and Marguerite had been the best of friends since the beginning of his memory, Reinmar was far from certain that he wanted their friendship to develop further in the way that everyone – not least Marguerite – seemed to expect. She was a pretty girl, after her bland and blonde fashion, but not as pretty as the dark girls with exotic eyes that Reinmar often saw in the square on market days, selling metal trinkets and medicinal charms.

While Marguerite stayed away, though, there was no relief from boredom available to Reinmar but daydreaming, and even his daydreams seemed to have grown stale from recent overuse. The comfort that he usually found in fantasies of flight and adventure was not to be found on that particular day, and in the absence of that comfort he had grown irritable and desperate. By the time the customer came into the empty shop, when Reinmar should have been glad for any distraction, his mood was too bad to be lightened by anything so slight.

Had the customer seemed more interesting in himself, Reinmar might have been able to rouse himself from his ill humour, but the only interesting thing about the man, at first glance, was that he was a stranger. Reinmar had plenty of time to study him while he prowled the racks, peering at the goods on offer. He was short – hardly half a hand's-breadth taller than Reinmar – and somewhat stout. His hair was dark, but not uniformly black, and there was two days' growth of black beard staining his jowls. The quality of his clothes suggested that he was more likely to have arrived in Eilhart by barge than in a carriage, although he was not costumed as a stevedore. His hands did not seem to be marked by habitual use of ropes or tools, nor did his face have the leathery appearance given by long exposure to the sun, but he certainly did not have the look of a gentleman.

Reinmar was not good at guessing any man's age, but this one posed a particular puzzle; he might have been anywhere between thirty and sixty. His eyes were narrow, dark brown in colour but startlingly bright whenever they caught the shafts of sunlight that filtered through the narrow windows.

The stranger looked like the kind of customer who knew exactly what he was looking for, although he obviously could not locate it in the racks, but Reinmar's mood was so bad that he let the man carry on looking for a full five minutes before his patience finally gave out.

'May I help you, sir?' Reinmar said, four minutes later than politeness and good tradesmanship demanded.

'You might,' the stranger said, coming to the counter as soon as the offer was made, 'if you can fetch Luther Wieland.'

Reinmar blinked in astonishment. Luther was his grandfather, and had been forced by his ill health to surrender the running of the business to Gottfried before Reinmar was born. The old man had been bed-ridden for the last six years.

'That I cannot do,' Reinmar said. 'My father – Luther Wieland's son – is in charge of the shop nowadays, and even he is not at home at present. I fear that there is no one to help you but me, but if you care to tell me what it is you want, I am sure that I can find it. I know my way around the cellars.'

The stranger stared at him, not in a hostile way but rather discomfitingly. 'Gottfried's boy,' he murmured, pensively. 'Gottfried's boy, and almost grown. What's your name, lad?'

'Reinmar.'

'Reinmar, eh? Very well, Reinmar – are you telling me that Luther Wieland is dead and buried?'

'No sir. But he has been in poor health for a long time. He takes no active part in the business.'

'What about Albrecht?'

Reinmar blinked again. Albrecht was Luther's brother, but Reinmar could hardly remember the last time he had come to the shop, and Gottfried rarely visited his house, which stood some way apart from the town. There had been some trouble between them, although Reinmar had no idea what had caused it. His father did not seem to like or approve of Albrecht, but Reinmar had no idea why, because Gottfried never mentioned the subject.

'Albrecht never had any part in running the business,' Reinmar told the stranger, uneasily.

'But he has a stake in it, does he not?' the stranger was quick to say. 'Albrecht is part-owner of the shop.'

'I believe he was at one time, many years ago,' Reinmar admitted. 'But to the best of my knowledge, my grandfather bought out his brother's interest long before I was born. My understanding is that when my grandfather dies, my father will inherit everything – everything in this house, that is. Albrecht has his own house. I believe he lives alone, except for an old gypsy woman who serves as his housekeeper. I'm sure that I would have heard had he died, so I assume that you can find him at home if you want to see him, but he is even older than my grandfather and might be just as poorly. I haven't seen him since I was nine or ten years old. I doubt that I'd recognise him if I ran into him in the market.'

'A close family,' the stranger observed. 'What a marvel of stiffness these little provincial towns are, where quarrels can last a lifetime and old friends can pass one another in the street every day, refusing to speak because of some long-forgotten insult that city folk would think utterly trivial.'

The contempt in his voice was not calculated to improve Reinmar's mood. 'What is it you want, sir?' Reinmar asked, pronouncing the final word as if it were an insult rather than an honorific.

The stranger took another step closer, and leaned across the counter in a confidential manner.

'What I need, Reinmar Wieland,' he said, in a voice hardly louder than a whisper, 'is a flagon of dark wine.'

Chapter Two

'I AM PREPARED to pay the market price, since it seems to be required,' the stranger added. The tone of his voice suggested that he did not think it should be required.

'I don't know what you mean by dark wine,' Reinmar told him, flatly.

'You said that you knew your way around the cellars,' the stranger said, resentfully.

'So I do,' Reinmar replied, with equal asperity. In actual fact, he did not know his way around the cellars half as well as his father thought he should, but he was certain that Gottfried had never mentioned 'dark wine'. The wines of Bretonnia, it was said, were red instead of white, but no one in Eilhart would ever have deigned to drink Bretonnian wine while good Reikish hock was available. The most colourful wines in the shop were sweet dessert wines made from grapes that had stayed on the vine till their skins had shrivelled to raisin-brown, but they were straw-coloured and Reinmar had never thought of them as 'dark' or heard them described in such a fashion.

The stranger had withdrawn slightly in the face of his uncertainty. 'Boy or not,' he said, in a low voice, 'you're the heir apparent. You should know your stock.'

'I do,' Reinmar insisted, again.

'There's nothing to fear,' the stranger said, leaning closer again. His dark eyes stared with a brightness that was surely unnatural, given that their lids were so heavy. 'I'm your cousin, if you hadn't guessed – or your father's cousin, at any rate.'

'My father has no cousins,' Reinmar retorted, annoyance giving him a steadiness that he might otherwise have lacked. 'My grandfather had but one brother, and my grandmother was an only child. Albrecht never married.'

'No,' the stranger said, his lips forming a humourless smile. 'Not the marrying kind, my father – but he acknowledged me nevertheless. If I am not known here, even in rumour, it must be Luther that kept the secret, for I am certain that my father wrote to him from Marienburg to tell him the news. I'm your cousin, in truth – but I have already told you that I'm willing and able to pay the full market price for the goods. If you cannot bring Luther to me, then you must take me to him. He will set your mind at rest.'

'He will not,' said a new voice, speaking from the door that connected the shop to the living-quarters of the house.

Reinmar and the stranger turned their heads simultaneously. Reinmar was surprised to see his father, having expected him to be out on business for at least two hours more.

'Cousin Gottfried,' said the stranger, easily. 'I'm glad to meet you, at long last.'

'I have no cousin,' Gottfried replied coldly. 'What is it you want?'

'He asked for dark wine,' Reinmar put in, anxious to avoid any accusation that might materialise regarding his apparent failure to do his job properly. 'I told him that I did not know what he meant.'

'Which was true,' Gottfried said, still speaking in a cold tone that he usually reserved for his servants when they had earned his most extreme displeasure – and occasionally for his son, when Reinmar had done something he reckoned very wrong. 'We have no such thing in our cellars.'

'Come now, cousin,' the stranger said, meekly. 'I assure you that you can trust me – and if you doubt me, there are things I could say to Uncle Luther that would set his mind at rest. Will you insist that I return in company with my father, when I had hoped to arrive at his house bearing an appropriate gift? I bring news – bad news, alas, but news that you ought to hear.'

'We do not keep the wine you want,' Gottfried said, firmly. 'We have not kept it for twenty years and more. No one in Eilhart keeps it now. There is none to be had for ten leagues in any direction.'

'You will forgive me if I take leave to doubt that,' the stranger said, smiling. 'Perhaps I should take my news to someone who will be grateful for the warning.'

Reinmar pricked up his ears at the mention of the word 'warning' but Gottfried was not to be tempted or intimidated. 'I will not give you leave,' he said, with all his typical sternness. 'No one in Eilhart doubts my word, and I expect a similar courtesy from strangers. I would be greatly obliged, sir, if you would leave my shop and never return. There is nothing for you here. Nothing. We are respectable tradesmen.'

The stranger murmured something that even Reinmar could not quite catch, although it might have included the phrase 'a contradiction in terms' – but the dark man was quick enough to draw back, and then to turn towards the door that led out to the street. 'Very well, Cousin Gottfried,' he said, as he opened the door and made ready to step out. 'I shall have to go to my father empty-handed – but if you never see me again, it will be the result of his instruction, not my desire. Will you tell me how to get to his house?'

'If it will be rid of you, I'll be glad to,' Gottfried said, ungraciously. 'Go up the hill until you pass the bounds of the town, then take the pathway that goes away to the right. Go through the gap between the two farms and on for a further five hundred paces. You'll see the slate roof of Albrecht's house on the upper slope, nested in the firs. If you miss the path you'll find your way easily enough – the ground's not treacherous.'

'Thank you, cousin,' the dark man said. 'I'm sorry that you did not want to hear my news. Good day to you, Reinmar.'

Reinmar might have replied had he not caught his father's eye, but the rejoinder died on his lips. The stranger stepped out into the street and closed the door quietly behind him. Reinmar found, somewhat to his own amazement, that his bad mood had evaporated, to be replaced by a fervent curiosity. It was the most exciting sensation that had possessed him for as long as he could remember.

The silence that fell when the stranger's footsteps had died away was profound. Reinmar resisted the temptation to demand an immediate explanation from his father, contenting himself with watching the elder Wieland carefully as he moved uneasily around the shop, making a show of peering into the racks as if taking stock. For several minutes Reinmar was prepared to assume that his father would eventually relent, but the older man's body became gradually less tense and still he kept silent.

Reinmar's mother had died when he was a small child, and Reinmar had always wanted to believe that Gottfried's lack of emotion was a defensive mask forced upon him by the loss of a beloved wife, but now he wondered whether the chill might have set in long before that. In the end, Reinmar could contain himself no longer. 'Did Great-Uncle Albrecht have a son while he lived in Marienburg?' he asked. 'Could that man be your cousin?'

'No one in Eilhart knows or cares what Albrecht got up to in Marienburg,' Gottfried replied, brusquely. 'We are respectable folk.'

Reinmar had only the vaguest notion of when Albrecht had gone to Marienburg or when he had returned, both events having taken place before he was born. No one had ever told him in so many words why Albrecht and Luther had quarrelled, but he suspected that it must have had to do with the business. Presumably Albrecht had felt that there was more to life than shopkeeping and had gone off to 'seek his fortune', leaving Luther to learn the ins and outs of the trade much as Reinmar was now doing. If that had indeed been the way it was, Reinmar could easily sympathise with Albrecht, but he had no brother of his own, and his father would be only too glad to remind him that Albrecht had not, in the end, found or made 'his fortune'. At some later date the prodigal had returned to Eilhart to live, by which time he no longer had any financial stake in the business and no friends in the town, where he had settled again as a virtual stranger. Nowadays, he was a recluse; even if Reinmar had been able to recognise him, the probability of 'running into him' in the market square was negligible.

'What is this dark wine that he wanted to buy?' Reinmar wanted to know. 'Do we have any in the cellar?'

'No we do not,' Gottfried replied, his coldness turning to passionate heat with alarming suddenness. 'It were best you had never heard of it, but since you have, you must believe me when I tell you that there has been none in this house for twenty years. We do not keep it and never shall.'

'Why? Because it is Bretonnian?'

'Bretonnian! It is worse than that, Reinmar. We do not keep such liquor.'

'But you did once,' Reinmar pointed out, inferring the obvious. 'Or grandfather did, in the days when you were his apprentice.'

'What my father did when I was your age does not concern you,' Gottfried said firmly. 'There has never been anything within these walls to taint your life or harm your soul, and so it will remain while there is breath in my body. I cannot deny that your great-uncle exists, since he lives little more than an hour's walk away, but his connection with this house was severed many years ago and can never be repaired. He has no legitimate kin, so we have no cousins in law – and this is a house in which the law obtains its due respect.'

'Are you saying that Great-Uncle Albrecht's house is one in which the law is not respected?' Reinmar asked curiously.

'I am saying that the dead past need not concern you,' Gottfried repeated. 'We do not keep the produce for which that man was enquiring. If he calls again while I am not here, send him away immediately. He is not to be allowed to linger here, and he is not to be allowed to see my father. Do you understand?'

'Not really,' Reinmar said.

'Then you must obey without understanding,' was the absolutely typical reply. 'I have said what there is to say.' To make that abundantly clear, Gottfried stamped back to the door which gave access to the stairway leading up to the bedrooms, and slammed it behind him.

Reinmar absentmindedly raised his hand to tug at his collar. His throat was dry and the warm air was so heavy that it seemed to require twice the usual effort to draw an adequate measure into his lungs. He was not in the least surprised by his father's unwillingness to tell him more, because there were a great many issues on which Gottfried Wieland was apt to offer opinions as if they were beyond all possible dispute. Yet most of the others were matters of propriety and etiquette. This was the first time Reinmar had been squarely confronted with the awareness that his family had secrets, although now he was forced to consider the fact, he realised that there were other clues he might have noticed, had he been more observant.

While Albrecht had hardly ever been mentioned, the fact that he was hardy ever mentioned had not seemed particularly significant. But now the matter had been so sharply raised the omission took on a new significance in Reinmar's thoughts. There was also the matter of his grandfather's illness. There was nothing unusual in the fact that the old man was an invalid who never left his room – there were at least four other houses in the neighbourhood whose attics played permanent host to an aged grandparent whose name had become legend – but Reinmar had observed since taking up his new duties that whenever older clients of the shop felt obliged to ask after Luther's condition there was always a slight discomfort or embarrassment in the pronunciation of his name. Although the customers always took care to say that they were pleased when he reported that his grandfather was no worse, they did not always contrive to match their facial expressions to their words. The impression Reinmar had gained was not so much that his grandfather was disliked as that the old man was feared.

As to the mystery of the 'dark wine', Reinmar had not the slightest idea what might lie behind it. What could his father possibly have meant by 'worse than Bretonnian'? Why had the stranger been so insistent that he was willing to pay the full market price for the product? What was the news that Gottfried had refused to hear, and why was there a warning in it?

Reinmar was still mulling over these mysteries when the shop door opened again and a second stranger came in. This man was much taller and paler than the first. He was dressed in clothes which were of better quality, though they were even duller in hue, being almost entirely black. His eyes were blue; his slightly hooked nose made them seem hawkish. Reinmar had never seen an eagle at close range, but this man seemed to have something of the eagle about him.

The second stranger barely glanced about him before coming to the counter. He reached into his pouch and brought forth a folded piece of parchment. He opened the bottom flap to reveal a patch of dark red wax into which a seal had been impressed.

'Do you recognise this?' he said.

'No,' said Reinmar.

'It is the seal of Grand Theogonist Volkmar,' the stranger informed him loftily.

Reinmar had heard the name of Volkmar before, although he had only the faintest idea of what a Grand Theogonist might be. Volkmar, so rumour had it, was a famous warrior who rode into battle on the War Altar of Sigmar. He was reputed to be the second most important person in the Empire, after Emperor Karl Franz himself – which presumably meant that any document on which his seal was set conferred considerable authority upon its holder. What the hook-nosed stranger was trying to impress upon Reinmar, therefore, was that he was a man of vast importance – certainly greater than the burgomaster of Eilhart and probably greater than the baron in whose fief the town lay. Reinmar had never seen the baron, who seemed to spend all his time in Altdorf.

'Is it?' was all the reply he could contrive.

He did not mean to seem sceptical, but the black-clad stranger took umbrage anyhow. 'Sigmar protect me from the ignorance of peasants!' he exclaimed, with a world-weary gesture. 'What is your name?'

Reinmar sensed that it would be unwise to point out that he was not a peasant. The stranger obviously knew already exactly what manner of man he was.

'I'm Reinmar Wieland,' Reinmar said, as politely as he could. 'Would you like me to fetch my father, sir? I believe he's at home.'

'Have you been at this counter all day?' the stranger demanded.

'Yes sir,' Reinmar admitted.

'Then it's you I want answers from, Reinmar Wieland. Since it seems to mean nothing to you, I ought to explain that this warrant entitles me to demand honest answers, and that any failure to give them is punishable by the severest penalties. I am the Grand Theogonist's special agent. My name is Machar von Spurzheim. Think carefully before you answer me. Has this shop been visited today by a man not known in these parts, perhaps half a hand's-breadth taller than you and rather portly, with near-black hair and a dark complexion?'

Reinmar took full advantage of the invitation to think carefully before he replied, but in the end he said, 'Yes.'

'When?' Von Spurzheim shot out the question like an archer loosing an arrow.

'Perhaps half an hour ago,' Reinmar told him.

'What did he want?'

Reinmar had anticipated the question, and had made up his mind that he would not hesitate. 'He asked for something called dark wine,' he said. 'I had never heard of it. My father came in while I was explaining that, and told the man that we did not stock such a thing.' He knew that he was being slightly economical with the truth, but instinct told him that it was the safest course when dealing with a Grand Theogonist's special agent.

'Is it true that you do not stock dark wine?' the black-clad man demanded.

'It is,' Reinmar confirmed. 'I asked my father what dark wine was, and he would not tell me, but he said that it was something in which we do not deal and never shall. He was very adamant about it.'

'Was he indeed? And did he tell the customer where else he might obtain what he sought?'

'No sir. He told him that there was no other possible source. There is no other wine merchant hereabouts – the nearest shop is in Holthusen, and that is ours too. Some of the vintagers who supply us will sell wine directly to their neighbours and occasional visitors, but I never heard of one who made dark wine and I have lived my whole life in and above this shop.'

'Fifteen years!' von Spurzheim scoffed.

'Sixteen, sir,' Reinmar corrected him, 'and nine months.'

'Do you know where the man went when he left the shop?'

'I heard his footsteps going along the street,' Reinmar said, with the utmost care. 'He had turned left outside the door and he was going uphill, in the opposite direction to the market square.' It was absolutely true, so far as it went.

'Good,' said the agent of the Grand Theogonist. 'I have taken lodgings at the burgomaster's house. If you see this man again send word to me, or to the sergeant in command of the men-at-arms at the inn on the market square – or, failing that, to the local constables.'

With that, he turned on his heel and left.

CHAPTER THREE

REINMAR WASTED NO time in running upstairs to find his father, but Gottfried insisted on coming down with him before hearing what he had to say. Gottfried Wieland was a great respecter of rules, and the cardinal rule of shopkeeping was never to leave the shop unattended. Once the two of them were back amid the display stock, however, the older man listened very attentively to Reinmar's account of the second visitor – and Reinmar watched his father's face grow deathly pale.

'Who is he?' Reinmar asked, as soon as he had told all he knew.

'A witch hunter,' Gottfried replied, in a low tone. 'An important witch hunter, if he carries the Grand Theogonist's seal, although I doubt that he got it from Volkmar himself. It's bad enough that there is any interest at all in Altdorf in this affair, although I suppose there will always be interest in Altdorf whenever evil in Marienburg is mentioned. No one now alive remembers the secession, but Wilhelm's heir is ever watchful. Did this witch hunter say how many men-at-arms he has with him? No, of course not – but if he can lodge them at an inn there can hardly be many. More might be coming, though, now that he knows that he is on the right track. Did you mention Luther or Albrecht?'

'No,' said Reinmar. 'It did not seem politic to reveal that the stranger called me cousin. Did I do right?'

'You did right,' Gottfried confirmed, although there was no hint of fatherly pride in the confirmation, 'but if he corners his quarry the relationship will come out anyway, and it would only require one ill-spoken word...'

He broke off abruptly as the door to the shop opened yet again. This time it was Marguerite who came in. She had found a reason to cut short the period of quarantine to which her wounded feelings had condemned poor Reinmar. 'Reinmar!' she said, breathlessly. 'There are soldiers in the square – they rode in on big black horses. They came with a witch hunter, it's said, hunting an evil magician who stowed away on a barge from Holthusen! That was the witch hunter himself who left your shop a few minutes ago!'

Reinmar did not know quite what to say to that, but probably would not have been allowed to get two words out in any case before his father intervened. 'I'll thank you not to bring gossip into this shop, young lady,' Gottfried said. 'And I'll thank you not to talk about our customers, whose business is their own.'

Marguerite looked crestfallen, but her excitement was irrepressible.

'Did he speak to you, Reinmar?' she asked, breathlessly.

'Yes,' Reinmar said – but he had no time to add anything else.

'That's none of your business,' Gottfried said. 'And the witch hunter's business is none of ours, thankfully.'

It seemed, though, that he was wrong. Marguerite was still holding on to the door, having been unsure of her welcome since the moment she had first seen Gottfried standing next to Reinmar. Now she was pushed gently but firmly to one side as two armed men entered the shop. Reinmar did not recognise the colours they were wearing; all he knew for sure was that they were not the Baron's.

'Gottfried Wieland?' one of them enquired, politely enough.

'That's me,' Gottfried said.

'Could you possibly come with us to the burgomaster's house, sir?' The spokesman was still speaking with a courtesy that seemed perfectly sincere. 'My sergeant, Matthias Vaedecker, would like a word with you, if you wouldn't mind.'

'Are you arresting me?' Gottfried asked, uneasily.

'By no means, sir,' the man-at-arms was quick to reply. 'But your name has been given to Sergeant Vaedecker as that of a man who might be able and more than willing to help him. Will you come?' There was no hint of a threat in his tone, but Reinmar knew from his accent that he was a city man, and he had been told often enough that city men did not always say what they meant, or let their meaning show in their manner.

'Yes,' Gottfried said. 'I'll come with you. Reinmar, be sure that you keep the shop open till nightfall. You must not leave the counter under any circumstances. Do you understand me?'

'Yes, father,' Reinmar said. He wondered, though, whether he did understand. He already knew that he had to keep the shop open till nightfall, and that he must not leave the counter. The fact that his father had taken the trouble to make the instruction explicit and to emphasise it so strongly must have some further significance – in fact, the words must have been spoken for the soldier's benefit rather than for his.

Reinmar and Marguerite watched silently as Gottfried went out of the door with the two men-at-arms, who turned right towards the market square as he closed the door behind him.

'Why do they think he can help them?' Marguerite asked Reinmar, when the silence became unbearable.

'I don't know,' Reinmar replied. 'But who knows more about a town than its only wine-merchant? Who better to consult as to its secrets?'

'Eilhart doesn't have any secrets,' Marguerite said, faithfully reproducing the common opinion of the region. 'It's a nice town. There's none nicer or safer anywhere in the Empire.' She spoke as if it went without saying that there could not possibly be anywhere nice or safe outside the Empire's bounds.

The sense of being in the nicest and safest town in all the world had always seemed to Reinmar to make the quality of his prison that much more treacherous, and to increase the sense he had had for more than a year of being trapped in a life for which he might be direly ill-suited. 'Yes it is,' he agreed. 'It always has been, and probably always will be.'

Reinmar could hardly wait for night to fall, so that he could steal up the stairs to his grandfather's room and interrogate him. In the meantime, he wavered between hoping that Gottfried would stay out of the way long enough for him to learn whatever Luther cared to reveal to him and dreading that his father might not return at all, having been thrown in jail on suspicion of having consorted with evil magicians.

Marguerite stayed with him for an hour, chattering about the possibilities opened up by the arrival of the witch hunter and his escort, but Reinmar easily resisted the temptation to tell her that the mysterious stranger they were hunting was his father's cousin. She went away again, having had no occasion to take further offence at his treatment of her, when the second wave of customers began to arrive in the shop, intent on trading rumours as well as buying wine.

Reinmar knew better than to trust the rumours entertained by labourers, who rarely knew anything and were ever wont to fantasise, but he could not help suffering pangs of anxiety when he was assured that the stowaway was a necromancer from the Cursed Marshes west of Marienburg, a sailor who had gone mad while cast away on a haunted islet in the Sea of Claws, or a daemonologist from the Howling Hills who had unleashed a host of evil spirits into the streets of Altdorf. He had no idea what a necromancer or a daemonologist was, and he suspected that his wide-eyed informants had no better idea than he, but the titles seemed pregnant with horrible disaster.

Just as the rush was easing, Machar von Spurzheim returned in the company of four armed men, one of whom he introduced to Reinmar as Sergeant Matthias Vaedecker.

'Your father has graciously offered to allow us to search his stock,' the witch hunter informed Reinmar. 'He assures us that he has never placed any dark wine in his cellars, and we believe him, but he shares our anxiety that there might be some hidden corner where old stocks lurk of which he knows nothing.'

The statement was, of course, absurd. Gottfried Wieland knew every jug, jar, cask and flagon in his cellars, and was not a man to tolerate the existence of hidden corners or unevaluated stock. If Gottfried had given von Spurzheim permission to search, his intention must be to clear away any slight shadow of doubt that might remain in the witch hunter's mind as to his innocence of any dealings in 'dark wine'.

'I will show you the way,' Reinmar said. He did, and lit all the lamps that were grouped at the foot of the stone stairs so that every last corner of the mazy cellars could be illuminated at will. He stayed to watch, as Gottfried would have wanted him to do, while the five men prowled the multitudinous racks, removing the stoppers from stone jars so that they might sniff the contents and turning the spigots on wooden casks to let drops fall onto the palms of their hands. They were not wasteful, nor did their tentative sampling of the produce lead to the least intoxication.

The search would have been quicker had all the wines in the cellars been kept in transparent bottles, but only the finest wines were ever dignified thus, and usually only in the shop itself. Glass was too precious a commodity to be wasted, and customers who were slow in returning their empties for reuse were always treated with prejudice. Gottfried Wieland was well known for his sternness in keeping count of such errors of omission, and for the infallibility of his memory.

Machar von Spurzheim insisted that Reinmar open every cupboard and chest, while Sergeant Vaedecker used the hilt of a dagger to rap on every wall, listening raptly for any hollow echo. The whole process lasted nearly two hours, but at the end of it the visitors seemed satisfied.

'Your stores seem to be running low,' von Spurzheim commented, as Reinmar led the way back up the stairs, 'and yet your casks and jars are clustered together. There is a deal of empty space.'

'That is true, sir,' Reinmar agreed. 'We have made space to take in new stock. Godrich and I will be setting out on a buying trip in nine days time. We will take the wagon south into the hills, visiting a dozen vineyards, and we shall return fully laden.'

'Who is Godrich?' the witch hunter wanted to know.

'My father's steward. One of the manservants will come with us to tend the horses and mount guard on our money and stock.'

'Will one be enough?' Vaedecker inquired solicitously. 'Are there not gypsies in the hills, and brigands?'

'My father has made at least a hundred expeditions of this sort,' Reinmar told him, 'and never lost a cargo. There has been petty pilfering by sneak-thieves, for which the gypsies may or may not have been responsible, but they tend to get the blame for every misfortune hereabouts whether it is theirs or not. There are always tales of brigands, and sometimes of monsters too, but my father says that it is all nonsense.'

'If only it were,' von Spurzheim said gloomily. 'These are bad times, and there is evil abroad in every corner of the Empire. Everyone to whom I speak hereabouts assures me that Eilhart is as good and safe a place as could ever be imagined, but my experience is that one of evil's favourite tricks is to lull potential victims into a false sense of security.'

By the time this speech had been delivered the party was back in the shop, and the sergeant had already unlatched the door. The night air that gusted in when he opened it was not unduly chilly, but it cleared away the lingering fustiness of the day in a matter of seconds.

'Thank you, Master Wieland,' von Spurzheim said. 'You have calmed our fears.'

'When shall I see my father again?' Reinmar asked.

'Soon,' the witch hunter assured him. 'I have a few more questions to ask, but he will be back by daybreak. We understand how anxious he is to resume his everyday routine.'

As soon as the door was closed behind them, Reinmar went down to the cellars to extinguish the lanterns, then put out the lights in the shop. He was now so impatient to consult his grandfather that he ran up the steps to the topmost floor of the house, where Luther Wieland had one of the rooms under the eaves.

The room was lit by a single candle, which one of the maidservants had brought with the old man's supper. The hour was so late that Luther should have blown it out and settled down to sleep, but he had heard too much commotion and had doubtless been informed that soldiers had been in and out of the shop earlier in the day.

'What's going on?' he said, as soon as Reinmar appeared. 'Why does no one bother to tell me what's happening in my own house?' The fact that Luther's supper-tray was on the table by his bed suggested that he must have received some news, but whatever the kitchen maid had told him had only increased his curiosity.

'We've all been busy,' Reinmar told him. 'Godrich is down at the warehouse on the quay and my father is at the Burgomaster's house. I was in the cellars, watching soldiers and a witch hunter while they searched.'

'What was the witch hunter searching for?' Luther wanted to know – but the guarded tone of his voice suggested that he probably knew very well.

'Dark wine,' Reinmar answered, watching closely to see how Luther would react to the phrase. He was disappointed. The old man's wrinkled features seemed quite impassive, and his eyes grew no narrower. His white hair was neatly tucked away within a black woollen cap, and his nightshirt had been freshly laundered that day, so his whole appearance was uncommonly neat and his manner equally crisp. His gnarled hands lay quite still upon the coverlet, the fingers relaxed.

'They found none, of course,' Luther said.

'Of course,' Reinmar echoed. 'Nor did they expect to – unlike the man who came to the shop this afternoon. The witch hunter appears to be chasing him, although he did not tell me what the fellow is supposed to have done and the man would not tell us his own news because he thought we were being unhelpful. There is wild talk of necromancers from the Cursed Marshes and daemonologists from the Howling Hills, but the man seemed perfectly ordinary to me – except, of course, that he claimed to be your nephew.'

Luther did not seem surprised by that either. The servants of the household were obviously better informed than they had any right to be, and the kitchen maid clearly had not hesitated to share her knowledge with the man who still desired to be thought of as her ultimate master.

'Did you tell the witch hunter that the other man claimed to be my nephew?' Luther asked.

'No,' said Reinmar, 'but he will find out eventually. If they find him at Great-Uncle Albrecht's house the witch hunter will come back here again, and his men might not be so careful to avoid spillage next time.'

'Albrecht's got more sense than to keep the boy in his house,' Luther assured him. 'He'll find some sort of hidey-hole for him, if he can't persuade him to go away.'

'According to my father,' Reinmar observed, 'Albrecht never had a son.'

'I never found it convenient, let alone rewarding, to tell your father everything,' Luther admitted. 'He has the kind of mind which cannot tolerate overmuch confusion. You, on the other hand, are probably cursed with far too much imagination. Yes, Albrecht had a son, although he was never wed. As to whether this man is really him… that's another question. Did you tell him where to find Albrecht?'

'My father did. Was he wrong?'

'No. If he is who he says he is, I suppose Albrecht might be glad to see him.'

Reinmar took note of his grandfather's use of 'might', but he had more urgent matters on his mind than the likely emotions of his Great-Uncle Albrecht on being confronted by his long-lost bastard son.

'What's dark wine, grandfather?' Reinmar asked. 'Father says that we used to stock it, twenty years ago.'

'So we did,' Luther admitted. 'A very tidy profit we made from it, too. A delightful vintage, taken in moderation – although there were few men hereabouts with pockets deep enough to take it in anything but extreme moderation. In times long gone it had generated a healthy westward flow of Marienburger gold, but that flow stuttered in the confusion that followed the secession and never fully recovered. My father never tired of telling me how that storm in a soupladle had ruined everything. There was still a demand, of course, but the chain of supply was disrupted.

'The dark wine became a pawn in a political game, charged with being an agent of evil on account of the dreams it nurtured. According to the priests of law it stimulated an appetite for unnatural luxury that ought to be stamped out. Can you believe that? All wine intoxicates, and all liquor stimulates an appetite for more – and why should anyone object? Dreams enrich life, no matter what hard-faced men like your father may think, and while there never was a man who did not take delight in luxury how can anyone possibly charge luxury with being unnatural? Believe me, Reinmar, there is no folly like the folly of excessive reason!'

Luther's voice had grown faint with effort, and his head sank back upon the pillow, but Reinmar was determined to hear more while he had the chance. He poured water from the pitcher beside the bed into his grandfather's cup, and put it to the old man's cracked lips.

'Thank you,' Luther said. 'What a curse age is! Had I but known, I'd have...'

He broke off guiltily, as if he had almost said something forbidden.

Reinmar did not want to press him too hard, while there was a tale he was prepared to tell. It was difficult to be patient, but he knew that he had to get the old man talking again, and hope that the flow of his conversation would regain its impetus. So he put the cup to the old man's mouth again, and lied.

'It's all right, grandfather,' he said. 'There's all the time in the world.'

CHAPTER FOUR

'AT ANY RATE,' Luther continued, when he could, 'attempts were made downriver to stamp out the trade in dark wine, and we found it politic to get out of it. There was still demand in Marienburg, and we might have taken a good profit from the service of that demand, always provided that we exercised discretion, but your father never had any sense of adventure. If I hadn't fallen ill, I'd have taken the chance, but your father saw things differently. He'd married, and he intended to start a family. He knew that I took a little of the wine myself occasionally, but that only made him more determined. Now, I suppose, he'll be more convinced than before that he was right.'

'He told the witch hunter that there was nowhere within ten leagues where the wine could be obtained,' Reinmar observed. 'Was he right?'

'How should I know, stuck fast to my bed as I am? There was none for me, at any rate, and I doubt that Albrecht's fared much better for all the sharpness of his thirst. I never knew where the vintage was trampled and stored – and it was usually bottled before it was delivered into my hands – but the fact that its producers used our family as agents suggests that Eilhart lay on the most convenient route to the Reik. If the dark wine and its kin no longer use the Schilder as a conduit, they must use another route, but how close it lies I cannot say. If certain rumours were true which said that the wines came from Bretonnia by means of a secret pass through the mountains, its makers may have had to go twenty or thirty leagues east or west in search of another such pass, but I never trusted that kind of talk. I always suspected that the source lay closer to home – in which case the present distribution route probably passes within a day's walk of the town.'

'As close as Great-Uncle Albrecht's house, perhaps?' Reinmar suggested.

That obtained a reaction from the old man, whose right hand twitched before forming a fist.

'Not as close as that, I think,' Luther said, in a low voice. 'Albrecht was never cut out for the wine trade, and when I saw him last he certainly didn't have the look of a regular drinker.'

'Why wasn't he cut out for the trade?' Reinmar wanted to know. He had grave misgivings about his own suitability for a life in any sort of trade. 'And what look does a regular drinker of the dark wine have?'

Luther chose to answer the first question and ignore the second. 'Albrecht had no talent for moderation,' he said dourly. 'The wine business may not require the iron discipline your father brings to it, but it does demand moderation.'

'Is that why you quarrelled – because his drinking was eating into the profits?'

'Is that what your father told you?' the old man parried. The conversation had obviously strayed too far into matters of which Luther was supposedly forbidden – presumably by Gottfried – to speak.

'Father never tells me anything that is not strictly related to the conduct of the business,' Reinmar answered, with more than a trace of bitterness. 'It was a guess.'

'Not such a bad guess,' Luther admitted. 'It was far more complicated, of course, but that was part of it. Albrecht always had a keen thirst, for wisdom as well as wine. He had ambitions to be a scholar, and more. Eilhart was never enough for him. He wanted to be a city gentleman, but his passion for prosperity far outstripped the patience that might have delivered it.'

'Is it such a terrible thing to want something more than Eilhart has to offer?' Reinmar asked, hesitantly.

'Perhaps not,' Luther replied, guardedly. 'But there are no reliable short cuts to prosperity, any more than there are reliable short cuts to wisdom.'

'And that, no doubt, is why the dutiful burgers and housewives of Eilhart are so smug in their ignorance, their small-mindedness and the extreme urgency of their desire to obtain full measure from the local tradesmen,' Reinmar said.

Luther cackled. Reinmar could remember a day when the old man's laugh had been far more robust, rumbling up from the belly instead of rattling in the throat, but time had taken its steady toll of the slowly-withering flesh. The family physician had despaired of finding any treatment that would even slow the progress of the sickness that was gradually but relentlessly consuming him.

'No doubt,' the old man agreed, his black cap bobbing as he nodded. 'But it was as well, in the end, that I refused to be quite as reckless as Albrecht, else you'd have nothing to inherit in spite of all Gottfried's industry and meanness. Albrecht never forgave me for it, but I was right.' There was a moment's pause while Luther considered the import of this conclusion. He was still nodding his head, but much more slowly than before.

'What does this man who calls us cousins want of us, grandfather?' Reinmar asked, when the black cap finally ceased its bobbing.

'I don't know,' Luther answered. 'If he is who he says he is, then he probably wants the wine to serve his own appetite rather than to sell – but if he is a secret agent of the witch hunter, he will be searching for evil to discover and uproot. Men like that sometimes find what they seek, even when it is not there.'

'What should I do?' Reinmar wanted to know.

'Your father will certainly instruct you to do nothing, or less,' Luther observed, speculatively. 'He would not thank me for offering different advice.'

'I would,' Reinmar admitted.

'Don't be too quick to say so,' Luther advised. 'But you could, if you so wished, go to visit your great-uncle. Whatever the situation is, Albrecht will doubtless be glad to be warned that there are witch hunters in the town, and I doubt that anyone else will take the trouble to tell him. If the man who claims to be his son is with him, he might well be glad of the warning too – and he is certainly the best person to explain why a man like Machar von Spurzheim might be looking for him.'

Reinmar was prepared to consider the possibility that had been set before him at his leisure, but there was still one question he wanted to ask.

'If one happened to have a flask of dark wine,' he said, casually, 'how much would it fetch, in today's money? My mysterious visitor wasn't very enthusiastic to offer the full market price, but he said he was prepared to pay it.'

Luther let out a sound that was almost, but not quite, a laugh. 'I haven't handled money for ten years,' he said, 'and I haven't seen a flask of dark wine in twenty. How would I know what prices are being asked in the markets of Schilderheim and Marienburg? It might be twice what Gottfried asks for a bottle of his best vintage, or it might be a hundred times – but your customer might not have been thinking in monetary terms at all. If he came here looking for me as well as for Albrecht, he may think of me as a man who was too fond of money in his youth to pay a fuller price for the kind of reward he seeks. If you see him again, he may deign to explain himself – but if not, you might be better off not knowing. Gottfried would certainly say so, and I owe him too much to go against his wishes. You, of course, might make your own decision.'

'I came to you for answers,' Reinmar said, 'not for more puzzles, each more enigmatic than the last.'

'We can't always get what we want,' Luther whispered, letting his head sink back into his pillow again. 'That should be the first lesson that every man learns from life – for it may be his last, if he learns it too late.' His eyelids had fallen shut.

Reinmar knew that he would get no more out of the old man that night. He also knew that he would have to be back at his counter at an uncomfortably early hour – but he knew, too, that if he put off visiting Great-Uncle Albrecht until the following night there would probably be no point in going at all. Machar von Spurzheim had all the daylight hours at his disposal, and would undoubtedly make full use of them. If Reinmar wanted to get to Albrecht before the witch hunter did, he would have to go now.

By the time Reinmar crept out of Luther's room the hour was so late that the great majority of the townsfolk would be abed, but he was still fully charged with the excitement of the extraordinary day and he did not even pause to wonder whether Albrecht might be peacefully asleep. He dared not leave the shop door unbolted so he used a route of his own, which he had established in early childhood, clambering out of the narrow window of his bedroom on to the bay above the shop, then letting himself down by a series of foot- and handholds cut by the removal of mortar from the cracks between the blocks of grey stone that made up the walls of the house.

The descent seemed more perilous every time he used it, but he was still light enough and lithe enough to negotiate it safely.

Gottfried had said that Albrecht's house was 'little more than an hours' walk' from the shop, but he had been thinking in terms of a leisurely stroll. Although he had no light but that of the stars to guide him, and it was not a route with which he was familiar, Reinmar contrived to make the journey in a few minutes less than the hour, arriving as the distant market bell chimed midnight.

It would not have been easy to find the house among the firs had it been unlit, but there was a lamp burning in an upstairs room which shone brightly through a gap in the conical crowns and guided Reinmar through the most difficult passage.

When he thumped the door with his fist there was no immediate response, and impatience made him knock again before the door was unbarred and opened a crack. It was not his gypsy housekeeper but Albrecht himself who answered it.

Albrecht Wieland must have been taller than his younger brother even in their youth, but Luther had been so wasted by his illness that Albrecht now seemed to have more than twice his brother's mass. He was not quite as tall as the witch hunter, but he loomed over Reinmar nevertheless. He was obviously not used to visitors; he had a candle-tray in one hand and a cudgel in the other.

'Who are you?' he demanded roughly. He had thrust the candle forward so that Reinmar's face was fully illuminated, but he obviously did not recognise his great-nephew.

'It's me, great-uncle. Reinmar.'

Albrecht seemed startled by this news, and slightly dismayed. 'Gottfried's boy? What do you want? Is my brother dead?'

'No. Is there no one else here? Have you had no other visitor today?'

Albrecht still had not stood aside to admit Reinmar to his house, and the perplexity on his face suggested that he had not the faintest idea what Reinmar was talking about. If the man who claimed to be Albrecht's son had set out to follow Gottfried's directions, he did not seem to have completed his journey. 'I never have visitors,' Albrecht stated, flatly.

'You'll have some tomorrow, great-uncle,' Reinmar told him. 'There's a witch hunter in town. His men took my father away and then searched the shop. May I come in?'

At the mention of the witch hunter Albrecht's ill-lit face had changed expression, anxiety banishing puzzlement on the instant. He had already begun to swing the door wide open and usher Reinmar in, and he looked fearfully out into the darkness before closing it again and replacing the bar in its slots.

'There,' he said. He was pointing to the poorer of a pair of rickety chairs. It stood beside a table strewn with the debris of at least three meals, half a dozen saucers pooled with sooty candle-wax, and various pieces of rotting parchment that might once have been deeds, letters or pages torn out of a book. Reinmar sat down gingerly, rocking the chair one way and then the other until he figured out which three-legged stance was the more comfortable. The room was suffused with a strong animal odour, although the scrawny cat asleep by the hearth seemed hardly big enough to be responsible. Albrecht's housekeeper – of whom there was still no sign – did not seem to be overly attentive to her duties.

Albrecht took the other chair, which was somewhat sturdier and equipped with arms on which he could rest his own. 'What would a witch hunter want with me?' he demanded.

'The man he is chasing told me that he is your son,' Reinmar informed him. 'He also told me that he was coming to see you, although he doesn't seem to have arrived.'

'Wirnt?' Albrecht seemed to be utterly astonished. 'Wirnt is in Eilhart?'

'He did not tell me his name,' Reinmar said. 'So you do have a son, then? My father didn't seem to know it. The stranger came to the shop asking for dark wine, and was disappointed when my father told him that we had none. Perhaps it was as well, given that the witch hunter came so quickly on his heels. The witch hunter's soldiers searched the cellars, although I cannot imagine that there is witchcraft in wine.'

'All wine is witchcraft,' Albrecht murmured, although his mind seemed to be elsewhere. 'What else is intoxication but a gentle form of magic, a pleasing disorder?'

'According to my father,' Reinmar told his aged relative, 'good wine is virtue incarnate, and even bad wine is a useful accompaniment to poor food. I am his apprentice, but he has never said a word to me of evil wine. That is the sense, I assume, in which this mysterious liquor is dark?'

'Wine comes in more colours than the burgers of Eilhart and Holthusen imagine,' Albrecht told him, still speaking rather absent-mindedly while he worried over possibilities that he was not yet inclined to share, 'and the dreams it stimulates are far richer and more various than your father or his neighbours can imagine. Luther knows – but Luther was always a weakling and a coward. There is no evil in wine, but there is evil in men, and even the finest wine can sometimes draw it out. The wine of dreams may reveal more than some men find comfortable. It is always the way of witch hunters and priests of law to blame the magic rather than the man, but scholars have another way of seeing.'

'In Eilhart,' Reinmar observed, 'the kind of learning you call scholarship is regarded with far more suspicion than wine.'

That remark brought Albrecht's mind back into focus. 'Do you think I need to be told that?' he demanded sharply. 'It was to escape such ignorance that I went to Marienburg, and let my brother steal my share of your precious shop by slow degrees. If your father imagines that he can send a witch hunter after the rascal of the family while keeping his own house clean he is mistaken. If I am guilty, in the witch hunter's eyes – and I am certainly innocent in my own – than Luther is guilty too, and if my past catches up with me your precious business is bound to be drawn into the enquiry. If Wirnt has any sense at all...'

He broke off, somewhat to Reinmar's annoyance.

'I don't understand what is happening, great-uncle,' Reinmar said. 'My father will not tell me, and my grandfather insists on respecting my father's wishes, for the time being – although he did suggest that I ought to forego my precious sleep in order to warn you that the witch hunter is here. Do you not think that I am entitled to know what danger I am in?'

Albrecht recoiled slightly under this assault, but he seemed to be made of stronger stuff than Luther. He drew his lips back to expose his yellow teeth, and teased the incisors thoughtfully with his tongue as he considered the matter.

'Although you would not know it to hear the gossip in the marketplace, we live in quiet times in a favoured place,' the old man said, eventually. 'Tradesmen are always grumbling, but the tradesmen of Reikland know nothing of how hard life is in less prosperous parts of the Empire or how desperate it was in Reikland in other phases of our history. There are rumours of terrible events in distant corners of the Empire, and horrors in Altdorf itself, but nothing has happened in my lifetime to compare with the great conflicts of the past. The siege of Praag has always been the stuff of legend in Reikland, and the Vampire Counts of Sylvania are bogeymen fit only to frighten naughty children in these parts, but you and I have every reason to be grateful that we were not born in a worse place or in an earlier era. You have not the slightest idea how grim reality is in less favoured localities, or what evil lurks in the wastes of the far north.'

'Tell me, then,' Reinmar suggested.

Albrecht hesitated. 'Your education is your father's responsibility,' he said, after a few moments.

'Your brother thinks the same,' Reinmar observed. 'He is too old, and too weak, even to think of defying my father by telling me things that my father would rather I did not know. But that is why I came to you: a scholar, and a man who can still stand upright. My cousin has come to Eilhart with a witch hunter at his heels. We are all under suspicion, it seems. My father has been taken away, and you may well be next. I need to know what is going on, and you are the only one who can tell me. You are the scholar of the family, are you not?'

Flattery, Reinmar had heard it said, would get a man anywhere. It was the flattery of being named the scholar of the family that loosened his great-uncle's tongue.

'Very well,' Albrecht said. 'Perhaps it is time that my nephew's son knew the family secrets – and I believe that he will hear a more honest account from me than from my brother or his son. Listen, then!'

Reinmar listened, more enthusiastically than he had ever listened to any lecture delivered by his father.

Chapter Five

'The relative peace that we enjoy was not cheaply bought,' Albrecht told Reinmar. 'The price my father's generation paid was fierce repression. If the scholars of Marienburg are right in their account of the world, much of that repression was necessary and wholly justified, but the forces of repression never know when to stop or relent. Trade in the wine of dreams – which is not the only dark wine but the one most commonly used and the one to which most men refer when they use the phrase – had been established for centuries before my father's time, but when it was investigated by agents of Magnus the Pious and his Theogonists it was quickly limited, and then proscribed.

'Suppression of the trade was by no means welcome in Marienburg, and may even have played some small part in the events leading to secession, but that was before my time. The trade went underground thereafter, at least in the lower reaches of the Reik, but it was tolerated by local people to whom it was a matter of custom. The main effect of the notional ban was, in fact, to increase curiosity among those who dealt in the wine as to the reason for its bad reputation. Yes, I used dark wine myself – more freely, I dare say, than Luther – and I would have continued to use it had I been able to stay in Marienburg or had I been able to secure a supply of my own when I returned to Eilhart. Once the traffic was taken out of the charge of our family, however, I found it as hard to come by as anyone else and I am too poor nowadays to support expensive habits.

'If Wirnt has fled Marienburg there must be further trouble in the city, completing the disruption of the dark wine's supply. If a witch hunter and soldiers are mere hours behind him, the trouble in question is presumably a crusade of sorts. Whatever Wirnt might have told you, I doubt that it is filial affection that has brought him here. He is more likely to be searching for the source of the wine of dreams. He might even be hoping that Luther can tell him where to continue his search.'

'He did ask for Luther before he asked for you,' Reinmar confirmed.

'He will probably come here too,' Albrecht said, mournfully. 'He is likely to go anywhere and everywhere in search of a clue, and he will draw the witch hunter after him. I only hope that someone can persuade him that the secret lies beyond the mountains. He will do less harm hereabouts if he goes in search of the famous secret pass without undue delay.'

'My grandfather does not believe that there is any such pass,' Reinmar commented.

'Nor does any man who knows the mountains,' Albrecht agreed. 'But it has been a convenient fiction for centuries – and the truth is that no one knows where the wine of dreams and its kin are made, or by whom, or by what process. Its makers guard their secret well, and wisely so.'

'What kin?' Reinmar questioned. 'How is other dark wine different from the wine of dreams?'

'The wine of dreams is one of several vintages allegedly produced by the same growers,' Albrecht said, uneasily, 'but the others are even rarer, and cater to more exotic tastes.'

'My father seems to think that dark wine really is evil,' Reinmar said, hoping to provoke further revelations.'

'Your father has never tasted it,' Albrecht retorted, with a sigh. 'Perhaps he is wise, although I have never admired that narrow kind of wisdom. It is as well that he has kept you clear of it, if there are witch hunters abroad. Luther might be a stronger man today if it had never passed his lips, but I cannot regret the visions I obtained from it. I am a scholar through and through and I have always been willing to pay a price for insight and inspiration. The witch hunter will find nothing here if he comes calling, and my crimes, if crimes they were, are too distant now to interest him. If you see Wirnt again, tell him that I would be glad to see him – but beg him to be careful, for all our sakes. You had best go now. If honest men are not abed when they should be it excites suspicion, and I dare say that you have duties to perform by day.'

'I have,' Reinmar agreed, dolefully. He had hoped to learn more, but he did not have the time.

'Come again, when this is over and done with. Your father disapproves of me, I know, but we are kin and he thinks worse of me than I deserve.' Albrecht stood up as he spoke, and Reinmar stood too, allowing himself to be ushered back to the door.

Reinmar removed the bar himself, although he had seen that the old man handled it without difficulty. 'I will come again,' he promised. 'I'll bring news, when there is more to bring.'

'Be careful,' Albrecht advised. 'Can you find your way by starlight? The moons are but crescents, alas.'

'I have good eyes,' Reinmar assured him, 'and there will be light enough in the streets, once I am among the houses again.'

He took the advice he had been given, and trod carefully until he was sure of his way – and even then he took pains to move discreetly, lest there was anyone nearby who had been told to stand watch and take note of his passing. He saw no one, but the trees were dense enough to conceal a dozen inquisitive watchers.

When he arrived back home the house seemed quiet. His ascent to the first floor window was as awkward as the descent, but he contrived to wriggle through the narrow window-frame without doing overmuch damage to his jerkin.

One of the servants had set a lamp beside the bed, although the wick had been compressed so tightly that the blue flame was hardly brighter than the starlight outside. Reinmar had already decided to go straight to his bed, so he did not bother to turn up the light – but he had barely knelt down to unfasten his shoes when he heard soft footfalls on the floor above.

Reinmar's first thought was that it must be Godrich or one of the other servants, but he moved to the door nevertheless, then slipped outside into the corridor in the hope that he might be better placed to hear. He closed the door behind him to cut off the glimmer of the light and held himself perfectly still while he listened hard.

The quality of the shuffling steps changed as whoever was abroad reached the head of the staircase leading down to the first floor, and Reinmar deduced from the sound that whoever was coming down was less sure of his footing than any of the servants would have been. A servant about his business would, in any case, have been carrying a candle – and this person was not.

Reinmar did not know what to do. If he stayed where he was, outside his bedroom door, the intruder – if it was an intruder – would have to pass by him to get to the stair which led down to the shop. In all probability, the man – if it were a man – would walk right into him. He was tempted to call out and wake the household, but did not like to do so while he had no idea what might be happening, so he waited while the footsteps approached.

He did not move, but he could hardly stop breathing, and the footfalls stopped abruptly while the other was still two paces away from Reinmar's station. There was a windowslit at the far end of the corridor, but the faint light that filtered through it was insufficient to let him make out a shadow unless or until the other placed himself directly in line with it, and the man seemed instead to be pressing himself against the wall, using it to guide him.

When he could bear the suspense no longer, Reinmar said: 'Who's there?' He felt direly foolish, for he was hardly likely to obtain a meek reply if the other had no right to be where he was, but it would have been worse to leap upon the other and engage in a tussle if it turned out to be Godrich or Gottfried.

The reply he actually obtained was an urgent 'Shh!' – a syllable which was inadequate to give him any clue as to the accent of the voice. Within a second or two, though, the sound was followed by urgent action, as Reinmar felt hands groping for his neck. Fearful that he was about to be strangled he tried to wrestle, but the other man was much stronger than he, and within three seconds he was tightly held, with a hand clamped over his mouth.

'No need to wake the servants, cousin,' a voice hissed in his ear. 'The fewer people know that I was here the better. Where's the door of your room?'

The hand relaxed to permit him to reply, although it remained poised to reassert its grip if he should try to call out.

'We have only to step to the side, Cousin Wirnt,' Reinmar assured his captor, extending his free hand to push the door inwards.

Wirnt bundled him through it, then let him go. After the darkness of the corridor the lamplight did not seem so dim, although it lent an eerie tint to the dark man's features. 'Who told you my name?' he demanded.

'Great-Uncle Albrecht,' Reinmar told him. 'Did my grandfather not tell you that I had gone to warn him?'

'Uncle Luther told me far less than I had hoped,' said Wirnt, bitterly. 'He's scared half to death, perhaps because von Spurzheim still has your father. How did they catch up with me so soon? That barge must have been even slower that it seemed, and von Spurzheim must have hired horses so that he and his favourites could ride ahead of the troop. Do you know how many locks there are between here and Holthusen?'

Reinmar knew exactly how many locks there were between Eilhart and Holthusen – the taming of the river's flow was a great source of pride in the town – but he did not bother to number them. 'You must go,' he said. 'Great-Uncle Albrecht said that he would be glad to see you in other circumstances, but that he cannot give you what you seek or tell you what you want to know. If you go up into the hills you will find it exceedingly easy to lose yourself. When the witch hunter has gone there will be time enough to renew old acquaintances.'

'To renew old acquaintances,' the dark man repeated, with a sneer in his voice. 'That is not why I came, cousin – nor did I come to hear nonsense about secret passes to Bretonnia. I must make contact with the vintagers, for their sake as well as mine. Vaedecker's platoon is the advance detachment of a much larger company, and von Spurzheim's spies are already abroad in the region. There has been treason in Marienburg and the authorities there know far too much – more than I, and more than your grandfather is yet prepared to admit.'

'You are not safe here,' Reinmar said, stubbornly. 'And while you are here, neither are we. You must go.'

Wirnt's expression was twisted with anger as well as anxiety, and for a moment Reinmar thought he would refuse – but then he relaxed. 'Aye,' he muttered. 'So I must. Will you come down with me, to let me out and bar the door behind me? I climbed up the same way I watched you climb down, but I nearly got caught half way in and half way out of the window, and I wouldn't care to try it again.'

'With pleasure,' Reinmar assured him, insincerely, as he turned to pick up the lamp. 'I hope you won't take it amiss if I say that I hope I shall not see you again for quite some time.'

The other man laughed dryly. 'No, cousin,' he said, as he followed Reinmar out of the room. 'I won't take it amiss. Now that I've seen Uncle Luther I know how the land lies – but don't think that this affair will be over when you bar the door behind me. Von Spurzheim won't stop searching, and it won't be easy to convince him that none of you can point him in the right direction. You'll be carefully watched, so you'd best not put a foot wrong.'

'How can I,' Reinmar protested, as he made his way to the shop door, 'when I know nothing?'

'That might not save you,' Wirnt said, while he waited for the bar to be removed. 'When witch hunts begin, all kinds of old resentments surface. Your neighbours might be denouncing all three of you as addicts of the wine and active sorcerers even as we speak. You might soon have to make new estimates as to who your friends are – and you might regret your rudeness to me.'

Reinmar decided then that he did not like his cousin Wirnt, and regretted that he had accidentally shown him a way into the house – a way that he could obviously use in spite of his generous girth.

'We are honest tradesmen,' Reinmar said, stiffly, as he held the door open to let out his unwelcome visitor.

'I'll be sure to remember that,' Wirnt promised – but the promise was a sneer, ill-befitting a man who had just exposed his kin to danger, and had refused to warn them when he had the chance, because they could not give him what he sought. Reinmar watched him until he had vanished into the night, and then took himself swiftly to bed.

Tired as he was, he could not sleep. It seemed to him that within the space of a few hours his whole world had been turned upside-down. Everything was different: his father, his grandfather, Eilhart and the wine trade. Every one of them had seemed so straightforward when the day dawned, dull and settled and secure. Now, they had all exposed to his sideways glance the suggestion of a darker underside, as ominous as it was mysterious. How could that be factored into his life? And how could it be factored into his dreams? Was there hope in this sudden upsurge of mystery as well as danger? Was there opportunity as well as threat?

Of one thing he was certain: he must discover more. And he must not do so meekly, waiting for others to tell him what they cared to when they cared to do it. He must work on his own account, with his own aims and his own ambitions. He was a child no longer, and he must reach his own accommodation with the enigmatic wine of dreams and its even darker kin. He would take nothing as given, no man's word as final. He must be his own man now – but he must discover more, if he was to be the kind of man he was anxious to become.

Chapter Six

In spite of the sleep-denying effect of all the ideas seething in his brain, Reinmar contrived to rouse himself in time to open the shop at the designated hour. He was almost immediately swamped by customers who had far more on their minds than a simple exchange of coin for jugs of wine. Several of them assured him that they had been expecting 'this' for years, although they were disinclined to specify exactly what 'this' might be. None of them mentioned dark wine in so many words, but more than one commiserated with Reinmar over the fact that the legacy of Luther's sins now seemed to be descending to his son and grandson.

'Not that the old man ever meant any harm,' Frau Walther assured him, 'or even that stuck up brother of his – but meaning no harm isn't the same as doing none, and chickens always come home to roost. There are evil things abroad in the forest now, so they say. The poachers always say so, of course, but when the woodcutters join in you have to take it seriously. You stick fast to the roads, now, when you go off on your tour of the vineyards, and watch out for the gypsies.'

'More soldiers are coming,' he was told by one of the constables' wives. 'All well and good for your trade, I suppose, but where there's soldiers there's trouble. They'll pass through, it seems, as soon as they've figured out where to head for next, but they'll be back when they've done whatever they've come to do, dragging trouble in their wake. There are advantages to being at the limit of the river's navigability, you know – this has always been such a decent town. We never needed soldiers here. Never.'

Gottfried still had not returned by the time the first rush was over, and Reinmar was becoming worried, although one of his loyal customers would have been sure to pass on the news if his father had actually been arrested. When Marguerite turned up, hungry for news, he had not the slightest idea what to tell her.

'People are saying that it's your grandfather's fault,' she informed him, hesitantly. 'They say that he first got sick because he dabbled in magic. Some even say that your Great-Uncle Albrecht is some sort of necromancer and that his housekeeper is a witch.'

'That's nonsense,' Reinmar assured her. 'Albrecht's just a harmless old man. His housekeeper might be a gypsy, but she's just a housekeeper. My grandfather just got sick – magic had nothing to do with it.'

'I don't think you should go out with the wagon next week,' she said. 'It's not safe.'

'We're wine merchants,' Reinmar said, patiently. 'All but the dregs of this year's harvest will have been trampled and casked by now, and last year's will have matured in the wood. We need to restock the cellar. It's just a matter of doing the usual rounds, filling up the cart. I'll have Godrich with me, and one of the labourers – probably Sigurd. Godrich and I have both been schooled in swordplay and Sigurd's practically a giant. Nobody's going to attack us – and if there are Reiksguard cavalrymen and foot soldiers in the region the roads will be even safer than usual. I'll be back inside a fortnight.'

'There are tales of monsters in the woods,' Marguerite persisted.

'There have always been tales of monsters in the woods,' Reinmar countered, 'and monsters in the mountains, and monsters everywhere else, but who do you know who's ever been harmed by one? All travellers tell tall tales, Marguerite – I'll probably bring back a couple myself – but the fact that they always live to tell them suggests that the danger isn't quite as bad as they make out. I'll be fine.'

Marguerite would probably have said more, but the door to the shop opened again, and when she saw that it was Gottfried she suddenly remembered whatever errand she had been running for her mother and beat a hasty retreat, leaving father and son alone.

'Have they let you go?' Reinmar asked, awkwardly.

'They never arrested me,' Gottfried was quick to insist. 'They wanted my advice, and I gave it freely.'

'They searched the cellars,' Reinmar pointed out.

'As I invited them to do. We have nothing to hide – nothing. I wanted to make that clear.'

'Everyone says that more soldiers are coming,' Reinmar said, tentatively. 'Do you know why?'

'Politics,' Gottfried said, succinctly. 'There is trouble in Marienburg, and the Empire is always intensely interested in trouble in Marienburg. Even after all this time, the secession still rankles. There are many in Altdorf who would be exceedingly glad to welcome Marienburg back into the Imperial fold, even if the opportunity were bought in blood. The witch hunter has friends in the Reiksguard who are prepared to indulge his whims, it seems, and he thinks that he might find something hereabouts to give him useful leverage over the burgers of Schilderheim and Marienburg.'

'The mysterious source of the dark wine, in which we do not deal,' Reinmar said.

Gottfried looked at him sharply. 'You've been talking to my father,' he said disgustedly. 'What did he tell you?'

'That there is no secret pass through the mountains,' Reinmar said, offhandedly, 'and that the dark wine isn't as black as some would like to paint it.'

Gottfried scowled. 'Old fool,' he said. 'I've decided to bring forward the buying trip. You leave tomorrow. It's been a good summer – the harvest must have come in on time, and the more industrious vintagers will be ahead of their normal timetable. You won't be expected so soon, so Godrich might have to improvise a little, but he and I will plan a route tonight.'

'You want me out of the way,' Reinmar said, flatly.

Gottfried hesitated momentarily, but then nodded his head. 'Yes, I do,' he admitted. 'We have nothing to hide and should have nothing to fear, but people hereabouts have long memories and agile tongues. Von Spurzheim will want to talk to Luther, and Albrecht too – and they may not find it easy to persuade him that they cannot help him. Old animosities might flare up again, and things could become unpleasant. I don't think anything bad will happen, but I want you out of harm's way, just in case.'

'I want to know what this is all about,' Reinmar told him, firmly. 'If I'm old enough to take a full part in the business, I'm old enough to be let in on all its secrets.'

'There isn't any secret.'

'Yes there is,' Reinmar insisted. 'Or there was, once – and however dead and buried it seemed to be this time yesterday, it's definitely not dead and buried now. You might be able to stop Luther talking to me, but you can't stop Albrecht and Wirnt – and if you won't tell me what this is all about, they will.'

'Who's Wirnt?'

'Your cousin. Albrecht's son.'

Gottfried raised an inquisitive eyebrow, and seemed to be on the point of asking how Reinmar knew that – but he had already deduced that Reinmar had been talking to Luther. In the end, he sighed and said: 'I've never known the half of it myself, and I've always been glad of that – but I suppose the time has come when it might be more dangerous to remain ignorant than to know what my father knows, and perhaps what Albrecht knows too. The authorities in Marienburg seem to have stamped out their end of the trade in dark wine, at least for the time being, but they won't be satisfied with that. They want the source eliminated, and having traced it back as far as this they won't be in any mood to stop short of their goal. If we can't help them, they're likely to assume that the "can't" is really a "won't", so we must hope that we can. You'd better come with me while I talk to my father – Godrich can mind the shop for an hour or two, given that it's so quiet.'

Reinmar felt a thrill of triumph as he realised that for the first time in his life he had forced his father's hand. He went up the stairs far more lightly than his heavily-treading father, although he had only had a little more rest.

Luther seemed distinctly uneasy when his son and grandson confronted him – unsurprisingly, given that Gottfried was in such a grim mood. The old man's gaze flickered uneasily from one to the other. 'I couldn't help it,' he said defensively, shrinking back beneath the coverlet. 'It wasn't me who let him in.'

Gottfried was startled, but not completely astonished. 'The stout stranger came back,' he quickly deduced. 'Albrecht's brat. He wouldn't take no for an answer – not from me, at any rate. He's not still here, I hope?'

'No, he's not,' said Reinmar. 'I saw him as he left. He's gone into the hills to hide – unless he decided to call on his father first.'

'What did you tell him?' Gottfried asked of Luther.

'What could I tell him?' the old man retorted, resentfully. 'We have no dark wine, and we don't know where it's made.'

'And what did he tell you?' Gottfried demanded.

'That his mother, when he found her, seemed hardly old enough to have given birth to him – but that she did acknowledge him, and that he continued to see her in spite of rumours that she was involved in dark magic. She was proud of him, it seems, and told him not to hate his father too much for having gone away and left him in the care of strangers. She introduced him to the wine. He said that the dreams were like coming home – as if they filled a hole in his heart that he had never quite been aware of before. It was as if he had never properly begun to live, until that moment. It was as if... but you have heard such talk before, and did not like it then.'

'I haven't,' Reinmar put in, quietly.

Luther was still staring at his son, waiting for permission to continue. Gottfried only hesitated briefly before he said: 'Tell him everything.'

Luther nodded, and made an obvious effort to collect himself, then shifted his gaze to his grandson. 'The dark wine is also called the wine of dreams,' he said, in a voice that was strangely dry as well as weak. 'There are other wines from the same source, all darker of hue than the sweetest Reikish and all of which give rise to dreams, but those who know what they are about speak of dark wine in the singular, and the wine of dreams likewise. A few who have had the opportunity to tire of the wine of dreams manage to cultivate an appetite for one or other of its peculiar kin, but their use has always been... esoteric.'

Reinmar wished that he might elaborate on that, but he did not.

'The wine of dreams is the kindest and most generous of the vintages produced by its makers,' Luther continued, 'and connoisseurs deem it the very essence of luxury, because the greatest luxury of all is youth and dark wine is a veritable elixir of youth. It has the power to preserve beauty, and zest, and a particular kind of innocence that none but the guilty can appreciate. Is it magic? Perhaps. Who can tell where nature ends and magic begins? All wine intoxicates, and it is surely conceivable that dark wine is merely the finest and purest intoxicant of all. Albrecht used to write to me, in the days when we were still as close as brothers ought to be, that he had heard scholars swear there is no magic in dark wine at all, while others praised it as the greatest magic known to man. A third party damned it as a snare – an alluring gateway to unspeakable evil – but Albrecht never kept company with men of that kind while he was pretending to be a scholar in Marienburg. Nor did I, in Eilhart.'

The old man paused to take a drink; it was Gottfried who helped him with the cup. This time, it was hock rather than water, but Luther still looked as if he would have preferred something far stronger.

'You would not think to look at me now that I was once a man of superabundant youth,' Luther went on, 'but I was. I never thought any less of myself because of it, although my father was a man of my son's stripe – worse, in a way, for he never allowed any kind of liquor to pass his own lips. It needs a sober man to deal in wine, he used to say. Cultivate a liking for the stock, and you'll pour your profits down your throat. You might think your father's love of moderation stern enough, Reinmar, but you never had the opportunity to measure him against a real pillar of rectitude.

'Albrecht took the brunt of our father's wrath and disapproval, and it drove him away. I was younger, and I learned to be sly. I was a drinker long before he found me out, and once I had tasted dark wine I lost my appetite for most lesser vices. But he did find me out, alas, and he was not an easy man to best in a dispute. He had his way, although he had to steal my own son to secure his final victory – and his gain was our loss, for my father never once considered the possibility of refusing to trade in the dark wine and its kin, which is what your own dear father did as soon as he had the whip hand.'

'It was the only way,' Gottfried muttered.

'Was it?' Luther asked, sceptically. 'What consternation there must have been in Marienburg when you made that decision! But only for a while. As the Schilder's assiduous lock-builders discovered long ago, the flow of a river can never be entirely gentled. When the spring meltwater runs from the mountains the gates must be opened wide, and the worst floods can only be diverted; you can only protect land here by diverting the floodwater there. The dark wine was like the Schilder; frustrated in its normal course, it only found other channels to the Reik – and once there, it vanished into the irresistible tide of river traffic.'

'This is no use,' Gottfried butted in. 'We need something to give the witchfinder. The only way to get him off our backs is to send him further along the trail. You must have some idea where the dark wine is produced, and by whom.'

'I don't,' Luther said, stubbornly.

'I don't believe you,' Gottfried said. 'Albrecht went to Marienburg, but you stayed here. You went up into the hills on yearly buying trips just as I have always done. Don't try to tell me that you never searched for the source of the dark wine.'

'The agents of the dark wine's producers always came to us.'

'And who were they? Where did they live?'

'They were gypsies – wanderers, without any permanent home.'

'People hereabouts blame such travellers for everything,' Gottfried said, disgustedly. 'Every time a chicken is stolen, the gypsies took it. Every time a milk-cow dries up, it was cursed by the gypsies. If a man gets a bellyache, it was never from eating unripe apples, but always because some gypsy crone looked sideways at him. Now you tell me that the gypsies make dark wine – doubtless from wild grapes gathered in some secret valley whose location is known only to their elders.'

'I did not say that they made it,' Luther pointed out. 'Merely that they brought it from its source – of which they had nothing, or next to nothing, to say.'

'But you did ask,' Gottfried said. 'As often and as cleverly as you could, given your fondness for the stuff. And you say they told you next to nothing. Why the margin, father? What little did they tell you?'

The old man let his head flop back on to the pillow, but there was a wry twist to his mouth as he realised that he had given himself away, and knew that he could no take refuge in his enfeeblement.

'Only that the source was magically protected – that a man might search for years without ever obtaining a glimpse of it, because it was accessible only to those of their own kind who heard the call and to those who accompanied them to see them safely to their destination.'

'What call?'

'How should I know?' Luther protested, his voice becoming feeble again as he wilted under his son's fierce gaze. 'I never heard it – and not for want of listening.' The last phrase was muttered.

'How can I give this to the witch hunter?' Gottfried complained, speaking more to Reinmar than to Luther. 'It's the kind of tittle-tattle you can hear on any street-corner. Gypsies and calls – old wives' tales, more like. It's a lie, put about to distract the gullible. You must know more.'

'It's what I was told,' Luther complained. 'Maybe I never quite believed it, but all the searching I did wasn't enough to teach me any better. There were other rumours, of monasteries built atop deep caverns, and strange flowers that grow underground, but I always discounted them. The wine of dreams isn't the produce of the grape – not entirely, at any rate – but no fruit can ripen except in the sun. If there's a valley whose entrance isn't hidden by magic it must be very well concealed in some other way. Perhaps Albrecht knows more. He's certainly had time to enquire since he scuttled back from Marienburg with his tail between his legs. Even hired a nomad to be his housekeeper, perhaps because of something she knew that the town's old crones did not. He's housebound now, but he certainly did his share of searching when he first came back and thought himself unjustly dispossessed. He was ambitious to set himself up as a rival then, but I dare say that the mysterious makers of the wine of dreams didn't want a disgraced brother of mine for a middleman. If I couldn't find the source in twenty years of searching, your witch hunter has a hard task on his hands. I wish him luck.'

'I need a name,' Gottfried said. 'I need something that will tell von Spurzheim which gypsies to question.'

'Who asks a gypsy's family name?' Luther retorted. 'Who obtains a reply if he does? The nomads keep the secrets of their kind. The witch hunter has only one advantage, in my estimation, and it may not be enough.'

'What advantage?' Gottfried demanded, exasperatedly.

'The season. Whatever fruit it is that gives dark wine its special qualities surely ripens when other fruits ripen, and there must be a cycle to its manufacture. If all living things are prisoners of the calendar, this season's crop should now be ready, and those commissioned to bring it away will need to be summoned soon. If von Spurzheim's spies can find the final link in the chain that stretches here from Marienburg, they have a chance of being led to the source – but if that opportunity is real, it'll only last for twenty or thirty days.'

'Guesswork of that kind is not good enough,' Gottfried told him, harshly.

'It is all I have to offer, as a man who has spent his life in the wine trade,' Luther retorted, stiffly – but his voice was very weak now and his head lolled back on his pillow, exhausted. His distress was obviously real.

'He's doing his best, father,' Reinmar murmured. 'He has no more liking for the prospect of being vigorously interrogated by the witchfinder than have you. If this liquor really is as insidiously evil as you suppose, its source would be jealously guarded, would it not?'

Gottfried sighed. 'I suppose so,' he conceded. 'I had better find out what Albrecht has to say – and you had better get back to your counter. Business goes on, no matter what.'

Reinmar almost told his father that he had already been to see Albrecht, but he strangled the impulse. Was he not playing his own game now? Was he not determined to make his own discoveries, so that he might make up his own mind?

'Are we really in danger?' he asked, instead.

'I hope not,' Gottfried replied, dryly. 'But it would be in the interest of everyone in town if the witch hunter were to pass swiftly through. We must hope that he finds what he is looking for, and that he brings his business to a swift and successful conclusion.' He looked down at Luther as he spoke, but the old man had pulled his black cap over his forehead and had closed his eyes.

Chapter Seven

Reinmar would rather have gone with his father to see Albrecht than mind the shop, but he knew that it was useless to protest. Godrich had better things to do than stand at the counter, and Reinmar knew that it would take far more than a mere witch hunt to make Gottfried Wieland consent to close his shop during business hours.

As it turned out, though, Gottfried's was a wasted trip. Albrecht was not at home, because Machar von Spurzheim had sent soldiers to arrest him and confine him in the town jail. They would have arrested his housekeeper too, but she had fled. The rumours that flew around the town were divided as to whether she had merely run away for her own safety or had gone to warn the secret vintners that trouble was on its way. As soon as Gottfried returned he threw himself into making urgent preparations for Reinmar's imminent buying trip.

As Reinmar had anticipated, Gottfried delegated Sigurd to serve alongside Godrich as his protector on the expedition. Sigurd normally worked on the quays loading and unloading barges, in which service he had built up an impressive set of muscles. Whenever the stevedores engaged in tug-o'-war competitions against the local land-labourers, Sigurd was the anchorman who tipped the balance, and in any local contest of individual strength he was the certain winner. He had never been trained in swordsmanship but he could wield a staff with terrific force and cunning, and his fists were as powerful as clubs. He was the kind of man in whose company any lesser mortal would feel safe, and Reinmar was glad to see him waiting with the wagon when he brought his own pack down from his room, not long after first light on the following day.

He was not so pleased, however, to find Matthias Vaedecker waiting alongside Sigurd, with a pack of his own. He was not wearing his military colours, although he was carrying a crossbow.

'What are you doing here?' Reinmar asked, in frank astonishment.

'I've been ordered to travel with you,' the sergeant said, airily. 'Herr von Spurzheim is anxious for your safety. There are rumours of monsters abroad in the hills.'

Reinmar's eyes flicked back and forth between the squat sergeant and the massive Sigurd. 'There are always rumours of monsters in the hills,' he said. 'Wise men know better than to take them seriously.'

'The truly wise man is the one who knows when rumours that are not usually to be taken seriously begin to carry evil import,' the sergeant informed him, coolly.

It seemed perfectly obvious to Reinmar that Vaedecker had actually been commissioned to spy on him, or at the very least to use the expedition as a cover enabling him to spy on the vintagers they intended to visit and any other travellers who might be abroad. He knew, too, that Vaedecker must be aware that it was obvious – but that was not a licence to say the words aloud. All Reinmar said, instead, was: 'Where's your horse?'

'I'm an infantryman,' the sergeant replied, mildly. 'The horses on which I and my companions arrived in Eilhart were hired, time being short while we still hoped to catch the man we were following before he disembarked. I shall be quite content to ride in the cart with you.'

When Godrich joined them, Reinmar asked whether his father knew about the sergeant's orders, but it was the sergeant who answered. 'He is perfectly agreeable,' Vaedecker assured him – and Godrich confirmed it with a discreetly sullen nod.

Gottfried came out of the shop a few minutes later to bid them all farewell, and he made a show of thanking Vaedecker for lending his services to the party. 'These are troubled times,' he said, blithely overlooking the fact that the only symptom of trouble so far visible in Eilhart had been von Spurzheim's arrival, 'and I shall feel much better knowing that Reinmar has a seasoned soldier with him. The combination of Godrich's wisdom, Sigurd's strength and your fighting skill should ensure his safe return and the profitability of the expedition.'

'I shall do my very best,' the soldier promised, 'to ensure that the journey is as profitable as anyone could hope.'

Not until the cart was loaded and Godrich had the whip in his fist did Gottfried hand over the purse containing the coins which Reinmar was to use in purchasing new stock. 'Remember,' he said. 'Be patient and clever in striking your bargains. Try not to seem so hard as to cause resentment, but always bear it in mind that we have an effective monopoly. Maintain an appearance of generosity – but make sure that it is only an appearance.'

'I shall do my best,' Reinmar promised. 'If anyone tries to take advantage of my youth and inexperience, I'll tell them that I'm so terrified of my father that I dare not offer them a penny more than the meanest figure I can calculate, lest I be flogged within an inch of my life when I return with a wagon half full and an empty purse. They will easily believe it, will they not?'

'They will,' Gottfried assured him – but his smile was not as broad as it should have been. 'Good luck, my son, and come back safe.'

Ordinarily, Reinmar would have chattered away to Godrich and Sigurd as the cart rolled out of town, but the presence of the sergeant was a powerful inhibiting factor. The only topic of conversation within the town that morning would be the arrest of Albrecht Wieland and its likely import, but that was not something that could be safely discussed in front of Vaedecker and Reinmar was not sufficiently desperate to cast about for a harmless substitute.

The road on which they left town was a good one, but their progress was slowed somewhat by the fact that there was considerable traffic in the other direction. Although it was the day before the principal market day, the flow of everyday produce like eggs and milk was swelled by the movement of heavier produce in preparation for the weekly orgy of buying and selling. The further they drew away from the town, in fact, the more traffic of that kind they encountered and the narrower the road became. Theirs was the uphill route, which made their progress even more difficult.

At first, they followed the course of the river, which flowed relatively smoothly for a league or so above Eilhart pool, even though it was not considered navigable by cargo-boats. There were plenty of rowboats on the water, and flat-bottomed ferries bringing carters and foot-travellers from the further bank, where the tracks were less comfortable. When they came to the first confluence of the Schilder with one of its lesser streams, they swung away south-westwards and the way became steeper. The peaks of the Grey Mountains were visible even in Eilhart, although the intervening hills supported the bleak horizon with a rich band of green, but the further they went into the forested slopes the more grey became visible from every ridge, and the true mass of the mountains became far easier to judge.

By midday they had left the best farmlands behind, having progressed into drier land better suited to vines than to grain or root vegetables. In the depths of winter, Reinmar knew, the sun could scarcely raise itself above the distant peaks and all this land seemed bleak and derelict, but when the sun was high and shone benignly down upon them the valleys seemed much richer. The best vines grew on southern-facing slopes, and were always on the farther side of their particular hills, so the faces to which the cart first came usually looked wild and unpromising. They were grazed by flocks of ragged goats. When the cart had moved around to the better side, the vineyards nestling into the hillsides were revealed, each one dominated by a grey stone house surrounded by labourers' cottages. A few such clusters were large enough to be reckoned villages, with their own inns, shrines and burial-grounds, but most were set some way apart from the dwellings that clung to the banks of streams and the coverts where fruit trees grew and foresters gathered.

Reinmar made his first purchases as dusk approached, and they lodged that night with the wine-grower. Reinmar offered no explanation of Vaedecker's presence and the grower assumed that he was present at Gottfried's request to afford extra protection for his son. This enabled Vaedecker to ask some subtly searching questions about possible difficulties they might face as they went higher into the hills.

'None that I can vouch for,' the grower assured them. 'There is a lot of talk of monsters and black magic, but such talk is always produced in quantity when settled folk want an excuse to harass the gypsies. The summer has been an awkward one – some farmers have had a mediocre but satisfactory harvest while others have seen their crops utterly ruined by fierce storms. That has lowered the demand for casual labour, leaving more travellers to roam the land in search of whatever pickings they can find, and the situation has inflamed the jealousies that always fester among such folk. Why me? the unlucky always say in such circumstances. Why me and not him? Who has cursed me with this foul misfortune? Any violence bred by such talk tends to be suffered by the gypsies as well as blamed on them – I doubt that anyone will trouble you.'

This sounded to Reinmar like good common sense, although Vaedecker did not seem entirely satisfied.

What they saw in the course of the next three days seemed to Reinmar to confirm his judgement. The higher hills were often subject to violent but localised storms, which could batter fields and buildings with hailstones even in the hottest months, and such visitations could blast the fruits of one man's yearly labour to smithereens while leaving his neighbour's crop untouched. In good years the neighbours would rally round, alleviating the disaster with a portion of their own surplus, but in years when their yields had not lived up to their own hopes the neighbours were less generous and resentments accumulated. The pent-up anger usually erupted in ways that would not threaten permanent relationships, rebounding on strangers and scapegoats. Whenever he saw groups of gypsies Reinmar noted clear signs of tension between them and the settled folk.

Reinmar had always been instructed by his father to make it a point of principle to treat gypsies no less politely than anyone else, because the seasonal labour provided by the nomads was vital to the production of good vintages. This was partly because time was so much of the essence in harvesting and processing the grapes and partly because many gypsies were not only skilled men and women but people with an instinctive feel for the art of wine-making. Without the contribution of the gypsies, Gottfried had often told Reinmar, the products they sold would be poorer, and the greatest loss would be suffered by the finest vintages.

For his own part, Reinmar had always been fascinated by the gypsies who came to the market in Eilhart, especially by those who attempted to earn coin by various kinds of exotic performance: fortune-telling, playing musical instruments of their own design and manufacture, and dancing. He had always felt that there was a little magic in gypsy music, which was as intoxicating in its own way as good wine.

With all this in mind, Reinmar made a particular effort to be courteous and friendly towards the gypsies the cart encountered on the road, and was slightly hurt by the fact that their responses were often curt and suspicious. At first he was inclined to attribute this entirely to the legacy of insults hurled at them by other prosperous folk, but he realised eventually that Matthias Vaedecker's presence was an additional factor. Without his colours the sergeant was supposedly in civilian dress, but that only made his possession of a crossbow more remarkable, and his attitude to the gypsies was not ameliorated by the conditions that modified the manners of his companions.

Eventually, Reinmar took Vaedecker to task for this while the cart was making its way through a particularly gloomy wood.

'You should not stare at them with such frank hostility,' he said. 'They are people like you or me, who will respond to a smile and a kind word as well as anyone. How would you feel if you were greeted everywhere with stony looks and signs supposedly designed to ward off the evil eye?'

'The nomad tribes are breeding-grounds for evil,' Vaedecker assured him. 'I do not say that they are all magicians, but I do say that any who are enthusiastic to sell their souls can readily find recipes for self-destruction and tutors in witchcraft. Their culture is corrupt – and if your father is to be believed, they are the ones who know where the dark wine is made.'

'If that were the case,' Reinmar informed him, unable to hide his irritation, 'a wise spy would make every effort to be friendly, helpful and cheerful.'

Somewhat to his surprise, Vaedecker seemed to take this observation seriously. 'You are right, of course,' the sergeant said, with a sigh. 'This is not the kind of work for which I was trained. I'm a fighting-man, not a secret agent. I'm used to meeting the enemy head-on. I'm a Reiklander through and through, but once a man has done a long tour in the north, where life is hard for everyone and evil clearly manifest, the south comes to seem like a land becalmed in a dream.'

'What do you mean?' Reinmar asked him, taken aback by the sudden rush of confidentiality.

'The people who live ordered and comfortable lives in towns like Eilhart assume that theirs is the way human life should be lived,' Vaedecker observed. 'They think that if only people everywhere were like them – hard-working, businesslike and scrupulous – the whole world would be like Eilhart, as prosperous and as happy as any community has any right to be. It isn't so. There are places in the world – places not merely on the borders of the Empire but actually within its bounds – where the wages of hard work and a businesslike attitude is an early and ignominious death, which end can only be postponed by fighting the enemies of order with every last fibre of strength and ounce of courage a man possesses.'

'So all travellers' tales say,' Reinmar remarked.

Vaedecker did not take offence at his scepticism. 'You hear tales of monsters in the hills, Master Wieland, and your automatic reaction is to say, laughing, that there are always tales of monsters in the hills. Well, Reinmar, I have fought whole armies of monsters, with darts and arrows, swords and clubs – and sometimes, in the end, with nothing but my bare and bloody hands. Monsters have come so close to tearing out my throat that I can never laugh when I hear the word. I have seen them so awfully arrayed in their hundreds before the pikes of my fellows and the lances of the guard that it sickens and disheartens me to hear men like yourself casually assuming that only fools could believe such things dangerous. I am a traveller of sorts, but I can assure you that the tales I have to tell are true, and even nastier than they sound. The world is not like Eilhart, my friend – and if the state of affairs that pertains elsewhere in the world of men ever spreads to Eilhart, you might find yourself awakening from that lovely dream in which you have lived your entire life, into nightmarish reality.'

Had these words been spoken while the cart was bathed in warm sunshine, or while the four men with it had been sat around a blazing fire in a grower's well-stocked hearth, they might not have seemed so threatening. In fact, the sky that was all-but-eclipsed by the branches of the looming conifers was blue only in the north. The mountaintops to the south were immersed in a thick blanket of grey cloud, whose trailing edges extended over them like an ominous awning.

In such circumstances, Reinmar could hardly suppress a shudder as the sergeant's words cut through him and penetrated his heart. He could find no adequate reply.

'So you will understand,' Vaedecker added, 'that I cannot look upon the gypsy folk with the same generous and trusting eye as you. I do not doubt that you are right, and that many of them are good and honest souls who mean us no harm – but the knowledge that even one in a hundred is not is quite enough to make a man like me uneasy. Still, I will follow your advice and try to suppress my feelings, not because it is polite but because it is politic. I am, as you have kindly reminded me, a spy – and I must do my very best to watch the folk we encounter as closely as I am watching you.'

The last sentence, with its veiled accusation, helped Reinmar overcome his embarrassment. He saw Godrich's head turned, and took note of the warning in the steward's eyes, but he ignored the silent advice.

'It must be an indignity for a fighting man like yourself to be reduced to spying,' Reinmar observed. 'Indeed, it must be a sickening come-down for a bold hero used to fighting legions of monsters to be chasing liquor-smugglers through the happiest lands in the realm.'

'Must it?' Vaedecker countered. 'I have stood face-to-face with beastmen and ogres and wished that I might be anywhere else in the world, about any other kind of work. Duty does not always compel us to spectacular exploits. I have always used my strength in the service of virtue, however menial my task – although I cannot expect that to impress men whose notion of hard labour is entirely determined by their experience of lifting and moving casks of wine.'

Even Sigurd frowned at that, but Sigurd was not the kind of man to react to slights. If he did not intend to move with crushing force he did not move at all.

'Peace, friends,' Godrich said, turning in his seat. 'The cart is not half full and we have a long way yet to go. The time will pass more easily if we can keep from quarrelling. We are not adversaries. In this matter of the dark wine we are all on the same side.'

Are we? Reinmar thought, but he held his tongue. He forced himself to nod, and to soften his expression. It was not an apology, but it was a gesture, and Matthias Vaedecker – who probably felt that he had spoken far too freely – was prepared to do more than match it.

'Aye,' he said. 'Your man is right. I'm not used to being set apart from my own kind like this, and I have become fretful. I meant no offence.'

'Nor I,' Reinmar felt bound to add. 'I have been here before, but always with my father to guide me. I suppose I too am a little uneasy – and I do not like to see those clouds gathering about the mountain-peaks. It is thunderheads of that kind which spit out the storms that cause so much consternation hereabouts.'

'We'll be fine till nightfall,' Godrich assured him, quick to take advantage of the change of subject. 'There's a village ahead with an inn and a blacksmith to see to the horses, so we'll be warm no matter what. With luck, the sky will be clearer in the morning.'

And without it, Reinmar thought, some of us may be looking for someone to blame for any hail that falls upon our luckless heads.

CHAPTER EIGHT

AS ILL LUCK would have it, things began to go wrong long before nightfall. The village that Godrich had welcomed as a potential haven did indeed have an inn and a forge, and even a market square of sorts between the inn yard and the town pump. When the cart pulled into that square, however, it seemed to be anything but an outpost of Reikish civilisation.

The conflict that was in full swing on the cobbles probably seemed to be a mere casual brawl to the battle-hardened sergeant, but it seemed bloody and bitter enough to Reinmar. No weapon was being wielded more deadly than a pitchfork, but he knew that cudgels could do an enormous amount of damage if plied with sufficient vigour, and there was no doubting the enthusiasm of the foresters and farm-hands who were laying about them with a fine fury.

The object of the local men's ire was a party of gypsies, no more than a dozen strong – including three women and two small children – whose even greater ardour was not nearly enough to make up for the deficit in their numbers. The fight had presumably begun in the middle of the square, but the gypsies had already been forced back against the wall of the inn. They had so little room for further manoeuvre that their attempts to stay together in a square formation, in which they could make some attempt to guard one another's backs, were futile. They were being forced into a thin line, with no space at all for retreat. Two had already gone down, one of them a boy no more than twelve years old. Now that their adversaries had them trapped it seemed that they would all go down one by one, each to be beaten black and blue by staves, boots and rake-handles.

Reinmar did not suppose that the gypsies' attackers intended to murder them, but it required no more than a glance to see that they were highly unlikely to be particular in judging the exact extent of the punishment they were handing out, even to the women and children.

Rising impulsively to his feet, Reinmar filled his lungs, ready to shout an order to desist at the top of his voice, but Godrich was too quick for him. Keenly aware of his own duty, the steward grabbed his master's son hard and jammed a gauntleted hand over the lower part of his face, with the fingers splayed to choke off his shout. Reinmar spluttered, but could not deliver his challenge. Furiously, he reached up with his own hands to drag the cloying glove away from his mouth, but the steward was strong as well as determined. Godrich was, however, sufficiently sensitive to the diplomatic necessities of the situation to round on Sergeant Vaedecker.

'Soldier!' he said. 'You have much to say of duty, and of the necessity of keeping order. Exercise your powers of discipline!'

Vaedecker was obviously reluctant, but his expression showed clearly enough that the appeal to his sense of duty was not misplaced. While he hesitated, though, Sigurd acted.

The giant did not jump down from the cart immediately, perhaps judging that the extra elevation would make his immense height seem positively supernatural at first glance. To emphasise the point even further he raised his massive arms above his head, holding his six-foot staff horizontally, before howling: 'Stop! In the name of the law!'

He had, of course, no real authority to speak for the law, but the village was by no means large enough to possess a constable, so there was hardly likely to be anyone in the crowd in a position to dispute his entitlement.

The loudness of Sigurd's cry was remarkable, but it was not nearly as remarkable as the echoes which fired back and forth from the walls of the inn and its stables, from the forge and from the opposite barn – and seemingly, though it must have been an illusion, from the peaks of the Grey Mountains.

The immediate effect of the command was as impressive as Reinmar could possibly have wished. The entire fracas was abruptly stilled, as every single combatant paused and looked around to see who had spoken.

Had they only seen four men in a half-laden cart drawn by two exhausted horses the foresters and farm-labourers might have returned to their work without delay, but Sigurd did not look like any mere man. Striking a pose in the blue twilight, with his arms upraised to the lowering sky, he must have seemed to anyone with imagination like Sigmar Heldenhammer reincarnate.

'Drop your weapons!' Sigurd shouted, following through his advantage.

Half a dozen staves and axe-handles clattered to the ground, all of them dropped by members of the attacking force. The gypsies, by and large, were not quite so startled and not quite so impressed – and that gave them a fraction of a second to reconsider their options.

'Run!' shouted one of their number – a man whose booming voice echoed almost as impressively as Sigurd's.

It was a wise decision. Any violent advantage the gypsies might have taken of the disconcertion of their attackers would have been very brief, and would have called forth a much stronger reaction. Flight, on the other hand, prompted no reflexive response.

Had the gypsies had more room they might have managed to contrive a safe retreat, even pausing to pick up their fallen. Even as it was, the man who had shouted the order contrived to snatch up the fallen child and managed to jostle his way clear, while five or six of his companions also managed to slip sideways from the battle-line before anyone thought to wonder whether it was worth trying to stop them. Unfortunately, the four gypsies who were furthest away from the edges of the inn-wall had no obvious escape-route available. Because they were in the centre, their adversaries were gathered more thickly in front of them, and whichever way they turned their path was blocked by bodies.

For five or six seconds after Sigurd first cried out no one was actually attempting to knock the remaining gypsies down, but that interval was not long enough for them to find a route out of harm's way – and when the mob realised that the objects of their hatred were in the process of escaping, they still had more than enough anger in reserve to make them stubborn.

Nobody shouted 'Stop them!' because nobody had to; the curious collective consciousness that mobs sometimes acquire restored a similar sense of purpose to each and every one of them. Sticks, fists and boots were raised again, but this time the fight separated out into three. One company of gypsies ran to the right, and was pursued; another went to the left, and was also chased. The third, unable to run, lashed out with whatever meagre force its members could contrive.

Given the uneven distribution of the attacking force, it was inevitable that the three-way split should be far from equal. The four gypsies who fled to the right were chased by five foresters, the three who fled to the left – one of them carrying the child – were pursued by four farm-hands. The four who were left to make their stand found themselves outnumbered almost four-to-one by various abundantly-muscled opponents. That would have been a very brief fight indeed if Sigurd and Matthias Vaedecker had not decided that the time had come to assert their authority in person.

Sigurd shouted again, repeating his instruction to let all weapons drop, but he had leapt to the ground by now and the second shout had amply demonstrated that the multiplication of his voice was not, in fact, supernatural. Vaedecker shouted too, invoking the names of Sigmar, Magnus, the Emperor and the Reiksguard, but any effect those august names might have had was ruined by the cacophonous echoes, which swallowed up the sense of what he said.

Neither Sigurd nor Vaedecker made the slightest attempt to break heads or knock men down. They were entirely content to haul their opponents back and shove them aside – but anyone hauled back and shoved aside by the giant stayed where he was put, and Vaedecker knew how to handle men firmly without doing them any permanent damage. It took them less than three minutes to scatter the remnant of the mob like ears of corn under the thresher – but by the time they had fought their way through to the people whose backs were to the wall not one of the four was still standing. Only two were able to raise themselves painfully to their feet as the square became suddenly quiet again.

Sigurd beckoned to Godrich, who finally consented to let go of Reinmar's mouth.

'Sorry, sir,' the steward murmured. 'Remember, I beg you, that we do business here, and must be careful.' Having said this, he went straight away to one of the fallen bodies – a woman's – whose condition was obviously causing Sigurd some concern. Vaedecker was checking the injuries of the other fallen man, so Reinmar went to one of those who had regained his feet.

'Thank you, sir,' the gypsy said, using the fingers of his right hand to test the flesh of his upper left arm for evidence of a break. 'They'd have killed us for sure were it not for your arrival. You're Gottfried the Merchant's son, are you not? My name is Rollo – your father would know my face.'

'What was the fight about?' Reinmar asked him.

'What is it ever about? Work and witchcraft. We brought in the vintage on the estate south of the village, and brought it in better than it deserved, while most of the local farms had a bad year. The chickens won't lay and the hunters' snares have been empty for weeks. All summer they've been whispering that we bought our luck at the expense of theirs – that we're in league with the monsters in the woods that have ruined the hunting. We were paid off yesterday, and thought to leave a little coin behind in their inn, as a token of our good intent – stupid, to think that such as they could understand a generous gesture.' While he was speaking the man moved to join his companion and Godrich, who were kneeling anxiously over the unconscious woman. Sigurd stood aside to give them room, and Reinmar thought it best to take a pace back – a pace which brought him into collision with Matthias Vaedecker.

Reinmar apologised, but the soldier had already forgiven him his clumsiness. 'The boy will be all right,' the sergeant opined, referring to the other seemingly serious casualty. 'The clubs knocked the wind out of him, and he'll have some ugly bruises, but there's nothing broken so far as I can tell. Perhaps as well – I don't suppose there's a bone-setter nearer than Eilhart, or even a barber, and letting the smith have at him would be likely to do more harm than good, by accident if not by design.'

'I dare say that you can set a bone, if you have to,' Reinmar said, his mind still on the other casualty. 'If not, Godrich can turn his hand to most things.'

'Never met a steward who didn't fancy himself a swordsman and a surgeon,' Vaedecker muttered, ungraciously, 'but they serve best of all when they only stand and wait.'

The gypsy who had spoken to Reinmar obviously had more faith in a steward's judgement, for he was anxiously begging Godrich for a verdict on the girl's condition.

'Not good, I fear,' Godrich said. 'She's taken a bad blow to the head. We ought to move her into the inn and make her comfortable on a mattress. There's not much we can do thereafter but wait.'

'Wait!' Rollo exclaimed. 'We cannot wait here! Not after this.'

'You'll come to no harm tonight,' the steward said. 'You've nothing to fear while we are with you. In the morning... we'll consider our options again.'

Rollo and his unhurt friend immediately removed themselves by a couple of paces from their rescuers and went into a huddle. After a couple of minutes they re-emerged, the spokesman saying: 'Tam and I must find the others, tell them what is happening and find out what they want us to do. I'll be back as soon after daybreak as I can. If you'll look after the boy and the girl till then, we'll be grateful – but after that, we'll have to be gone. Those louts may still think they have a score to settle.'

'We'll keep them safe tonight,' Reinmar promised, speaking swiftly lest Sergeant Vaedecker had other ideas. 'We'll wait for you in the morning, before we move on to sample the vintage you've brought in.'

'Thank you, sir,' the gypsy said. 'It's a fine vintage, all things considered, and I'm glad you'll be getting the benefit of it. I'll see you in the morning – but you needn't wait. We'll find you easily enough wherever you may be, and I'd as soon not have to come back here.'

In the meantime, Sigurd had gone to the door of the inn, which had been firmly closed and barred while the fight had raged, and had begun to hammer upon it.

The innkeeper must have been watching from a window, as would anyone else in the village who possessed a window, but when he opened the door he pretended to be astonished by what he saw.

'Godrich!' he exclaimed, in the manner of a man greeting a long-lost cousin – or perhaps more generously than that, Reinmar thought, having recently seen the greeting his father had given to an actual long-lost cousin. 'You're early this year. Come in, come in!'

'Help me with the girl, Sigurd,' Godrich said. 'We must lift her very carefully, supporting her head, and we must lie her down as gently as we can. If you and Sergeant Vaedecker would care to bring the boy, Reinmar, it will save time.'

The innkeeper did not extend his act so far as to ask what had happened or who the injured people were; he merely stepped aside to let his unexpected guests convey their own unexpected guests into his sitting-room.

'I'll send a boy to take care of the horses and the cart,' the innkeeper offered, when both burdens had been safely laid down.

'That's very kind of you,' Godrich said, 'but Sigurd and I will see to that. You know how anxious we always are to see that no harm comes to our cargo.'

'Of course,' said the innkeeper. 'I'll see what I can find in my own cellar – but the food's poor, I fear. The hunting's been terrible all summer, and it's hardly been worth holding a market. I'll probably have to import supplies from the lowlands to see us through the winter – and that won't sit well with the people hereabouts.'

'We've supplies of our own,' Godrich assured him, with a slightly contrived sigh, 'which you're welcome to share for tonight, of course.'

'Very kind,' said the innkeeper. 'Very kind.'

'Too kind by half,' Matthias Vaedecker muttered in Reinmar's ear. 'Considering the number of friends you've lost by breaking up that fight, slipping our host a slice of ham won't even begin to make amends.'

'Too late now to disapprove,' Reinmar observed, dryly. 'When the fight was on, you did the right thing.'

'I did,' the sergeant agreed. 'But did you? I'm just a soldier passing through, but you're a wine merchant. It must be difficult, though, feeling obliged to support both sides in a dispute like that.'

'It's easy enough,' Reinmar assured him, 'if you stick to the principles of common sense and decency.

He expected Vaedecker to scowl, but in fact the sergeant smiled, and clapped him lightly on the shoulder. 'Enough for one day, friend,' he said. 'Let's get some rest, and some food. There's nothing like a good fight to build an appetite – and that farce out front was certainly nothing like a good fight.'

Reinmar looked at him suspiciously, but he could not see any hidden meaning within the feeble joke so he eventually condescended to smile and nod. Then he went to the pallet beside the fireplace, where Sigurd and Godrich had laid the girl down.

He had not realised before how beautiful she was, but now the lamplight shone full upon her face he realised that she was quite exceptional. She was of the same general type as the girls he had often seen dancing for pennies in Eilhart's market square, with glossy jet-black hair, a dark complexion and soft full lips, but she seemed more delicate and exquisite than the robust and slightly coarse dancing girls. Although she was unconscious her facial muscles did not seem relaxed. She was, in fact, wearing a troubled expression, as if her sleep had delivered her into a disturbing dream.

Far from making the girl seem less appealing, the troubled expression awoke a fervent pity in Reinmar, and he yearned to be able to dive into her dream and rescue her from its nightmare threats. While he watched he saw her lips move, and for a moment he thought that she was about to wake, but whatever words she was trying to form remained inchoate and soundless.

Reinmar knelt down beside the nomad girl and bowed low over her head, but there was nothing more to hear. From this angle, though, he could see the blood matted in her hair where she had been struck by a cudgel, and he could make out the contours of the ugly bump swelling up beneath the bloodstain. If her skull was split, he supposed, she would certainly die – but human heads were notoriously hard and resilient, and she was probably far less frail than she seemed. At least, he hoped so.

'Don't be afraid,' he murmured. 'No harm will come to you. I swear it.'

'Don't promise too much,' Godrich murmured. 'She's in a bad way.' Reinmar was afraid that he might be right. Even so, he was prepared to promise anything within his power.

Chapter Nine

As was usual, Godrich instructed Sigurd to sleep on the wagon. Because the innkeeper's barn was separated from the inn itself by a considerable space, and because he judged that the risk to the stock was far greater than it was on most nights, the steward decided to join his labourer. He apologised to Reinmar for leaving him alone with the soldier to take care of the two wounded gypsies, but assured him that he would be ready to come to their aid at a moment's notice – as Vaedecker would doubtless be ready to come to his.

When Reinmar demanded extra pallets so that he and Vaedecker could sleep beside the stricken pair the innkeeper shrugged his shoulders and sent his boy to stuff a couple of linen sacks with straw. He did not apologise for the quality of the straw, nor did he assure them that he would be ready to answer any further whims at a moment's notice. This failure of customer service presumably reflected his suspicion that the evening's events might leave an awkward legacy of bad feeling festering in some of his regular clients.

'We had to break it up,' Reinmar said, defensively, when he and Vaedecker had been left to their own devices.

'Agreed,' the sergeant said wholeheartedly. 'I'm not such a stickler for propriety as to say that fighting should be reserved entirely for soldiers, but I can't stand to see people going at it without the least semblance of military discipline. Reminds me of the unruly creatures we sometimes have to face on northern campaigns. If people like us can't do our bit to keep order, who can?' His tone made the words sound less than wholly serious, but Reinmar suspected that he meant every word.

'You talk of creatures, monsters and ogres,' he said. 'Don't you ever have occasion to fight men when you're off on your adventures?'

'Oh yes,' said Vaedecker. 'Mostly men – but the distinction isn't always as clear as you'd imagine. Men can be marked, you see, when they turn against the ideals of civilisation, order and empire. It's as if they begin to become creatures as soon as they forsake the discipline of being human. The further they go in opposition to the ideals of order and harmony, the more bestial they become – and in the end, there's nothing left of them but monsters. Some liken it to sliding down a slippery slope, but a businessman like you might find it easier to imagine it in terms of finding the obligations of human society too taxing, and the evasion of that tax slowly compounding into full-scale fraud.'

'You don't like businessmen very much, do you?'

'Never think that, lad,' Vaedecker said. 'I know as well as anyone what rewards the Empire reaps from healthy trade along the Reik. What I worry about is that such folk often come to consider themselves immune from the threats and temptations that afflict the rest of us, and they're not. People like your grandfather and his brother think they can dabble in black magic the way they might dabble in tax evasion, but they have no idea what they're playing with. They don't realise that the risks they run aren't just borne by them but by the rest of us. It's bad enough when nomads and gypsies dabble in magic, but at least they're on the fringes of society, not really part of its fabric. In his prime, Luther Wieland was at the very heart of society in Eilhart, and his corruption could have been a direly serious matter. You can't imagine how great a debt you owe to your father's strength of mind. Had he not purged your business of the dark wine the whole of Eilhart might now be as sick, frail and mad as the old man.'

'He's not mad,' Reinmar protested. 'He's just old.'

'Older than he would be if he'd never taken a sip of the wine of dreams,' Vaedecker opined. 'But the false youth he'd have obtained had he continued to drink it would have been bought at a terrible price, paid by everyone with whom he came into contact – including you.'

'So you say,' Reinmar countered, the criticism calling forth his natural stubbornness. 'But I hear talk of that kind all the time, and none of it ever matches my reality. There are monsters in the hills, I hear – but the only monsters I have seen have been brutes attacking women and children with clubs, rakes and pitchforks. The north has so many monsters that they gather into armies to harry the Reiksguard and the knights of every other order, so you tell me, but the only military action of yours that I have observed was the search of my father's cellars. The tales that are told of the Empire's glorious history ramble on about the great war against the skaven, the great war against the Vampire Counts of Sylvania and the legendary victory of Magnus the Pious over a monstrous horde at the gates of Kislev, but are there skaven or Vampire Counts in the world now? And what is Kislev but a neighbour state with which we trade? Do you see my difficulty, sergeant?'

'Only too well,' Vaedecker agreed. 'But you do not see mine. I do not know for certain whether there are vampires in the world now, but I believe it. As for skaven – if that is the name for men-become-beasts who take their stigmata from the common rat, then yes, there are skaven in the world now and I have spilled their blood myself. Now Kislev, it is a state of sorts, where men struggle hard to do what men must do to retain their manhood, including trade, but it is a state under perpetual siege by every kind of evil, after a fashion that you cannot seem to grasp. I suppose I should hope that the scales of innocence never fall from your eyes, but I cannot. If you were my son, Reinmar Wieland, I would want you to understand what kind of a world it is in which you live, however harsh the lesson was.'

'Bravo,' said a weak voice. 'Might I have some water?' It was the gypsy boy, who had obviously recovered consciousness some time before, and had been waiting for an opportunity to make himself heard.

Reinmar filled a leather cup with water from a jug which the innkeeper had left for them on the table.

It was not until the boy had drunk it, wincing at the slightest movement of his head, that he noticed the second casualty. 'Marcilla!' he said, angrily. 'What have they…?' He could not finish the sentence.

'She's still alive,' Vaedecker was quick to say. 'She's taken fewer bruises to the body than you have. When she's slept off the head-blow that knocked her out she'll probably be fine.' He was promising far too much, but he obviously did not want the boy to become too agitated. By way of further distraction he added a question. 'Is she your sister?'

The boy made as if to nod, thought better of it, and whispered: 'Aye. We're twins, but not alike – like enough, though, that I might have been felled by the blow that hit her, without even taking a bruise to my own skull.'

As he spoke the boy used his arms to drag himself across the floor, without even attempting to crawl, let alone to walk. When he arrived beside his sister he touched the back of his hand gently to her forehead.

'I knew it,' he said. 'She has a fever. Half of this ache in my head is hers. I can feel the fury of her dreams, and…' He broke off abruptly.

'And what?' Vaedecker asked, mildly.

The boy did not answer. In response to his touch, however, the girl roused slightly. If, as the boy said, her condition was compounding his, the slight alleviation of his condition must have echoed in her own. Her eyeballs were moving rapidly from side to side beneath closed lids, and her lips trembled. A few muttered words escaped them, too ill-formed to be comprehensible, except perhaps for one.

Reinmar was at first perfectly certain, although it took no more than a couple of seconds for profound doubts to return, that one of the words she spoke was 'call'.

Even if it was, he told himself, sternly, it might mean nothing. The word has a perfectly ordinary everyday meaning. And she might not have said 'call' at all; the syllable might have been conjured up by my own imagination, primed by what my grandfather told us on the eve of our departure.

He might have told himself more, but he was not given the opportunity. Matthias Vaedecker had seized his arm and was gripping it hard. 'What did she say, Master Reinmar?' he demanded. 'What did she say?'

He knows, was Reinmar's reflexive internal response. He knows what it means for a gypsy to hear a call. But what he said aloud was: 'I don't know, sergeant. My ear was only a little closer to her lips than yours.'

'What did she say?' Vaedecker asked the boy.

'She's dreaming,' was all the boy would say. 'She's hurt – but you're right. She cannot die. It won't be allowed.'

Reinmar saw that Vaedecker's first impulse was to demand a further explanation of the last remark, but he saw the sergeant clamp his mouth shut, as if in response to a reminder that he was now a spy, duty-bound to play a long and careful game.

When the sergeant released his arm Reinmar reached out to touch the boy, as reassuringly as he could. 'If your twin is as sensitive to your condition as you are to hers,' he said, 'would it not be a good idea to rest your bruises and to try to sleep?'

The boy turned to him, evidently surprised by his perspicacity, or perhaps by his concern. 'Aye,' he whispered. 'Is my father hurt? Why are we here?'

'Your companions were wise enough to retreat in the face of far superior numbers,' Vaedecker told him. 'They were pursued, but I suspect they're fleet enough and clever enough to make good their escape. One man had to pick up and carry a young boy – might that have been your father?'

The boy nodded warily, although the gesture was obviously painful.

'The fight would have gone much worse for you had we not come along,' the soldier added. 'We broke it up, saving a few hundred bruises and perhaps a life or two. Two others who remained – they named themselves Rollo and Tam – judged that we were fit people to look after you, and defend you from any further harm. They promised to return in the morning. You'll be quite safe until then. You have my word on that. I'm no knight, but I am a soldier – and I am sure that your father would know this man, even if you do not. He is Reinmar Wieland, son of the wine merchant Gottfried Wieland, whose stock you help to produce and refine.'

The boy was nodding more easily now, and it did not seem to be causing him too much discomfort. 'I have heard of you, Master Wieland,' he confirmed. 'I may have seen you, also, when we were both too young to take note of it. My name is Ulick.'

'I will see you safe, Ulick,' Reinmar promised. 'Your sister too. Now, will you take my advice?'

The boy nearly nodded again, but this time felt that even mild discomfort was uncalled-for. 'Aye,' he said. With some effort, he managed to raise himself to his knees and crawl back to his own pallet. He laid himself down with a deep sigh, seemingly satisfied that he could trust his companions to keep their word.

'We had best do likewise,' Vaedecker murmured, and Reinmar agreed.

All of Reinmar's confused ambitions had been reawakened by the suspicion that the girl's delirious mutterings were connected with the strange tale his grandfather had told him before he had set out, but there was no possibility of keeping sleep away after the exertions and privations of the previous few days. He fell unconscious as soon as he laid his head down – but he dreamed extravagantly while he slept and he awoke before any of his immediate companions, with a sense of urgency and anticipation already upon him.

Ulick and Marcilla both appeared to be sleeping soundly and peacefully, although the boy seemed to have become very cold. Reinmar's gaze lingered far longer over the girl, whose features were now possessed by a serenity he had never seen in any human face. Her skin was very smooth, quite flawless in every respect.

Marguerite's skin had the usual bloom of youth, but close inspection showed up a host of tiny blemishes: freckles, small patches of dead skin, blocked pores, unruly hairs a shade darker than those upon her head. Marcilla's loveliness was subject to none of these minuscule compromises. She was so neatly formed, so seemingly polished, that it was hard for Reinmar to believe that she was a product of nature. She was more like a statue brought to life – not one of the military memorials carved from grey stone or cast from bronze that could apparently be seen outside the town halls of every Schilder port but something lovingly formed from Tilean marble, like the ancient busts which were occasionally displayed inside the town halls, as treasures plundered in the course of centuries-old military expeditions.

Her helplessness added to her charm, and the longer Reinmar looked at her the more protective he felt towards her.

He reached out a hand to stroke her face, and her eyelids slowly lifted to display a pair of eyes so wondrously dark as almost to be black rather than brown. The eyes were staring straight at him, but Reinmar was not convinced that the girl had really awakened. There was little or no consciousness in the incurious stare, and he had the strangest feeling that something other than her everyday mind might be using her eyes to appraise him.

Apparently, he passed the appraisal. A slight smile began to ease the corners of her mouth.

'It's all right,' he whispered. 'You're safe.'

Her lips stirred, very slightly – far too slightly, he would normally have assumed, for any audible words to have escaped them. And yet, he did hear words, whether they were spoken or merely imagined.

'I have heard the call,' she seemed to say. 'I must obey.'

'So you must,' he murmured, as her eyes fell shut again and she relaxed back into a deeper sleep – but as he continued stroking her cheek he noticed that her flesh had taken on a sudden chill. He took up the cloak under which he had been sleeping and draped it over her body.

Matthias Vaedecker raised his head then, his eye immediately attracted by the swirl of the cloak. 'Is she awake?' he asked.

'Not yet,' Reinmar said. 'She seems well enough, given the nature of her injury. I think she'll live, if she is given time enough to recover.'

'That's good,' the sergeant acknowledged. He frowned slightly before adding: 'I suppose it would complicate things for us if her kinsfolk cannot collect her.'

Reinmar went to the outhouse behind the inn to relieve himself, then continued to the barn to see if Godrich and Sigurd were awake. They were – and Sigurd was already in conversation with the gypsy spokesman of the night before. They were arguing, but not fiercely.

'Reinmar,' Godrich said, as soon as the steward clapped eyes on his master. 'You remember Rollo. The two within are brother and sister, it seems, and they have a cousin even younger who was also hurt last night. Their father has sent Rollo to ask us whether we will keep the two of them with us until we are well away from the town, so that he can collect them from a far safer place. That would allow him to avoid any further trouble with locals who are still intent on giving the rest of his family a battering. I am not so sure, however, that the girl is fit to travel on roads as bad as those hereabouts in a cart that's already overloaded. She shouldn't really be moved at all.'

Godrich obviously wanted support for his own view, but Reinmar knew that there were times when it could be an advantage to seem naive. He pretended not to understand what was required of him.

'I think the boy will be much better today,' he said. 'As for the girl, we've taken on no more than half our intended cargo, so I think we can make room for her. Since the roads are so ill-made, it will probably be best in any case if Sigurd, the sergeant and I walk behind. We can wrap the girl up well enough to prevent her taking a bruise from every lurch.'

'We have business to transact,' Godrich protested. 'We are not nursemaids – and she really was badly hurt.'

'We saved these people from being murdered,' Reinmar stated. 'We have an obligation to see that they remain safe from their would-be murderers. We shall keep them with us until it is safe to let them go, even if that requires us to shelter them for several days.'

If the steward expected any support from Matthias Vaedecker he was sorely disappointed. The sergeant had come into the barn while they were talking, to tell them that the innkeeper had brought fresh water from the well and an allegedly-new loaf of bread. When he heard what Reinmar was saying he became thoughtful – but by the time the steward turned to him he was quick to add his own endorsement.

'Master Wieland is right,' he said. 'The scoundrels who set upon these folk last night are probably lurking in the pines, brooding on their defeat and awaiting their opportunity. We have to keep the boy and the girl until we're well away from here.' Without waiting for Godrich to comment he addressed Rollo directly, saying: 'Tell your elders that we'll look after them well until they can be collected in perfect safety.'

It sounded like generosity, but Reinmar knew better. The sergeant had heard from the witch hunter what Reinmar had heard from his grandfather: that the source of the dark wine might be protected by magic, but that a way thereto could be opened for those who 'heard a call' and anyone who accompanied them 'to see them safely to their destination'.

Reinmar did not feel able to criticise the soldier for his deceptiveness, given that he was keeping his own counsel, but he did feel that his own motives were far purer. He wanted to know what all the fuss was about, and he was determined to keep an open mind about all the matters of which Vaedecker seemed so fearfully certain.

'Very well,' said Godrich, accepting defeat. 'I suppose we shall be able to conduct our business just as well – and if your assurances are to be trusted, our guests have already played their part in guaranteeing us a good return in these parts. We shall be glad to do as you ask, Rollo.'

'A thousand thanks,' the gypsy said. 'You are good men, and we shall not forget this.'

'How is the girl, really?' Godrich asked the sergeant, when Rollo had gone.

'Very poorly,' Vaedecker admitted. 'But Reinmar may be right. If we can keep her well wrapped up, she might well be safer with us for the next day or two than anywhere else in this treacherous land – and she's a rare beauty.' He cast a knowing sideways glance at Reinmar as he made the last pronouncement, but Reinmar looked away and pretended that he had not heard.

Chapter Ten

By the time the horses had been fed, watered and hitched to the wagon Reinmar could see that Godrich's mood had darkened somewhat. The breakfast they had eaten, while by no means good, should have made him feel better, but any effect of that sort had been more than outweighed by his gloomy contemplation of the early morning weather. The northern sky, from which the last traces of night had still to be erased, was clear enough, but the grey pall that had squatted down upon the mountain peaks the night before had intensified even further. In the west it was so dark as to seem black even by day; in the east, with the sun directly behind it, its leaden gloom was only slightly alleviated by an ochreous yellow tint.

'Storms are gathering,' the steward opined. 'The clouds will spit them out like great gobs of catarrh. If we run into one this afternoon, after we've left the vineyard–'

'We'll pull into the shelter of the pines and raise the canopy,' Reinmar said. The underside of the cart was fitted with three iron bands which could be removed and arched over the body of the wagon, secured in slots on the side-walls to serve as a frame for a protective awning. The awning would be able to withstand a buffeting wind, provided that the wind's force was broken by surrounding trees, and it would keep rain and hail at bay if it had a little help from the overhanging crowns of mature conifers.

'It would be better by far if we did not need to,' the steward muttered. 'Still, the storms are always localised, and usually brief. The likelihood is that they will miss us altogether, and will not trouble us for long if we are unlucky enough to run into one.'

Although Reinmar had been obliged to volunteer to walk with Sigurd and Sergeant Vaedecker in order to lighten the draught-horses' load he was not very enthusiastic to do so. He was relieved when the soldier assured him that he and Sigurd had bodyweight enough between them to render his slim measure irrelevant. Ulick also pronounced himself capable of walking, but Vaedecker disagreed with that too, so Reinmar and the gypsy boy ended up sitting to either side of the unconscious Marcilla, helping to make sure that she was not thrown about whenever the wagon-wheels slipped from one rut into another, or had to negotiate a fallen branch.

They were so high in the hills by now that carts were relatively scarce, and those used by the local farmers had all been home-made, usually with scant regard to the imperial standard gauge. The result of this was that the deep ruts that were worn by conventionally-built carts into the fabric of conventionally-built roads, which ordinary traffic followed like inset rails, were replaced hereabouts by a confusion of different rut-patterns. Even that would not have been so bad had the roads not been mostly used by riders and men afoot, whose hoof- and boot-prints blurred and broke the ruts. Although pack-trains were uncommon this far from the nearest pass through the mountains their occasional passage had wrought even greater havoc with the surface, the weight of the packs having forced the iron-shod hooves of the mules deep into the rain-softened surface, creating a vast and disorderly expanse of shallow pits. This made the labour of the two horses pulling Reinmar's cart that much harder, and made Godrich's task as driver four or five times as difficult as it was at the best of times.

The continued threat of the clouds would probably have made the steward's mood very dark indeed by early afternoon had they not had such a good morning at the vineyard. As Rollo had promised, the harvest had been more abundant than the quality of the season had led them to expect, and the work that had gone into the making of the wine had been artful as well as neatly-timed.

'This is wine that will mature very well indeed,' the steward confided to Reinmar. 'It is for vintages such as this that cellars were intended. This will be a real investment.'

The grower knew this too, of course, but Reinmar had not forgotten what Gottfried had told him about the value of their virtual monopoly. He felt that he had given his generosity quite enough indulgence for one day. He struck what seemed to him – and to Godrich – to be an exceptionally good bargain for an exceptionally large purchase.

The success required a good deal of rearrangement in order that Marcilla could still be comfortably accommodated, but that was accomplished without requiring too much of Sigurd's mighty shoulders, and the party was on its way again a few hours after noon.

By this time, the girl seemed a little better, and Reinmar was somewhat reassured that he had done the right thing. She opened her eyes briefly when Ulick fed some water to her, but she was not yet ready to take anything solid. There was no sign of her other relatives.

'Where will you go for the winter, when you are all united again?' Reinmar asked the boy, when they were once again making steady progress southwestwards, towards the furthest of the vineyards at which they were due to call.

'I don't know,' Ulick said. 'Sometimes we make a winter camp and provision it before the snows arrive, but the hunting has been so bad this year that we would have too little meat to salt away. We might make a trek northwestwards, to join up with other clan-members, or we might go due north into the lowlands to find what lodgings we can in the towns. People do not like us there, but they are never as violent as those madmen last night.'

The boy did not sound sure of any of these possible objectives, and he left Reinmar with the impression that there were others carefully unmentioned.

'Winters are usually mild in Eilhart itself,' Reinmar observed. 'If the uplands have a bad time, though, we feel the effects in spring when the meltwater swells the Schilder. River traffic can be halted for days on end, and if the thaw comes quickly to the hills the river always bursts its banks somewhere. My father and I have never been flooded ourselves, but the parts of the town below the docks are sometimes swamped. Can you still tell whether your sister is dreaming?'

Ulick looked at him a little sharply, but accepted the question as common curiosity.

'She is calm,' he said, 'except...'

After a few moments' silence, Reinmar said: 'Except what?'

The boy shook his head, but he obviously knew how discourteous it would seem if he refused a reply, so he said: 'There is something she and I must do when she is well enough.'

Reinmar knew that it was a risk, but he decided to be bold. 'She has heard a call,' he said. 'You and she have work still to do, bringing in another harvest.'

The boy looked at him suspiciously. 'I am in the trade,' Reinmar reminded him. 'My grandfather is Luther Wieland, whose task it once was to start the wine of dreams on its long journey to Marienburg, via the Schilder and the Reik. My great-uncle went to Marienburg to become a scholar, guided in his ambition by dark wine.'

'Why is the soldier with you?' the boy asked.

'My father thought the cart needed extra protection. There are rumours of monsters abroad in the hills.'

For a moment or two he feared that the boy would dismiss the rumours, and the reason with them, but Ulick's eventual reaction was more surprising than that. 'Yes,' he said. 'I suppose that was wise. We have as much to fear as anyone else, it seems, although I do not know why they are gathering. Do you?'

'Do I know why the monsters are gathering?' Reinmar repeated, not sure he had grasped the true significance of the question. 'How would I?'

Ulick shrugged. 'Perhaps no one does,' he said. 'Marcilla is calm enough, I suppose. I think she would sense it if we had anything to fear... although she gave us no warning of that mob last night. Perhaps, since she heard the call, she has grown deaf to aught else.'

'What kind of monsters are gathering?' Reinmar asked. 'The rumours that have reached Eilhart are vague.'

'The kind that cannot be safely glimpsed except at the limit of vision,' the boy replied, unhelpfully – but then he added: 'Beastmen of a wolfish stripe. More dangerous in packs than those which have no discipline at all, though not as reckless. This is wineland, after all, and the very heart of it.'

'Have you seen them?' Reinmar asked, wondering why his jaw suddenly felt slightly numb.

'Only in my dreams,' the boy replied, glumly. 'The worst place of all, some would say – for I could not see them so clearly in my mind's eye were I not fated to look into their actual faces. It were best, I think, if we could obey the call quickly, but Marcilla is hurt and my father has not managed to catch up with us. Who could have thought that foresters with axe-handles and farm-boys with rakes and pitchforks could disrupt the plans of masters such as ours? What a world we live in!'

'What a world,' Reinmar agreed. His mouth had gone so dry that he had to take a swig of water from the jug he kept beside him. He offered it to Ulick, but the boy shook his head, pointing instead to his sister. Reinmar nodded, and tried to bring the neck of the jug to her lips.

She had responded before, but weakly. This time, she did more than open her lips reflexively. As the water splashed upon her teeth she opened her eyes, and was able to raise her head slightly. Reinmar immediately reached out to help her, and with his support she managed to raise herself up even further, so that she could drink more deeply and more comfortably. By the time she had slaked her thirst she was definitely awake.

She did not attempt to say anything, but she looked up into Reinmar's face, met his eyes, and did not look away. She looked at him as if she had always known him and always trusted him. It seemed to Reinmar, in fact, that she was looking at him as if she loved him.

He knew that it must be wishful thinking, but he was convinced that it was not entirely so. She was definitely looking at him, languidly and very tenderly. He felt his heart lurch in response, and felt a lump form in his throat, and knew that he loved her too. If this was how it felt to be the victim of a magic spell, he thought, it was not so bad – but he did not think that love could really be reckoned a kind of magic.

'We're safe, Marcilla,' Ulick said. 'This is Reinmar Wieland, son of the wine merchant to whom the vintage we helped prepare was promised. He has collected his portion of the crop, having stepped in to save us when the local louts set about us last evening. Father will collect us as soon as he is able, but for now we are in good and sympathetic hands. We shall do what we need to do when we can.'

Marcilla smiled, but paused for a moment longer before testing her voice. 'I have seen him in my dreams,' was what she murmured.

She said it lightly, as if it were of little significance, but Reinmar had just been listening to Ulick's account of what his own dream visions might signify. 'Well,' he said, 'you can see me now in the flesh. The dream has come true.'

'Not yet,' she murmured.

What Reinmar inferred from that was that she had seen more in her dreams than his face. However deaf the call that she had heard might have made her to other influences, it obviously had not made her blind to other possibilities. 'You have nothing to fear,' he assured her. 'While you are with me, I will do my utmost to see that you come to no harm, and if there is anywhere you wish to go I shall do my very best to see that you reach your destination safely.'

'Thank you,' she said, faintly, 'but I have not so far to go, now, and time is not yet pressing.'

Her flawless face still seemed perfect, even in the unkind light, but her flesh was suddenly startled by the fall of a raindrop, which struck her upon the cheek. As it ran away like a tear another caught her on the forehead.

Reinmar suppressed a curse as he looked up in some alarm. The cloud directly overhead seemed as featurelessly leaden as ever, but he could see darker vapours snaking across the sky from the south in the grip of some high capricious wind, and he guessed what was about to happen. At the same time, the realisation struck his steward.

Godrich immediately reined in the horses and looked from side to side in search of a thick stand of trees. The slope they were negotiating was not overly steep, but they had been caught on an upgrade and the ground to either side of the track was horribly uneven. They were in a wood of sorts, but the trees were scrawny and widely spaced and the terrain was dominated by a thick undergrowth of ferns and grasses.

Sigurd and Vaedecker had already run up to stand abreast of the steward's driving-seat. 'Forward!' the sergeant said. 'We must hope to find better ground ahead.'

'You're right,' said Godrich, quickly. 'We need to find a place where we can safely shelter – but we ought to raise the canopy while we roll, if we can.'

'We can,' Sigurd said, having already ducked under the wagon to unfasten the iron bands that would serve as supports for the awning. As Godrich moved the horses forward again the giant began to bend the bars across, one by one.

The first two flexed readily enough, but the third had become brittle with rust and it splintered as soon as Sigurd threw his weight upon it. The end that he had bedded in its slot whipped back like a spring and hurtled away from the wagon, leaving the astonished giant holding the other end like a ludicrously bent broadsword. Sigurd cursed and dropped the useless piece that he still held.

'We must still get the canopy up if we can,' Reinmar said, having already unearthed the cloth from its lodging in the box beneath Godrich's seat.

'There's a better wood ahead,' Godrich told them. 'Let's hope there's a covert where I can roll off the road safely.' The wagon had crested the ridge, sliding slightly to one side as the ground beneath its wheels was slickened by the rain. 'I think we can reach it if we don't get bogged down,' the steward added.

Becoming bogged down was a real danger, Reinmar realised, for the rain had thickened so much in less than a minute that it was pouring from the sky as if from a bucket.

Ulick pulled the cloak that had served Marcilla as a blanket over her head, and told her to draw herself into a huddle, which she did. Then the boy drew his own arms about his head, while Reinmar and Vaedecker wrestled with the canopy-cloth.

The wind had grown stronger, but it was not yet strong enough to drag the sheet from their hands, and they contrived to get it over the pair of half-hoops that Sigurd had managed to erect. It sagged badly at the back, but they pinned it down with casks of wine in order to prevent it billowing up like a sail and catching the wayward wind. The sound of the rain on the stretched cloth was thunderous – and was soon joined by actual thunder after the dimly-lit interior of the wagon was briefly illuminated by a distant lightning-flash.

Sigurd had joined them by now, so the space was very cramped, but Marcilla was able to peep out from beneath the cloak now that the awning was in place, and she was able to move her legs to make a little more room.

The cart moved steadily forward, although the rain blurred visibility to the point at which Reinmar could not make out the wood that Godrich had spotted – nor, for that matter, could he see the road that would take them there if all went well.

'I think it's all right,' Godrich called back. 'There's a gap in the trees into which the cart will probably fit, and the ground looks tolerable. We'll lurch a bit, but... curse you, what's the matter?'

It took Reinmar a second or two to work out that this last remark was addressed to the horses, which were whinnying, and trying to pull themselves up.

'Not now, you fools!' Godrich protested. 'That's shelter – for you as much as for – oh no! In Sigmar's name, *no!*'

The terror in the steward's voice made Reinmar sit bolt upright, and caused Matthias Vaedecker to go scrambling for his weapons.

Reinmar was wearing his own sword but Sigurd had stowed his staff and he too had to go grubbing around in the cargo, his huge shoulders lifting the badly-secured awning. Even Ulick reached down reflexively to snatch up the broken end of the iron strut that Sigurd had dropped at his feet, which he took in hand as if it were a dagger.

Reinmar contrived to get far enough forward to look over the back of Godrich's driving-seat, but it was difficult to see anything at all through the driving rain, except for the backs of the horses. The animals, normally so placid and willing, were rearing up on their hind legs, struggling against the collars and harnesses that bound them to the struts of the cart.

There were straight-boled trees thirty or forty paces away, whose high crowns vanished into the low-lying cloud, but it was difficult to discern exactly what it was that was moving between the boles.

The shadows looked almost human – but not quite human enough. Reinmar remembered all too clearly what Ulick had said about 'beastmen of a wolfish stripe'.

Vaedecker cursed as he took up a position parallel to Reinmar, resting his crossbow on the wooden ridge of the seat to steady his aim. 'Sit still!' he muttered, to Godrich, as he placed the dart and made ready to fire. He took careful aim before doing so, and that interval gave Reinmar the chance to peer a little more intently at the faces of the figures emerging from the wood – the faces that should have been human had they been fitted to the general gait of the creatures, but were instead hairy and elongated and full of bestial cruelty.

Forewarned by Ulick, Reinmar was able to put a name to what he saw, and the name was 'Beastmen!'

Then Vaedecker released the string of his crossbow, the bolt flew true to its target – and all hell broke loose.

Chapter Eleven

The beastmen came forward in a group, although it was impossible for Reinmar to tell exactly how many there were – at least seven, he thought, and perhaps as many as ten. Some came to the left of the horses and some to the right but one actually leapt up between them, pausing for balance on the yoke that connected their collars before using their rain-slicked backs as stepping-stones to launch itself at Godrich.

The steward had dropped the reins, but he had not had time to release the string tying his sword into its scabbard, and the beastman was upon him while the weapon was still undrawn. He tumbled over the back of the driving-seat, his head catching the top of the iron arch which Sigurd had set in place to support the awning. All of a sudden, the beastman was in the wagon with them, and there could be no further doubt as to its monstrous nature.

The creature's arms, though very hairy, were fundamentally humanoid, and its shaggy legs too, although its huge feet were massively clawed. Its head was not quite the head of a wolf, although it was certainly as furry; it had the fangs and the slavering jaws, but its eyes were set further forward than a wolf's and its ears were more like a cat's. Its snout was more like a pig's and it had two vestigial horns set atop its furrowed brow.

Had it only had claws and teeth for weapons the beastman would have been a formidable opponent, but it also had an artificial weapon in each hand – a thick-bladed knife in the right and a club in the left. Perhaps that was not entirely to its advantage, though, because as Godrich sprawled, knocked silly by the blow to his head, there might have been time enough to rip his throat out with those awful teeth – but instead of doing so, the creature raised its knife ready for a disembowelling blow.

That was all the interval Sigurd needed.

The beastmen had not made a sound, but Sigurd let loose a howl far longer and far louder than any mere animal could have contrived, and his hand shot out to seize the beastman that had invaded the wagon by its hairy throat. As he took the creature's neck in his grip Sigurd straightened his body, standing upright.

The canopy burst as the giant's huge head and shoulders went through it, the jagged rip spreading back and forth along the taut cloth to rend it in two – and there was sufficient elasticity in the release to send both halves whipping outwards into the faces of the beastmen who had run to either side of the wagon.

The beastman Sigurd held was as big as Reinmar, and more sturdily built, but the giant lifted it off its feet with contemptuous ease, and crushed its throat with his fingers. By the time his arm had straightened above his head he was holding a mere trophy aloft, displaying it to the rain-filled sky and to the beastmen which had recoiled from the whiplashing fragments of the canopy.

It was a truly awesome sight, but Reinmar could not help thinking that its dignity was more than slightly ruined by the fact that the slain beastman's slackened bowels released a cargo of stinking shit, which showered Matthias Vaedecker's back as well as a dozen rattling casks. Vaedecker did not respond as Reinmar would have; he was too busy taking aim with the second bolt that he had fitted to his crossbow.

Reinmar had no doubt that the shot would have been a second hit had all else been equal, but the terrified horses had realised by now that the source of their fear had moved from front to flank, and they were determined to take the opportunity thus presented. No one was holding the reins, but it would have done no good had Reinmar managed to snatch them up. It would have taken more than merely human strength to stop the horses bolting.

Godrich had lined up the wagon with the gap in the trees into which he had intended to move in search of shelter, but the steward had not had time to ascertain whether the ground was flat enough to be safely traversed. It now transpired that it was not.

As the horses fled and the wagon followed, the whole assembly lurched into a hole and out again, bouncing the casks of wine so vigorously that the ropes holding them in place creaked under the strain. Reinmar, Ulick and Marcilla bounced too, far more freely and far more painfully.

Matthias Vaedecker's shot went wild, and even Sigurd lost his balance. Had the cart been unladen the giant might have recovered his balance with a single adjustment of his stance, but both his feet were planted in narrow spaces, with casks and boxes to one side and fallen bodies everywhere. He lurched, he staggered, and in the end he accepted that he could not stay where he was.

Rather than fall where he stood, the huge man threw the corpse of the beastman over one side of the wagon and made use of what leverage he had to move to the other, leaping into the air. He obviously intended to clear the side of the cart and land two-footed, but the wagon's lurch had cost him too much co-ordination. His foot caught the side of the vehicle as he jumped, tripping him, and he went over flailing his arms, obviously knowing that he was bound to fall.

The wagon continued its forward course, the wheels hitting more ridges and potholes, and not in any kind of order. Reinmar knew that it would be a miracle if none of them broke – but he saw that there was a more urgent danger as the horses careered into the trees. With no one to steer and no native understanding of side-margins and turning arcs, nor any way of communicating that would have allowed them to change course in unison, the panic-stricken animals dragged the left side of the cart against the bole of a tree. The tree's rough bark scraped the wagon along its entire length, splintering several of the timbers and tearing away the fragments of the canopy that had flopped to that side. Both of the remaining iron bands were dislodged from their sockets.

The iron struts rebounded like springs, soaring away in the opposite direction before the runaway horses contrived a second collision, more brutal than the first, between the right-hand side of the wagon and another tree-trunk.

This second collision stopped the wagon dead, and the pins to which the horses' harnesses were secured were ripped out of their wooden beds, disconnecting the animals from the cart. One of the wagon's shafts fractured, and the horses disappeared into the wood, separating as they went. The ragged remnants of their harnesses were not strong enough to bind them together.

For a moment, Reinmar was relieved, not merely for his cargo – which was still secure – but for the four bodies that would have been very badly battered and bruised had the headlong ride continued.

Then he remembered the beastmen.

Temporarily left behind when the horses lurched forward, the beastmen were less than thirty yards in arrears, and now they were coming after their prey. Their first target was the fallen Sigurd, who still had not risen after his heavy fall.

Reinmar heard Matthias Vaedecker curse again, but the sergeant did not hesitate over what needed to be done. With Godrich also out of action, at least for the moment, there was no way that three of them could hold off eight or nine beastmen. To stand any chance at all they needed Sigurd – and that meant they had to defend Sigurd while he was down, until he had time to raise his huge bulk up again and start lashing out with those massive fists.

Vaedecker threw his crossbow aside, drew his sword, and leapt down from the back of the wagon. Then he charged, without waiting to see if anyone was following where he led. As he charged he let loose a fearsome battle-cry, which would certainly have give pause to a human enemy but did not seem to impress the beastmen at all.

'Come on,' said Reinmar to Ulick, as he leapt down behind the soldier and followed him into the fight. Like Vaedecker, he did not wait to see whether Ulick would obey his summons, but he saw from the corner of his eye that the boy had indeed followed him, even though he was only armed with a twisted piece of rusty metal.

It was touch and go whether the beastmen would reach Sigurd's fallen body before Vaedecker did, and both parties put all the effort they could into the winning of the race, with the result that it was a virtual tie.

The beastmen had numbers on their side, but Vaedecker had training, and a far better weapon than any of the beastmen. The sergeant was already sweeping his sword across in a broad horizontal sweep as he arrived by Sigurd's side, and the beastmen were sprinting too hard to stop and jump back. The best they could achieve was to peel away to either side, and neither of the leading two could do that fast enough to avoid the blade. Both were cut about the torso. Although their ribs protected them from fatal damage, the long cuts fountained blood.

It was not so easy to reverse the sweep as the second wave of beastmen arrived. One of them was able to duck inside the soldier's guard, throwing itself upon him as if to wrestle him to the ground. Had he recoiled reflexively, Vaedecker would indeed have gone down, but he had the trained responses of an infantryman, schooled to hold his line no matter what. Vaedecker body-checked the beastman with brutal stubbornness, and smashed his fist into the ugly animal face.

The beastman was far from frail, but it had not bulk enough to win that kind of match and it lurched away. There were two more ready to leap in after it, but Reinmar and Ulick had arrived by now and they each lashed out at a different target.

Reinmar's sword was short and light, built for stabbing rather than sweeping, and he remembered his schooling well enough not to attempt any move for which the weapon was not designed. Although the beastman he targeted managed to avoid his move, it had to throw itself sideways to do so, losing its balance and sprawling on to all fours.

Ulick's piece of iron was not designed for any kind of thrust at all, and the boy was slighter than Reinmar, but he too enjoyed success of a sort. He fetched his enemy a very painful blow upon its upraised arm, and not only made it squeal but caused it to raise its other arm defensively, ruining any blow it might otherwise have aimed at Vaedecker.

When these thrusts had been made, however, the cart's defenders had done what they could for the moment, and there were still three beastmen coming forward.

Reinmar realised that he simply had not time or space to fence with these opponents. The weapons the beastmen carried were meagre, but there were simply too many of them. Three men could not stand against them for more than a matter of minutes.

But four could, if the fourth were Sigurd.

The giant must have been winded by his fall, and probably bruised, but he was not the kind of man to worry about bruises. Once he had managed to suck air back into his evacuated lungs he was ready to rejoin the fray, and all he had to do in order to accomplish that end was to stand up.

That was not as easy as it sounded, given that he had defenders standing over him and attackers eager to displace them, but mere convenience was not an issue. Sigurd was obviously intent on standing as soon as he could stand, and he left it to his friends to get out of the way as soon as they saw him make a move.

Unfortunately, that was not as easy as it sounded either.

Sigurd stood up in the very heart of the brawl, forcing his massive bulk into a space that was simply not there. His fists shot out in two directions – aiming, of course, for beastmen – and he shrugged as he stood, as if to clear the space he needed. No less than three beastmen were sent tumbling – but so was Reinmar. From the corner of his eye he saw Ulick duck under a flailing giant arm, and he saw Vaedecker move with an awesome sense of purpose to a new position, but a fast-moving fist clipped him under the chin and sent him flying.

The sword flew from Reinmar's hand and he just had time to think, as he was taken off his feet, that when he landed – flat on his back – he would be wide open to attack by a plunging dagger or flashing teeth. It would be even worse for him if he struck his head and was knocked unconscious.

Perhaps he had enough presence of mind to react to this awareness, or perhaps it was only blind luck, but in the end he fell upon his shoulders, without whacking the back of his head against the ground. He was indeed wide open to attack, but he did not lose consciousness. He retained full possession of his faculties.

He saw a beastman make as if to fall upon him, and for a split second thought he was doomed – but Sigurd was well aware of the fact that he had just knocked over the man to whom his safety had been entrusted, and the good servant was not about to let his mistake become fatal. As the beastman leapt, Sigurd's arm lashed out in a great horizontal arc, the palm of his hand held flat – and as it impacted with the beastman's neck Reinmar heard the snap that broke the creature's spine.

And as soon as that, it was over.

Suddenly, there were no more enemies to fight. No more beastmen were leaping forward with murderous intent. Save for the one that had just fallen and would never rise again, all eight or nine of them were in full flight, scattering in every direction. They had been eager to fight three men, though two of them had swords, but they were not willing to face three and one fallen if one of the unfallen were Sigurd.

But it was not a victory. Although none of the cart's defenders had been seriously wounded, and all were now ready to renew the fight if necessary, they were stranded. The horses had run off into the driving rain, and the wagon had taken such a battering that it would be a virtual miracle if it were still roadworthy. It would almost certainly require repair, and the horses would require recapture – which could not be achieved without dividing the party.

Now there was no possible room for doubt that there were monsters abroad in the hills; for once, the rumours were true. Had Reinmar's world not turned upside-down already, it would have turned upside-down then – but as things were, he felt grimly unastonished. He had set out on this expedition determined to make discoveries of his own, and he had made them. He suspected that he now knew more than any of his companions, including Vaedecker, about what was happening and what it might signify. He was proud of that, and firmly intent on keeping the advantage.

'Why did they attack us?' Ulick asked. The question presumably sounded more innocent to Sergeant Vaedecker than it did to Reinmar, given that Vaedecker had not been party to their earlier conversation.

'They didn't,' Vaedecker said, scowling as he used the toe of his boot to turn over the second of the two monsters that Sigurd had killed. 'Strictly speaking, we attacked them. They must have taken shelter in the wood when the rain began – and then we came along, driving at them like madmen. If I hadn't fired that first bolt, they might have run away without a fight – but once I'd killed one, they had to react. So we had to kill two more, and leave at least three wounded. Now, they'll either be too terrified to come within half a mile of us, or so angry that they'll be after our blood with real determination. We'll have to hope for the first. The real question is: why are they here? I take it that the woods in these parts aren't normally home to packs of beastmen.'

'No,' said Reinmar. 'They aren't.'

'You may not have liked the idea of rough soldiers coming to your nice, prosperous little town, Master Reinmar,' Vaedecker said, with a certain relish, 'but I've got a shrewd suspicion that you'll soon be grateful that we came. I think we're going to be needed. This expedition is hereby cut short – we return direct to Eilhart as soon as we can. But first, we have to get the horses back.'

'And the wagon fixed,' Reinmar said. 'Let's hope Godrich is well enough to lend a hand – he's the only one with the knowledge and the skill to get it moving again.'

'But first we need the horses,' Vaedecker insisted. 'We need to get to them before the beastmen do, and we need to get them back here safely. Sigurd!'

The giant was not supposed to be taking orders from the soldier, but he did not so much as glance in Reinmar's direction for confirmation. 'Yes,' he said, 'I'll go. You'll have to guard the wagon.'

Reinmar knew that Sigurd didn't really mean 'the wagon'. He meant that he was trusting Vaedecker to look after his master, and his master's other servant.

'Take the boy,' Vaedecker commanded. 'You might need more than one pair of hands.'

Ulick was under no one's orders, and Reinmar expected him to protest that he had to stay with his sister, but in fact the boy nodded meekly. He too appreciated the need to regather what they needed with the maximum possible speed, before the beastmen could regroup and plan another attack.

Sigurd immediately strode off in the direction which the horses had followed, with the gypsy boy hurrying after him.

'What do we do about that?' Reinmar asked, pointing to the beastman whose neck had been broken.

'Nothing,' Vaedecker replied. 'The one we have to attend to is Godrich. As you say, he's the one whose knowledge and skill will allow us to patch up the wagon, if it can be patched at all.'

As if the bleakness of his tone had not lent a keen enough edge to the import of his words, lightning flashed upon the mountain peaks far to the south, then flashed again and again as a whole chain of strikes extended across the range. The sky was filled with the crackle of distant thunder, and when it finally died away the steady hiss of the rain that fell all about them seemed twice as loud as it had before.

'This is it, Reinmar,' Matthias Vaedecker said. 'This is where it begins.'

'Where what begins?' Reinmar wanted to know.

'Reality,' the sergeant retorted. 'The dream is dissolving, and the nightmare is free. This is when you begin to find out what the world is really like.'

CHAPTER TWELVE

THE STORM CLOUDS had already blown over, and the rain had ceased as abruptly as it had begun, but thick cloud still lay across the southern half of the sky. The sun's light was beginning its slow fade towards darkness.

When Reinmar and Vaedecker had sheathed their blades and toiled back to the cart they found Godrich sitting up and nursing his head between his hands. He seemed very groggy, but when Reinmar scrambled back on to the wooden boards he roused himself and said: 'It's just a bump on the head and a twisted ankle. I'll live.' He was already looking about him, his careful eye judging the extent of the damage that the cart and its cargo had sustained. Appearances were not encouraging, although the steward's expression suggested that he had feared worse.

'Where's the girl?' Vaedecker demanded, suddenly.

Reinmar was surprised by the urgency in the sergeant's tone. He had not thought the soldier to be a caring man.

Godrich looked around, uncertainly, while Vaedecker snatched up the cloak under which the gypsy girl had been huddling, shaking it as if she might somehow have slipped into its lining. It was Reinmar who spotted her, already fifty or sixty paces away from the wagon – and he would have lost her in the trees had he not caught that brief glimpse.

'There!' he said, pointing.

Marcilla vanished almost as soon as he spoke, but Reinmar had time to notice that she was walking with a sureness of step that seemed unnaturally mechanical and measured, as if she were in some kind of trance.

Vaedecker cursed, almost as volubly as he had during the fight.

'Mind the cart well, steward,' he growled, although Reinmar formed the impression that he did not care overmuch at that point in time whether the cart was minded carefully or not. 'Come on, Reinmar.'

Reinmar was surprised, but he obeyed readily enough, jumping down behind the sergeant and moving off in the direction the girl had taken – which was at a right angle to that in which the horses had fled. He had gone a dozen paces before he realised that the soldier was not in the least concerned for the girl's welfare. Vaedecker was following her because he had heard the word 'call' in her delirium, and knew what significance that word might have in the context of his spying mission.

They did not catch sight of her again as soon as they might have expected, and they drew apart by slow degrees so that they could cover more ground, although the sergeant called out a warning lest they lose sight of one another entirely.

By the time he caught another glimpse of the slim figure as it went gliding between the trees, Reinmar was beginning to wonder whether he would be able to find his way back to the cart. It was impossible to stick to a straight course while moving among thickets and fallen logs, and he was no longer sure of his exact heading – but Marcilla seemed certain enough of hers, and she kept on going, heedless of any threat which might be posed by inhuman creatures of any kind.

Reinmar had never had any particular fear of the forests that decked the foothills of the Grey Mountains, although they could be dismal and ominously quiet. He had slept beneath the trees on previous expeditions that he had made with his father, and would not have hesitated to do it again on this trip had it been necessary, even in this relatively gloomy region which he did not know well – but now that he knew that there really were monsters in the hills, every step that separated him from the cart seemed a step into the dangerous unknown.

Oddly enough, however, Reinmar feared more for Marcilla than he did for himself. The gypsy girl must have slept rough far more often than he, in far worse places than this. But she was ill now, and wet through in spite of the cloak he had draped over her sleeping body. While she was entranced she might easily step into a ditch and take a heavy fall, and would not be able to raise the slightest defence against a beastman. The ground over which they were walking was very uneven.

It was not until Vaedecker shouted 'Hulloa!' that Reinmar realised that they had lost sight of one another – but when he replied they were able to reset their paces instantly on a convergent course.

The sound of Reinmar's answering call seemed to rouse Marcilla slightly from her waking dream. She paused for a fraction of a second, but she did not look back. Whatever force held her seemed to tighten its grip in response to her hesitation, refusing to release her. Blurred echoes of the two shouts lingered in the air for a second or two, as if Vaedecker had been answered by a dozen distant voices emanating from the darkest part of the forest, away to the south-east.

They were now no more than fifteen paces behind Marcilla. There was no further danger of losing her, but still Reinmar hurried on in order to catch up. Vaedecker matched him stride for stride.

Reinmar called out again, this time addressing himself directly to the girl – but the only answer he received was from the eerie echoes. He hurried forward even faster and soon drew level with the gypsy, but Vaedecker hissed a warning at him.

'Don't touch her!' the sergeant said. 'Let her go where she will – and let her take us with her.'

The instruction banished any last lingering doubt that Reinmar might have entertained as to the sergeant's purpose. One way or another, Machar von Spurzheim had discovered the little that Luther Wieland knew about the source of the dark wine, and his sergeant was not about to pass up the stroke of good fortune that had delivered Marcilla into his care at exactly the right moment. This was his mission, and he had an unexpected opportunity to complete it. It was not, of course, Reinmar's mission, and Reinmar knew full well what Gottfried would say, if and when he heard that his son had gone haring off into the forest after a sleepwalking gypsy instead of remaining with his cargo, but he put the thought aside. He had taken the girl under his protective wing, and he was determined to protect her. He could not leave her to wander the forest alone, or with none to look after her but a soldier intent on using her as a guide to a secret place.

In any case, Reinmar's own curiosity had been excited by tales of the wine of dreams. What would Luther or Albrecht have given, he wondered, for the chance that had casually been thrown into his lap? How many expeditions of this kind must Luther have undertaken in his youth, without ever experiencing such an outrageous stroke of luck?

Reinmar had drawn level with Marcilla again, and he could see the expression on her face. He had expected it to be blank, but it was not. He saw that the girl seemed deeply anxious and agitated, as if lost in an inner turmoil she could not dispel.

'Don't touch her,' Vaedecker warned him, again. 'Whatever troubles her, it is but a dream.'

'We don't know that,' Reinmar muttered – but he kept his hands by his sides.

'Where are we going, Master Wieland?' the sergeant asked him. 'You know these parts better than I. What lies beyond this wood?'

Reinmar looked about him, although he knew full well that he had not the slightest chance of catching sight of a landmark he knew. They were travelling roughly east-southeast, and they were travelling uphill, but he had no notion at all of what might lie in that direction or what might lie beyond the ridge that they would presumably attain in due course.

'I have no idea,' Reinmar confessed. 'I dare say that there are farms and hamlets hereabouts which have no access for carts. The ground is too uneven to permit the building of roads. Even a man on horseback would have great difficulty following deer-trails through a wood of this kind. This is territory for walkers, and any produce brought out of it must take a long and winding course to anything remotely resembling a market. Have you seen any sign of human habitation since we left the cart – the markings of a woodcutter's axe, or a hunter's snare?'

'None,' the soldier admitted. 'But the road cannot be much more than a few hundred paces away, and this is habitable land

– or would be, were there not half-human monsters lurking in its coverts.'

'What are we to do when night falls?' Reinmar asked him, tacitly accepting the fact that they would follow the girl wherever she led for as long as it took, leaving the cart and its cargo to the protection of Godrich and Sigurd. 'We have no lantern. Without our packs, in fact, we have nothing but the contents of our pouches, our blades and our sodden clothing – and yours, if you'll forgive the observation, is distinctly malodorous.'

'The least the rain might have done for our cause was to wash the beastman's stink away,' Vaedecker agreed, glumly. 'But we've a while till the twilight fades, and no matter what magic may be guiding her steps, the girl still needs her eyes to tell her where to place her feet. If she doesn't get to where she's going before darkness falls, she'll have to stop and wait.'

Silence fell while they trudged on for a while, but the agitation within Marcilla's half-eclipsed soul was beginning to communicate itself to Reinmar, and he did not want to be left at the mercy of its horrid uncertainties.

'Why did you instruct me to come with you?' he asked the soldier. 'I thought you didn't trust me.'

'Why did you come?' Vaedecker countered. 'I know you don't trust me.'

Reinmar was slightly taken aback by the question, because he was genuinely uncertain of the answer. In the end, he said: 'I did not want the girl to come to harm. Not from any source.'

Vaedecker laughed dryly. 'Young men fall in love too easily,' he observed. 'Show them a pretty face and a helpless form, and they're lost. Still, better that than the lure of the dark wine. I'd rather you were here as a hero than a merchant – but whatever your reason, I'd rather have you under my eye. I'm a soldier, not a fool; if this mysterious source is protected by monsters which hunt in packs, I'd far rather that I didn't have to face them without a friend to guard my back.'

'A friend?' Reinmar echoed.

'Are we not friends, Master Wieland? We did not wake as friends this morning, I suppose, but we stood side by side to fight monsters this afternoon. We've a basis for friendship now, have we not?'

'I suppose we have,' Reinmar granted, although he knew that Vaedecker must have reasons of his own for making the claim.

They were still heading upslope, with no sign of a ridge before them – but the trees grew much taller hereabouts, with higher and more elaborate crowns. A few of the conifers typical of the wider region could still be seen, but the dominant vegetation hereabouts was deciduous and the leaves had already begun to yellow on the branches. The ferny undergrowth was nourished by a rich leaf-humus, which enabled the curling fern-leaves to grow man-high, but the going was not so very difficult.

Reinmar realised that the trees between which they passed must be very old. They had held dominion here for so long that not a single sapling had found space to grow up for thirty years or more. The woods beside the roads were extensively worked by fellers and coppicers, and always had young growth mingled with old, but this was obviously a place where few men ever came, and to which none brought axes.

Marcilla's stride had begun to falter, not through any loss of resolution but because she was near exhaustion. She had not taken a drink since the rain had wet her lips, and she had not eaten for far too long. The blow to her head had taken a great deal out of her.

While Reinmar hesitated, uncertain as to whether to take a hand, she stumbled – and would have fallen had he not then stepped swiftly forward to catch her.

He would have helped to ease her back into her stride if he could, but as soon as her progress was interrupted she collapsed like a puppet whose strings had snapped. He found himself holding her up, cradled in his arms. She was fast asleep, but still dreaming. Her eyes still moved behind closed lids, and her expression was by no means serene.

Vaedecker cursed yet again.

'What now?' Reinmar asked. 'Do we wait until morning? We have neither food nor water to help her regain her strength. She might have recovered if she'd stayed with the cart, but she's much worse now.'

'The call she has heard cannot make concessions to her condition,' the soldier muttered. 'The magic, if magic it is, cannot know or care that she had been hit over the head and knocked silly. If we were not here, she'd probably lie down and die, but since you're here to carry her there's still a chance that she might live. Let's hold her course while we can, at least until we reach the top of this cursed slope. Once at the top, I'll climb into the crown of one of these wooden giants, to see how the land lies ahead.'

Reinmar adjusted Marcilla's position in his arms as best he could before he moved on, this time following the sergeant's lead. The girl had seemed slight enough when she was moving under her own volition, but now that she was a dead weight she seemed very heavy indeed, and Reinmar was not sure that he could carry her far without collapsing himself.

Fortunately, the top of the slope was not so very far away – and when they attained it, Vaedecker immediately set himself to climb a tree. Reinmar looked around for somewhere that he might set his burden down, but the ground was rutted with root-ridges, and the spaces in between were thick with ferns. The vegetation was still very wet; it certainly would not dry out before nightfall, and the same was true of Marcilla's clothing. Reinmar looked down at the top of her head. The wound she had sustained was very obvious from this angle.

Reinmar looked back the way they had come, trying to estimate how much distance they had put between themselves and the wagon. There was no shelter to be had there, but some of the spare clothing in the packs would be reasonably dry, and there was food and water on the cart – not to mention plenty of wine. Would it be so very bad, he wondered, if he and Vaedecker lost their one and only chance to gain admittance to the place where the wine of dreams was fermented? To refuse to go back, given their circumstances, might be to volunteer for a great deal of hardship and strife.

Matthias Vaedecker dropped down from the lower branches of the tree that he had climbed.

'Good news,' he said. 'There are two clusters of buildings visible in the valley beyond. The forest thins out, and there's a lake. Its waters look grey and gloomy in this light, but I dare say it's a pleasant enough spot when the sun shines. The buildings are grey too. The larger group is on the shore – it seemed to me to be capable of accommodating a whole community. The other is closer to the forest's edge, directly in the path of anyone heading for the lake or the larger edifice. The nearer cluster looks like a common farmhouse and its outbuildings – two barns and perhaps a henhouse – but I could see no sign of labourers or livestock. It's valuable shelter, if we could be sure of a welcome there.'

'If,' Reinmar repeated, dubiously.

'Well, Master Wieland,' the sergeant said, decisively, 'I suppose it's up to you to see that you do obtain a welcome. If you turn up on the doorstep with the girl unconscious in your arms and near to death, they're hardly likely to turn you away – and if they ask you who you are and what your business is, you're Reinmar Wieland, grandson of Luther Wieland the well-known wine-merchant, out in search of new stock. I believe they'll be prepared to entertain you, whoever they may be.'

'And what about you?' Reinmar demanded, with only slight resentment of the manner in which the other was trying to manipulate him. He had his own plans, after all – and he was the one in the best position to make further enquiries and further discoveries.

'I'm a soldier,' Vaedecker told him. 'I can look after myself for a while – and now we're here, if here is the place we've been trying to attain, I need to take a long look around. I'd prefer it if no one knew that I was here – all the more so if it's true, as rumour has it, that strangers are not supposed to be able to find their way here without supernatural aid. Spies work best where they're not expected.'

'Aren't you worried about leaving me to my own devices?' Reinmar asked, wryly.

'I'll be close at hand till you're safe indoors,' the soldier assured him. 'After that, I'll have to trust you to look after all our interests as best you can.'

Reinmar only hesitated for a moment before nodding assent to the plan. He might indeed be made far more welcome if he and the girl were unaccompanied by another man. Even if his hosts were suspicious of him, they would owe him a debt of gratitude when they realised that she could not possibly have completed the journey on her own, and they might be pleased to hear his name. If they were makers of dark wine, or even if they were merely agents of its distribution, the Wielands had been their allies once, and if they knew of von Spurzheim's exploits in Marienburg they might well feel that they were in direr need of allies now than they had ever been before.

He readjusted Marcilla's position in his arms so that when he set off his load was fairly evenly balanced. Now that he was travelling down the slope instead of up the going seemed easier, although he had to be careful not to trip over a trailing root, or slip on a patch of mud.

The trees grew more densely lower down the slope, but he contrived to find a path through them without losing his bearings. He hardly noticed when Vaedecker vanished into the trees. Although he looked around from time to time in the hope of seeing where the other man was, Reinmar could not catch the slightest glimpse of him – but he did not assume that he was unobservable himself.

Because Reinmar was descending into a valley, the sun – which was setting behind the mask of cloud – descended into shadow a little faster than he had anticipated, and he began to wonder whether the twilight would last, but as soon as he became anxious the trees began to thin out again. He was profoundly glad when lighted windows showed ahead, giving him a target for which to aim.

'Well,' he said to himself, in a whisper, 'here I am. I always longed for an adventure, and now I am in the middle of one. Let's hope I can acquit myself in a manner that I can remember gladly for a lifetime.'

Chapter Thirteen

In the descending gloom, Reinmar could not judge exactly what manner of farm the buildings and their surrounding land might constitute, but he was too tired to worry unduly about matters of detail. He could smell the smoke of chimneys, lightly flavoured with the odours of recent cooking. He could also hear the clucking of chickens away to the left of the house – a sound which was deeply reassuring.

The door of the house opened long before he had a chance to announce his presence, and a thickset man – presumably the farmer – came out to watch him approach. The man carried no weapon, but there was a measurable tension in the way he held himself. After surveying Reinmar from top to toe, as best he could given the fading light and the obscuring effect of the unconscious girl, the farmer relaxed a little – but only a little.

'I am Reinmar Wieland, wine merchant,' Reinmar told him.

'Are you, indeed?' the farmer said. 'My name is Zygmund. What is your business here?'

'I lodged last night in a village half a day's ride east of here,' Reinmar explained, 'with my steward and my servant. We saved the lives of a gypsy girl and her brother, who had been attacked by local ruffians, but we were not in time to save them from a beating. When the wagon was bogged down by a sudden storm the girl wandered off. She was delirious from a blow to the head, and did not know what she was doing. I followed her till she fell, utterly exhausted – but it is too late now to make my way back to the wagon, and I have no food or water. If you could spare a little, and let us rest in front of your fire until our clothes are dry, I'd be very grateful. I fear that the girl might die in my arms if I cannot set her down soon.'

There was little change in the stout man's manner, which remained tense and suspicious, and Reinmar grew similarly tense while he waited for a response.

'Wieland, did you say?' said the farmer, eventually, as if he were struggling to recover some faded memory from his long-lost youth. 'I believe I know the name. Come in – and welcome.' The belated addition of the last phrase eased Reinmar's anxiety slightly, although it did not sound entirely sincere.

The main room of the farmhouse was tidier than the room in which Reinmar had talked to Albrecht, but its whitewashed walls and crude furniture were very similar. Reinmar deposited his burden on the hearth-rug, and Marcilla responded by stretching herself out to catch the heat of the fire, although she was still asleep and dreaming.

Zygmund had an equally sturdy wife, who disappeared into the kitchen when asked to find food, while her husband went out to fetch more logs with which to build up the fire. The day had never become warm and the rainstorm had cooled the air considerably, so there was a chill in the dampened air, but it disappeared when the farmer returned and reset the fire so that it would blaze up again.

Their host retired again, eventually coming back with a loosely-packed pallet and two thick blankets. 'It's none too soft,' he said, apologetically, 'but the straw is clean and reasonably inanimate. The blankets will keep her safe and warm, if you take her wet clothes off. You'll have to sit by the fire until your own clothes dry on your body.'

Reinmar accepted the offerings gratefully. He took off Marcilla's dress, having covered her with one of the blankets to protect her modesty, and hung it over the arm of a wooden chair.

The farmer's wife brought half a loaf of bread and the remains of a haunch of venison. Reinmar immediately began slicing the meat with his knife, then broke the bread into more manageable chunks. By the time he had finished this dissection two cups of wine had been set by the hearth. Reinmar took one up and tasted it. He was surprised at first to find it reasonably good, until he realised that it must have been obtained from the very same vineyard that he had visited earlier that day.

'Not the worst of the vintage, by any means,' he murmured. The farmer had withdrawn again, and could not hear him – in fact, Reinmar slowly realised, he must have gone out again.

The woman brought in a pitcher of water. 'Would you like me to help you feed the maid?' she asked. 'The poor thing seems worn out.'

Reinmar shook his head, bitterly regretful of the fact that poor Marcilla was far worse than merely worn out. 'Did I see another building in the valley?' he asked, absentmindedly.

'Aye,' the woman said, slowly. 'That's the monastery. Zygmund's gone there to ask for help for the maid. The monks have some skill in curing.'

'Monastery?' Reinmar queried, remembering what Luther had said about further rumours relating to the dark wine's source. 'How many monks live there?'

'Don't rightly know. No more than sixty, at a guess.'

Sixty! It was a larger figure than Reinmar had expected to hear. So far as he knew, monks were more given to brewing beer than making wine, but they had perforce to be able to turn their hands to anything – and monks, it was said, had first discovered the trick of distillation that allowed wine to be converted into stronger liqueurs. It was plausible that the wine of dreams might be the invention of monks – but was it blessed Sigmar these monks worshipped, or some other deity? And how much more truth might there be in the tales that Luther Wieland had gleaned while he searched for the source of the wine of dreams?

Reinmar noticed that the woman was studying him with a curious expression that had a little anxiety in it as well as a little perplexity. He turned his head away, hoping that it did not seem to be a guilty gesture. Either way, she took it as an invitation to leave, and he continued feeding himself morsels of bread and slivers of venison. He persuaded Marcilla to take a little water in spite of her unconsciousness, and even a little wine, but when he soaked a piece of bread in water she could not take it into her mouth.

Although he was worried, and did not feel at all safe, Reinmar found himself relaxing as exhaustion sapped his wakefulness. Once he had finished the half-loaf he would almost certainly have drifted off to sleep had he not heard the door of the house opening yet again.

He looked up blearily, expecting to see Zygmund, but the farmer was not with the two men who came in. They were clad in monkish habits, with satchels thrown over their shoulders. They must have been abroad during the earlier rainstorm, because their robes were still wet. The dampness of the dark grey cloth caused the habits to emit a musty odour like nothing Reinmar had ever scented before.

The monks were both tall and thin of face. When they eased back their damp cowls to expose the tonsures hollowed in their thick jet black hair Reinmar saw that they both had eyes which were as uncommonly bright as they were uncommonly dark. There was something peculiar about that brightness, but Reinmar could not tell exactly what it was.

The two newcomers looked quickly round the room, then came to the fireside where Reinmar sat and Marcilla lay.

With barely a nod to Reinmar, one of the monks set his satchel aside and knelt beside the girl. He laid his hand upon her forehead, then against her cheek. He seemed genuinely concerned – but his companion was studying Reinmar with great care and obvious curiosity.

'She's feverish,' the kneeling monk reported. 'This head wound has hurt her badly, and I fear for her life. You did well to find shelter, young man – I only hope and pray that it is not too late to save her. Did you have to carry her far?'

'Quite a way,' Reinmar said, his anxiety greatly renewed by the monk's uncompromising diagnosis. 'I was very lucky to find the farmhouse, because I was utterly lost. I'm sure that I couldn't have found my way back to my wagon. Is she so very ill? My steward thought that she would recover, although that was before she went wandering off after the storm had soaked her clothes.' He made room so that the two newcomers could dry their wet robes in the full heat of the flames, while the monk who had remained standing threw more wood to the hungry fire.

'It's a bad day to be out and about,' the kneeling monk remarked. 'The storm caught us all by surprise, it seems, and it certainly has not helped your friend. She has been wet through, and then exhausted. If she was not in mortal danger before, she is now. I'm Brother Noel, by the way, and my companion is Brother Almeric. Our house is on the far side of the lake. Perhaps you caught a glimpse of it as you came down the slope.' His tone was amicable enough, but slightly guarded.

Reinmar knew that the two men did not know quite what to make of him, although Zygmund must have told them his name and profession. He repeated it anyway, for the sake of emphasis as well as politeness.

'I'm Reinmar Wieland, wine merchant of Eilhart. The girl is named Marcilla, so her brother told me. She has hardly said two words herself since we rescued her from the louts who had attacked her in a nearby village.' He looked down fearfully, knowing that he had no experience on which he might base an accurate assessment of her plight.

'Wieland the vintner?' Brother Almeric said, thoughtfully. 'We used to know a man of that name once, did we not, Brother Noel?'

'We did,' his companion confirmed. Reinmar wondered whether 'we' was supposed to signify the two monks themselves, or merely their community.

'My grandfather Luther used to visit these parts regularly,' Reinmar informed them. In spite of his concern for Marcilla he knew that he must keep in mind that he had another agenda to follow. 'Unfortunately, he fell ill and had to resign the management of the business to my father Gottfried before my father had been fully trained, and he lost contact with some of our former suppliers. Now that I am old enough to play my part, we hope that we might regain some of the trade that we lost.'

'Indeed?' said Brother Noel. 'We are inexperienced in matters of trade, I fear. We ourselves have little intercourse with the villages in neighbouring valleys, although the man whose house we are in has always been a good neighbour. He does a good deal of bartering on our behalf, and we have other friends in the region.' He spoke as straightforwardly as Reinmar had, but Reinmar was sure that he knew perfectly well what 'the trade that we lost' might mean.

'I fear that I have eaten all the bread,' Reinmar said, 'but there is a little meat, and the cup of wine the farmer's wife brought for Marcilla is virtually untouched.' He was still looking anxiously down at the girl, and he reached out a hand to touch her troubled face as he spoke her name. She was very feverish, now that the fire had warmed her again.

'We have bread of our own,' Almeric retorted, gruffly, 'and wine too. Better wine than this.'

'Indeed?' said Reinmar. 'I thought this an unusually pleasant vintage. I bought a healthy fraction of the crop from which it came this very morning.' He only hesitated for an instant before adding: 'If you have better, I'd be glad to taste it.'

Brother Almeric did not seem enthusiastic to respond to that request, but he looked to his companion for advice.

'Did you, perchance, come here in search of the monastery, Master Wieland?' Brother Noel asked, lightly but warily. 'Our wines had a certain reputation once, among connoisseurs of sweet liqueurs as well as those who knew their medicinal value.'

'I had no idea that the monastery existed,' Reinmar assured them. 'Had the gypsy girl not led me such a dance I'd have passed the valley without ever knowing that it was here – but I'm always interested in good wines. I am, as you will readily appreciate, a mere apprentice still in the process of learning the trade, but I'm eager to build the family business up to its former profitability and esteem. Can you help her? Zygmund said that you had some skill in curing – that is why he fetched you, is it not?'

While Reinmar was making this careful speech Almeric had opened his satchel and had taken out the end of a stick of bread, somewhat begrimed, and a small stone bottle. The bottle's stopper was securely clamped in place with leaden wire.

'We can help her,' Noel said, 'if you will consent to allow Brother Almeric to give a modest draught of this liquor to the girl. I do not think that it will enable her to recover her senses now, but it will work to her advantage in the long run. It has remarkable powers of revivification, and the members of our order have always enjoyed unusually good health.'

It was not until these words were spoken that the full import of what he was doing came home to Reinmar. He had been playing his part in spite of his anxiety, and had led himself into a trap. What Marcilla was being offered, he realised, must be one of the dark wines. If the judgement of Gottfried Wieland

and Machar von Spurzheim could be trusted, he was being asked to let the monks dose her with the very essence of evil. On the other hand, he thought, the only people he knew who had actually tasted the dark wine were Luther and Albrecht, both of whom spoke of it in far warmer terms and both of whom were still alive to tell the tale. Neither, it seemed, had become a hopeless addict, and neither had come to any swift or permanent harm as a result of its use.

For several seconds he was in an agony of indecision so intense that he could not form a syllable of protest when the decision was taken out of his hands. Almeric had knelt down beside his companion, who moved aside. The stopper had already been removed, and Almeric put the neck of the bottle directly to Marcilla's mouth.

She had been unable to take more than a tiny sip of water or ordinary wine, but as soon as this liquor touched her lips she raised her head slightly, and when the liquid entered her mouth she drank it greedily. Reinmar extended a hand as if to stop him, but there was no real force in the gesture and Brother Noel reached forward to take his wrist, gently but firmly.

'She needs it, Master Wieland,' Noel said, quietly. 'Believe me, I beg you – she really does need it.' Marcilla's eyes had fluttered open, but only for a moment. She sighed deeply as she closed them again, and then she sank back again, returning to sleep. She did seem more at ease now, and not quite so hot.

'You see,' said Brother Noel. 'She really did need it. I do not say that it will cure her, but it will make her far more comfortable.' The tone of his voice had not changed at all, but his words seemed to Reinmar to have taken on a distinctly ominous edge.

'Thank you,' Reinmar said, uncertainly. 'You're very kind.'

'You may try the wine yourself if you wish,' Noel went on. 'It will likely be stronger and sweeter than any you have tasted before, but I think you will find it rewarding. Your companion obviously has the greater need of it, but you seem to have suffered a little yourself. It is a marvellous aid to recuperation. It cannot undo a wound, but it can revive the spirit and ease distress, and you do seem to stand in need of some such treatment. At the very least, you will find it interesting, in your professional capacity.'

Reinmar swallowed hard. Anxiety had made his throat dry, and he certainly had a thirst, but he felt sure that this was the wine in which his father had always refused to trade. The arguments that had come to mind when the wine was offered to Marcilla were as sound now as they had been then, and he knew that he could not possibly continue to maintain his pose as a possible buyer of the wine if he refused even to taste it, but he knew that this moment of decision might be the most crucial he had ever faced in his life.

He knew that his father would have insisted that he refuse; he knew, too, that his grandfather would have urged him to try it for himself. In the end, though, it was his own decision and no one else's.

'I'll need to clean my palate,' he said, eventually.

Carefully, he drained the last dregs of the wine that the farmer's wife had set out for him before pouring himself a draught of water. This he swirled around in his mouth, as any expert taster would before turning to a new vintage. By this means he established that he only intended to sip the wine that was being offered to him, and would then spit it out.

Brother Almeric removed the loosened stopper from his bottle for a second time, and poured a parsimonious fraction of its contents into the waiting cup.

Reinmar looked into the interior of the wooden vessel, but its sides were so darkly stained that it was impossible to judge the colour of the liquid it now contained. The fluid was slightly viscous, and had a remarkably heavy fragrance – sweet but rather cloying – which he did not find entirely pleasant.

I am my own man, he thought. From now on, I make my own decisions, and I am true to my own dreams.

Then he took a tiny sip of the dark wine, and let it linger for a moment on his tongue.

Chapter Fourteen

Reinmar really had intended to spit the drop of wine into the fire when he had tasted it, but as its taste unfolded and extended the unexpected complexity of the sensation gave him an altogether pleasant shock. He let the liquid lay upon his tongue for a moment longer, and then another, until its warmth and fragrance had suffused the whole interior of his mouth.

When he finally did spit, there was hardly anything left to emerge, and the drop of sputum that sizzled briefly in the fire seemed almost derisory.

The aftertaste that the liquor left behind on his tongue reminded Reinmar of the scent of certain exotic flowers which the gardeners of Eilhart received as bulbs and seeds from distant Tilea, to whose cities they had allegedly been brought by spice-caravans. He decided that it was far more pleasing than he had anticipated, and could easily imagine why some men thought it a taste worth recapitulating.

'It is rather fine, is it not?' Noel said. 'It is a vintage once treasured in many of the noblest houses of the Empire, although the troubles which presently afflict the realm have all but destroyed the steady commerce we once enjoyed. No one outside the monastery knows the secret of its making.'

Reinmar inhaled deeply, letting the air cool his tongue and drawing a last breath of that curious fragrance into his lungs. He felt a shock of brief intoxication like nothing he had ever experienced before. He did not quite know what to say, but felt that some comment was necessary. 'It is very unusual,' he murmured – but was instantly ashamed of the inadequacy of the adjective. To cover his embarrassment, he said: 'I am surprised that it is not better known in Eilhart.'

'We had assumed that it was still valued there,' Brother Almeric murmured, 'but we live sheltered lives.'

Is he claiming innocence? Reinmar wondered. Is he trying to persuade me that he has no inkling of the reputation that dark wine has in the world beyond the valley?

'It is not so very surprising that you do not know the wine, even though you are a vintner,' Noel put in, as if to clarify this point. 'In the seclusion of our valley we have lost any real sense of the extent and complexity of the world. We leave it to others to disseminate the meagre surplus we produce as they see fit, although we obtain real benefit from it as an aid to meditation and communion with the god to whom our order's service is dedicated. To a successful businessman like you, our hidden valley and its little secrets must seem tiny and remote, hardly worthy of interest in a commercial sense.'

'I would not say so,' Reinmar answered, thinking that he might as well be bold. 'Chance and misfortune brought me here, but the product of your secret process might yet turn my misfortune to our mutual advantage.'

Brother Almeric did not seem convinced of Reinmar's sincerity, but Brother Noel was still looking at him with all apparent benevolence. 'You would be welcome to visit the monastery tomorrow, Master Vintner, if you have the time,' he said. 'I hope that the maid is not as seriously hurt as she seems to be, but if perchance you were to be further delayed...'

'I would like that,' Reinmar said.

Brother Noel and Brother Almeric bid him good night then, although their clothes were still not dry, and they left him huddled over the fire.

As they drew the door shut behind them, Noel called back: 'We shall see you tomorrow, Master Wieland. We'll return to see how the girl is faring, and we'll take you to visit the monastery afterwards, if you care to come.'

'I shall look forward to it,' Reinmar promised – and having done so, wondered whether he ought, after all, to be reckoned a bold adventurer, or something more akin to a fly that had wandered into a spider's web. He ran his tongue around his mouth one last time, but the taste of the dark wine was already exhausted. Then he looked down at the lovely face of the gypsy, which seemed even lovelier now than it had before.

She stirred slightly, but not as if she were disturbed or anxious. If she was still dreaming, her dreams must have become far more tranquil – but the wound on her head seemed uglier now than it had ever been, and he realised that Noel had been right to judge that it was even worse than Godrich had estimated.

'Sleep well, my love,' he said, recklessly. 'You have done what you were required to do, and I can only pray that you'll be safe.'

After a few minutes' silence Marcilla stirred again, more vigorously this time. Reinmar bent over her anxiously, but there did not seem to be any cause for alarm. Her eyes opened and she peered at him intently, as if she were trying to remember who he was. Then she looked sideways at the fire, and down at the rug on which she lay. He had stretched the pallet out beside her but had not yet had a chance to interpose it between her body and the rug.

'We had to take shelter,' he told her. 'We are in a farmhouse in a valley, not far from a monastery.'

She nodded as if in reply, but he was not convinced that she understood what he had said. The mention of a monastery certainly drew no reaction.

'Two monks brought you medicine to drink,' Reinmar went on. 'It seems to have helped make you a little better.'

Mention of something to drink drew a more positive response, and the gypsy girl looked around until her eyes lighted on the cup. Reinmar poured a little water into it and offered it to her. She was able to take it in her hand and put it to her own lips. Perhaps because she had seen him pour the water she paused in surprise when she sipped. He guessed that there must have been a little of the monks' wine still clinging to the cup's interior, which the water had absorbed. Marcilla drank more deeply, and more greedily. Reinmar watched as the initial shock passed and her surprise was displaced by dissatisfaction.

'Is there no more?' she asked, weakly.

He reached out for the water-jug, but that was not what she meant. She shook her head.

'It was some kind of sweet wine they gave you,' he said, guardedly. 'I had never tasted it before.'

'It is very sweet,' she murmured, passing her tongue over the inside of her mouth. 'Very sweet indeed.' She passed the empty cup back to him and he put it aside. She seemed dazed, as if her mind were balanced on the very edge of reality. He coaxed her into rolling sideways on to the pallet. He would have been glad to talk further, but by the time she had made herself more comfortable she was drifting off to sleep again. He was so very tired himself that he could not regret the necessity of postponing further discussion until morning. He laid himself down beside her on the rug, not caring that her body shielded him from the direct radiation of the fire.

He fell asleep almost immediately.

Although he slept as deeply as might have been expected, given his extraordinary exertions, Reinmar's slumber was troubled from the very outset by strange dreams.

He had put the encounter with the beastmen firmly out of his mind while he pursued the day's subsequent adventures, but the guard he had put upon the memory collapsed as soon as he lost consciousness, and the moment he began to dream he was revisited by the day's horrors.

He remembered the first awful sight of that initial bestial face, and its instant compounding with the knowledge that there was a whole pack of such creatures, advance scouts of a monstrous army.

He remembered the leap that had carried the first beastman into awful collision with his father's steward, and the sickening thud as Godrich's head had hit the iron hoop supporting the wagon's ill-fitted canopy.

He remembered the way the beastman's bowels had opened as Sigurd had made the most of his killing grip, and the way Matthias Vaedecker's shirt had soaked up the stink of the alien creature.

He began to remember all these things at once, so that the memories piled up like a heap of autumn leaves, shed by the day's experience but not yet shrivelled into the mulch of experience. One by one they had been difficult enough to bear, but detached from time and whipped into such awful confusion they seemed ten times worse. They told him not merely that his life would never be the same again, but that the sixteen years he had so far lived had been spent behind walls of ignorance: walls that had always been under siege by all the monstrous lusts and hazards in the world, even though he did not know it.

Reinmar resisted the images as best he could, by mustering all his will to the task of remembering Marcilla's beautiful, innocent, sleeping face – but all he contrived to do was to interpose a frail and translucent veil between his frightened eyes and the frame in which all his horrors were contained.

To understand his past in this new light – or to fall a little way short of understanding, as is often the way in dreams – was almost too much for him to bear, and it was not in the least unnatural that he should have begun to dream of other things: of the possibilities of the future rather than the burden of the past.

Alas, the potentialities of the future had been transformed along with the legacies of the past, and Reinmar's dreams became even more phantasmagoric when they turned in that direction.

The beastmen of his earlier dream had seemed fearsome enough, but they were poor things by comparison with the chimeras of his subsequent dreams, which had horned heads like bulls or bison, and extra limbs which ended in claws instead of hands. But the most terrifying thing about them was something he could not see but only suspect, which was that beings of their kind concealed an awesome intelligence beneath their monstrous masks, and were capable of hearing words that were spoken anywhere in and out of the world.

He kept trying with all his might to use more comforting imagery as a ward against the horror, but every time he tried to conjure Marcilla's beauty it lasted for but an instant before metamorphosing into something far more terrible. Her eyes would inflate until they were huge and green, and her flowing black hair would turn vivid white, and her body would manifest all kinds of bizarre decorations, tattooed as well as painted. Her hands would turn into long, scissor-like claws and her hindquarters would sprout a remarkable tail, terminating in a barbed fluke.

It was all too much to bear, but the only way in which he could refuse to bear it was to shatter the images into countless shards of thought, reducing the fugitive coherency of his dream-consciousness to a mere dust of madness – and even in that panic-stricken retreat he glimpsed a possibility more awful than any he had ever glimpsed before, because he realised that something similar could happen to a waking mind. To shatter a nightmare was of no permanent consequence, but to shatter the waking mind in like fashion was to give way, irrecoverably, to madness.

Reinmar had never suspected himself of any tendency to madness, and had never considered himself ready prey for such a fate – but he knew now that there was no man alive who was free of such potential, or immune to such a fate.

His subsequent nightmares were as disordered and senseless as nightmares ever could be. By the time he finally awoke they were already beginning to slip through the net of memory, but there were certain images which were sufficiently powerful to be deeply graven upon his returning consciousness. Before he opened his eyes to greet the new day, Reinmar was all too easily able to recall some of these fugitive moments to mind.

At one point in his dream, he thought, he had been trying with all his might to scale a rough-and-ready mountain path, which led to a castle in the clouds. A terrible wind had made every step difficult, plucking at him as though with savage claws and bloodying his arms when he raised them in his defence.

More than once, he was certain, he had managed to reach the closed door of the dark citadel, and had cried out to be let in. On each occasion the door had opened, though only by the merest crack, to let the bright light within spill out upon his face – but he had not been made welcome. The light that had bathed him had been cold and cruel, cutting into him like the invisible claws which had assailed him on the path, and driving him back. Somehow, though, he had gained entry to the enigmatic fortress, and had scurried into the shadows clustered about a great hall, like a mouse in fear of the household cat.

At another point in the dream, he remembered, a beautiful woman had come to him while he lay upon a broad bed. She had been far more beautiful of face than his beloved Marcilla, but that was only to be expected because – as he had discovered upon turning towards her – she was not entirely a woman, but was at least in part a daemon. She had a forked tongue like a serpent and legs which ended in monstrous, two-taloned claws, and her torso was decked in polished and multicoloured scales, whose dominant hues were pink and blue. This white-haired succubus had pleaded with Reinmar – most urgently, it seemed – to desert his appointed bride and go with her to share a better kind of ecstasy.

Although he had felt the force of temptation he had resisted. At least, he was sure when he tried to remember the dream in the morning that he must have resisted... although he could not quite remember what he had said to this awesome siren, or what he had done to detach himself from the pressure of her deadly green gaze and the avidity of her embracing arms. He could remember the sheen of her silver-white hair, like the gloss on a swan's wing, and the exotic promise of her swaying, voluptuous body, and the hungry smile which showed the points of her pearly teeth, but no matter how hard he tried he could not remember how he had escaped his awful predicament.

Nor could he remember now how he had escaped the invisible claws that had harried him incessantly while he attempted to attain the fortress of his desire – except that he was not sure that they had always remained invisible. He could conjure up the briefest imaginable flashes of chimeras even worse than the bison-headed beasts, compounded out of scorpions, vile reptiles and vaguely humanoid limbs.

Was this, he wondered, after he had woken up but before he had opened his eyes, the kind of dream which visited all adults once in a while, from which only youth had kept him safe? Or was it the kind of dream which only visited those who had taken a sip of the dark wine and failed to follow through the intention to spit it out?

Memory failed him then, when he tried to recapture more of the fugitive dream, and he consented to open his eyes instead. Then he sat up and stretched himself, looking sideways at the recumbent gypsy girl.

She was very still, and silent.

At first, he thought that Marcilla was still suffering the effects of exhaustion. It was only by degrees that he realised, while he tried to rouse her, that hers was a much deeper sleep than any mere tiredness could cause. Her flesh was unnaturally cold in spite of the fact that the last embers of the fire still gave out a little heat.

Several minutes passed while Reinmar shook her harder and spoke to her in increasingly louder tones. His voice must have become hysterical, for Zygmund's wife flew into the room in a panic, as if expecting to find the pallet on fire. The woman knelt down to look at Marcilla and touch her fingertips to the sleeping girl's forehead. Then she called out to her husband, who came bustling into the room in his turn.

Reinmar took up Marcilla's arm, holding it by the wrist, but he could find no pulse at all.

'She was supposed to get better,' Reinmar insisted. 'She cannot be dead. She was only cold, and wet – and we set her before the fire, with a warm blanket. She was getting better.'

By this time Zygmund had joined him on his knees beside the pallet. The farmer tried to find a pulse, as Reinmar had, and apparently failed. His wife passed him a lacquered box, which he polished briskly on his sleeve before putting it to her lips – after which the shiny surface remained quite unclouded.

The farmer rocked back on his heels, putting his weight on his ankles, and looked down at the slender body.

'She is a gypsy,' he observed, fatalistically. 'She heard the call, but the effort of obedience was too great for her.'

'She cannot be dead,' Reinmar insisted. 'She cannot! I love her!'

'I fear that she is, whether you loved her or not,' Zygmund told him wearily. 'There is nothing to be done.'

Chapter Fifteen

It seemed to Reinmar as if the minutes that followed were a renewal of his nightmare – that part of it, at least, when the very air and light had cut him like knives, and there had been no respite. They were like a dream in another sense too, for they made little permanent impression on his memory or his intelligence. They seemed to flow in a very disjointed fashion, and when he tried to collect himself in order that he might take charge of the flow of events, he could not do it.

'She is not dead!' he exclaimed, although he knew by now that saying it could not and would not make it so.

'Alas, my son,' said the farmer, gently, 'she is.'

'Then she must have been poisoned – poisoned by that cup of wine which the monk gave to her!' Reinmar knew that it was a dangerous thought to voice in his present company, but it was the only possible cause for his terrible distress that his distraught mind could seize upon.

The farmer shook his head, seemingly more in sorrow than in anger. 'You drank from the cup yourself, I dare say,' he said. 'I fear that the girl was not as strong as you hoped. Whatever left the dark bruise on her head injured her badly. Her heart has failed her, and there is no more to it than that. The exertions of yesterday must have drained the last dregs of her strength.'

It occurred to Reinmar that this explanation put the blame partly on him, and he was about to deny it hotly, claiming that Matthias Vaedecker was the one who had insisted on letting her go where she wished, but his common sense reasserted its authority over his tongue. The heat of his anger was transformed on the instant into an icy chill of despair.

Marcilla was dead, and no matter what cruel stroke of misfortune it was that had stolen her soul away, she was lost and gone forever. That was the whole truth of it. She was lost, and gone forever – and he had wasted the last opportunity he had had to talk to her, and perhaps to make love to her.

While he was still lost in grief, Noel and Almeric returned, as they had promised to do. They too examined the gypsy girl, and Noel confirmed that she was dead. They immediately set about making preparations for a funeral, while Reinmar sat numbly by, unable to assist or protest.

Four more monks eventually came with a stretcher, ready to carry Marcilla's body away. With Brother Noel and Brother Almeric beside him, Reinmar followed them as they trudged through a small wood to the shore of the lake and then moved around it to the burial-ground which the monks had established on the near side of the complex of buildings that constituted their monastery.

Time seemed to have stopped, and Reinmar felt that he was moving through a new kind of dream, in which he was reduced to utter helplessness by the flow of events. His body moved mechanically, as if he were in a trance, barely conscious of what was happening. Somewhere deep inside him was a more vivid fraction of his soul, which was far too conscious, but it could not assert its empire, bound and pinned down as it was by grief.

On another day, Reinmar might have taken note of the fact that the lake was rather beautiful, deep blue in the reflected light of a clear sky from which the cloud had retreated in order to take a much tighter grip on the peaks of the Grey Mountains. On another day he might have found much to delight him in the water-lilies and bulrushes which grew profusely in the shallows. Today, however, he was as blind to the water as he was to the meagre fields surrounding it.

A grave had already been dug, within ten yards of the cracked and mossy wall surrounding the burial-ground, whose only markers were wooden. The moss-encrusted wall had a curiously musty odour suggestive of antiquity and ruin – a subtle stench which might have been more offensive had it not been for the competing reek of the freshly-turned earth, which seemed to Reinmar to be dreadfully heavy and dank. The nearest building to the burial-ground was a temple – dedicated, Reinmar supposed, to Morr, the ruler of the underworld.

Reinmar watched numbly while the girl's shrouded body was laid in the grave. When the burial was over and done with, however, he did not have the slightest idea what to do with himself. Although he was now but a stone's throw from the monastery, its grey walls seemed frightful and forbidding, like the ominous citadel of his dream, and he no longer wanted to go there, although Brother Noel and Brother Almeric renewed their invitation. Almeric tried to press him, but Noel drew his companion away.

'The boy has had a shock,' he said. 'I think he needs some time to himself.'

Almeric conceded the point, and it was Noel who said to Reinmar: 'We have other duties to attend to. When you are ready, come to the door of the main building and ask for me. I will leave instructions that you are to be admitted. We are very sorry for your loss.'

Reinmar could contrive no better response than a mere nod of the head, and the monks withdrew, leaving him alone in the burial-ground. He soon decided that he could not stay there, and began retracing his steps towards the farmhouse. All the vague plans he had made in the course of the previous evening seemed to have been rendered redundant by the tragedy of Marcilla's death, and his one remaining impulse was to go home – which meant, in the first instance, finding his way back to the wagon and rejoining Godrich and Sigurd.

He had hardly made up his mind that that was what he must do, though, when he was thrown into confusion all over again. Almost as soon as he left the shore of the lake and moved back into the small wood to the south of the farmhouse he was seized by the shoulders and dragged from the path by Matthias Vaedecker.

Vaedecker drew Reinmar into the shelter of a clump of trees, looking this way and that to make sure that no one had seen him. The monks had returned to their huge grey house, and there was no sign of Zygmund or his wife, or any of the labourers who helped maintain the farm.

'What happened?' the sergeant demanded.

Reinmar had hardly been able to speak to the monks, but Vaedecker suddenly seemed to him to be a friend: someone in whom he could confide. His dumbness and stupidity evaporated, and he began to weep.

'She seemed to be improving again once we had reached shelter,' Reinmar told the sergeant, trying to scrub away the tears with his sleeve. 'She even managed to speak a few words, but when I awoke this morning I found her deeply unconscious. I think her heart stopped while I watched. The monks who came to the house last night gave her something to drink – the dark wine, I suppose it must have been – but it seemed at the time to be helping her.'

'Did you take any?' Vaedecker asked, sharply.

Reinmar had a denial ready on the tip of his tongue, but his resolve wavered before the soldier's penetrating gaze. 'The merest sip,' he admitted. 'I had told them that I was a wine merchant, and could hardly refuse to taste their wares. I did not swallow it.' The return of his instinctive defensiveness made him feel as if he were standing before his father, trying to justify some minor sin of omission. Mercifully, the illusion had the effect of stemming the embarrassing flow of his tears.

'Forgive me, my friend,' the sergeant said, taking due note of his distress, 'but I must ask you these questions. Did you recognise the taste of the wine – and did you dream after tasting it?'

'No to the first,' Reinmar said. 'I've never tasted anything like it before. Yes to the second – I certainly dreamed, but my dreams were nightmares, not at all the kind of experience that would make me avid to drink more deeply of their cause. In fact, I wish…'

But he did not know exactly what he wished, and the futility of bringing his confused desires into focus brought him to silence again.

'Perhaps it is time we began to trust one another a little better,' Vaedecker said. 'How much has your grandfather told you about the dark wine, its properties and its source?'

Reinmar laughed briefly. 'Not nearly enough,' he said. 'I wish I had been told enough to make a sensible response to customers who came enquiring for it. I wish I had been told enough to make a sensible response to witch hunters who came looking for the customers. In fact, I was told nothing at all until even my father conceded that my ignorance was more dangerous than a little knowledge. I think you know at least as much as I do. You read as much into Marcilla's delirious mutterings as I did, so you must know the tale which says that the source of the dark wine can only be found by those who have heard a call, and their companions. Doubtless you have also heard that it provides a special intoxication and that it preserves the appearance of youth. If you know more, I'd be glad to share your wisdom – or does the trust of which you speak work one way only?'

'You're the only ally I have in this place,' Vaedecker pointed out. 'If I cannot trust you, I'm in trouble. I cannot help feeling that you might be in more danger of suffering the dark wine's worst effects than most, given your family history, but I suppose I must hope that you're your father's son and that he is the man he seems to be. I have been told a little more, and although I dare not treat any item of information as certain, I'm prepared to act on the assumption that what I know is true. There is one thing I certainly ought to share with you. In spite of appearances, the girl might not have been dead.'

Reinmar felt that he had been struck. 'If you thought that,' he said, in a terribly dry voice, 'why did you not say so before they set her in the ground.'

'If I am right,' said the sergeant, grimly, 'she will not remain in the ground for long. I think they will wait to see what you do before proceeding, because they do not know as yet whether you are a potential ally or an enemy – and I suspect that they might consider you a prize worth capturing, even if there is a certain risk involved. They cannot be certain, you see, whether the girl was the only one who was guided here by a supernatural instinct. They may suspect, given your family history, that you also might have heard a call of sorts.'

'I didn't,' Reinmar said, flatly.

'I believe you,' Vaedecker said. 'But it might be a good idea to let the monks think that you did, if they want to.'

'And why should they want to?'

'I have no more idea than you how the dark wine is made, or from what kind of fruit,' the sergeant said, 'but Machar von Spurzheim has had cause to interrogate a good many gypsies during the last few years. The magic which brings the chosen few to the valley is no mere matter of recruiting carriers to bear it away into the world. The gypsies who hear the call are special children, marked for some kind of sacrifice. They come here never to return, I have been told, but not to die – at least, not as we normally understand death. They come here to be transformed.'

'Into what?'

'Into things not human, or only partly so.'

'Like the beastmen we fought yesterday?' Reinmar asked, quickly – but the image which had sprung immediately to mind was one of the creatures he had glimpsed in his dreams.

'Worse, I think. Those seemed to me to be mere creatures, capable of fighting but not much else. If they are daemonic at all, the daemonic part of their natures is not very active. Von Spurzheim's reluctant informants have spoken of more terrible compounds of human and animal attributes, whose daemonic glue is much more powerful. They also speak of a second stage of metamorphosis, which is fundamental to the manufacture of the dark wine and other equally sinister concoctions. Did you grandfather mention those?'

'He said that the makers of the wine of dreams produce other liquors, geared to more esoteric tastes.'

'Esoteric? Is that how he put it? Did he offer any further explanation?'

'No.'

'Well,' said Vaedecker, 'the wine that is so popular in certain quarters of every town between Eilhart and Marienburg is peddled as the ultimate luxury of consumption, and the bloom of youth which it preserves as the ultimate luxury of life – but luxuries pall when they become familiar, and the greatest luxury of all is the one which remains just out of reach. Some of those to whom the dark wine becomes overfamiliar eventually demand more piquant sensations. Dreams are not enough. Youth is not enough. The inner daemons which make them increasingly avid for the dark wine eventually make them avid for something even darker. Luxury never leads to satiation, but always to cruelty, and overindulgence in dreaming always leads, in the end, to a love of horrors. For some of its consumers, at least, the wine of dreams is but an introduction to its more demanding kin – but none of the dark wines can be made without human sacrifice, and children like Marcilla are part of the price the gypsies pay for the favour of darker gods than are worshipped by civilised men.'

The longer Reinmar pondered this speech, the less clear its import became. 'What, exactly, are you saying?' he asked. 'That the monks intend to disinter Marcilla, and revive her from her deathlike trance in order that she might complete her metamorphosis into some kind of half-human monster? That she will then undergo some further transformation, in the course of which the dark wine will somehow be extracted from the substance of her flesh and the essence of her soul?'

'So we have been led to believe,' the soldier confirmed. 'It might be that those we questioned had no real knowledge, but had to invent something under the pressure of our questions. There was talk of a monastery too, and of a secret in its cellars, but nothing explicit.'

'My grandfather said that he had heard some such talk,' Reinmar admitted.

'We have heard his name mentioned more than once,' Vaedecker admitted in his turn. 'When Luther Wieland became too fond of the dark wine, it is said, and subsequently fell ill for lack of it, his father and his son conspired to break an important link in the supply-line which led from this valley to Marienburg. The missing link was by-passed soon enough, but the whole chain has now been shattered by von Spurzheim and his allies, working back upriver from Marienburg. If the monks hope to rebuild the traffic they can only begin from here – and Eilhart is a ready-made site for a first base. Luther's father is long dead, and the monks must be attracted to the notion of instituting a new conspiracy of grandfather and grandson to undo the work of the old.

'I think they will come to you again, Reinmar, if you do not go to them – and they will take far more interest than they appeared to do last night. They will probably flatter you, and make what appears to be a generous proposition. If you will trust my judgement you will appear to be tempted – but you must go along with them just so far, and no further. You must win their confidence, as far as you can, and then you must betray it. Our real purpose must be to find out everything we can about what goes on here, and then to escape, marking our path as we go, so that no mere spell of concealment can blind us to its approaches when we return with an army at our backs.'

'You don't ask much,' Reinmar observed, sarcastically. 'I'm my own man, not a servant of the witch hunter.'

'I ask what was asked of me, if the chance arose,' Vaedecker told him, sharply. 'The chance has arisen, far more readily than I could ever have hoped. I must make the most of it, or fail in my duty – and I am not the kind of man who is given to failing in his duty. I need your help, and I am asking for it as one virtuous man to another. You are your own man, but you are also your father's son, and a citizen of the Empire. I'm very sorry that you grew to like the girl so much, and then saw her die, but I have a mission to fulfil and so have you. Are you with me, or against me?'

Reinmar hesitated, but not for long. 'If this is the source of the wine of dreams,' he said, 'we must find out what we can. And if there is the slightest chance that Marcilla is not really dead, we must certainly find out.'

'Good,' said Vaedecker. 'Go now, while I hide myself again – but when they come for you, keep your wits about you. Wear your sword.'

When Reinmar eventually returned to the farmhouse Zygmund and his wife did not ask him whether he would soon be on his way. They seemed to assume, in fact, that he would be with them a while longer. The woman gave him food, somewhat better than the bread and meat they had provided when he and Marcilla had arrived, and a jug of the same good wine.

While he was still eating, the two monks came in again and sat down with him. 'Well,' said Brother Noel, 'we have now offered our prayers to the god of death and dreams for the safe deliverance and good care of the gypsy girl. We are very sorry for your misfortune.'

'The girl obviously made a deep impression on you, and you must have thought that you had saved her life,' Almeric added. 'Saved her for a better kind of life, perhaps.' He spoke lightly enough, but he was plainly curious to see how Reinmar would respond to the tantalising hint. Reinmar concluded that Vaedecker was right. They did not know quite what to make of him and were anxious to take his measure. They had not waited long to see whether he would accept Noel's invitation.

'I would have taken the girl with me to Eilhart if she had been agreeable,' Reinmar informed them. 'I would have continued to protect her. I loved her.'

'I'm sure you did,' Noel said.

'Have you come to offer me a cargo of your precious wine?' Reinmar asked the monk, sounding a slight but carefully-calculated note of interest. 'I admit that it had a good odour and an unusual sweetness, but the promise that it would ease my sleep and make my dreams pleasant was unfulfilled.'

'You did not take enough to obtain that effect,' Noel told him.

'Perhaps not,' Reinmar admitted. 'Having thought about the matter, though, I realise that there is not much demand for sweet wine in Eilhart and Holthusen. Were I to buy a couple of casks of your wine I would probably have to trade them on, at least as far as the Reik – perhaps as far as Marienburg.'

Reinmar saw Almeric's eyes narrow in response to the mention of Marienburg, and noticed once again the peculiar quality of their radiance. When he looked back at Noel he saw the same strange glow in his eyes, but Noel forced a smile.

'Our agents have found new customers since your grandfather lost interest in us,' Noel said, in a neutral tone, 'but our order has always valued tradition. This is a sad time for you, I know, but it might be best for you to put your loss behind you and find what distraction you can in matters of business.'

'That's easy for you to say,' Reinmar observed, 'but not so easy for me to do.'

Brother Noel was not so easily put off. 'We have consulted our fellows at the monastery,' he said, gently, 'and we have been authorised to sell you a little of our stock, if you are prepared to take it. The name of Wieland is fondly remembered by the older brothers, and our superior was attracted by the notion that we might be able to rebuild one of our oldest bridges to the outside world. We enjoy our seclusion, to be sure, but it is not good even for men of our kind to be entirely isolated from the greater society of men. If the price were right, we would be prepared to let you take a sample case of our wine, ready-bottled in good crystal glass. We have our own glass-blowing shop, you know, and were almost as famous at one time for our bottles as for the wares they contained. You are, of course, very welcome to taste our produce again if you wish to make sure of its quality. But if you are not interested…'

'I suppose I might be,' Reinmar said, with a contrived sigh. 'But I am acting at present solely as my father's agent. He instructed me to be very careful with his money, and to stick very carefully to the route which he had planned. He might not be pleased to hear that I had deviated from his scheme and bought wine from someone other than our regular suppliers.'

'We were numbered among your regular suppliers once,' Brother Almeric pointed out. 'Were we not, Brother Noel?'

'We remember your grandfather's name very well,' Noel confirmed. 'He never came here, but we used to send our emissaries to deal with him. Zygmund's father knew him, I think – perhaps Zygmund met him, as a boy.'

'The farmer appeared to recognise the name of Wieland,' Reinmar agreed, reflectively. 'My steward will be worried about me, though, and I really ought to try to get back to the wagon before nightfall. I really ought to…'

He trailed off, hoping to leave the impression that he really did not know what he ought to do, and did not quite understand his own motives.

'Any business we do could be concluded before sunset,' Brother Almeric observed. 'The day is not so very far advanced. Perhaps you should give the wine another chance. When you tasted it last night the circumstances were far from ideal, and the girl's unfortunate death has obviously unsettled you. If you will come to the monastery, you may sample a number of the vintages we have in store. You are obviously a man who knows the value of wine.'

Reinmar continued his show of hesitation. 'If only my steward were here,' he said, eventually, 'I would feel much happier. I don't even know that my wagon is safe. We were attacked by monstrous beasts, and it was damaged. Although they ran off they might have returned. Are the environs of the valley always haunted by monsters?'

'Not usually,' Almeric said. 'Zygmund told us that he had heard rumours, but we did not take them seriously.'

'Should you wish to purchase some wine,' Brother Noel assured him, 'we could instruct Zygmund and one of his men to carry it safely to your wagon. They are skilled men, and would be pleased to help with any necessary repairs. It should not take us long to conclude our business – and this is an opportunity that you might never have again.'

'Well,' Reinmar said softly, 'I suppose that is true.'

CHAPTER SIXTEEN

WHILE HE WALKED back to the monastery in the company of Brother Noel and Brother Almeric, Reinmar tried to take more careful note of his surroundings and of the buildings towards which they were moving. Because they were walking along the valley floor his vantage was not ideal, but he had a reasonably good view of the slopes on either side of the lake. They were heavily wooded, and there was no sign of a vineyard.

The temple by the burial ground was not so very different from the Temple of Morr in Eilhart. The main part of the building was surmounted by a rounded dome. Its narrow windows were filled with leaded lights, so that the interior might be invisible from without while being softly illuminated within by the colour-stained rays of the sun.

Behind the temple there was a huddle of subsidiary buildings, presumably storerooms where tools were kept and perhaps a closeted shrine for private prayer. Then there was an open space separating the temple from a single-storeyed U-shaped edifice which Reinmar assumed to be the monks' living-quarters. That too was augmented by a set of wooden outhouses, but most of them were hidden from view by its bulk.

The grey stone of the temple and the living quarters was considerably darker than that from which the Wieland house was constructed, and the architectural style of the monastery complex was sterner and more angular than the one in which the grander houses of Eilhart were cast. Even so, the contrast between the buildings and their woodland setting did not seem as strong as Reinmar had expected. The stones comprising the temple and its outbuildings were square and sullen, while the trees were green and full of the vivid enthusiasm of high summer, but there was something about the way that the weather had worn and pitted the fabric of the monastery, while mosses and creepers had made themselves at home upon its walls, that suited the man-made constructions to their natural surrounds.

Reinmar also realised while he walked that this was not at all the same kind of woodland as the one through which he and Vaedecker had trekked the day before. Its trees grew less straight and its greenery was more confused. The hard berries which decked its thorny bushes were bright with warning colours to bid the birds beware.

Reinmar could not suppress a shudder as the three of them passed the burial-ground, and he could not keep his eyes from the freshly-turned earth with which the monks had covered Marcilla's body.

'It would be best if you could put her from your mind,' said Brother Noel, quietly. 'The living must give themselves to life, while the dead have business of their own. You are sad because you found her beautiful, but those who are chosen are chosen, and those who are not must choose instead to live.'

'Chosen?' Reinmar repeated. 'Who chose her?'

Almeric looked sharply at him, but Noel remained solicitous.

'It is but a manner of speaking,' the monk assured him. 'All men and women are born with appetites and potentialities already established in their souls. We have freedom of choice, but not of desire. We are guided to our different fates by yearnings not of our own making. Each of us has to find himself, and those who find themselves in the wine of dreams are as fortunate in their way as those who find themselves in monastic discipline or the machinations of trade.'

While he was delivering this speech Noel guided Reinmar into the quadrangle protected on three sides by the U-shaped building. It was rimmed by cloisters, where more monks were abroad. Most bowed to their visitor as they passed but none spoke to him, although one took Brother Noel aside and whispered something in his ear. It seemed to Reinmar that whatever news was passed by this means was unwelcome; Noel frowned deeply before rejoining Almeric.

The two monks did not take Reinmar to the main door, but to a smaller one set in one of the wings. He had no chance to explore the mazy corridors within, because he was taken into the first room that presented its door, to the left of the entrance. There was a table within, on which three small casks had been set, along with a jug of water, three glass goblets and a ladle. There was also a leather bucket on the floor. The goblets were neatly formed, but they could hardly be reckoned exquisite examples of the glassblower's art.

'These are three of our most recent vintages,' Almeric told Reinmar. 'All are now in short supply, so we cannot offer you more than a drop of each to taste. We shall be forced to ask high prices if you wish to buy – but I think you are better placed now to estimate their worth than you were last night.'

The casks were not spigoted, but their tops were loose and Almeric used the ladle to fetch a tiny measure from the first, which he tipped into the first of the goblets. Reinmar accepted it, and touched it to his lips. He took the whole measure into his mouth – there was little more than a drop – and let it lie on his tongue for a moment or two before spitting it into the bucket. He suspected that he was being tantalised, and that the monks expected him to become greedy for a more generous portion, but he was determined to resist any such temptation. He swilled out his mouth with water before taking a second meagre drop from the second goblet, and then repeated the whole sequence for a third time.

All three samples were the same sweet wine, but Reinmar could discern the subtle differences imposed by ageing, and knew without having to be told which vintage was the youngest and which the most mature. He did his best to consider the offerings as a winemaster would, focusing his entire attention on the taste sensations and putting aside all thought of dreams. Noel watched him closely throughout, his expression clouded by thought – and perhaps by doubt.

'I saw no vines as we approached the monastery,' Reinmar remarked, offhandedly. 'Nor did I see any other sign of elaborate cultivation, save for Zygmund's vegetable-plots. Where do you grow the fruit from which the wine is made?'

'That is our secret,' Almeric told him.

'What fruit is it?' Reinmar asked. 'If it is a grape, it is none that is grown elsewhere in the surrounding hills.'

'That too is a secret known only to the members of our order,' Almeric told him. 'All you need to know is that the wine is good, and that we can send consignments to Eilhart three or four times a year if there is enough demand.'

'We normally buy once a year from each of our suppliers and store the casks in our own cellars,' Reinmar said. 'It is more convenient for everyone concerned.'

'Not for us,' Almeric said. 'We prefer to store our supplies until they are needed. Our agents only sell what is required for imminent consumption.'

'I do not know the market,' Reinmar said, carefully setting out his stall for a hard bargaining session. 'I do not know who your regular customers are, or the price they usually pay. I would be taking a risk if I were to make an offer for the produce. My father might be very angry if I were to turn up with goods that he is not expecting, for which he has no ready-made buyers. I ought to consult him before making any decision – but I shall be happy to return here, if he thinks the matter worth further exploration.'

'That is not possible,' Almeric said – but Noel immediately put a hand on his arm to instruct him to be silent.

'How do you like the wine, Master Wieland?' Noel asked, quietly. 'How does it sit upon your tongue? Do you feel an affinity for its special qualities?' He seemed disappointed by Reinmar's attitude, and his own had undergone a marked change since the other monk had whispered in his ear. If someone had brought intelligence from Eilhart, Reinmar thought, there might be more contained in it than news of Machar von Spurzheim's arrival. Even if the message had not come so far, it might say that he had been seen with Matthias Vaedecker, a witch hunter's man.

Now that Noel had raised the question, however, Reinmar was forced to consider it earnestly. He did like the wine, although he had nothing left of it in his mouth but the aftertaste. It had sat upon his tongue very comfortably, as if there had indeed been an appetite inborn in him that he had never before understood or had the opportunity to serve. And he did, indeed, feel an affinity for the prospect of luxury that it held out to him. But honesty was not the game he had come to play.

'It is too sweet and too rich for my taste,' he said, cautiously. 'The people of Eilhart are used to plainer and simpler wines, whose taste is brisk and clean. That is what I have been brought up to value. If my own taste were to determine my decision, I might be disinclined to make you any offer – but I will admit that the wine is of good quality, and it is certainly interesting. I wonder, though, whether there are too many imponderables to allow me to strike a wise bargain.'

Almeric seemed to be ready to argue with him, but Noel's hand was still resting on his companion's arm and it was Noel who spoke. 'I understand your reluctance,' he said, amiably. 'It requires a certain boldness to be adventurous in trade, and you are evidently a careful man. We will not press you. Produce like ours requires a sympathetic distributor, and we had better search until we find one. We shall bid you farewell. I'll accompany you back to the farm and ask Zygmund to guide you back to your wagon.'

'That's not necessary,' Reinmar said, trying hard to overcome his astonishment at the abrupt closure of negotiations. 'I can find my own way easily enough, and Zygmund has been far too kind already.'

Brother Noel made no protest. 'As you wish,' he said. 'I am sorry that we could not find common ground.'

Brother Almeric did not seem satisfied, but he had divined that the situation had changed since they all set out from Zygmund's house. He said nothing as Noel led Reinmar back to the door.

'I am sure that you have business of your own to attend to, Brother Noel,' Reinmar said, as they stepped out into the sunlight. 'I can retrace my steps easily enough, and will make better time if I travel alone. I need to reach the wagon before dusk.'

'Very well,' Noel said. 'I wish you a safe and profitable journey home, Master Wieland. I am truly sorry that we could not do business, but if you cannot commit yourself to the wine the loss is yours.'

'Perhaps we shall meet again,' Reinmar ventured.

'Perhaps we shall, if it is our fate,' Brother Noel echoed, although the tone of his voice suggested otherwise.

Reinmar immediately set out to walk back to the farm, intending to pass by in clear sight of Zygmund and his wife and to continue towards the neck of the valley at least until Matthias Vaedecker rejoined him. This time he refused to look into the burial-ground as he walked past it.

He never reached the farmhouse, because Vaedecker appeared by his side at almost exactly the same spot as before, in the wood between the farm and the monastery.

'You should not risk being seen here,' Reinmar complained.

'I was wrong,' Vaedecker told him, without any preamble. 'They did not wait before taking the girl from her shallow grave. Almost as soon as you had passed the burial-ground on your way to the wine-tasting they came for her. They are obviously in a hurry. Did you see anything in the big building – anything that von Spurzheim will be glad to know?'

'Nothing at all. Where did they take her?' Reinmar demanded.

'Into the temple,' Vaedecker said, glumly. 'They have not come out again, although I could see no sign of them when I went to peep through the door that they had left ajar. Nothing at all, you say?'

'A cloister and a single room,' Reinmar told him. 'They did not give me a tour, and when I established my starting-point for what I expected to be a lengthy bargaining session, they took my apparent reluctance to deal at face value. Brother Noel apparently decided that he would rather be rid of me than work for my conversion. One of the other monks whispered in his ear while he passed through the cloister. The gypsies may have sent word to say that the wagon had an extra passenger, and that he is a witchfinder's spy; if so, any inclination they had to trust me would have disappeared on the instant.'

'Something has happened,' Vaedecker said, pensively. 'It may have been a message from outside that instilled a new urgency in the monks. If they are discomfited, that is our advantage. We must find out more while we still have the chance.'

'If Marcilla is not dead,' Reinmar reminded him, 'we cannot leave her here. If they intend to harm her, we must do our utmost to save her.'

'We must certainly try to find out what has become of her,' Vaedecker agreed. 'If we are lucky, we might come out of this with exactly what von Spurzheim needs, and the answer to a riddle that has lain unsolved for centuries – but it will be dangerous. We have no idea what odds we might be facing. Are you ready?

'If there is a possibility that Marcilla is alive,' Reinmar insisted, 'I would risk anything.'

'It is not the best possible reason,' Vaedecker told him, 'but it's the right pledge. We are comrades in arms, then?' He offered his hand, as a token of the compact.

'Comrades,' Reinmar agreed, clasping the hand as firmly as he could.

Chapter Seventeen

Vaedecker led Reinmar to the edge of the wood, then told him to wait while he scouted ahead. While Reinmar obeyed he offered up a quiet prayer to the god of death and dreams, imploring him to concentrate his attention upon this little place, in order to make certain that his servants here were scrupulous in keeping to their vows. Reinmar suggested to the god, in a suitably humble fashion, that if there were those in this valley who had betrayed their monkish vows, then perhaps Morr might spare a little of his wrath to help a son of Eilhart in an hour of need.

Whether Morr would hear this prayer or not, Reinmar could not judge, but he was prudent enough to offer others, both to Sigmaer and to the goddess Verena, whose scales of fairness were the symbol of honest trade. He hoped that she would not disregard it, even though he had never been so wholehearted in his veneration to think of himself as a devout follower.

When Vaedecker returned it was to report that members of the company of monks were tending the vegetable-patches which lay without the walls, feeding their animals, and otherwise going about their everyday business, but that the temple was silent and seemingly unoccupied.

'No longer,' Reinmar replied, drawing Vaedecker behind the bole of a tree and pointing.

Two hooded priests had just come from the temple, bearing spades. They passed through the lich-gate into the burial-ground, and went immediately to the reopened grave, which they began to fill again with earth. Reinmar watched them, his eyes hot with patient anger, until they had finished and returned their tools to one of the wooden outbuildings.

'Now we shall see,' said Vaedecker, as the two monks returned to their cloister. 'Not the front door – there's another at the back, in a secluded court.'

The wall at the rear of the temple was so pitted and overgrown with creeping plants that they had no difficulty in climbing over it and letting themselves down into the courtyard. The small door which they found there was latched within, but there was a narrow gap between the worn edge of the ancient door and the stone wall, and Vaedecker was able to lift the latch with the blade of his sword in order to let himself in.

The corridor inside was very gloomy, but the last rays of twilight sent light enough through the slit-windows to let Vaedecker find his way, and he moved cautiously into the heart of the building, listening carefully for footsteps. Reinmar followed.

They had gone only a few steps, and had not yet reached the door that gave access to the altar-space, when Reinmar heard the sounds of softly-slippered feet approaching from the other side. There was nowhere to hide, and no time to get back to the door through which they had come, so he was not surprised when Vaedecker stayed where he was.

The door opened. The monk who came through was hooded, and he carried a smouldering taper although he had no lamp or candle with him. While other sounds were masked by the creaking of the door upon its rusty hinge Vaedecker moved very swiftly past the monk, sliding his left arm around the man's throat to take a choking grip. In his right hand he still held the sword which he had used to open the latch on the outer door, and he touched its point gently to the monk's cheek while whispering in his ear to warn him to be quiet.

'Go back the way you came,' the soldier murmured, 'and make not a sound, lest it be your last.'

He pushed the man back into the altar-space. There was a candle on a table set beside the door, its recently-extinguished wick still glowing faintly.

'Relight it!' Vaedecker commanded.

The monk had breath enough to blow his taper into brightness, but when he touched it to the wick of the candle he was panting with anxiety, and his hand was trembling. It took more than ten seconds to warm the wax sufficiently to make the candle take light.

When the tiny flame was finally alive the monk turned to look at his assailants, and said: 'Who are you?'

Vaedecker's only answer was to push back the folds of the monk's cowl so that his face became visible. The man was considerably older than Vaedecker and much thinner – it was obvious that he would not be capable of putting up a fight, and he did not seem inclined to try.

'I need two sets of robes like yours,' Vaedecker said, gruffly.

'There are none here,' the monk replied – but his eyes had flickered sideways to a cupboard, and Reinmar moved quickly to open it.

There were several sets of robes inside, most of them ornate and ceremonial – but there were two plain robes, and Reinmar took them both. He offered the more capacious of the two to Vaedecker, and put the other one on himself.

'Thank you,' said the sergeant to the monk. 'But from now on, I require you to be honest, else I'll feel obliged to cut your throat.'

'You have no business here,' said the monk, in a low tone.

'I disagree,' Vaedecker said. 'I saw a body disinterred, and I need to know why, and what you intend to do with it. Show me!'

'She is beyond your help,' the monk said, stubbornly.

'If that is so,' Reinmar put in, 'then we have only vengeance to seek against those who placed her there. But you must show us anyway.'

'I cannot,' the monk insisted, but Matthias Vaedecker was not about to tolerate any refusal. The soldier pressed the point of his blade a little harder, and drew blood.

'There is an odour about this place,' the sergeant whispered in his captive's ear, 'which reminds me of the stink of necromancy. As a virtuous man, I do not hesitate to kill whenever such a stench reaches my nostrils.'

'Necromancy!' the monk spluttered, as though stifling a cry with difficulty. 'There is no necromancy here!'

Reinmar scowled. 'Is she alive?' he hissed. 'Tell us now or my friend will cut your throat. Is she alive?'

The monk's eyes dilated with fear, and he nodded his head. 'The wine does not kill those it chooses,' he whispered, 'although it stills their hearts and relieves them of the need to breathe. But she is chosen. She is gone from the world of men. Go, I beg you – there is nothing for you here.'

Vaedecker pressed harder – not lethally, but with sufficient force to cut the frightened monk more deeply. He gasped, so tortuously that Reinmar could almost believe that his windpipe was half-severed.

Terrified as he was, however, the monk shook his head. 'I am bound by vows which I dare not break,' he said. 'I dare not.' The way in which he said it suggested that his fear of breaking his vow was almost as great as his fear of the blade at his throat. 'What do men like you know of the lord who rules our lives and our souls? Go, I beg of you.'

There was such an awful sincerity in the man's voice that Reinmar was frightened. Despite having paused to say his prayers, he had not thought as he climbed over the wall surrounding the temple grounds that he was entering the domain of a god. Now he faced up to that notion and its implications, including the probability that this domain might belong to a god even sterner and darker than the one that men called Morr.

Matthias Vaedecker did not hesitate at all. 'Show us the way!' he whispered again, his voice overflowing with menace. 'Lead and live. Refuse and die!' It was obvious to Reinmar that the soldier meant what he said – and it was obvious to the monk, too. It proved, in that moment of extremity, that the man had underestimated his own ability and power of choice.

'This way,' he croaked. 'But it is a sacrilege you will regret.'

Wearing their stolen robes over their own clothes, with their faces well-hidden by the cowls and Vaedecker's unsheathed blade all-but-covered by a loose fold of his costume, the two intruders followed the captive monk. As they passed the altar, Reinmar noticed a staff propped up against it, and immediately picked it up. Its head was carved, as priests' staves usually were, having been fashioned into the shape of a raven's head with the beak extended in line with the staff. It seemed to Reinmar by no means unsuitable to be carried by a priest of Morr, but it was not unsuitable to be carried as a weapon either. He had his sword, but if his disguise was to be of any use it might be prudent to have a weapon that could be carried more openly.

The domed chamber in front of the altar was bare of all furniture, as custom dictated. It was strange in only two significant respects. Firstly, the great oaken doors which should have stood perpetually open in a temple dedicated to Morr were shut and barred. Secondly, the hollow dome was ornately decorated in a curious fashion, which made it resemble the spreading petals of some vast flower. This resemblance was further enhanced by an intricately-woven rope, as thick as those used to tow barges along the Schilder, hung down from the dome into the atrium, as if it were a pendulous style extending the flower's stigma in order to facilitate pollination.

Opposite the closed doors was the symbolic gateway which Reinmar would have expected to see in any temple of Morr, consisting of two plain pillars and a heavy black lintel. Behind it there was a tapestried screen depicting ravens in flight against the background of a stormy sky. These were the universal emblems of Morr – but Reinmar realised as he saw them here that they might equally well be employed as emblems of any other god of death and dreams, if there were any others of that kind in the mysterious and unknowable realm of the gods.

In the temples and shrines of Morr that Reinmar had previously had occasion to visit the screens behind the inner gateway were never thrust back or drawn aside. There would, of course, have been no point in doing so, for in those other places they invariably stood against blank walls, but the true reason was not a practical one. Such gateways were symbolic of the threshold of death, which the soul could cross but the body could not, and their screens were symbolic of the curtain of ignorance that had been placed across the threshold in question by decree of the gods, so that no man might know his fate in the Great Beyond. It was inconceivable, supposedly, that a screen of this kind should ever be moved in such a way as to permit a living being to pass through.

In this temple, however, the screen was hanging loose, so that the monk who was leading them could draw it aside like a curtain and pass by into some mysterious space beyond the gateway. Reinmar could not help but catch his breath when he saw what was happening, but his stride did not falter at all. He already knew that the boundary between life and death was somehow blurred in this uncanny place, in fact as well as allegory.

When all three of them had passed through, Vaedecker took the screen from the monk and closed it behind them.

The space behind the gateway was small; it was no more than a covert cut into the wall of the temple, which here seemed to be founded in native granite, not on quarried stones. It had no floor at all, but was simply the mouth of a fissure. The cleft did not appear to have been hollowed out by pick and spade, and Reinmar guessed that it was entirely natural. Human artifice had, however, added to it a spiral staircase of wrought iron, lit by candles mounted on spikes, three to every complete turn of the stair. The steps were very steep, and Reinmar estimated that each rotation took them four fathoms or more into the depths of the earth – and yet the stairway wound about the central pillar no less than eighteen times before their descending feet touched level ground again.

So the rumours Luther had heard had more truth in them than he would credit, he thought. The real secret here lies far beneath any mere cellars.

At the bottom of the spiral stair there was a tunnel, very neat and round in section. Again, Reinmar was certain that no human hand had had any part in making the passage; it was as if some huge and patient worm had bored through the rock a thousand or a million years before. How many pairs of slippered feet had passed along its length since then he could not guess, for they had not yet succeeded in eroding any kind of track. Like the staircase, the tunnel was lit by candles set on spikes placed fifteen paces apart. Reinmar counted nineteen candles before he saw, over the shoulders of the two figures hurrying ahead of him, the light at the end of the tunnel.

For one careless and unthinking moment he presumed that the bright light must be daylight – but then he remembered that the sun must be near to setting by now, even if it were possible for the tunnel to have brought them out on to a hillside somewhere in the forest. Whatever this bright glow might be, he realised, it could not possibly be the bountiful light of day.

He remembered what his grandfather had said about fruits never ripening except in the sun, and realised that the old man might have made a wrong assumption. As the two cowled figures before him came to the tunnel's end, Reinmar was able to move alongside them again.

They had entered a much broader space, having passed into a vast cavern, more huge by far than the domed atrium of the temple from which they had come. The floor of this awesome area was smooth but not flat, undulating like a range of gentle hills in miniature. Its walls and ceiling were formed even more peculiarly, their undulations being so pronounced that the roof seemed to be festooned with countless bulbous fungi – but Reinmar could only see this indistinctly, because white light blazed so dazzlingly from the rounded extremities of these protrusions that the fissures between them were hidden by the glare.

What a light that is! Reinmar thought. What fruits might ripen in its glare!

The thought was forced upon him, for the floor of the cavern was thickly planted with flowers, which grew to far greater size than any he had ever seen before. There were hundreds of them arrayed before him, of several different kinds. Each one was mounted on a stalk as thick as a man's leg, from the base of which sprouted four gargantuan leaves. The immense flower-heads were vast and bell-like, compounded of eight, ten or twelve close-set petals. Every one that Reinmar could see hung downwards, every stalk being curved into the shape of an inverted hook.

Had the flowers been coloured as gorgeously as the flowers which grew in the best garden in Eilhart they would have been very beautiful indeed, but they were not. The predominant colours were four in number: jet black, livid white, pale blue and rosy pink. Some of the flowers were plainly coloured, but there were a few in which the colours were mixed as stripes, white paired with black and blue with pink. The stems and leaves which carried them, far from reproducing the green shades of the forested hills, were a curious creamy white colour.

The scent of the flowers was more subtle than their size implied, but while Reinmar stood there lost in amazement the fragrances teased his nose, gradually filling his mouth and throat with a sickly sweetness. He recognised the particular bouquet of the wine that Noel and Almeric had given him to taste, but it was mixed with other scents that seemed sharper and more piquant.

There were pathways in the flower-forest, three of which diverged from the entrance at which they stood, but the undergrowth to either side of each pathway was abundant, and seemed impenetrable. Although the floor of the underworld was very uneven, deeply pitted and grooved, the flower-stalks did not seem to be bedded in soil-filled hollows. Instead, each stalk widened out into a complex base not unlike the holdfasts by which the sturdier kinds of river weed clung to the rocks and boulders of the Schilder. It was not easy to judge from where they stood, but Reinmar thought that each stem was a bundle of four or five threads, which separated as they neared the ground, each element broadening and becoming more lumpen, its texture taking on the appearance of petrifaction, as it met and merged with the cavern's stony floor. Vegetable flesh and stone seemed ultimately to be fused together, without any distinct junction.

When he had studied these vegetable marvels for half a minute, Reinmar was convinced that the radiance which lit this eerie underworld must be very different in its quality from the light of the sun, or from the silvery light of the twin moons and the stars. This was an alien light, which he had never seen before.

The flowers with which he was familiar, fed on the golden light of the sun, reproduced in their character something of the colour, the warmth and the sweetness of that glorious light. It mattered not whether they grew wild in the shady glades of the forest, or whether they were carefully nurtured in the gardens of Eilhart; the light which nourished them was the same. These flowers had a different mode of sustenance, and in every aspect of their character they gave evidence of that disparity. They were not without colour, nor without warmth, and certainly not without a kind of sweetness, and yet all these things were strange – and, to Reinmar's eye, quite wrong.

Vaedecker plainly felt the same. 'What is this place, Reinmar?' he whispered in an awed tone. 'What have we found?'

Chapter Eighteen

'You have found something that is forbidden to the sight of men like you,' the captive monk hissed, in reply to Vaedecker's question. 'This invasion will not be forgiven.'

Vaedecker ignored him. The soldier was still searching with his eyes. The space immediately outside the entrance of the tunnel belonged more to the upper world than the nether one. It was cluttered with tools and various other items of apparatus, including ladders, tables and empty crates. There was obviously a good deal of work to be done hereabouts, but none was being done at present – not, at least, within sight of the underworld's entrance.

This, Reinmar decided, must be the place where the fruit was grown from which dark wine was pressed, if it really were the product of a wine-press. But was it? Given that the dark wine was not the produce of any ordinary grape, ought he to assume that it was made by a similar method? Now that he had seen the massive flowers which grew here, he wondered whether it might not be the result of a very different process. Was it possible, he wondered, that the liquor might in fact be made from the nectar manufactured by these enormous and extraordinary blooms?

Nectar, he knew, was made by flowers to attract and nourish the insects which carried their pollen away to fertilise their neighbours. Nectar was the currency in which flowering plants paid for sexual intercourse, the lubricant of their trade in the seeds of identity. Nectar was, on the other hand, the luxury of insects: the most delicious food imaginable.

These flowers were of a different sort; there was no hum of insects audible in the underworld. Their dutiful pollinators were presumably human: monks, who were content to gather their reward instead of consuming it, so that they could transmit its currency and its luxury to the world outside. There, it became an object of trade like any other – or, perhaps, quite unlike any other.

The monk who had brought them down the spiral stair and along the tunnel took a step backwards, as if he assumed that his task was done.

'Wait,' said Vaedecker, quietly but sharply. 'We need to know which way they took the girl's body. Which path?'

'I have shown you too much,' the monk replied, his face as white as chalk in the unnatural light. Now that he was in the presence of the giant flowers he seemed more frightened of them than he was of Vaedecker's blade, no matter that the blood was still seeping sluggishly from the cut in his throat. Even so, he raised his arm to point to the middle path.

Vaedecker's eyes narrowed as he made a calculation, and then he lifted his sword above his head. The terrified monk ducked away from the blade, but when the soldier brought it down he made sure that it was the flat of the blade that landed on the monk's tonsured pate. The first blow only knocked the man to his knees, but a second strike rendered him unconsciousness.

Reinmar made as if to kneel in order to check that the man was still alive, but the sergeant grabbed his sleeve and dragged him away.

'We must hurry,' he said. He was still speaking in a low voice, anxious that his words did not echo from the walls in case there were monks abroad in the underworld, hidden from view by the flowers. 'If he lied, we'll find out soon enough.'

The soldier moved off between the gargantuan plants, passing beneath a rough arch formed by two of the flower-heads, and Reinmar followed. He was anxious to see more of their structure, so he threw back the capacious hood that had concealed his face while he and Vaedecker had descended the stair. This allowed him the freedom to look up into the bell-like corollas to see what was inside.

He was not overly surprised to discover that each of them had a single pendulous style, which seemed to be hanging limply in the manner of the thickly-woven rope which hung from the dome of the temple. Shadowed as they were by the flowers it was difficult to tell what colours the styles might be, but most were pale. He could not see the nectar-glands that were presumably clustered about the base of each style, because the more distant parts of the interior of each flower-head were hidden even from reflected light.

Having looked up, he looked down again, to study the tangled structures at the bases of the stems. These holdfasts were highly irregular in shape, but as soon as Reinmar began to inspect them more closely he detected shapes within each mass that reminded him somewhat of human bodies laid supine and mysteriously bloated. A fifth 'limb' which sometimes appeared to be present seemed, in accordance with this fancy, to be the head of the recumbent form, which had become so molten and misshapen as to seem part of the bedrock.

Although he cursed himself for his stupidity when he finally realised the appalling truth, it took time for Reinmar to accept that this impression was more than mere macabre fancy. He might have realised it sooner had it not been for the fact that some of the forms seemed very far from human – but that, he eventually realised, was because they had only been half-human to begin with. The tangled 'roots' which bound the gargantuan plants to the cavern floor really were bodies bloated and transmogrified by alien flesh. Some had been human, but some had been beastmen whose limbs had extended into claws instead of hands and feet and whose misshapen heads had been horned.

'Do you see –?' he asked of Vaedecker – but the sergeant did not let him finish.

'Be quiet,' he retorted, hoarsely. 'I see what you see. Keep looking – and be on guard!'

The advice was good, for it had hardly been voiced when Reinmar caught sight of robed figures ahead of them. Vaedecker immediately reached up to take his hood and flip it over his head again, before moving sideways to take cover behind one of the massive stems. Reinmar copied him, taking cover behind a stem some eight or ten paces to his right.

Peering around the stem, Reinmar saw that half a dozen monks were gathered together, all but one facing away from him. There was a slight susurrus of voices, but the monks were standing quite still. It seemed that they were waiting for something significant to happen. Reinmar could not see the face of the one monk who was facing them – for which he was duly grateful, since it implied that the man in question could not see him – but he could see that the man was holding aloft a staff decorated at the head with the effigy of a black flower, whose 'petals' were fashioned from ravens' wings.

It was not until a momentary gap appeared in the rank of six that Reinmar was able to see more – but when it did, he had to suppress a gasp of horror and alarm.

In the space between the line of six and the man with the staff the naked body of the gypsy girl had been carefully laid out, supine, within a shallow depression in the cavern's floor that extended away to the left of the path that they had followed, close to a junction at which it crossed another.

It was almost as if the polished rock were getting ready to hug her, and welcome her to its adamantine bosom.

Reinmar understood, now that he had seen what he had seen, that some of the holdfasts which supported the stems of these astonishing plants had indeed once been the bodies of human beings – those who had 'heard a call' that summoned them here. He understood, too, that although they had undergone some monstrous mutation and transfiguration which had made them part stone and part alien flesh, they still retained faint echoes of their previous identity.

He became suddenly and horribly certain that these luckless persons had never died and were not dead even now: that their human souls were within them still, eternally imprisoned in strangeness. The beastmen, he presumed, were in a similar state – but he could not bring himself to care overmuch about that. Marcilla was a different matter.

'If this is not your doing, Morr,' he murmured, not loud enough for Vaedecker to hear but not quite silently, 'then I beg you to send down your most fervent wrath upon these people without delay, whatever consequence it may have for me.'

But the God of Death and Dreams, after the invariable habit of all the gods to whom men pray, gave no evidence of having heard this prayer, nor any evidence at all of his concern.

The monk who had held the staff aloft above Marcilla's naked body lowered it again, looking down at the motionless form that lay exposed before him. Then he pushed back the cowl which had covered his head – and Reinmar could not help but start with shock, because he could see the exposed face between the heads of two of the six, and saw how it caught the white light which flooded from above.

The monk's features seemed to catch fire with a similar glow of their own, as if the light were taking on substance as it gathered about the man, caressing his cheeks and forehead lovingly. His eyes, in particular, seemed fiercely ablaze, and Reinmar realised that the uncanny brightness which he had perceived in the eyes of Brother Noel and Brother Almeric when he first saw them was a feeble presentiment of what it one day might become. The monk's skull was quite hairless, and his features seemed abnormally rounded – his nose snubbed and his chin like a tide-worn pebble – but his flesh had a curious glossy polish, as if it had the texture as well as the colour of a tarnished tooth.

The celebrant extended his arm, and with the foot of his staff he began to make a series of passes over Marcilla's naked body. While he did so he crooned a long sequence of liquid syllables in some arcane language whose like Reinmar had never heard. When this part of the ritual was complete the monk changed his grip upon the staff, so that he held it near the foot, and extended its ornamented head towards the bell of a black flower which loomed above him.

The model fashioned from ravens' wings that surmounted the staff was but a hundredth the size of the huge entity above it, but as the symbol extended, so the thing which it symbolised began to move towards it, lowered very gently by the gradual relaxation of its massive stem.

Again the celebrant began to make a complex series of passes in the air, still chanting all the while. From time to time the remainder of the company joined in to add their voices to a periodic chorus, or to answer some particular syllable – but positioned as they were, there was little danger that anyone would notice either of the uninvited guests.

As the rite drew towards its close, Reinmar saw that the pendulous style within the bell of the flower had extended itself, so that its tip now extended beyond the rim of the corolla. It had not done so by any process of engorgement or uncoiling, but rather by stretching itself in an elastic manner. Its basic colour was not amber, as he had at first imagined, but a creamy near-white hue similar to that of the leaves which spread from the stalk in fanlike fashion. It was darker because the white was faintly streaked with pink.

The style writhed very slowly, in a manner which reminded Reinmar of the head of a luckless and bewildered earthworm come unexpectedly to the surface of the soil. Marcilla lay quite still beneath the enormous dome of the flower: unseeing, unfeeling, unbreathing.

The officiating priest began to lower his ornamented staff, and the tip of the style dipped down more urgently, as though trying to pursue it. But then the celebrant stepped aside and moved unhurriedly away, to allow the flower-head to continue its slow descent.

It seemed to Reinmar that the flower was now aware of Marcilla's cold presence, and he choked back an exclamation of horror. The tip of the style had extended at least half a yard beyond the rim of the corolla now, and its writhing had become more excited. Down and down it came, while Reinmar held his breath in terrified anticipation.

The moment the lascivious style touched Marcilla's pale flesh, she moved. It seemed to Reinmar that she was trying to squirm away, and would have moved more urgently had her limbs not been deadened by the drug she had been given. It was as if she were stirring in her sleep, trying to awaken from a bad dream in which her entire body had become mysteriously immovable.

The style touched her again, drawing its tip along the length of her arm, as slow and gentle as the caress of a lover's finger. Again she moved, restlessly but impotently. It was as if she were trying with all her might to awake, but could not. Her body was cold and stiff, her flesh as white as marble in the unnatural light, and the power of intention was insufficient to move her reluctant limbs.

But she certainly was not dead.

She was not dead.

Reinmar clenched his jaw very tightly, but he gripped his stolen staff more tightly in his right hand and adjusted the position of his feet so that he was set to leap forward. He did not know how far this ritual would go, but he wanted to be ready to act as soon as the moment seemed ripe. With his left hand he fumbled at the cord holding his sword in its scabbard, but the shock of what he had seen made his fingers clumsy and the knot would not come undone.

The tip of the vermiform style stroked Marcilla's naked arm, then moved down her torso and along her thigh towards the knee. When it reached the calf it reversed its motion, making a long and languorous pass as it moved over the contours of her abdomen and breast, very gently and very delicately. Every touch, it seemed, brought her a little closer to life and consciousness. She began to make sounds – not cries of alarm but deep, slow moans.

Reinmar saw that Marcilla was now able to move her limbs a little. It seemed that the touch of the writhing thing within the black bell was restoring warmth to her muscles. Reinmar had no doubt that her heart was beating again, but he had no idea how strong and fast that pulse might be.

At some stage, Reinmar presumed, this monstrous creature would have to transmit its seeds into the gypsy girl's body. He knew only too well what her destiny was supposed to be – the seeds would take root in her living flesh, ready to begin the patient work of transforming her substance – but he could only guess what intermediate stages there might be. Would she be allowed to wake, to see what fate awaited her? Or would she remain locked in her dream as the blood coursed through her veins and her fever grew?

He could not believe that she would be allowed to know what was really happening. He clung to the hope that the dream in which she was lost – itself a product of the wine of dreams – would be a dream of paradise, and that no matter what became of her as she lay in the crack in the cavern floor she would know nothing but happiness. In time, no doubt, she too would live as a plant, producing a glorious flower-head of her own, and any consciousness that remained in her bloated and petrified head would be the awareness of bright and eternal light.

Was that, he wondered, how every plant and flower in the world imagined the heavens?

All the while, the priests continued their incantation, murmuring liquid syllables in a language that Reinmar did not recognise. All the while, too, he tried to free his blade with his left hand, but the unpractised fingers still could not undo the knot and he did not dare release his ready grip on the staff.

Marcilla seemed to be coming closer to consciousness all the while, although she had not yet reached the brink – but as she recovered more power of movement, the nature of her movements changed. As the pendulous style continued to caress her, she ceased her futile attempts to wriggle away and moved more responsively, as though the tickling touch no longer irritated her.

But she was coming back towards the very brink of wakefulness. Reinmar was certain that there would come a point when it would need no more than a rival touch to bring her out of her dream. If she could only be snatched back from the edge of disaster at that propitious moment, she might still be saved. She would be fully alive again, and her dream could be broken. If he acted at exactly the right time, he might still save her. If not, she would lie in that shallow pit, uncoffined and unburied, until her transformation was complete. She would melt into the welcoming rock while the first ivory-white shoot sprang up from her navel, extending its tender leaves to bask in the white fire which poured from the pitted ceiling of this world-in-miniature.

He could not let it happen.

Reinmar let go of the knot securing his sword and struggled to control himself, knowing how difficult it would be to complete the course of action he intended. His most urgent need was that Marcilla would be able to flee with him when he ran, so that they might make their reckless break for freedom together. They would have to climb the spiral stair together and quit the grounds of the gloomy temple which stood sullenly above them, without any delay. There were six men to be felled here, but there might be as many as fifty or sixty more who would join the chase as soon as the alarm was raised. It would not be easy to outrun them in the forest – and even if they managed to reach the wagon, and Godrich and Sigurd had contrived to mend the wheel...

Reinmar looked across at Matthias Vaedecker, and the sergeant immediately glanced sideways to catch his eyes – but the signal Vaedecker sent with a quick gesture of his hand was a command to be still: *watch and wait.*

For the moment, Reinmar obeyed – but he knew that he would not be able to maintain his obedience for long.

Chapter Nineteen

Reinmar wanted nothing more than to rush forward, swinging his staff with deadly force, but he forced himself to be still for a few moments longer. He knew that Vaedecker was right, and that he had to wait until the caresses of the loathsome flower had brought Marcilla all the way back to life – but he also knew that he must not wait an instant too long, lest everything be lost. He had to discover that precious moment when she would be best capable of conscious thought and movement, but had not yet suffered the final act of pollution which would lead inexorably to her destruction. He waited, tense and taut with the agony of uncertainty as to how long he could safely delay.

In the meantime, the worm in the flower's mouth, which seemed to grow pinker with every moment that went by, continued its measured dance upon the floor of Marcilla's tender flesh, exploring her contours and teasing her with the revivifying effects of its touch.

She was now able to reach out towards it, as if she were trying to catch it as it passed, but she was still sightless and slow, while the worm-thing was quick and clever. It evaded her groping fingers.

Reinmar watched and waited, although the tension in his heart and limbs was becoming unbearable.

Marcilla began to writhe more urgently, and there was no question that her limbs had regained the greater part of their strength – but still she could not open her eyes. She was lost in her dream, without the least inkling of where she was or what was happening to her. Perhaps, Reinmar thought, she imagined herself still safe on the hearth of the farmhouse, slyly pleasured by the hallucinatory power of the sweet wine that she had quaffed before sleeping.

Then, just for an instant, the style paused in its writhing and drew back a little. The tip parted, to expose a deeper structure within: the stigma, which presumably bore the spores of destruction. The stigma was golden yellow in colour, like the summer sun of the world above, and it glistened with mucus.

The tissues of the style parted, like eyelids at the moment of awakening.

Marcilla parted her own eyelids at long last, and looked up into the great black hood of the flower which hovered over her, and into the sightless daemonic eye which threatened her. She opened her mouth uncertainly, as if she did not know whether to scream or to cry with glad delight – but no sound came from her trembling lips.

Reinmar, as certain as any man could be that it must be now or never, did not bother to look to Matthias Vaedecker for permission. He let out a howl of fiendish glee as he bounded forward, with the raven-headed staff raised up high, to snatch his beloved away from the cruel attentions of his dreadful rival.

The five monks who still had their backs to him began to turn in alarm as soon as they heard his war-cry, but in their confusion they bumped into one another, their limbs becoming entangled as they raised their arms to defend themselves. The only one exempt from this confusion was the sorcerer-in-chief, who had been officiating at the rite.

As soon as he moved, Reinmar felt the gaze of the chief monk's unnaturally radiant eyes upon him, and he knew that however stunned the others might be, the man who had invoked the attentions of the black flower was dangerous. To meet this challenge before it was properly laid down, Reinmar changed his grip upon the staff, holding it as if it were a spear, with the ornamented end directed forwards. He charged into the other five celebrants, knocking them sideways without making any attempt to ensure that they stayed down once they had fallen. He made straight for the worst of his enemies.

The wooden beak of the raven's head was angled thirty degrees and more from the line of the shaft, and it had not been sharpened, but the weapon was still spear enough to strike through the coarse cloth of the spellcaster's robe and carve a bloody wound upon his breast as it rebounded from his ribs.

The stricken man fell backwards, letting loose a pathetically faint cry of anguish as the force of the blow drove the breath from his lungs.

Reinmar's left hand was free to seize the vermiform style of the flower, and this he reached out to do. Had it begun to recoil into its bell he would not have been able to reach it, but the flower made no defensive response at all. If anything, it actually moved its gaping mouth towards him, extending its wormlike tongue in his direction as if it were curious to touch and taste the attacker who had sprung so unexpectedly from the ranks of its worshippers.

The golden stigma seemed more like a staring eye than ever, but it was entirely blind to Reinmar's purpose.

Reinmar's mind had become suddenly clear as he discharged his pent-up tension in furious action. Perhaps, he thought, the plant was entirely innocent of the ways of the upper world. Perhaps it knew nothing of nature red in tooth and claw, of violence and predation, or of anger and jealousy. Perhaps, having been lovingly tended by the patient priests in this deep, secret and nightless cave, it had no experience of any kind of attack whatsoever. Or perhaps, after all, it was only a flower, devoid of any intelligence or reflex, helpless in its vegetable impotence.

For whatever reason, the tip of the style was still there to be seized and held when Reinmar reached out, and seize it he did.

He had expected it to be sticky and cold, but it was silky and warm. There was the slightest of thrills to the touch, as if it were trying to renew the life even in him, who had never suffered any simulation of death.

Reinmar pulled, as hard as he could, in order to draw as much of the length of the thing from the maw of the flower as might be drawn, and to make it as taut as he could. Then he shouted to Matthias Vaedecker, who was hurrying to his side. 'Strike!' he yelled. 'Sever the thing from its root!'

Vaedecker seemed to be angry, and was certainly cursing volubly, but he hacked at the style, slashing at it from a height, determined to sever the cord with a single blow. The strike was almost too successful. Stretched as it was, the plant's peculiar organ was already under considerable tension, and its soft flesh offered little resistance to the sharp blade. It snapped so suddenly that Reinmar nearly fell backwards, with the piece which he had severed coiled about his hand.

He stumbled so badly that his knee struck the ground, and only then remembered that there were enemies all around him, eager to grab him and pull him down. Luckily, they were still confused and he had a firm grip on the staff. Reinmar tried to swing the staff from side to side, as Sigurd would have done, but he had nothing like Sigurd's strength, and the staff had insufficient momentum to knock anyone down. He was fortunate that no one snatched it from his grasp, or struck him while his knee was on the ground.

The flower, which could never have known injury before, recoiled from the shock spasmodically. Reinmar saw that its great stalk, which had moved with such stately grace before, shuddered briefly before erupting with a titanic convulsion, whose whiplash effect caught a couple of the priests as they exclaimed in horror, and sent them tumbling like ninepins.

The part of the style that was left for Reinmar to clutch writhed in a similar fashion, but it could not contrive to grip his hand. He gladly let it fall into the crevice beside Marcilla's body, where it continued to squirm. It shed no blood or ichor, but the flesh which had been cut across showed red and raw within its paler sheath, and the blind golden eye that had so briefly opened was tightly closed again.

Marcilla was certainly awake. She screamed, with far greater effect than Reinmar or the priest he had struck down with his makeshift spear.

As the scream cut through his confusion, dispelling a little of his wild anger, Reinmar became suddenly aware that Matthias Vaedecker's sword was red with blood. The soldier was holding it in both hands, hacking first to the left and then to the right with brutal efficiency.

Reinmar saw one man's face cleaved in two from temple to jaw, so that the features came away like a mask. He saw another with his throat slashed, clutching both hands to his neck as if he might somehow seal his carotid arteries and secure his windpipe. He saw another lurch back clutching his belly, though he had too few fingers to stem the flow of his uncoiling intestines as they slid through a great gaping wound. He became belatedly aware of the fact that Vaedecker was calling him a fool, and howling at him to run – and he saw that other priests were approaching from three different directions. They were coming in ones and twos, but they were not bumping into one another in alarm and confusion, and they were armed with iron-bladed spades, sharp-tined forks and huge wooden staves. If he and Vaedecker waited for them to gather in full force, they would be considerably outnumbered.

Reinmar was neither shocked nor sickened by the sight of so much blood; he still had a plan to execute. Marcilla's newly-opened eyes had been dazzled by the white light and she had thrown up a hand to protect them, but she was evidently well aware of the fact that she had woken into a frightful nightmare. Her distress seemed boundless. Reinmar, still staggering from his temporary loss of balance, caught the girl's right wrist in his left hand, and tried to drag her to her feet. For one hideous moment he thought that she could not rise – that there was insufficient life in her to allow her to stand up, let alone to run – but the fervent insistence of his grip ultimately proved irresistible.

'It is Reinmar, come to save you!' he shouted at her, although her scream had died by now and he did not need to yell in order to be heard. 'We must run for our lives!' So saying, he began to run himself, keeping such a tight hold of her wrist that she had to follow him or fall.

Immediately there formed in front of him a ragged rank of three newly-arrived priests, but he held the staff before him like a spear. He was eager to thrust and slash at them. Had they been fighting men of any kind – soldiers, or common ruffians, or even careful tradesmen – he would not have stood a chance, for their makeshift weapons, which amounted to two massive clubs and a rusty cleaver, would have been worth far more than his slim wooden shaft, but these were not fighting-men at all, and the violence which they had already seen must have seemed to them to be the most outrageous sacrilege imaginable. It was not that they did not wish to impede and capture him – indeed, they probably wished it as avidly as they could – but they did not know how to act in concert to achieve that end. None of the three, it seemed, could quite grasp the fact that he was part of a potentially powerful company; each and every one of them displayed in his eyes the consciousness of being face-to-face with an armed madman, and each one was caught up by hesitation and uncertainty.

Reinmar crashed through them boldly and recklessly, swinging his puny weapon as bravely and boldly as if it were Sigmar's mighty warhammer. Not a hand was laid on him as he went past, bringing the bedazzled Marcilla behind him. Once he was past them, however, they were quick to turn and eager to make up for their failure to check his charge. Reinmar could not help but howl out his exultation when he realised that he and Marcilla were free of immediate danger, but it was only exultation and not triumph. He knew that the priests would pursue him and harry all the more determinedly because they had failed to stop him when they had the chance.

He turned sideways, and with a single fluid motion swept Marcilla up on to his left shoulder – and such was the fever of his excitement that she seemed to weigh no more than any of the ordinary burdens which he hoisted thus a dozen times in every working day. Then he set off, moving away from the enemies who were still clustered about Matthias Vaedecker, trying to dodge his busy sword.

As he ran in what seemed to be the safest direction, Reinmar was only vaguely aware that the path he had taken was not the one that had brought him to the spot where Marcilla's violation was taking place. It was not one of the two branches of the fork that would have taken him deeper into the underworld, but he knew it would not take him directly back to the entrance. Given the way it was angled, though, he felt sure that it would take him back to the wall of the cavern, so that he and Vaedecker could make their way along it and could make a stand against it if they had to. In the meantime, Reinmar raced along the meandering and uncertain path as fast as his legs would carry him, hurdling one encroaching root-ridge after another as a hunted stag might bound through a forest's leafy glades.

He was so completely absorbed by the necessity to put distance between himself and the pursuing priests that he must have taken a hundred expansive paces before he realised that

Vaedecker was not running after them. He realised too that, burdened as he was, he had no hope of outstaying his pursuers for more than a few fleeting minutes.

As soon as Reinmar realised that they had been separated he shouted Matthias Vaedecker's name, but the three priests who were pursuing him had set up a clamour of their own, and the echoes of more distant cries were resounding from the bright-lit ceiling in such awful confusion that Reinmar could not tell whether he would be heard or not. He dared not hesitate, and was quick to convince himself that the best thing to do was to follow the path until he reached the boundary of the cavern and then to turn to his right, working his way along the wall until he came to the tunnel that led to the spiral stair. Vaedecker would surely make his own way back to the same place.

Reinmar did not doubt that he could outfight his pursuers if he did not exhaust himself too soon. He was young, well-nourished and thoroughly used to hard work. Although his principal duty was to man a counter, he had moved more than his fair share of casks up and down the steps to his father's cellar. He had also been schooled in fighting. These priests, whose god of death and dreams was known to them in the flowers of this horrid field of unnatural death, were much older men than he, and their thinness was obvious to the most cursory glance. The two who carried oversized clubs – which must surely be pestles, normally used to crush and pound vegetable pulp in a mortar – seemed barely able to lift them, and certainly would not be able to wield them as if they were cudgels. The three undoubtedly toiled as other men toiled, but their strength had been sapped by the austerity of their vocation. The most dangerous man, Reinmar decided, was the one armed with a cleaver. When he reached the wall and had to turn, he decided, that must be the one he put out of action first.

For a further fifty strides Reinmar managed to maintain the distance he had put between himself and his pursuers, but then, in spite of their obvious tiredness, they began to gain on him. His own legs were beginning to grow leaden, and he knew that they would buckle soon. He tried again to cry out for Vaedecker, but he could not do it; his breath was too desperately needed to sustain his flight. Remembering that he was only a man after all, with a man's limitations, he began to feel the true weight of the burden that he carried on his shoulder, and the true strain upon his aching legs.

Had he not reached the cavern's boundary at that moment he would have been forced to make his stand on the path, with the heads of the dreadful flowers nodding all around him, but he saw the wall looming up ahead. Even better than that, he saw a gap in the wall: a shadowy covert whose interior was not illuminated by the appalling white light of the underworld but by ordinary yellow candlelight.

Reinmar's first thought was that the covert must be a way out, even though it was not the entrance through which he had come. His second was that if it offered a way out it must also offer a way in, where more enemies might be lying in wait for him. For that reason, he did not make directly for it, but decided instead to make his stand with a solid glowing wall at his back.

He laid Marcilla down beside the wall, telling her to be still, and immediately turned to face the three monks. He saw the expression of triumph in their weirdly-glowing eyes as they converged upon him, but he knew that it was premature.

CHAPTER TWENTY

HOLDING THE raven-headed staff before him as if it were a half-pike, Reinmar charged without waiting for his assailants to come to a standstill. It was the right move; they tried to stop when they saw him coming but they had too much momentum and their efforts only made them ungainly. One stumbled and fell, carried forward in spite of himself by the momentum of his unwieldy club. The one who came on most recklessly of all, though, was the man with the cleaver, who raised it as if to strike Reinmar's head from his shoulders.

He never got the chance. Reinmar slammed the head of the staff into his breastbone with all the force he could muster, and the priest was stopped in his tracks. The cleaver flew from his hand and soared harmlessly past Reinmar's left shoulder to rebound from the cavern wall.

Reinmar immediately swung the staff around so that its blunter end thumped into the midriff of his third opponent, and bought just enough time to turn and pluck up the cleaver from where it had fallen.

No one was shouting any longer, and the echoes that had resounded from the ceiling of the underworld a few moments before were silent now. Reinmar used the cleaver to slash at the throat of the man he had winded. He expected the blade to shear right through the soft flesh, but it was nowhere near sharp enough. It stuck and stuck fast, and as the man fell his weight wrenched the weapon from Reinmar's hand. He still had the staff, but he was well aware of its limitations.

While his two remaining opponents struggled to recover from the blows he had already struck, Reinmar finally found the opportunity to use his skilled right hand to loose the knot that held his own blade in place. He drew it from its scabbard just as they came forward again.

Had they been fighting men, they would have known what to do, but they were not. It was absurdly easy, even for a man who had never killed a human being before that day, to inflict mortal cuts on both of them. Reinmar struck one about the head, the other full in the chest – and it was fortunate, as it happened, that the first blow was so effective, for he had to put his foot on the second man's rib-cage and heave with all his might to free his blade again.

Then there was silence, and an appalling stink.

Marcilla was rising to her feet, her eyes full of horror. She was dumbstruck, but her hands were fluttering. At first, Reinmar thought that she was reaching out to him. Then he realised that she did not know who he was, and was trying, ineffectually, to ward him off.

He loved her, and she did not even know who he was. She had said once before that she had seen him in her dreams, but she did not seem able to remember that now.

'It's all right, Marcilla,' he assured her, surprised by the hoarseness of his voice. 'I'm a friend, and these men were your enemies. This way!' He caught her right wrist in his left hand and drew her towards the shadowed covert and the candlelight within. She resisted, but only for a second; it seemed that she took the decision to trust him, perhaps by virtue of the kindness in his tone and perhaps because she remembered, dimly, that she had seen him before.

When he first saw that the space within the covert was a blind cave, with no means of egress from the underworld, Reinmar felt a stab of fear in his belly – but the fear was quickly overwhelmed by wonder as he realised what the covert was.

Five stone vats were arranged in a rough arc against the right-hand wall of the space. These, it seemed, were the mortars which partnered the pestles that the two monks had tried to use as clubs. Three of them were brimming with wet pulp, but the other two were less than half-full. At the rear of the cave, near the ceiling, a spring of water gushed from the rock, the waterfall descending to a shallow pool. The overflow from the pool ran into a crack that carried the excess water away into the bowels of the underworld, but water had been drawn off into a number of large open barrels. There were more barrels positioned near the vats, with huge filter-funnels set atop them.

Reinmar had no difficulty deducing that when the pulp had been crushed in the mortars it was filtered into these barrels, producing a solution. There was no sign of yeast, either physical or odorous, and he concluded that although the filtered solution was probably a mere substrate, the process by which the wine of dreams was made did not involve orthodox fermentation.

The wooden shelves that skirted the left-hand wall of the cave were not entirely full, but they were laden with various small sealed casks and stone jars, and a considerable number of glass bottles. Many of the bottles were empty but some were not, and what they held was a dark fluid whose odour could not be entirely confined, and whose sweetness overwhelmed the much more delicate scent of the pulp in the mortars. There were also a number of smaller phials, set in a position of privilege in a covert-within-the-covert. All but two of these were empty, or nearly so, but those last two were nearly full.

Reinmar picked up one of the phials and carefully removed the stopper. The perfume that rushed into his nostrils was so incredibly powerful that he immediately replaced the stopper, and then had to stand stock still while his head cleared. His eyes had begun to weep, and he felt utterly helpless – but once the fluid was safely confined again he recovered soon enough.

This, Reinmar realised, was where the wine of dreams was actually made. The substances dissolved from the pulp obviously gave it some of its texture and some of its complexity, but the eventual product was obviously highly diluted – and the most active ingredient of all was that which was kept in the phials and added drop by drop to the bottled liquor. He was sure now that it was the nectar of the uncanny flowers, patiently gathered by the monks.

Luther's assumption that the making of the wine of dreams must be subject to the same seasonal cycle as any other vintage was quite wrong, Reinmar realised. Here there was probably no alternation of day and night, let alone an alternation of winter and summer. That was why Almeric had said that the monastery could supply wine three or four times a year – but the process by which the nectar was produced must be slow, for this store was far nearer empty than full.

Marcilla had drawn back against the unadorned wall to the left of the entrance, but when Reinmar dropped her hand she made no attempt to run, or even to move further away from him. He took off his stolen cloak and gave it to her so that she could cover her body. She hesitated, perhaps because its skirts were so liberally stained with blood, but she put it on regardless.

'I'm a friend,' Reinmar said again. 'Stay close to me, and I'll defend you with my life. Only trust me, and we'll win through.' In the meantime, his gaze flicked back and forth along the row of vats and the huddled masses of the barrels, and he wondered what he ought to do now. Had the vats been made of wood he might have been able to overturn them, but they were stone, and he knew that even Sigurd would have laboured in vain to upset one. Even the laden barrels were too heavy to be easily overturned – but the bottles were brittle as well as light, and the phials were lighter still.

No more pursuers had followed him as yet, but Reinmar knew that he only had a minute or two to spare if he hoped to make his escape. He had to get back to the entrance before it could be sealed. With luck, though, a minute or two ought to be enough. He put the phial he had already opened into his pouch, and threw the other full one, unopened, into the rock where the stream made its way into the further depths. It vanished from sight, and he had no doubt that it was irretrievable. He followed it with two other phials which still had a few drops of fluid in them.

The crack in the rock was too narrow to accommodate a bottle, but he was not afraid of the scent of the diluted wine. All he had to do to reduce the stocks of the final product was to race back and forth along the shelves on the left-hand wall, tumbling bottles, flasks and jars from the shelves, letting them smash upon the floor as they fell – and that is what he did.

It only required fifteen seconds of running amok, picking up any stone jars that would not consent to fall and hurling them this way and that, to wreak utter havoc in the storeroom. The odour of the spilled wine quickly became strong enough to intoxicate, but it was nothing like as strong as the perfume of the pure nectar, which had threatened to immobilise him. The giddiness he felt only made him wave his arms about more furiously, until there was nothing left on any of the shelves and his feet were surrounded by shards of broken glass. The floor of the cavern was sticky and sweet, but the spilled wine was already draining towards the exit-hole into which he had cast the phials.

The thrill of destruction was delicious, and the rising odour of the wine of dreams merely served to make it more piquant still.

'What have you done?' Marcilla whispered, finding her voice at last.

'I have revenged you,' he told her, trying to keep his own voice firm and level. He kept on talking, hoping that it would help to calm his thundering heart and painting breath. 'I have taught these unholy monks a much-needed lesson as to the proper price of human flesh and human souls. Now, we must go. We must find Vaedecker, and the way out.

'You killed those men,' the gypsy whispered.

'So I did,' he admitted. 'But what I have seen of this vile world below the world would drive any virtuous man to murder – even one who did not love you. If ever there were men who deserved to die... Come with me now, I beg you!' So saying, he took Marcilla by the wrist again, as if to draw her out of the cave – but she was a little stronger now, and she resisted.

'Please,' he said, softly. 'You do not know me now, but I love you. If you cannot trust me, we are both doomed.' He looked deep into her lovely eyes, hoping that she could measure his worth accurately, and know him for what he was. She lowered her head, and stopped trying to pull away from him. Perhaps she had remembered, at last, that she had seen him in her dreams. He drew her towards him, and hugged her tightly, hoping that the gesture would reassure her.

'We must go now,' he said. She seemed to have understood that necessity, for she made no effort to hold him back. They departed from the storehouse of the wine of dreams without a backward glance at the wreckage they left behind.

Once out of the covert, Reinmar began to move rapidly but stealthily along the wall of the underworld, in the direction which, he hoped and trusted, would bring them to the spiral stair. Mercifully, although there was no path, the way was fairly clear. Marcilla followed, not needing to be hauled along. The coldly glowing wall was to their left. To their right, great ebon bells hung down from ivory stalks – enough of them to make a carillon. As they passed along the subtly curving wall, though, the black blossoms gave way to pink, and then to pale blue, and then to black and white in combination. Reinmar watched them all the while, fearful that if a single style should extend like a sinuous tongue from any one of those huge hoods to coil itself about his neck or any part of Marcilla's person then he might have a far sterner fight on his hands than the cadaverous monks had been able to offer.

It seemed, though, that the flowers were lost in some dream of their own. If they were capable of caring about anything at all, they clearly did not care about the loss of Marcilla, even though she had been chosen for their use and called to their service. Reinmar sent a silent prayer of gratitude to Morr – whose wrath, he now felt sure, must have aided him considerably in his desperate rush to snatch his beloved from the jaws of a fate far worse than death. The success of his mad dash now seemed evidence enough that Morr was severely displeased by these heretic priests and their macabre garden of lost souls. When he had finished his prayer of thanks, however, Reinmar was quick to send another, imploring further help. He knew that he was not yet safe, and that there was ample time for further intervention in this adventure. As soon as he had made this further plea his heart leapt, for he saw another breach in the shining wall of the cavern and recognised it as the gateway through which he and Vaedecker had entered the underworld.

The monk knocked unconscious by Vaedecker still lay unmoving, and alone, at the tunnel's entrance. This sight renewed Reinmar's strength. Gladness surged through him as he passed beneath the last of the awesome blooms and was suddenly among the man-made confusion of barrels and bottles, ladders and tables. He regretted that he had sheathed his sword when he heard rapid movement behind him as soon as he had passed into the antechamber. But when he whirled about he saw that it was Matthias Vaedecker hurrying after him, bloodstained sword in hand.

The soldier's expression was grim. 'You should not have moved away from me without my signal,' Vaedecker said, angrily, 'and after having moved, you certainly should not have hurled yourself upon them without so much as a sideways glance. Are you mad?'

'Are there any left to chase us?' Reinmar asked, ignoring the rebukes.

'I think not – no thanks to you,' Vaedecker growled.

'On the contrary,' Reinmar told him. 'I did my share, and none can say otherwise.' As he spoke, the memory of the man with the cleaver stuck in his throat came back momentarily to haunt him, but he was too tired to shudder and far too wrathful to feel ashamed.

'You had better pray that they are even worse fools than you,' Vaedecker told him. 'If even one has had the sense to run to the stair instead of racing to meet our blades, then we're done for. Our only hope is to be up and away before anyone on the surface realises what has been done down here.' He knelt down as he spoke and put his fingers to the throat of the unconscious monk, checking for a pulse. 'He'll sleep for a while yet,' he opined. 'I suppose I should slit his throat, but he'll be no threat to us if we move quickly. It appears, Master Wieland, that I underestimated you. I did not think you the kind of man to start a war so recklessly. We came here as careful spies, not a two-man army set to run amok.'

'You were the one who came as a spy,' Reinmar reminded him. 'I came to save Marcilla, by any means necessary. It seems to me that the war began as soon as the monsters in the hills became real. I started nothing.'

Vaedecker shook his head, but not unsympathetically. 'The war began in Marienburg,' he said. 'I've been on the march with von Spurzheim ever since – but if our battleground had not been decided already, you've probably determined it now. Had we contrived to slip away we might have brought the fight here while they did not expect us, but whichever evil god has made this place will surely take it amiss that we have slaughtered his servants. Whatever is waiting for us at the head of the stair, and however quick a getaway we make thereafter, there will be a full gathering of our enemies now – and those half-humans who attacked us before will likely be the least of the assembled army. You have no idea what you have done, Reinmar Wieland.' The sergeant was trying hard to be censorious, but the grudging approval beneath the criticism was obvious. Vaedecker might have come here as a spy, but he was a warrior first and foremost.

'No,' Reinmar replied, 'I have no idea what I have done – but I could not stop at half-measures when I saw what they intended to do with Marcilla, and I did not.'

'You killed the three who went after you, then?

'Oh yes. And I did what I could to spoil their harvest. I found their storehouse, and I spilt the wines within. I doubt there is a single flask, of glass or stone, that is still intact.' He said this proudly, expecting to earn a further increase in the soldier's esteem, but Vaedecker only knitted his brow. Clearly, he had little or no idea what the consequence might be of any interference with the monks' own supply of the wine of dreams, and he did not ask for further details of what Reinmar had done.

'Well,' the sergeant said, 'sometimes the recklessness of youth has the advantage over the skill of the tactician, even though shrewd tacticians usually live longer than hot-headed heroes. Since we are committed, I suppose we must do as much damage here as we can.'

Having said that, the soldier went into the tunnel to fetch out one of the candles set to light it, and applied the flame to the leg of one of the tables. Given the untidiness of the various objects heaped around the entrance, it was obvious that a fire would spread quickly, and would not be easily extinguished. There was no way to judge whether its spreading fumes would be able to hurt the horrid flowers, but they would certainly help to prevent any pursuit from the underworld.

'Now,' Vaedecker said as soon as the fire was well and truly alight, 'we must tackle that stair. If we get trapped half way, the blood we have so far shed will seem a trivial thing. Are you ready?'

He spoke the last words over his shoulder as he looked back to make certain that Reinmar and the girl were behind him. They were close on his heels as he moved swiftly along the tunnel – Reinmar certainly did not want to linger while the smoke was billowing in every direction.

'I'm ready,' he said, and meant it.

Chapter Twenty-One

'I don't understand,' Marcilla whispered, although she consented to be drawn towards the stair. 'Where am I, and what is happening?'

'Don't worry, my love,' Reinmar implored. 'The world we know awaits us up above, and we have every chance of making good our escape. Only trust me, and I will see you safe.' He would have felt better had he not caught sight of the expression in Matthias Vaedecker's eyes while he spoke these words. Vaedecker immediately turned his gaze forwards again and said nothing, but if Reinmar read him right the soldier was of the clear opinion that they would do far better, even now, to leave the girl behind, no matter what her subsequent fate might be.

They arrived at the foot of the spiral staircase while the air they breathed was still unpolluted.

'You go first,' Reinmar said, as evenly as he could, 'I'll follow.'

'See that you do,' the sergeant muttered, setting his foot on the first step. Marching with all the military precision he could muster, Vaedecker began to climb – and Reinmar followed, in his own fashion.

As they climbed the staircase Marcilla began pulling against Reinmar's clutching hand, mewling piteously, but Reinmar would not let her go and while he insisted she had not the strength to pull away from him. He felt a cold shock of fear in his heart as the possibility occurred to him that the false death induced by the drug – including a sojourn in the grave – might have disturbed her very profoundly, even to the extent of leaving her utterly and irredeemably mad. When he looked back at her, though, it seemed that her eyes, though bewildered, were lit by reason.

'Have patience,' he whispered, 'I am Reinmar Wieland, your deliverer. We must climb, dear heart, as fast as we can, for we have been in some tomblike world beneath the world, and must scale this wearisome stair in order to return.'

She swayed, and might have fallen had he not held her so tightly. 'This is the strangest dream of all!' she said, weakly.

He shook her again, and said: 'This is no dream, my love! This is real, and all might still be lost if you will not climb. Come up, my love, come up!'

He pulled her up the steps behind him, but he knew that he could not drag her all the way. She had to climb by the effort of her own will, and by the strength of her own frail limbs.

Help me, Morr! he begged silently. *God of Death you may be, but I beg you now to help my darling live, until the proper time when you must claim her – for I understand full well that I have saved her for you as well as for myself!*

Whether his prayer was heard or not, he could not know, but Marcilla did begin to climb, though her unshod feet had begun to bleed and her ankles were further stained by blood that had leaked from the habit that Reinmar had given her to wear. As Reinmar forced himself to go round and round, ascending the flight, she followed meekly, holding hard to the rail as she came. Once she was in motion, and only had to repeat what she did over and over again, she began to climb faster and faster, and Reinmar climbed before her, believing that every step they took, away from the uncanny white-lit underworld toward the golden radiance of the sun, was a tiny salvation in itself.

How long it took them to reach the top of the spiral staircase Reinmar could not tell. He did not attempt to count the candles as he passed them by, nor the steps on which he trod. His body was still perilously close to the limits of its endurance, and his legs ached terribly. It was as if his entire being were flooded by a kind of fire, which would not let him build any chain of consecutive thoughts, but burned a single intention into his consciousness: the intention to put one foot in front of the other, as relentlessly as he could, in the hope and faith that he would eventually be brought to the end of his course.

That he did, and continued to do, until the three of them came at last to the head of the stair, and the loose screen that separated the world to which they were returning from the one which they had fled.

Matthias Vaedecker drew the screen aside, and looked out into the space behind the altar. Then he moved rapidly forward, so that he could look out into the temple itself. Reinmar had not realised that the soldier was so tense and tired until he heard the sigh the sergeant released when he saw that the building was empty.

'We are fortunate, Master Wieland,' the soldier said. 'If any alarm had been raised in the living quarters they'd surely have set an ambush here. We still have to pass the farmhouse, but that should be easy enough. By the time the monk we left at the foot of the stair recovers, and goes into the underworld to see what we have done, we shall be long gone. Even so, it will be best if we can escape unseen.'

They left the temple by the same door they had used before, and hurried away from it in the direction of Zygmund's farmhouse. Vaedecker led the way in an unhurried fashion, making careful use of whatever cover he could find. Reinmar knew that it would not be easy to pass the farm buildings without being seen, but it would not be a disaster if they were; even if Zygmund had labourers with him they would think twice before attacking two men armed with bloody swords.

They stayed within the wood as long as they could, and were still hidden by bushes as they came to the edge of the farmer's fields. From that vantage point Reinmar could see that there was a group of five men gathered on the path that led to the farmhouse. They were standing still and seemed to be engaged in an intense discussion. Two of them, who had their backs to him, were unrecognisable save for the fact that they wore monastic robes – but one of those facing the two monks, who towered above them both, was unmistakable.

'Sigurd!' Reinmar exclaimed, exultantly. 'It's Sigurd, come searching for us!'

Vaedecker put out a hand to warn Reinmar to be still, and Reinmar obeyed the injunction willingly enough – but Marcilla had recognised someone too, and Reinmar had relaxed his grip on her hand sufficiently to let her pull away and run out of the wood into the open ground ahead of them.

'Ulick!' she cried. 'Ulick! I am here!'

Vaedecker cursed, but it was only habit and not alarm. Reinmar remembered what he had been told about the valley being hidden from everyone except those who had heard a call. If that was true, then he and Vaedecker had only been able to find it by following the girl. Sigurd must, therefore, have needed a guide of his own – and none but Ulick could have led him here.

For a moment or two Reinmar preserved the hope that the fifth and partly-hidden man might be Godrich, but as soon as he began to run after the girl, by which time all five faces had turned towards him, he saw that it was Zygmund.

Matthias Vaedecker followed him. He moved in a more careful fashion but he had given up all hope of remaining concealed.

As he drew closer to the waiting men Reinmar saw, not at all to his surprise, that the two monks were Noel and Almeric. Theirs was by far the greater shock as they recognised the figure running towards them as Marcilla. Almeric was white with amazement, and Noel's eyes blazed with alarm. The monks knew full well that the gypsy girl had never been dead, but they certainly had not expected her to emerge into the light of day again. When Ulick ran to meet his sister the two monks stood still, rooted by confusion.

By the time Reinmar had drawn level with the girl again he knew that the monks must have guessed how it had come about that the gypsy was here. The fact that she was clad in a monk's robe, whose drying stains were very obvious, had told them that she had been won back by force, and that the fight had been bloody. The monks could see as well as Reinmar, however, how severe their disadvantage was. Even if they and Zygmund had been well armed, they would have stood no chance at all in a fight against Sigurd and Vaedecker. Brother Noel put a calming hand on Almeric's arm, and whispered a command to Zygmund, presumably instructing him to be still. By the time Marcilla had embraced her brother, while the sergeant had arrived alongside Reinmar so that the two of them stood face to face with the two monks, Noel had decided his policy.

'You do not understand what you have done, Master Wieland,' said Brother Noel, quietly. 'You would have been wiser by far to leave quietly, when you had the chance. How many innocent men have you harmed?'

'I have saved an innocent girl from a horrible death-in-life,' Reinmar retorted, having had just as much time as his adversary to make ready for a battle of words. 'I have harmed none who did not deserve to be harmed, and every mortal blow I struck was in self-defence.'

Almeric winced when he heard the word 'mortal' but Noel had already turned his head to meet Matthias Vaedecker's eyes. 'And you, I suppose, are Machar von Spurzheim's man? You have come out of hiding to assist this fool in his mistaken endeavour.'

The fact that Vaedecker had managed to enter the valley, Reinmar deduced, must have been the substance of the whispered message that had changed Noel's attitude to him. Perhaps one of Zygmund's labourers had been sent out to investigate Reinmar's account of the broken wagon and had stayed long enough to learn – presumably from one of the gypsies who had come to collect their kin – how many passengers it had carried, and how many had followed the bemused girl when she wandered off.

'I am a soldier,' was Vaedecker's calm reply to Noel's taunt. 'I do my duty, to Reikland and the Empire, and the good gods.'

'Duty that compels you to spill the blood of unarmed men,' Brother Noel observed, somewhat inaccurately. 'Well, we all have our obligations. You had better go back the way you came, since we cannot stop you – but you had better tell the witch hunter that he will never find this valley, though he searches for a century – and you would be very wise to leave the girl and boy with us, where they belong.'

'No!' said Reinmar, anxiously.

Vaedecker was not about to make any concession to a man he regarded as an enemy and an agent of evil. 'I think not,' the soldier said. 'While they are in our care we might be better equipped to find this place again than if they were not – and I certainly intend to return when I can, with an army at my back. There is work to be done here.'

Reinmar could see the bitter anger in Brother Noel's bright eyes, but the monk was well in command of himself and his voice remained quite level. 'You have not the slightest inkling of what you have done here,' he said, 'or what its consequences will be. One draught of the wine of dreams might have been enough to save you, Master Wieland, but I fear that it may be too late now.'

Wait until you find out what I have done to your precious stores, Reinmar thought. You will understand then that it is later than you think. But what he said aloud was: 'One draught was all it took to send Marcilla to horrid damnation – or would have been, had I not loved her enough to prevent it.'

'Is that what you think, Master Wieland?' Noel countered. 'If so, you're a fool and worse. You have not even begun to understand the world in which we live, or what it means to live at all. I believe that you might now have appointed yourself to that majority of the human race which is fated to die young and wretchedly, when you might have joined the ranks of the chosen – and in cheating the girl of her destiny you have robbed her of the kindest fate of all. You came here as an invader, accepted our hospitality, told us lies and then turned violently against us. I do not know how many you have hurt and killed, but you should not have drawn your sword at all, and you will have the penalty to pay. You have turned your back on hope, and there is nothing in the world for you henceforth but suffering. You might have enjoyed a good life enriched by the wine of dreams, but your inheritance now will be a desiccating thirst that can never be properly slaked no matter how you try. You have one last chance to do a virtuous thing, and I ask you one last time: leave the girl and her brother here!'

Reinmar put his hand on the hilt of his sword, and it required a considerable effort of his will not to release it from its scabbard. 'I have seen everything!' he said, waspishly. 'I have seen exactly what is done with those who are chosen by whatever vile god you worship. I have descended into your little hell, and I have come out of it a better and wiser man than I could ever otherwise have been. I know now what life is worth, and how it must be defended. I am ready to do what I must – and the girl will stay with me, until she and I have yielded our last breaths in defence of our humanity. I have nothing more to say.'

When Reinmar had concluded his bold speech he saw Matthias Vaedecker smiling, albeit grimly, and he knew that he had pleased the soldier at last. Brother Noel and Brother Almeric, on the other hand, wore expressions of a more thunderous kind – but they seemed to have conceded that there was nothing more to be said.

'We should go now, Master Wieland,' Sigurd said, speaking for the first time. 'The gypsies are with Godrich. They will help him to defend the cart if anyone or anything should attack it, so he is perfectly safe, but we ought to be on our way. Your father will want us to see you safely home without further delay, and I will not disappoint him.' Reinmar understood that the giant was issuing a subtle warning to the monks.

'He's right, Master Wieland,' Vaedecker said. 'This argument is nothing but a delaying tactic. We should not allow it to distract us.'

'Do you think we will chase you?' Almeric demanded, bitterly. 'Shall frail ascetics harass you with sticks and curses, while you cut us to ribbons with your blades? Go – but never think that you are free. You have incurred a debt this day that will not easily be settled.'

Reinmar reached out to take Marcilla's hand again. 'Come,' he said. 'We must go now. You too, Ulick. The call you heard was bait in a terrible trap, intended to draw you to your doom. You must come with us, to Eilhart. It is the only place of safety available to you.'

The monks said nothing to that, but Zygmund contrived a wry grin. Somehow, it seemed more threatening than anything the monks had said, for they seemed hardly human now in Reinmar's eyes, while the farmer was a man like a million others in Reikland.

'You who are chosen would do better to stay, child,' Noel said – but he clearly did not expect his words to have any effect. It only required Sigurd to extend a huge hand and place it on the boy's shoulder to dispel any possibility of hesitation.

'Did they hurt you?' Ulick asked Marcilla.

She shook her head, slowly. 'It seems so,' she said, wonderingly, 'but I hardly know what was hurt and what was merely dreaming. I have seen this man in my dreams, but it seems that he is real, and my deliverer.'

Matthias Vaedecker did not wait for this speech to be concluded. He had hurried ahead to lead the way, leaving Reinmar to grab the girl's hand and follow swiftly behind. Sigurd pushed the boy gently ahead of him before he brought up the rear, looking behind him all the while to make sure that no one came after them. The farmer and the monks would have been fools to try, and they remained standing where they were, watching the five hurry past the farmhouse towards the neck of the valley and the wood beyond.

Reinmar looked back into the valley once while he was still able to see the expressions on the monks' faces. He found them still very sullen – but whatever anger there had been had already ebbed away, to be replaced with perplexity and anxiety. They were afraid, he supposed, of what they would find when they went into the underworld – as they had every cause to be. They would have need of their burial-ground now, not merely as a ruse but as a final resting-place for at least half a dozen of their company – and when they went to inspect their reserves of the wine of dreams, they would know the true extent of the blow that had been struck against their trade.

While Reinmar was still looking back, Brother Almeric took something from his pouch. Reinmar thought at first that it must be a weapon, but when the monk lifted it a little higher out he saw that it was a crystal flask, half-full of amber liquid. The troubled monk put it to his lips and took a sip, then passed it to his companion.

Reinmar turned away – but even as he turned he heard a mysterious voice whispering in his ear, which said: 'You do not know what you have done. She is already chosen. You may believe that you have saved her for another wedding, but she can never be yours. And for what have you saved her, after all, but a short and brutish life full of trials and tribulations, and an end in misery and pain?'

The voice was sourceless, and Reinmar was certain that none of his companions had heard it – but he was not afraid, and he felt no need to reply. He had done what he had to do, and he was proud of himself for having done it. Marcilla was his now, until she was Morr's, and he intended to keep her.

Chapter Twenty-Two

They passed through the wood without incident, marching steadily in spite of their wretched state. They found a dozen gypsies waiting with the mended wagon, including Rollo and Tam. The travellers were astonished and displeased to see the manner in which Marcilla was dressed, but Godrich – seeing the parlous condition that Reinmar and Vaedecker were in – asked them to wait for an explanation.

Exhaustion caught up with Reinmar almost as soon as he reached the cart, but he managed to give the steward a muttered and sketchy account of what had occurred.

The sergeant confirmed his story at every stage with swift nods. 'We must go, and go quickly,' Vaedecker said, when Reinmar had finished. 'The monk poured scorn on the notion that they might chase us, but the attendants of the underworld were only too ready to fight, even when they had no weapons to hand. If they stay where they are it will be because they can work greater mischief there. Can you persuade the gypsy and his chieftain to let us take his son and daughter with us – or, better still, to come with us to Eilhart himself?'

'I'll try,' Godrich said. 'But you must let Sigurd see to your wounds while I do it.'

Until that moment, Reinmar had not noticed that he was wounded, but when he took stock his bruises and grazes seemed trivial enough.

Vaedecker asked for water in which they might both bathe, and insisted that Reinmar clean himself. 'We must put on our spare clothes,' the soldier said. 'A man who keeps the blood and filth of his enemies about his person is asking for infection. Ulick, you must ask one of the women to see to it that Marcilla is bathed and properly dressed.'

The boy nodded, and drew Marcilla away while Godrich went into a huddle with Rollo, Tam and an older man. By the time that Reinmar was washed and dressed in clean clothes the discussion was over, and Godrich was able to report back to him. Reinmar had put on his belt again, and his pouch with it, although both were flecked with drying blood. He had no intention of leaving the pouch to one side, or transferring its contents to another, while it still held the phial that he had taken from the storehouse in the underworld. Nor had he any intention of telling Vaedecker or Godrich that he had the phial. For the present, it was his secret and his alone.

'They're scared,' Godrich eventually reported, meaning the gypsies. 'They've seen the body of the beastman. They know that the local people will think them in league with the monsters, even though the elder has no more idea what the monsters are, or why they are here, than we have. I have managed to persuade him – not without difficulty – that there is no privilege in being chosen, and that the path to the hidden valley leads only to death and destruction. He says that we can look after Ulick and Marcilla, since we are willing, but that Rollo and Tam have work to do, spreading the word of what has occurred among the gypsy folk. There must be a meeting of some sort, it seems – and petty magic to be worked, I dare say. They do not know what the result will be, but Rollo says that he will come for his kin as soon as he can, when the time is right. I agreed to that – don't contradict me, Master Reinmar, I beg of you, whatever your own intentions may be. We must go, and swiftly. I don't know what we shall find at home, but we must hope that your father has the situation under control.'

Vaedecker, who had been listening, said: 'Whatever control is exerted now, there will surely be trouble soon. What we must hope is that von Spurzheim has gathered an adequate fighting force and that it is ready to march. This is war, my friend, and the crucial conflict will be upon us far sooner than we had expected.'

Godrich contented himself with a nod by way of reply, and he went back to the gypsies to bid them a friendly farewell. Then he got up onto the cart, and called out that anyone who intended to ride should get aboard. The only one who did not respond was Sigurd; Matthias Vaedecker was far too tired to walk.

Almost as soon as they were under way it began to rain again, but it was a mere drizzle compared with the storm that had hurried them into their confrontation with the beastmen. The four who were riding on the cart with the casks found shelter enough under pieces of the ruined awning, which they draped over their shoulders. It was not strictly necessary for them to huddle together, but Ulick and Marcilla wanted to be as close as possible, and Reinmar wanted to be close to Marcilla, so the three of them ended up side by side.

As the horses picked up speed Marcilla asked Reinmar what had happened to her before she awoke in the underworld and put on the bloodstained robe. Reinmar was not certain at first how much he ought to tell her, but in the end he decided that she might need to know the truth, so he told her the full story, in as much detail as he could remember. Ulick listened raptly – and so did Matthias Vaedecker, although he kept his eyes half-closed.

'I remember the flower,' Marcilla confessed at one point. 'I thought I had dreamed it, and that in my dream I was a flower myself, with no desire but to meet and merge with my mate.'

'It was the wine of dreams,' Reinmar said. 'It is seductive, but it is evil. Whatever you have been told by its consumers is a lie.'

'But you are in the trade yourself,' Ulick objected. 'You told me so.'

'So I did, and so I am,' Reinmar agreed, quietly. 'But I am no consumer. I am beginning to understand now, what a wreck the wine of dreams has made of my grandfather, and I do not think that it has done his brother any good. Had my father been less of a man than he is, I too might have had the sickness in me that might have called me to the valley.'

'You found it,' Ulick reminded him. 'It's said–'

'Because I was with Marcilla,' Reinmar was quick to put in. 'She was the one who led us there, as you led Sigurd.'

'Who was it that brought the message while you were tasting the wine, Master Wieland?' Matthias Vaedecker said suddenly. 'Anyone could have told them that I had entered the valley, and that I am a soldier without colours – but who told them that I am Machar von Spurzheim's man?'

'I did not see the messenger; only the monk who conveyed the news to Brother Noel,' Reinmar answered. 'Rumour moves rapidly in these parts. It isn't surprising that news of von Spurzheim's arrival in Eilhart travelled as quickly as we did. Anyone could have carried it.'

'Your great-uncle's housekeeper is a gypsy,' Vaedecker reminded him unnecessarily. 'She was not there when we arrested him.'

'Eilhart is a market town of two thousand souls, and an important river port,' Reinmar reminded the soldier, in his turn. 'There are always travellers passing through – hundreds of them, brought by road and river alike. Anyone could have brought the news.'

'Including Albrecht's son, Wirnt,' Vaedecker said. 'Could it have been him?'

Reinmar was momentarily at a loss for words. By the time he realised that his silence might be as eloquent as any confession it was too late to speak.

'Don't worry, Master Wieland,' the sergeant said. 'I mention the name because I trust you now, not because I don't. You have proved yourself to me, and I'll gladly tell von Spurzheim that we can rely on you. I don't blame you for letting the name rest unspoken, given that you are kin – but I think you know now how dangerous that kind of kin might be.'

'I think I do,' Reinmar agreed.

'When it comes to a fight, Master Wieland – and it will – you had better remember that danger. The greatest power our enemies have is not that they can release daemons upon the world, but that they can twist their knives inside the hearts of those we know and love, turning cousin against cousin, brother against brother.'

While he spoke, Reinmar felt Marcilla's head slump against his shoulder, and knew that she had gone to sleep again. That made him very anxious, for there was no way to know how natural her sleep might be or what dreadful dreams might visit her therein – but he knew that he ought to pay attention to what Vaedecker was saying.

'Can men like Noel and Almeric really release daemons upon the world?' Reinmar asked, wonderingly.

'They are pawns in the game,' Vaedecker told him. 'As are you and I – but even pawns are sometimes granted an insight into the greater reality that underlies the surface of the world we know. You and I have been granted an insight of sorts today, although I don't know whether we should count ourselves lucky. We have seen a kind of garden, tended by men on behalf of something far more powerful and far more playful.'

'Playful?' Reinmar questioned. 'You think that a nightmare like that might only be play?'

Vaedecker's half-closed eyelids widened for a moment. 'Do you take encouragement from a word like that?' he said. 'You should not. Quite the reverse, in fact. It might not matter so much to a world like ours that there are evil gods, no matter how powerful they might be, were they not playful as well.

'I have heard the table talk of fat shopkeepers and petty aristocrats, my friend. If there are evil gods, they say, who have the power to snuff out our lives with a breath, why do they not do so? If they can unleash daemons upon the world, why do they not send forth irresistible armies of them? If they have powerful sorcerers at their beck and call, why are such magicians not forever knocking on our doors and demanding tribute? If they delight in turning men into beasts and monsters, how is it that there are men in the world at all, let alone men who eat and drink as well as we do, and enjoy such respect from our servants and our neighbours?

'The real tragedy, my newly-hatched hero, is not that the evil gods are powerful but that they are playful. I do not know whether they hate us or love us, or which of those possibilities ought to be reckoned the worse, but I do know that they like to tease us and tantalise us and test us and terrify us. Yes, they can send daemons into the world, but they do so with exceeding discretion. Yes, they delight in turning men into beasts and monsters, but they delight even more in confusion. Yes, they have powerful sorcerers at their beck and call, but they delight in letting men of that kind hope and believe, absurdly, that they are the masters, and gods and daemons their servants. They are playful, and that is the most horrible thing about them, for all the terror we experience and all the blood we shed is but play to them.

'I think you saw today exactly how playful the evil gods can be, even if you did not understand the significance of what you saw. If you think we have escaped the god who made that garden, think again. You might be more securely in his playful grip now than you would have been had you drunk your fill, and more, of the wine the monks tried to sell you.'

'You did not seem to think so while we were climbing that stair,' Reinmar answered him. 'You seemed to think that escape was possible then, and I did not see you pause before seizing the opportunity.'

'I have been in the game for a lifetime,' Vaedecker said, wearily. 'I know nothing else – and I know, too, that once a man has taken arms against the dark gods he had better do everything he can to stay in the game and win what victories he can, else he will suffer more terribly than he can imagine. I am trying to warn you that you will not always find the fight as easy as it was today. All you have really accomplished is to raise the stakes for conflicts yet to come.'

'Now you sound like Brother Noel,' Reinmar retorted. 'I would never have taken you for one of those profoundly solemn men who think that the best thing of all is not to be born, and after that to die young!'

'I'm not,' Vaedecker said. 'I'm a pawn who understands what it means to be a pawn, a fighting man who knows how desperate a real fight is. So far, Master Wieland, you have killed a few old men armed with garden tools – but you'll find that you cannot stop at that. Even if you had not insisted on bringing the girl away, the powers ranged against us would never let you stop at that. The real fight is yet to come, and when it comes to you, you'll have to watch out for the enemy within and the enemy behind as well as the enemy before you.'

Reinmar realised that the soldier was indeed trying to give him the best advice he could, not to frighten him but to prepare him. But he realised, too, that the kind of fight the soldier was anticipating was not the only one he had to look forward to. There would be a conflict of a far more intimate kind awaiting him at home, when his father would want an account of everything that he had brought back with him, and every transaction he had made with suppliers of every kind. That was, for the moment, the prospect that filled him with greater trepidation, for it seemed far more vexatious than any business that could be conducted with a blood-stained sword.

'If they will not have us in Eilhart,' he murmured in the ear of the sleeping gypsy, far too softly to be heard by anyone else, 'then we shall try our luck in Marienburg.'

He was astonished when Ulick immediately spoke out, as if in reply, but when he heard what was said he realised that the boy had been listening as carefully as he to everything that Matthias Vaedecker had said.

'You should not have come here, sir,' the gypsy boy said to the soldier. 'You should not have followed my sister when she answered the call. This may be a game to you, but it is life and death to us. You should not have interfered.'

'If we had not interfered,' the sergeant replied, 'you and she might be lying dead in the shadow of a barn, beaten to death by louts. If we had not continued to interfere, your throats might have been torn out by wolf-men. And if we had not insisted on interfering till the very end, your sister's guts would be incubating a monstrous plant while her flesh turned slowly to stone. A little gratitude would not come amiss.'

'You don't understand,' the boy said, although he spoke uneasily. 'Our kind is not your kind.'

'Your father thinks well enough of my kind to entrust you to my care,' the soldier pointed out. 'Whatever he thought before of calls and choosings, he has a different opinion now.'

'But you have said yourself that it is not finished,' Ulick countered. 'Because of what you've done, there will be a terrible fight. You've brought a curse upon our heads.'

'No,' Reinmar said. 'That isn't so. What I did, I did in order to lift a curse – and if I must fight again to save us, I shall do it. And again, and again, and again. I have found something worth fighting for.'

Mercifully, Vaedecker did not challenge him as to whether he had indeed lifted any curse, or who might be included in the word 'us'. Instead, the sergeant let his heavy eyelids descend all the way. Even though the cart was rattling more than it usually did as it raced down a slope and the rain beat relentlessly upon the cloth that covered his shoulders, the soldier let his head fall forward upon his knees.

Reinmar knew that the sergeant could not possibly be any more tired than he was himself, but his own thoughts were too confused and restless to allow him even to contemplate sleep – so he sat where he was, keeping very still for Marcilla's sake, and tried with all his might to think of the future, and all the possibilities it held. When his right hand began to tremble, he told himself that it was only the chill of the rain, but he knew that it was a lie. He did not feel cold at all.

So what if I have killed a man, he said to himself? And if there were three, how is that any worse than if there were only one? Would they not have killed me, had I paused to think of mercy, however weak and badly armed they were?

But the hand continued to tremble, and would not stop no matter how he hugged it to his breast.

It was a long way home, and it seemed much longer. He fretted in this manner through every tedious inch of it – but in the end, he did come safely into sight of the lights of Eilhart. Reinmar knew that he would find his father worried and anxious, and not at all prepared to welcome a gypsy as his son's beloved, and he knew that the battle of wills that lay ahead of him at home would be long and hard – but that was a battle he knew how to fight. As for the others of which Vaedecker had warned him, there was nothing he could do but wait until they began, and learn to fight them as he went along, as best he could.

Chapter Twenty-Three

It had been dark for an hour when the cart finally rolled to a halt outside Gottfried Wieland's shop. The horses should have been rested long before, but Godrich had kept them up to their work, on the assumption that they would have plenty of time to recover from their extraordinary exertions. Their load had been lightened for the last few miles because Reinmar and Vaedecker had walked with Sigurd. Vaedecker had not ridden in the cart since sleeping for thirteen hours after their escape from the valley, having recovered his strength easily enough.

Reinmar had not been so fortunate; although his exertions had taken a far greater toll of his limited strength he had hardly been able to sleep for more than an hour at a time during the days and nights following his adventure in the underworld, waking as soon as uncomfortable dreams began to disturb him – and it seemed that he had lost the knack of finding any kind of dream that was other than profoundly uncomfortable. Marcilla had slept far longer, far more deeply – and, if appearances could be trusted, far better – but she seemed to be in a perpetual daze whenever she awoke.

They had not been attacked while they were on the road, either by men or by monsters – but sometimes, when they looked behind them as they rested, they had seen shadowy figures lurking in the woods or on the ridges of the hills. As if to combat this ominous sign, however, the further they descended from the hills the more benign the weather had become. The kindness of the daylight and the increasing familiarity of the terrain had brought a little peace of mind to all of the travellers.

Matthias Vaedecker had taken the first opportunity to wash the clotted blood and other stains from the clothes he had worn when he entered the valley, and Reinmar had followed his example, but neither of them put those clothes on again when their replacements became soiled. Neither of them was able to think of the clothes they had worn in the underworld as clean, no matter how thoroughly they were scrubbed.

Gottfried Wieland was waiting in the street to welcome the cart, having received advance notice of its approach from a watchman. He had three labourers ready to convey its cargo to the cellar, and the waiting crowd was swelled to more than twice that number by other anxious faces. Machar von Spurzheim was with them, with two attendant men-at-arms. Godrich's wife and son were also there, and so was Marguerite. The reactions of these individuals were as varied as might be expected, even though none of them could have had any advance indication of what had befallen the members of the expedition.

While Godrich took Gottfried aside to whisper a report, and Vaedecker did likewise with the witch hunter, Reinmar found himself face-to-face with Marguerite, who seemed very enthusiastic to hear a full account of his adventure. He, for his own part, was anxious to know what had happened in the town while he had been away.

'We brought these two gypsies away from a village where they were attacked by farmhands,' Reinmar said, allowing Ulick to take responsibility for putting a protective arm around Marcilla's shoulder. 'Then we were attacked in our turn. But as you see, we are all alive and unhurt. Had the soldier not been with us it might have been different, but he and Sigurd make a fine team. What news is there of my great-uncle?'

'He is still in prison,' Marguerite told him. 'More soldiers have been arriving in the town every day – and others who certainly are not soldiers, though they may be fighting men of some sort. Three warehouses by the quays have been converted into barracks, and there are officers billeted in every inn and lodging-house. There are men sleeping in stables and storerooms, and their quartermasters are acquiring provisions on a massive scale, although they seem very reluctant to pay a proper price. The market has become a battleground. Some of the townsfolk are sealing their houses and moving their entire households downriver; others are sending their wives and children away but keeping their menservants at home, fearful that their houses might otherwise be requisitioned or looted. No one knows when or whether the soldiers intend to move on again, or where they will go if they do. What is happening, Reinmar? Is there really an army of monsters gathering in the hills?'

Reinmar was saved the trouble of improvising an answer to this question by the intervention of his father, who hauled him away in a peremptory fashion. Gottfried told Marguerite to go home, without bothering to be overly polite. She made not the slightest move to obey, and followed them into the shop so that she could hear what Gottfried had to say, and what responses Reinmar might make.

'Am I expected to find a room for these gypsies?' Gottfried demanded.

'We have plenty of rooms, father,' Reinmar said, obstinately. 'We gave them protection, and we have good reason to believe that they still need it.'

'Reason enough to leave the wagon and go haring off into the wilderness? Reason enough to leave Godrich alone when he was hurt and the cart broken? Reason enough, even though you had been attacked?'

The effect of these questions was to stimulate an anger that Reinmar had long held in reserve, and his replies would undoubtedly have caused more trouble. He had no time to make them, though, because Marguerite was rudely thrust aside for a second time as Machar von Spurzheim strode into the shop.

'Leave the boy be,' the witch hunter instructed, ignoring the amazement which took immediate possession of Gottfried Wieland's face. 'He has been brave as well as reckless, so my sergeant says, and his bravery may have won considerable gains for our cause. You can welcome him home in your own fashion later – for now, I have need of him and he must come with me.'

Gottfried opened his mouth to protest, and the words nearly escaped before he remembered who he was talking to, and how delicate his dealings with the witch hunter had been. Had his face been more brightly lit it would probably have exhibited his ire very clearly, but the lamp happened to be placed in such a way that he was in shadow – not that von Spurzheim was watching, for he had already reached out a hand to take Reinmar by the arm, and was already drawing him towards the door.

'Make the girl comfortable, I beg of you,' was all that Reinmar had time to say to his father before he was hustled out into the street again. 'You must keep her safe.'

'Do as the boy says,' von Spurzheim added, as he paused briefly in the doorway, having positioned himself squarely between father and son. 'The boy and girl might be vital to our enterprise. It is in everyone's interest that you keep them safe.'

Reinmar could not see how his father reacted to this instruction, but he could imagine it well enough. Given that Gottfried was the son of one man suspected of involvement in sorcery and the nephew of another, he could hardly afford to offend a witch hunter, but necessity would not make the indignity any easier to bear.

While von Spurzheim marched Reinmar through the streets Matthias Vaedecker and the other men-at-arms fell into step behind them, and Reinmar was uncomfortably aware that it would seem to any onlookers that he had been arrested – all the more so because they were not moving in the direction of the burgomaster's house, where von Spurzheim had established himself as a guest, but towards the town jail, where Albrecht Wieland was still being held under guard. Reinmar was also uncomfortably aware of the fact that if von Spurzheim demanded the privilege of searching him, the presence of the phial in his pouch might indeed give cause for his arrest and incarceration.

Although the streets were by no means crowded once they had moved away from Gottfried Wieland's shop, Reinmar did not doubt that there were eyes aplenty following his course. Every house that had a curtained window, whether glazed or not, had the curtain in question moved slightly to one side, so that the apprehensive dwellers within might keep track as best they could of the trouble that had visited their town.

'Don't be afraid, lad,' was all that von Spurzheim said to him while they strode through the streets. 'Sergeant Vaedecker has told me what you did, and I'm exceedingly grateful to you, no matter that your motives might not have been as pure as I could have wished.'

There was no reasonable reply that Reinmar could make to this, so he contented himself with silence, until they reached the blockhouse where the town constables discharged their official duties, and where felons were kept until the assizes at which they were tried. Once they were inside, von Spurzheim wasted no time in taking Reinmar to the windowless room in which Albrecht Wieland was confined.

Reinmar was glad to see that his great-uncle did not seem to have been badly maltreated; the old man had no obvious injuries and he did not look as if he had been starved. The pallet on which he had been sleeping was crude but it provided reasonable relief from the hardness of the stone floor and the stink from the iron bucket in the corner was not too awful to bear. Albrecht was obviously startled to see Reinmar in the company of Machar von Spurzheim, but he appeared to be completely in control of his faculties and his only reaction, once the initial astonishment had faded, was to knit his brows in concentration. Matthias Vaedecker closed the door of the cell behind him, leaving the other two men-at-arms outside.

'Your grandfather's brother has been helping us, Reinmar,' von Spurzheim said, when Vaedecker had come to stand beside him. 'His memory is a trifle vague when it comes to names and places, but he usually remembers his old friends once we have laid their names before him. There is a community of scholars to whom he once belonged, in whose activities we have long been interested – but there is little left of it now. Unfortunately, he does not know what has become of his son, Wirnt, or his former housekeeper. His house has been watched night and day, of course – as has your own, merely as a precaution – but no visitors had arrived when the sentries were last changed. It's possible that Wirnt is in Holthusen, where a few of the so-called scholars still remain, but he may have gone southwards, towards the place which you recently had occasion to visit. I hope that you will tell your great-uncle all about your adventure, so that he might have a clearer idea of the evil nature of the business in which he has involved himself.'

The last words were obviously intended to elicit a reaction from Albrecht, but Albrecht was ready for some such move and his expression hardly changed.

'Fortunately, Magister Albrecht,' von Spurzheim went on – pronouncing the word 'Magister' as sarcastically as he had earlier pronounced the word 'scholar' – 'Reinmar has been far more helpful to our cause than we could ever have hoped; he is obviously his father's son. He has succeeded where you and your brother apparently failed. He found the source of the wine of dreams at the first attempt, which inclines me to believe that it cannot have been so very difficult after all. Not only did he guide Sergeant Vaedecker there, but he penetrated its deepest secrets, and then brought about their escape. And there is more, is there not, Reinmar? What was it that you did, exactly, when you were briefly separated from the sergeant?'

Reinmar hesitated before replying. His eyes were fixed on his great-uncle's face – more by virtue of concern for the old man than because he was avoiding the witch hunter's eye – but he knew that the game being played here was being directed by von Spurzheim, and he was not at all sure that he wanted to play it by von Spurzheim's rules.

'I discovered the method by which the wine of dreams is made,' he said, softly, although he knew that it was not an adequate answer to the question. 'Those who drink it, and value it, can have no conception of its origins or they would never let it pass their lips, no matter how sweet it might be.'

'It is made by plants nourished on human flesh,' von Spurzheim said, by way of amplification. 'But you were better placed than Sergeant Vaedecker to understand exactly how the process works, were you not?'

'I only saw a storeroom,' Reinmar said. 'Nothing more. But I saw no fruit, nor any kind of press. I saw large mortars where vegetable flesh was ground, and vats into which the resultant fluid was decanted. The flowers that produce the wines of the underworld were so vast that I could not help but wonder whether the wine might be their nectar, but I can't be absolutely certain. People are fed to those plants, great-uncle. Those who are chosen hear some kind of summons in their dreams. Young people, with their whole lives before them, are drugged with the wine, and then the seeds are planted in their living flesh, within an underworld whose rocks shine with a strange and dazzling radiance. I'm sorry, but it's true.'

'The false monks who grow these murderous flowers attempted to sell Reinmar some of their most recent vintages,' von Spurzheim added, when it became clear that Albrecht still had nothing to say. 'He refused them, even before he knew what they were. But when he found the storeroom, he did know. What did you do then, Reinmar? Even Matthias seems uncertain.'

'Had I been able to upset the stone vats and spill their contents, I would have done it,' Reinmar said. 'I could not – but I smashed every vessel I could lay my hands on and emptied the contents of those I could carry into a channel that drained into the depths of the world. I can't be sure what proportion of their stocks I spoiled there, but I suspect that the shortages in the river towns and Marienburg will grow far worse before they can begin to improve.'

'I had hoped, Magister,' von Spurzheim said, in seeming imitation of the softness of Reinmar's voice, 'that you might be able to advise us as to the possible effects of that scarcity.'

When Albrecht spoke at last, it was to say: 'I have no idea. I have been out of touch for far too long.'

'But you have seen men driven to distraction and madness by lack of the wine, have you not?' von Spurzheim persisted. 'You, of course, are possessed of an enviable strength of mind and body – more so than your brother Luther, I dare say – but you have seen others whose dependency was greater. Have you not seen men driven to self-mutilation, suicide and murder, and others reduced to mere gibbering wreckage while their nightmares marked their flesh with agonising scars?'

'I have seen men distressed,' Albrecht admitted, dully, 'who blamed their distress on thirst for the wine and dreams that had turned from good to bad. Some men are less able to tolerate nightmares than others – but those who were driven to violence were violent before they ever took a sip of the wine.'

'Do you think so?' von Spurzheim said. 'I am not so sure.'

'You seem to have discussed the matter with at least as many people as I ever did,' Albrecht replied, stonily, 'and more persuasively too. I dare say that you are better placed to guess than I am, even though you have never deigned to put your own tastes to the test.'

Von Spurzheim laughed, but the lightness of the laugh was contrived. 'Perhaps I am,' he said. 'At any rate, I have plans to make. I dare say that you have private matters to discuss with your nephew, so I'll leave you alone. Matthias will collect you in a little while, Reinmar – I have a few questions still to ask you, if you aren't too tired.' He did not wait for a reply but left the cell with Vaedecker, who opened the door and then closed it behind them.

Reinmar was not fool enough to believe that it was safe to talk. Someone would undoubtedly be listening – but the door was thick, and Albrecht was by no means hard of hearing. He drew his great-uncle to the corner of the cell that was farthest from the door, and lifted his lips close to the old man's ear before he said: 'Are you all right? Have they hurt you?'

'They had no need,' Albrecht murmured. 'They have already found out more than I can tell them as they came from Marienburg. They have kept me here to make sure that I do not talk to Luther, who is prisoner enough in his own home, with a very dutiful jailer. Not that I blame Gottfried. It is all true, then? I suppose the witch hunter would not have let you come here otherwise.'

'It's all true,' Reinmar confirmed. 'The magic of the dark wine is rooted in horrors. It has to be stopped. Von Spurzheim is right about that.' Not for a moment did he contemplate the possibility of confiding to his great-uncle that he had a portion of the active ingredient of the wine of dreams – or one of its darker kin – in his possession.

Albrecht did not seem to know what to say next, but he decided in the end. 'It's probably too late for advice, but you must be careful,' he murmured very softly. 'Whatever you might think, I cannot believe it was luck or cleverness that guided you to a place that no man of Eilhart has ever been able to find. There is a clash of schemes here, and von Spurzheim's coming will surely prompt a response of some sort. Be very, very careful, else you be crushed or cut to shreds in the collision. If they will let you go, go – to Holthusen, at least. Those who are fleeing the town are the wise ones. Follow them if you can.'

CHAPTER TWENTY-FOUR

WHEN REINMAR CAME out of Albrecht's cell, Matthias Vaedecker locked the door behind him. The sergeant stayed behind in the blockhouse while Machar von Spurzheim took Reinmar out of the constables' lair and led him across the square to the town hall. Once they had arrived there, the witch hunter led the way to a room that presented as dramatic a contrast as could possibly be imagined to the one Reinmar had just been in. Its walls were hidden by velvet hangings and the floor was thickly carpeted. All the chairs had lavishly-upholstered seats and the enormous leather-topped oaken table at which Reinmar was invited to sit was piled with more pieces of parchment than he had ever seen in one place.

Von Spurzheim sat opposite, moving his hands on the table top in such a way as to part the scraps of parchment into two roughly-equal heaps, one to each side. Then he leaned forward, planting his elbows in the space he had cleared. 'Well, Master Wieland,' he said. 'It seems that I have something for which to thank you.'

'You should let my uncle go now,' Reinmar said. 'He's harmless.'

'Perhaps he is,' the witch hunter answered. 'Your father has made me the same assurances about your grandfather. But we have not quite cleared out the nest of vipers that was lodged in Holthusen, so there are others free with whom he might join up, possibly forming a company that would be stronger for his presence. Your cousin Wirnt warned them of our approach, you see, as he had earlier warned others, including your grandfather and your great-uncle – unless, of course, that was you.'

Reinmar said nothing to that, and von Spurzheim spread his hands dismissively. 'It doesn't matter,' he said. 'I'm sure now that you have only done what you thought was right. You're a man who knows the meaning of duty, Matthias says. He also says that you're a fool, but that may be too harsh a judgement. There are matters I'm bound to keep secret even from him. I confess that I don't quite understand why, but I too am a man of duty and when I am forbidden to speak of things I do not speak of them. It makes my job more difficult, but I am also bound not to complain. If I asked you to go to Holthusen for me, to help smoke out Wirnt's friends, would you do it?'

'I have been advised to leave Eilhart,' Reinmar replied, cautiously, 'but I doubt that my family would approve of my doing so as a spy. I don't think I ought to leave my father – and I can't leave the gypsy girl.'

Von Spurzheim frowned slightly at that, but he did not seem surprised. 'Your loyalties are still confused,' he observed. 'That is natural. Even if I could tell you everything that I know, you might not see the situation any more clearly. But you will listen, I suppose, to what I can tell you.'

'Of course,' Reinmar said.

'Very well. When you went into that strange underworld with Matthias Vaedecker, you caught a glimpse of something that very few innocent men have ever been unlucky enough to see. I do not simply mean the underworld itself but something far greater, of which it is but a tiny part. The world you know is not nearly as safe and secure as it seems; it exists in the shadow of a terrible threat, which manifests itself in many different ways. Matthias knows far more of this evil than most men, but he has only faced its most direct and brutal manifestations. Men like me are commissioned to deal with subtler threats – threats which do not crowd upon civilised lands from their unruly borders, seeking to diminish us by crude force of arms, but which emerge by stealth even in the best strongholds of order and humanity.

'Even in Eilhart, Master Wieland, you must have heard rumours saying that all is not well in the cities of the Empire. Even in Altdorf, in the very heart of the greatest Empire of men that there has ever been, there have been eruptions of horror and violence. The appetites that men possess are part of our precious humanity, but they are also portals to the heart and mind through which subtle invaders may pass. Some men are vulnerable because of their pride and their propensity to wrath, some because of their love of luxury and intoxication. Others are betrayed by their own inquisitiveness and hunger for strange sensations. The health of humankind is always under siege, from diseases of the body and diseases of the spirit – and great cities make fine breeding grounds for all manner of sicknesses.

'The phases of decay are easy to see, for those who are educated to see them. First, self-indulgence; second, addiction; third, desperation. All men begin by thinking, as your grandfather once thought and your great-uncle still professes to believe, that they can taste such temptations as the wine of dreams without becoming dependent on them – but all men find, as your grandfather did, that once they are increased such appetites can never be diminished to what they were before, nor abandoned without painful cost. Once men become slaves to the wine of dreams their thirst becomes so magnified that it requires stronger and stranger liquors to slake it. It has the reputation of being the indulgence of superior scholars and arrogant aristocrats – something which confers an enviable status on its users – but its purpose is to spread a cancer within the highest ranks and wisest enclaves of human civilization.

'Imagine, Reinmar, if you will, the magnitude of the conspiracy required to convey the wine of dreams and its darker kin from the underworld beneath the Grey Mountains to a city somewhere in the Empire. Imagine, too, that that is merely one part of a greater conspiracy, which has all the Empire's cities in its sights – not merely Marienburg and Altdorf but Nuln and Talabheim, and even far Middenheim, despite the distances involved. But imagine too a counter-conspiracy, directed by the defenders of all that is good in humankind and Empire: a conspiracy which attacks the cancer as it grows in a city and begins to squeeze the evil life out of it, while painstakingly tracing its extension along the Talabec, the Stir or the Reik itself.

The conspiracy has been the work of centuries, and the counter-conspiracy likewise the work of generations. The principal arena of concern has shifted half a dozen times, as has the balance of the contest, but in the present generation there has been a crucial shift in that balance, at least in respect of the wine of dreams.

'The present artery of the dark wine's supply is by no means the first to have been cut, but we have believed for some time that it is the most direct, and the one which has brought us closest to the source. We have not merely mapped the line along the Reik to the Schilder, to Holthusen and then to Eilhart, but each link in the chain has been so carefully broken that the supply-line has been decisively severed. I would dearly like to say irrevocably instead of decisively, but I dare not. Such hopes have been entertained before, and have failed. This may be the closest we have ever come to the source, and might well be the best opportunity we have ever had to destroy that source, but... do you see my difficulty, Reinmar? Can you see why I dare not take what you and Matthias have told me entirely at face value?'

Reinmar was puzzled, at first, and quite at a loss to see what von Spurzheim was driving at – but then he began to understand.

'It is far too convenient,' he said. 'The timing is too perfect. My grandfather and Albrecht have searched long and hard for the source of the wine of dreams – and other men like you have done so, for their own reasons – but none ever found it, until the day when you arrived in Eilhart, having erased almost every element of the supply-line. You think that a trap was being laid for you – a snare, carefully loaded with bait.' It was an idea that had not occurred to him before, but now that it had he saw exactly how monstrous the coincidence was. Could it be, he wondered, that Marcilla had led him into the hidden valley? Had she been placed against the wall of that barn in the village merely so that he might rescue her? If so, she could have been more than a pawn, with no inkling of the plot... but if Matthias Vaedecker and Machar von Spurzheim were right about the slyly playful nature of their enemy, it was certainly conceivable. And how, after what he had seen in that awful underworld, could he doubt the awful subtlety of its designer?

But even if Marcilla had led him to the valley, Reinmar thought, how much of what happened thereafter had been included in the plan? Surely the architects of the trap could not have expected him to find his way into the underworld itself? That must have been the point at which the carefully-laid plan began to go badly awry. There was no way that any one could have anticipated that he would find the storeroom and destroy its stocks. If he had been drawn into a trap – as even Albrecht had thought likely – then he had contrived to turn the tables on those who had laid down the lure, and had turned the advantage they hoped to win into a disaster.

'I was supposed to find the valley,' Reinmar said, trying to think the matter through. 'I was supposed to follow the girl on my own – Sergeant Vaedecker was an unexpected complication. The monks were supposed to test my attitude to the wine very carefully, winning me to their cause if I could be won – but when the gypsies sent word that the sergeant had come into the valley with me Brother Noel decided that it would be best to let us leave as soon as possible. He did not know, of course, that Vaedecker had seen Marcilla disinterred and that I would insist on following her. I saw the astonishment on his face when he saw Marcilla and realised what Vaedecker and I had done, and I am perfectly certain that he had never imagined for a moment that we would do what we did – but even then, he thought that the bare bones of the plan were still in place. He wanted you to think that the valley could be found, and that Ulick and I could lead you to it. Why?'

'You do understand my problem,' von Spurzheim said, nodding his head. 'In all probability, you and the boy – quite innocently, I don't doubt – would have led my hastily-gathered troops into an ambush or a magical trap. If there are valleys which are impossible to find, there might be others that are impossible to leave. More soldiers would come eventually, of course, and my reports have been transmitted back to Altdorf at regular intervals, but if I and my trusted lieutenants could be destroyed now, the work we have done could be undone and our cause set back by years.'

'Not now,' Reinmar said. 'Now, for the first time, you know exactly what you are dealing with – and it will not be easy to rebuild a chain of supply if there are no goods to supply.'

Von Spurzheim smiled at that, and nodded in acknowledgement, but he did not seem entirely reassured. 'I'll grant that you really did see far more than you were supposed to see,' he said, 'and that having seen it you took brave and altogether unexpected action. I believe that you did strike a real and telling blow against our enemies, and that you disrupted their scheme magnificently – but we may be sure that they will react, as swiftly and as effectively as they can. What do you think they might do now?'

Reinmar had not the slightest idea. 'Brother Noel and Brother Almeric took care to warn me that I had done myself more harm than good, even before they knew that I had wrecked their storehouse,' he recalled. 'The sergeant warned me to expect reprisals – but I never paused to wonder about the wider consequences of my actions.'

'How extensive was the underworld, Reinmar?' von Spurzheim asked him, quietly.

Reinmar realised that he had not the faintest idea. He had seen only that fraction of it that lay close to the entrance beneath the temple. Although he had run in panic once he had plucked Marcilla from the cleft in which she had been set, he had ended up at another covert in the same wall, not more than a couple of hundred paces away. In the other direction, the underworld might have extended for miles – or for tens of miles. The Grey Mountains were vast, providing a barrier many hundreds of miles long that separated the Empire from Bretonnia, passable only at widely-spaced intervals. Even if the cave he had visited were no bigger than the valley it underlay, how many similar underworlds might there be?

He realised that even though he had seen too much, he had not seen enough. He had no idea of the enemy's true strength, and no basis for guessing what new plan might now be put in place of the one that had gone awry.

'Perhaps, for your sake, I ought to send you to Holthusen anyhow, even if you will not be my spy,' von Spurzheim said. 'Alas, there is nowhere in the world that is truly safe, and the cities of the Empire are less safe now than they were. I have no idea how useful you might be as bait in a trap of my own setting, but you will understand that I have to consider the possibility. Perhaps I should let you make your own decision – but I still have to make mine. Should I set off tomorrow for this valley of yours, using the boy or the girl as a guide, and risk an ambush? Or should I stay here and wait, hoping that the enemy will now be angry enough to fight on any ground, no matter how disadvantageous? If I do stay, can I defend the town successfully? If I were to ask the townspeople, I dare say they'd beg me to be gone, not caring in the least whether I went forwards or back – but the townspeople don't know what you and I know, do they?

'By daybreak, I suppose the wings of rumour will have carried some account of your exploits into every last shop and house – but the people who listen to those rumours will not know a quarter of what you and I know. I have the reputation of being a good tactician, but every man of my kind still alive has that, because the first defeat he suffers is usually his last. I would ask for advice, if I thought there was anyone in Eilhart capable of giving it, but there is not. Everyone here who knows anything worth knowing is, for that very reason, untrustworthy. Even you, Reinmar. Even you.'

Reinmar pondered that for a few moments – but he was not tempted to bring the phial out of his pouch and hand it over to the witch hunter. If everyone who knew anything had to be reckoned as being untrustworthy by the Wieland family, then von Spurzheim was surely the least trustworthy of all. 'I still have only the faintest idea who or what it is that we are fighting,' Reinmar said, dubiously. 'If they come, should we expect men or beastmen, or something even worse – daemons, perhaps?'

'I don't know,' von Spurzheim admitted. 'But I'm glad to hear you say "we", because I do want you on my side. I can't tell you exactly what form the enemy will take, but ought to warn you to expect the most dreadful beastmen you can imagine, and things more frightful still. That way, at least, you will be mentally prepared. Always remember this, though: these monsters can be successfully fought. Their power is limited, in ways I cannot pretend to comprehend. Even daemons, it seems, can only enter our world for brief periods, and their tenure here is always fragile. While they are here they can be hurt like any mortal creature. If you can keep your head and use your brain, you have advantages of your own which most of your enemies have not. Whatever else they are, they are no great thinkers, and such discipline as they have is very weak indeed. They can be beaten. Whatever may happen, remember that. They are not invincible. Powerful, vicious, treacherous, insidious... but not invulnerable.'

'The people of Eilhart,' Reinmar observed, wryly, 'are not used to making do with such small crumbs of comfort as that.'

'Well,' said Machar von Spurzheim, standing up as he spoke and moving towards the door of the room, 'I hope, as you undoubtedly do, that they will not be forced to get used to it – but I dare not be optimistic. Go home now – but think on what I have said. If you really have contrived to harm the cause of our enemies, rather than merely serving as an instrument of their cunning, the choice of battleground may not be left to me. If you have invited vengeance, it will probably be swift in coming, and you will obtain more than your fair share of our enemies' attentions. Sleep, if you can – and pay close attention to your dreams.'

While he was concluding this speech the witch hunter ushered Reinmar from the room, but he left him to make his own way down the stair and out into the street.

Reinmar walked home alone, nervous of every footfall and shadow because of the possibilities that von Spurzheim had suggested to him, and wondering all the while what kind of welcome his father would by now have prepared for him.

Chapter Twenty-Five

Reinmar was expecting anger, recrimination and complaint, but that was not what awaited him. Gottfried Wieland seemed, instead, to have decided to make himself abnormally calm and full of concern. He had obviously had a long conversation with Godrich and Sigurd, and had fully absorbed all that they had to tell him.

'The boy and girl are safely lodged,' the wine merchant assured his son. 'They shall have all the usual privileges of hospitality until their own folk come to claim them. Have you seen Albrecht?'

'Yes,' Reinmar replied, slightly disconcerted by the politeness of his father's manner. 'I think the witch hunter will release him in the morning. If so, it might be as well for him to go to Holthusen – grandfather too, if he is able to travel. Eilhart is not safe. Even if the soldiers march on in search of the valley, there might be trouble here. That might be my fault, in part.'

'No it's not,' Gottfried said, still acting out of character. 'It's no more your fault than mine, and no more mine than my father's. Our neighbours might prefer it if the blame were to stop here, but it can't. Eilhart has been a quiet and peaceful town for generations, and there's not a family here who does not know that a price has been paid for that quiet. There have been many here more tolerant of the traffic in the wine of dreams than I, and even I made no serious attempt to stop the trade, being content to divert it away from my shop. It might have been better for everyone if the witch hunter had not traced the trade-route this far, but now that he has there is no one of even moderate means who can honestly claim that his own prosperity has not been fostered by the trade. Whatever happens, Reinmar – to this house, or to the town – it isn't your fault. I don't know what the witch hunter said to you, but Godrich has told me that you conducted yourself nobly as well as bravely, and I am proud to hear it.'

Reinmar had never heard such a speech from his father's lips before, but he was too tired for overmuch astonishment or gratitude. All he could say was: 'Thank you for understanding.'

'You must go to bed now,' Gottfried said. 'But when you dress yourself in the morning you had best strap on your blade. I have no idea what tomorrow may bring, and nor has any other man, but I fear that we may have need of the ability to defend ourselves.'

'They are not invulnerable,' Reinmar said, feeling that he ought to make the effort. 'The witch hunter was enthusiastic to press that point. They can be beaten.'

'I know that,' his father replied. 'I have lived my whole life with that hope and expectation, else I would long since have gone the way of my own father, or those who have suffered fates far worse than his. Now bid me goodnight, and go.'

For once, Reinmar was glad to do as he was told.

There were half a dozen hiding-places in Reinmar's room that were capable of accommodating the phial that he had stolen from the underworld, and he was very glad to have the opportunity of relieving himself of that particular burden for a while. He placed it in the hidey-hole that he had always considered the best: a crevice in the brickwork that could be artfully concealed by a strip of mortar that gave no indication to an inquisitive eye that it was not firmly bound to its setting.

When he was finally able to lay his head upon his pillow Reinmar immediately sank into oblivion, and was afterwards certain that he remained in that peace for several hours – but long before he woke he was troubled by dreams whose turbulent substance eventually coalesced into a remarkably coherent vision.

It seemed to Reinmar that he was lifted from his bed and that he floated out of the open window of his bedroom, whereupon he was drawn into an erect posture before beginning a stately ascent into the dark and starry sky. He put his arms out on either side of him as if they were wings, and was careful in the meantime to hold his legs straight and his ankles tight together.

When he was high enough to look down on the roofs of all the houses in Eilhart, Reinmar's ascent was halted and his head was tilted slightly forward so that he could look down. It seemed to him that the town was surrounded by a great ring of roseate mist, in which blue and purple shadows moved. Among those shadows were groups of squat and ugly humanoids, and chimerical beings in which human parts were combined with animal, or animal elements with insectile, but they were no more than shadows and the mist had not yet encroached upon the boundaries of the town. Wherever there was a light on the streets, however – and there were many more than usual, particularly by the docks, where so many soldiers had been quartered – there were fluttering moths.

While Reinmar strained his eyes in order to see these moths more clearly they seemed to grow in size. Wherever he looked, the larger moths immediately began to detach themselves from the crowds clustering about the lanterns and moved upwards towards him, as if in answer to his curiosity. As more and more moths began to fly up to him, Reinmar began to wonder if he too might be alight like a lantern, not with fire but with some strange, pure white radiance that belonged deep in the heart of the world.

As the moths began to spiral around him they were certainly illuminated by some sort of light, and he was able to see that instead of insectile bodies and heads, they had the bodies and heads of female manikins, although their deep green eyes were large and compound and each of them had only a single breast. As they fluttered about him, though, he saw that the legs of each seemingly-human body were fused together, and wrapped around by a long tail. Their wings were very beautiful. The pale blues and rose-pinks that were their predominant colours were arrayed in whirling confusion, which became even more dizzying as the wings beat rapidly back and forth.

A sourceless voice whispered in his ear, instantly recognisable as the one he had heard as he quit the hidden valley to which – he now felt certain – he had been carefully lured.

'It is not too late, my child,' the voice said. 'Others stand condemned, but there is hope for you. Whatever harm you did, you conserved the possibility of setting matters to rights when you accepted a measure of my power – a measure far more potent than its volume implies. You were right to guess that the nectar of the flowers is the vital ingredient of its virtue, but you did not witness the careful process of dilution and adulteration to which it is normally subject. The phial you have contains pure nectar, and there is as much virtue in a single drop of that syrup as there is in a case of the wine you were give to taste. You fear, and rightly so, that you offended against my purpose when you spilled the bottled wines, but I am the kind of master who knows the value of forgiveness. An instrument at the heart of a rival camp has abundant opportunity for reparation, and for reward. The best victories are won by stealth, and the best of all are those in which the enemy does not know the manner or the extent of his defeat.

'You shall see horrors in the days to come, my child, that will make you understand what a paradise my garden in the underworld should properly be reckoned – but I can promise you that you shall not be torn apart, nor burned alive, nor shall your mind dissolve into madness. This I do freely without asking any recompense at all. I am content to tell you that you do have the means to make recompense, not merely to me but to those whom you love, and that I in my turn have the means to grant you pleasure far beyond the meagre capacities of common men.

'As you make your choices in the days to come, ask yourself only this: what, in life, is truly worth having? Has time any value of its own, or is it the quality of each moment rather than the quantity of all that provides the better measure of happiness?'

Reinmar might have fashioned a reply to this speech had his throat and mouth not been frozen, but he lacked the power to move his jaw or exercise his vocal cords. He knew, however, that no reply was required or desired. When the oration had concluded, the moths began to crowd about Reinmar more closely, their flight-paths spiralling inwards towards him. He could no more brace himself against the anticipated collisions than he could speak, so he simply waited for the impacts – but he felt none. It seemed that the moths entered his body as easily as they might have flown from shadow into starlight, meeting no resistance whatsoever.

Alas, whatever kind of light it was that attracted them to him was far from kindly, and as soon as they were inside him they burst into flame. He felt each one flare up, as if it were an element of a galaxy of tiny suns illuminating his breast and his belly, his skull and his groin. He felt not the slightest hint of agony in the process of annihilation, for the flash in which each tiny form was consumed was a blaze of pure pleasure, an eruption of incandescent ecstasy. The bliss of it was so extreme that although he could not close his eyes he ceased to see, blinding himself by the exercise of his will.

It was not until the entire company of moths had been obliterated that Reinmar accepted sight again and looked down.

Now he saw fire of a more brutal kind, flooding the town of Eilhart with a keen hunger for consumption, avidly embracing every beam of wood and every bolt of cloth, reducing every carriage and every boat to ash. He heard the agonised screams of the fire's victims, but he could not feel the heat of the flames nor smell the billowing smoke. Nor could he make out with any significant clarity the kinds of shadows that danced in the flames, joyously wielding claws and blades to deadly effect. It all seemed to him to be no more than play: a great game of pleasure and pain, which had begun long before he was born or the Empire founded, and would endure not merely long after he was dead but long after the Empire had been forgotten by history and legend alike.

And then he woke up, to find himself being shaken more roughly than could possibly have been necessary.

When he condescended to open his eyes, he found that daylight was shining strongly behind the curtain obscuring his window, but he was still convinced that the hour was unreasonably early. He would have asked what time it was, but he was still being shaken so insistently that his teeth would only have rattled in his mouth.

He was astonished to find that the man who was shaking him was his grandfather, Luther, who should not have had strength enough in his arms to lift a bowl of gruel. The old man was kneeling by the bed, as if he had crawled there on his hands and knees – as he would surely have been forced to do unless some miracle had restored his strength – but his arms were possessed by a fury that could not have been entirely his.

'Reinmar!' the old man whispered, plaintively. 'Do you have the wine? Did you bring the wine?'

Reinmar did not have to ask what wine the old man meant. Nor did he doubt that the measure that was in his possession really was, as the dream voice had assured him, far more powerful than its volume suggested.

'Stop it, grandfather!' Reinmar complained, fending off the furious hands. 'I'm awake.'

'I need the wine,' Luther said, hoarsely. 'Far more than Albrecht or his whelp. If you only knew what dreams I have had! I need the wine, Reinmar, for pity's sake. I am soon a dead man, and must have it now or never. I must have it now, or I cannot face my death. If you brought some from the source, you must give it to me and not to any other. You owe me that, child, for I have been a far better friend and father to you than any man alive.'

Reinmar finally succeeded in gripping the old man's hands in his own and forcing them to be still. 'What dreams?' he asked, roughly. 'What dreams?'

'They're coming, Reinmar,' Luther whispered, his huge eyes staring madly into Reinmar's own. 'They do not love violence for its own sake, but when they turn to it they are terrible. The monsters are coming, Reinmar, and Eilhart is doomed. As soon as they are fully gathered they will come, and I must have the wine. You must give me what you brought, even if it's but a single flask. I must have it. I must.'

It was confusion rather than cruelty that made Reinmar continue his stubborn refusal. Even if he had acted immediately, though, he would not have been able to bring the phial from its hiding-place in the wall in time to let Luther drink from it, because his father and Godrich had already come into the room, searching for the old man.

'He brought nothing,' Gottfried said, as he descended upon the old man in order to tear him away from his grandson's bedside. 'He was not such a fool, for he knows the value of sanity. He did everything in his power to make sure that no dark wine would come out of that place for a long time to come, because

I have taught him the ways of the world far better than you ever taught them to me. Whatever monsters come, the men of Eilhart will stand against them with no wines but mine to slake their thirst and fortify their courage.'

While he was speaking, Gottfried had lifted his father up like a sack of flour. As soon as he had finished he handed the old man over to Godrich as if he were, indeed, an item of household provision. Godrich held Luther a little more tenderly, but moved quickly enough to carry the old man out of the room and back to his own bed.

'I'm sorry for that, son,' Gottfried said. 'I'd have let you sleep longer if I could, but it might be best that you're awake. Marguerite is with the gypsy, but she seems to be doing no good.'

'Marguerite?' Reinmar repeated. 'What is Marguerite doing with Marcilla?'

'The gypsy girl has a high fever, and there's not a doctor left in town except for those who've been commandeered by the officers to help make their men battle-fit. Marguerite's hardly a wise woman, but she has patience and a tender touch, and she offered to sit by the sick-bed.'

Reinmar suspected that it was neither patience nor tenderness that had led Marguerite to volunteer such charity, but rather jealous curiosity about the girl that he had brought out of the hills. He did not say so. Instead, he asked his father to leave him while he used the chamber pot and got dressed, promising to look in on Marguerite and Marcilla before he came down to breakfast.

Although he put on the same bloodstained belt that he had worn throughout his adventure in the hills Reinmar was careful to find a new pouch. He left the phial where it was, glad to be free of its ominous presence for a little while longer. He followed his father's advice, and made sure that the scabbard of his sword was securely bound to his belt.

Ulick was with Marguerite by Marcilla's bedside, and it was he who reacted first to Reinmar's appearance. 'She is dying, sir!' he said, in obvious anguish. 'She has refused the call, and her senses have fled.'

Reinmar picked up Marcilla's arm from where it lay on the coverlet. Even the wrist was hot, and the pulse within was racing. Her lovely face was flushed deep red, and her lips were moving silently, as if she were reciting some secret spell.

'It's only a common fever,' Reinmar said, although he doubted it. 'It was brought on by over-exertion and exposure to the rain.'

'She has demanded wine,' Marguerite said. 'We have given her water, but it only made her demands more clamorous. In the end, I let her have a little hock, but she spat it out. She's incoherent now, but whenever she says anything aloud, she asks for wine. I don't know what wine she means, but if you have any you might have to let her have it. I don't know whether it will save her, but I fear that nothing else will.'

'She does not know what she needs,' Reinmar insisted. 'She has never known what is good for her. The fever will pass, in time.' If Marcilla was to have what she craved, she would have to wait until he and she were alone; he dared not trust Ulick or Marguerite with the knowledge that he had the phial.

Marguerite stood up, and placed herself squarely in front of the man who had been her likely husband since the day she was born. 'Why did you bring her here, Reinmar?' she demanded.

He knew that he could put her off with a lie. He could have said that Sergeant Vaedecker had recognised her value, and the boy's too, as an invaluable means of locating the hidden valley. He could have said that Machar von Spurzheim had ordered him to keep her safe. He could even have said that taking her in was a simple act of kindness and mercy. Instead, he told the truth. 'Because I love her,' he said, bluntly. 'I have saved her from a terrible fate, and I am determined to keep her safe forever, if I can. I have defended her against monsters, and I will continue to do so, no matter what monsters may come against me in future.'

Marguerite flinched twice as Reinmar set out his statement, but by the time he had finished she had done flinching.

'Everyone says that the monsters in the hills are massing for an attack,' she murmured. 'Everyone says that there will be a battle, and that the witch hunter has already delayed too long in waiting for reinforcements. I saw families arriving in carts from the farmlands when I stepped out into the street this morning, and others packing carts in order to go to the docks. Were there not so many barges arriving laden with soldiers and their weapons there would be none to bear those who want to flee downriver, but the traffic is steady in both directions. The superstitious see omens in the moths that cluster about the lanterns, swearing that they are not moths at all but spirits sent to spy on us, that the attackers might lay their plans in careful detail. The whole world is turning upside-down, Reinmar – but I did not think that you would turn with it. I see that you have put on your sword, even though you are at home. I always thought when I watched you at practice that you might one day fight for your father, or for your shop, or for Eilhart, or even for me, but I had never thought that you would ever fight for a gypsy whore who is already confirmed in the worship of evil.'

'She is a girl like any other,' Reinmar said, stiffly, although the speech had cut him deeply. 'It is her beauty alone that makes you jealous, and jealousy alone that makes you insult her. If you are not here to help her then I wish that you would go. I can look after her myself.'

'You cannot and shall not,' Marguerite contradicted him. 'Von Spurzheim has already sent word to your father asking for you. You are his darling of the moment, it seems. You'd best beware – however good a man he is, he's dangerous company. Almost as dangerous, I dare say, as your grandfather the repentant sorcerer.'

'Grandfather was never a sorcerer,' Reinmar told her. 'Nor was my Great-Uncle Albrecht, who was at least a scholar. I think Ulick can be trusted to give his sister as much care as she needs until I return, so you may still go.'

Marguerite had been looking into his eyes all the while, but now she looked down at her feet. 'I'll stay,' she said.

'To help?' Reinmar asked.

'To help,' she answered, stoutly. 'If there is anything I can do to save her, I shall not fail.'

As if in answer to that promise, the gypsy girl's soundless muttering suddenly became audible, and Marguerite knelt beside her, raising her head a little from the sweat-drenched pillow on which it lay. 'Wine!' Marcilla demanded, hoarsely. 'I need dark wine! Please! If I have not wine I shall never rest.'

Reinmar could not help but wonder whether the proximity of the phial of nectar was sufficient in itself to excite Marcilla and Luther alike, but he put the thought from his mind. However strong their cravings became, he thought, answering their demands would neither be helpful nor moral. The darkness of the wine was malice and destruction, no matter how its sweetness might amplify the appetites of its victims.

'I must go,' he said, brusquely. 'I need bread to stock my stomach before I go to see von Spurzheim.'

'You need more than bread to stock your stomach,' Marguerite replied. 'You need sense to stock your head. You need eyes to see what is good and what is not, instead of delusions born of glamour.'

'I shall return when I can,' Reinmar said, dutifully ignoring the insults and speaking as much to Ulick as to Marguerite. 'Keep her safe, I beg you, until the fever fades. Give her as much water as she can take, and food if she is able to eat.'

Having said that, he turned on his heel and left the room, hurrying down to take his breakfast and face his father. He half-expected that all his father's dourness and critical exactitude would have returned by now, but there was no sign of it. Gottfried managed to be perfectly civil as he told his son that he would man the counter while Reinmar went to see von Spurzheim, and positively tender when he insisted that Reinmar should eat his breakfast first.

CHAPTER TWENTY-SIX

AS SOON AS he had eaten a hurried meal, Reinmar set off for the burgomaster's house in search of Machar von Spurzheim. He had only to step outside the door of his father's shop to understand what Marguerite meant about the carts that were bringing farmers' families and their possessions into town while the local inhabitants were packing up to leave.

The exchange was not as nonsensical as logic might suggest. A town full of soldiers was a far safer place than a hamlet, if there really were an army massing in the surrounding hills, but that army was bound to need provisions and if the worst rumours were true, its officers were not the kind to pay their way or to hold back their troops from looting. From the viewpoint of a farmer who had already harvested and sold his crop, Eilhart would appear to be a haven simply because it offered the meagre safety of numbers; the townspeople, on the other hand, would be thinking in different terms. Many of them would have relatives or trading-partners in Holthusen, and the larger town must seem to them a very desirable haven by comparison with one that had no protective wall or local garrison and was likely to be stripped of the greater part of its wealth. Eilhart would have to be defended, if the need arose, by soldiers who had no local relatives or property to shape their priorities, who would undoubtedly become more desperate as time went by in their requisitioning of food, weapons and manpower.

Reinmar was stopped three times on his way to the square by people who knew that he was recently returned from an expedition into the foothills of the Grey Mountains. They all wanted to know if he had actually seen monsters. When he told them that he had, and that Sigurd and Matthias Vaedecker had even contrived to spill the blood of beastmen, they nodded grimly. They were not surprised; what he had to say merely set the seal on their anxiety. Two of the three also knew that he had been closeted for some time with Machar von Spurzheim, and they asked him what the witch hunter intended to do. He told them that he did not know, but that the decision might be taken out of the witch hunter's hands if the attack began too soon. It was the enemy, Reinmar conceded, who would determine the time and place of the conflict to come. He ended by echoing yet again the assurance that however monstrous the forces arrayed against the town might be, they were not invulnerable – but he was not surprised when his questioners could take no comfort from it.

No one asked after his great-uncle, or even his grandfather.

When he reached the burgomaster's house, Reinmar was immediately sent on to the blockhouse, where he found von Spurzheim in the company of the town constables, carefully examining a map. The witch hunter broke away from his conference as soon as Reinmar appeared, and took him to one side.

'There's no further need to keep your great-uncle in a cell,' he said, 'but he insists on returning home. I've told him that his house is too far out of town, and that we can't possibly extend our defensive perimeter that far, but he is adamant. If you could persuade him to come to your father's house you might save his life.'

'That's a task better suited to my father,' Reinmar pointed out.

'Aye,' said von Spurzheim, 'but your father was as reluctant to see Albrecht as Albrecht is to see him, while both seem happy to let you serve as go-between. For his own good, I hope you can persuade him – but if you can't, I wish that you would at least see him safely home. I still have two men watching the house, but I intend to withdraw them before nightfall.'

This speech rang slightly false, and Reinmar had no difficulty understanding what von Spurzheim really wanted of him. He had refused to go to Holthusen as a spy, but the witch hunter still thought that he might be useful in some such capacity. Von Spurzheim did not seem inclined to give him a formal commission, but would certainly demand a full account of any conversation that took place as Reinmar guided Albrecht home – and of any contact that Albrecht might subsequently make with his elusive son.

Even so, Reinmar thought, I have enough reasons of my own to comply. 'I'll need two horses,' was what he said aloud to von Spurzheim. 'Albrecht is too frail to walk home, and if I'm to come back alone I'll need to come quickly.'

Von Spurzheim nodded. 'I'll have two horses saddled,' he said. 'You're wise to wear your sword, but such intelligence as I can gather from the farm folk suggests that the enemy forces are still fairly widely scattered. If anything happens tonight it will probably be little more than a skirmish.'

One of the constables took Reinmar down to the cells and unlocked the door to Albrecht's.

'Will you come home with me, great-uncle?' Reinmar asked. 'We are a little crowded now, but we can set down a pallet for you in my room or Luther's, as you please.'

'I can't,' was Albrecht's reply.

'If you suppose that your past adventures in Marienburg will guarantee you immunity from the forces ranged against the town,' Reinmar said, soberly, 'I fear that you may be sadly mistaken.'

'I don't,' the old man said. 'The gratitude of princes is a bounteous thing compared to the gratitude of the darker gods. If you suppose that I would be any safer in your father's house than in my own then you're sadly mistaken. Granted that I am lost, I would rather be lost in my own place.'

'In that case,' Reinmar said, 'I'll come with you. I've sent for two horses, if you're well enough to ride. If not, I'll find us a carriage.'

Albrecht lifted a grey eyebrow. 'Is that wise?' he said.

'Why not?' Reinmar countered. 'If there's no safety for you in my father's house, there's none for me either.'

Albrecht gave in, evidently grateful for the favour of his nephew's company as well as a horse to ride. As von Spurzheim had promised, the two mounts were saddled and waiting by the time the two of them emerged blinking into the late morning light.

As soon as he had mounted his horse, Albrecht craned his neck to look at the cloud-clad peaks of the distant Grey Mountains. 'Tonight will be clear enough,' he judged, 'but tomorrow won't. When those clouds come scurrying northwards, bearing icy fogs and thunderstorms, worse things will follow in their train.'

'What things?' Reinmar wanted to know, as soon as they were out of earshot of the busy square. 'Where are these monsters coming from, great-uncle?'

'Who knows?' was Albrecht's reply. 'The mountains hereabouts were never host to dwarfish settlements, so far as history and legend can inform us, but you seem to have found that they are hollow nevertheless – and the fact that we know of no passes which lead conveniently to Bretonnia does not mean that none are known to unhuman beings. Then again, we are not so very far from the Cursed Marshes that lie beyond Marienburg. If von Spurzheim's forces have come so far since they began their campaign, their adversaries might easily have moved in parallel. What matters is not where these creatures came from, but how many have arrived. Six by six they will come, and thirty-six by thirty-six, while the witch hunter's men form up in tens, but we shall not know how the balance lies until the battle is actually joined, and perhaps not until it's ended.'

'Von Spurzheim seems to be assembling a considerable force,' Reinmar said. 'He has abundant support from the Reiksguard as well as men under his direct command – and if the fight is brought to us, the farmers and the townspeople will all take up arms to defend what is theirs. Eilhart will not lack for passionate defenders.'

'I dare say,' the old man replied, pensively. 'But I have drunk the wine of dreams, and I have heard the testimony of those who have probed its deeper secrets. The attackers will likely use mercenary troops, just as the defenders will, but those who are more fully committed to the cause will take such pleasure in the fury of battle as merely human beings can hardly comprehend. I have sipped darker wine than the wine of dreams, and I drew back from its grip, but as your new friend reminded me last night, I have known those who were only avid for more – and I have glimpsed the pleasure that such people take in torment and murder. You can have no conception of the ecstatic quality that some minds find in the furthest excesses of bloodlust. If you imagine that the strength men gain from defending home and hearth is the most powerful motive there is, you're mistaken.'

By this time Albrecht's house was in view. The surrounding woods gave such ample shelter that Reinmar had not expected to catch a glimpse of the spies von Spurzheim had set to watch it, and he did not. He was, however, startled to see that a thin plume of smoke was curling from the chimney. Although Albrecht had not been home for several days and his housekeeper was supposed to be long gone, someone had lit a fire that morning. Given that the late summer weather was more than warm enough, it had to be a cooking fire.

Reinmar's first thought was that the witch hunter's spies must have been uncommonly careless to let someone take up residence – but his second was that he himself had been unwary. Von Spurzheim probably knew full well that the house was occupied, and by whom, but he had decided that Reinmar might serve him better as an informant or agent provocateur than any company of constables and men-at-arms.

Albrecht had seen the smoke too. 'Wirnt?' he murmured, half in expectation and half in trepidation. The old man rode a little way ahead so that he might dismount and go to the door before Reinmar had quit the saddle, and he hurried inside while Reinmar took his time about tethering the two horses. Reinmar did not bother to take the animals round the back of the house to the stables, because they had not come far enough to need the water-trough.

When Reinmar went inside he expected to see the man whose visit to the shop had been the trigger of this whole affair, but what he actually saw was a woman. The quality of her clothing testified that she was not a housekeeper, although she did indeed have a kettle and a frying pan set upon the stove. She was not young, by any means, but she was handsome enough and her eyes were bright with intelligence.

'It's good to see you, Albrecht my love,' she was saying, although Reinmar took note of the fact that Albrecht had made no move to embrace her. He leapt immediately to the conclusion that this was Wirnt's mother, fled from Marienburg in Wirnt's wake and hastened on her way by the pursuit of Machar von Spurzheim's zealous witch hunters.

'Are you mad, Valeria?' Albrecht asked her. 'The house is watched – and if it were not, it might be more dangerous still.'

'I doubt that,' she replied. 'Yes, the house is watched, by more than one man. If the soldiers were to try to seize me, they might find me more dangerous than they imagine. The weight of the years has begun to weigh on me for want of the wine of dreams, but I am not without resources. Who is the lovely boy?'

'Luther's grandson, Reinmar Wieland.'

'One of us?'

'The Wielands have not traded in dark wine for many years,' Albrecht told her. 'I suppose I must take the blame for that, at least as much as Luther – but Reinmar has been to the source, it seems, and has escaped with his life.' Reinmar noticed that he had not actually answered the question he had been asked.

Answer or not, this news intensified Valeria's interest remarkably, and she stared hard at Reinmar, as if her eager eyes were avid to drink every detail of his face. He could not guess exactly how old she was. The flesh that sat upon her bones seemed on close examination to be almost as thin as Luther's, and her greying hair almost as filmy, but she had a kind of hauteur that somehow preserved her beauty in spite of such reductions. If she had come on horseback she must have changed after stabling her animal, because her gown was no riding-dress. It was pale blue in colour, with crimson embroidery, and the swirling design of the ornamental threads put him strangely in mind of the moths that he had seen in his dream.

'Did you bring wine away with you?' she asked him, abruptly.

'No,' he said, though the lie pricked his conscience slightly. 'But I saw something of how it was made, and how the plants were nourished whose nectar is its base.'

'They grow in human flesh,' Albrecht put in, as if to save Reinmar the embarrassment of explanation.

'Of course they do,' the old woman said, although Reinmar could not believe that she knew the truth in any detail. 'To what finer purpose could human flesh be put? What greater luxury can there be than to serve the cause of luxury itself – to become pure pleasure. What higher hope can the soul have than to be distilled into the elixir of life? Are you sure that you did not bring a little of it with you? Why else, I wonder, would you have been called? And why else would you have been sent home to us?'

'I was not sent to you,' Reinmar told her, hoping that it was true. 'I will concede that I might have been led to the source of the wine of dreams in order that a trap might be set, but if I was returned to anyone, it was to the witch hunter. The trap, if trap it was, went badly awry when I took the opportunity to pollute the purity of the wines that were in store. When you say that you have resources with which to protect yourself against capture, do you mean that you are a sorceress?'

Valeria clucked her tongue at that. 'I am a scholar,' she told him. 'Sorcery is magic worked for evil ends, but I have only been interested in knowledge – which is, in itself, the highest good of all. Scholarship is my resource, and my vocation, as it was Albrecht's in the days when he was my lover.'

Albrecht might or might not have muttered 'One of them' – Reinmar's eyes were still fixed on the old woman's rouged lips, and could not discern the words by sound alone.

'I know many men who would disagree with you,' Reinmar said evenly, 'and think themselves fully entitled to do it.'

'You know many fools and country bumpkins who would disagree with me,' Valeria replied, matching his level tone satirically. 'You know men who are fearful of knowledge itself, lest it threaten the ignorant empire of their stubborn beliefs. You know men who have tasted knowledge and have drawn back from it, terrified that they might forfeit the good opinion of their stupid neighbours merely by becoming wise. Perhaps you even know witch hunters, who are avid to destroy everything that threatens their cowardly confidence in the simplicity of goodness. But you do not know anyone who is entitled to disagree with me.'

'You should not have come here, Valeria,' Albrecht said. 'It isn't safe.'

'I did not come here because it was safe,' Valeria retorted, tartly, 'but precisely because it is unsafe. Were I safe, I'd have naught before me but the grave and naught but dreams to haunt my slow passage thence. I'd rather take a risk and have a chance to answer my need. Have you seen our son?'

'No.'

'No?' Valeria seemed genuinely surprised. 'Well, doubtless you shall. It will be a pleasure and a privilege, will it not, to be together again? A family reunited in its cause. Do you know where my son is, Reinmar, by any chance?'

'No,' said Reinmar. 'I have seen him, but he seems to have vanished. I gave him directions to this house, but he never arrived. Perhaps he has gone to find a flask of dark wine for his beloved mother – not realising that there is none left to find.'

'Is there not?' Valeria countered, still staring at him curiously. 'You have the odour of a liar about you now, for which I don't blame you in the least. You've tasted the wine, have you not? You've savoured its promises.'

'The merest sip,' Reinmar assured her. 'I got nothing from it but bad dreams.'

'Poor boy,' she said, sarcastically. 'Your left hand hardly knows what the right is doing – but you would do far better to throw in your lot with us than with von Spurzheim. Perhaps you have, but don't quite know it yet. Are you in love, perchance?'

Reinmar had no idea what reply he ought to make to this, although he was determined not to give way. He glanced at Albrecht, hoping to judge the old man's opinion, but Albrecht had sunk into his rickety armchair and already seemed lost to the world, save for the hungry expression that came into his eye as he contemplated the kettle and the frying-pan. In the end, Reinmar was saved the trouble of answering by the sound of a thunderous knocking at the door, which must have been made by the hilt of a sword rather than a mere fist.

'That will be von Spurzheim's men,' Reinmar said, jumping effortlessly to the conclusion. 'They must think that I have had time enough to judge the situation, and have come to arrest you.'

So saying, he went to the door and opened it, although it would have been perfectly adequate to shout an invitation to enter, because he had not barred it when he came in.

He threw it open gladly – but the gladness shrivelled and died on the instant when he saw who it was that had knocked.

Brother Noel stood on the threshold, accompanied by Brother Almeric. The knocking had indeed been made by the hilt of an unsheathed sword, which Noel still had in his hand. It was stained with blood.

Chapter Twenty-Seven

Reinmar leapt back to give himself time to draw his own blade. Mercifully, this operation went smoothly, and his prospective opponent had been inconvenienced by the narrowness of the doorway as well as his own surprise. Brother Almeric, who was unarmed, had stepped back rather than forward, and by the time Brother Noel had moved into a striking position Reinmar's guard was up. There was a brief moment when Noel seemed to be on the point of lunging forward, but then he thought better of it. Perhaps he had observed that Reinmar had been properly trained in the use of his weapon, or perhaps he was mindful of his own tiredness.

'You are full of surprises, Master Wieland,' the monk said, as he moved slowly, keeping the tip of his sword raised, as if to threaten Reinmar's throat. 'Have you come to spoil our plans all over again?'

Almeric was not so well composed, but he made no attempt to take a position beside his companion. 'Kill him,' he said. 'What are you waiting for?'

'Forgive my friend's impatience,' Noel said, his eyes still fixed on Reinmar's face in a hawk-like manner. 'He is unused to violence. Like the men you attacked and slaughtered in the underworld he has been a lifelong devotee of tranquillity and patience – but he becomes fretful when things go awry.'

'But you are not unused to violence,' Reinmar guessed, stepping backwards warily in response to Noel's forward movement.

'I came late to my vocation,' Noel admitted.

Valeria spoke over Reinmar's shoulder then, her lips no more than a few inches from his ear. 'Put up your swords and close the door,' she said, in the manner of one well-accustomed to being obeyed. Reinmar was about to object that the matter was not so simple, but the monks reacted more swiftly. Almeric came in and closed the door behind him, but did not bar it. Noel dropped the tip of his sword, although he did not return it to its sheath. Reinmar hesitated for a moment, but the odds were obviously not in his favour no matter how poor a fighter Almeric was. He lowered his own blade, but he kept it in his hand, ready to raise it again if he were threatened.

'I'm sorry, my lady,' Almeric said to Valeria. 'We tried to approach with all due discretion, but the two watchers were widely-spaced and overly vigilant.'

'They were one too many,' Noel added. 'I wounded one, but both are riding to the town as we speak. Time is short, but I think we can guarantee you safe passage if you come away now.'

'Have you brought wine?' That seemed to be Valeria's only concern.

'Of course, Lady.' Noel immediately reached into his pouch and brought out a crystal flask. Valeria relaxed as she saw it, as if a great anxiety had been lifted from her – but Reinmar saw that Albrecht tensed, as if confronted with a danger he had not expected to face.

Reinmar considered the possibility of attempting to break the flask. Noel was distracted and the weight of his blade had dragged its tip further down. The opportunity was there to knock the bottle aside and start a brawl – but Reinmar did not know whether he would be one against two, three or four, and if Noel was telling the truth about both sentries having gone for help no reinforcements would arrive for a quarter of an hour.

Valeria took the decision out of his hands by seizing the flask from the monk's hand. She wrestled the stopper free, then raised the bottle to her lips and drank, deeply and avidly.

Valeria's greying hair still had more than sufficient darkness in it to reveal that it had once been jet black, and the manner in which her fine skin sat neatly upon the bones of her face implied that she must have been exceedingly handsome in her youth. As soon as she had lowered the rouge-stained rim of the flask from her lips the turgor began to return to her cheeks. Her forehead became smooth and pale. Her hair darkened by degrees until it was as evenly black as a raven's wing. Her eyes brightened until they were actually luminous, their irises flooded with radiant blue. Her lips became fuller, and the false colour seemed to fade into her flesh. The teeth that she was no longer ashamed to show became much whiter and more even.

The greatest change of all, however, was not in her appearance but in her presence, which seemed so greatly magnified that it filled and dominated the room.

Only a few moments before, Valeria had been one human being among five, a mere element of a greater company in spite of her assumption of dominance. She might have stood among a crowd of thousands now without seeming a mere particle of no unique interest. As soon as the wine of dreams had taken effect she became the obvious centrepiece of the assembly, the pivot around which everything else was arrayed, and upon which all attention had to be focused.

Reinmar felt that he could understand why a person – especially a woman, given the ordinary way of the world – might risk a great deal in order to obtain that kind of presence.

Valeria held out the half-empty flask to Albrecht – from whose point of view, Reinmar knew, it must seem half-full.

Albrecht hesitated.

Reinmar was tempted to say 'Don't', as his father would certainly have wanted him to do, but the advice died on his tongue – not because he was afraid to voice it in such company but because he was afraid that it might not be the right advice. Albrecht knew far better than Reinmar did what price he might now have to pay for a draught of that quality, and death would only be a part of it – but what life had Albrecht left to lose?

Unwilling as yet to settle his hesitation, Albrecht took refuge in a question addressed to Brother Noel. 'Was it Wirnt who summoned you?'

'No,' Noel said, keeping his eyes on Reinmar. 'It was another messenger who came to tell us that the lady would meet us here, and to inform our friends as to the increasing strength and defensive disposition of von Spurzheim's forces. Do you know what this imbecile has done, my lady?'

The 'imbecile' he meant was, of course, Reinmar – but Reinmar made no immediate protest.

'Albrecht says that he found the source,' Valeria said, absent-mindedly, 'but that he was allowed to escape with his life.' She seemed intoxicated by the return of her strength, and she was studying the length of her right arm with obvious approval.

'Is that what you told them, Master Wieland?' Noel asked. 'Did you tell them what a hero you were, because you killed a few old men who had never learned to wield a weapon skilfully and lacked the strength in any case? I suppose you think yourself a master of improvisation because you ran amok in our storeroom, and a master of deception because you stole the one remaining measure of the unadulterated nectar. You think yourself privileged by fortune because you escaped from the valley unhurt and because I have not run you through, although I have had every chance to do so. But what, if we examine the case more carefully, have you made of yourself by ignoring the offer we made to you? A thief, a murderer, a coward and a fool. Lady Valeria, we must be away from here before the Reiksguard comes thundering along the road.'

'Yes,' Albrecht put in, 'go, Valeria, before you bring the witch hunter's wrath down upon us all.'

Valeria did not appear to be listening. She was looking at Reinmar too. 'Did you really take the nectar?' she asked.

Reinmar wanted to lie, but when he opened his mouth no sound came out. Valeria put her right forefinger into her mouth and sucked it for a moment or two. When she took it out again she reached out and touched it, still moist, to Reinmar's lips. He wanted to draw back, but he could not do that either. Her bright blue eyes held him in thrall, and he knew that if she ordered Noel to strike him now, he would not be able to parry the thrust.

While the finger lingered on his lips he could not taste the wine of dreams, but he could smell it. The odour eased into his nostrils, and into his brain. It brought back the memory of both his dreams – not merely the dream of being taken up above the town to watch its destruction by fire but the earlier one, when he had fought a hostile wind to climb a mountain to a castle in the clouds, and there had been seduced by something quite unhuman and yet more desirable than any human woman ever could be. He reminded himself that that had only been a dream, whereas Marcilla was real, but with the intoxicating scent in his nostrils he could not entirely trust his judgement.

Valeria was very beautiful now – more beautiful, certainly, than Marcilla. But was she only human?

She smiled at him, and her smile was glorious.

She removed her finger from his lips, and he drew them in reflexively. He tasted the dark wine as soon as it touched his tongue, but it was only the merest drop.

'You may come with us, if you wish,' Valeria said. 'Or stay, if you prefer. There will be fighting, and a great deal of killing, but I want you to know that that is nothing to do with us. Our part is very different, for we are scholars and honest tradesmen. Don't be frightened by what you have done, for it will make little difference in the end. All significant choices remain to be made, and you are still free.'

'He won't come with us,' Noel said, harshly. 'Like father, like son.'

'Don't be unkind, brother,' Valeria said. 'We know no more of the final scheme than he does, and he may yet play his part far better than we.'

'Come away, my lady,' Almeric put in, his voice taut with alarm. 'We have no time.'

'Of course we have,' she told him, negligently. 'We shall steal the horses on which my dear cousins arrived, to prove our apparent wickedness – but you will understand in time, dear Reinmar, what virtues are ours.'

Almeric was already hastening the rejuvenated sorceress towards the door, and she consented to be guided although she still looked back at Reinmar. The monk let her go in order to open the door and look out, anxiously scanning the trees. 'All quiet,' he said. 'If there is another watcher still out there, he will not dare come into the open. We must beware of crossbow bolts, but if we move quickly we needn't fear pursuit.'

'Fear pursuit?' Noel echoed. 'We are not the ones who need fear pursuit.' Valeria had already passed from Reinmar's view, and so had Brother Almeric – but Noel could not stop himself from pausing, as he left the room, to add to his farewell speech.

'Thank you for the horses, Master Wieland,' he said. 'Given the shortage of our present supply, I think you'll find the measure of the wine of dreams that your great-uncle holds in his hand more than adequate compensation. You'll doubtless be contacted again about the one you stole.' Once he had finished, though, he wasted no further time before disappearing, slamming the door shut behind him.

Reinmar did not bother to go to the door to see which two of the three had claimed the two fresh horses, or what recourse the other had instead. He stayed where he was, staring at his great-uncle and the flask the monks had left behind.

Albrecht refused to be ashamed. 'Is it true?' the old man asked him. 'Did you bring wine out of the underworld?'

'The nectar of the gods itself, apparently,' Reinmar conceded. 'I could not be certain that spilling the contents of the jugs and bottles would render them irrecoverable, but removing the most essential ingredient was bound to reduce their supply.' He told himself that it was not quite a lie, but failed to convince himself.

'And you hid it in the shop?' Albrecht queried.

'I hid it,' Reinmar admitted, refusing to confirm the latter part of the conclusion to which his great-uncle had jumped.

'Luther will probably find it,' Albrecht judged. 'As soon as he goes to sleep he will be visited by a dream. If he does not, the two gypsies will. Reinmar, you have not the slightest idea what you are doing. Do you think that everyone else in Eilhart is as disciplined as your father, merely because they are careful to maintain that appearance in public? Are you really so certain that your father is exactly what he appears to be? Or the witch hunter? We are dealing with the ultimate temptation, and you have just seen one of the rewards that temptation offers. It is the kind of temptation that can all too easily set man against man, husband against wife, and father against son. This is war, Reinmar. Indeed, this is the ultimate war. Who can you trust with what you have brought out of the underworld?'

Reinmar understood that the last question cut to the heart of the matter. Who could he trust? Who did he trust? Von Spurzheim? Matthias Vaedecker? Godrich? Sigurd? Marguerite? Himself?

'What are you going to do, great-uncle?' Reinmar asked, as he finally resheathed his blade.

'I am going to mind my own business, for as long as I have the opportunity,' Albrecht Wieland replied. 'If you ever had that option, you have lost it now. Do you have the least idea what kind of game you are playing?'

'I think so,' Reinmar said, speaking more honestly but still in some need of convincing. 'I am a pawn, it seems – but I was not supposed to find my way into the underworld. They had no idea that I would care so much about the fate of a girl I had only just met, and they did not know that Vaedecker would see them dig her up as soon as they had buried her. I was supposed to return to Eilhart with Ulick, offering von Spurzheim a way to find the valley – but I suspect that his men would have been led to a different and more dangerous place, where they would have fought at a great disadvantage. Once Vaedecker and I had seen too much, the plan had to be recalculated. They still hope that I will serve their purpose, using our existing business to establish a new supply-route for the wine of dreams and its darker kin. They desperately need some such link with the Reik towns, and they will not kill me while there is a chance that I might provide it, no matter how I have annoyed them. Von Spurzheim guessed that my discovery of the valley was bait in a trap, and he would not have hurried into it in any case. He will build what defences he can within the town, and I suppose that his enemies will try to stop him before he gathers sufficient reinforcements. Eilhart has no choice but to help him, and pray to all the good gods for his victory – and because I am part of Eilhart, that is what I must do.'

Albrecht shook his head slowly and sighed. 'Such is the nature of the wine of dreams,' he said. 'Its promises always lead to nightmares in the end. Go back, Reinmar, as fast as you can, and make what preparations you can for the battle. It will be fierce, I think. Von Spurzheim and the Reiksguard will have to draw on every last vestige of their might and endurance.'

Reinmar would not have obeyed the injunction to leave immediately had his ears not caught the sound of hoofbeats, but he knew that he did not want to be standing in Albrecht's house, watching the old man clutch a flask of the wine of dreams, when soldiers burst in, seeking revenge for the wounding of their comrade.

'Bar the door behind me,' he said, and immediately went out to meet the approaching troop.

He was very glad to see that the newly-arrived party was led by Matthias Vaedecker rather than some Reiksguard knight. The dozen men who were with him were all von Spurzheim's followers – a rather motley crew, although Reinmar did not doubt that they knew their business very well indeed.

'It was the two monks who attacked the sentry,' Reinmar told the sergeant. 'They came to meet a woman – a sorceress, I suspect. If you have not been tracking her from Marienburg, she has been tracking you. She was old until they gave her dark wine to drink, but she is younger now.'

'Did you put up a fight?' Vaedecker wanted to know.

'No,' Reinmar confessed. 'Had they threatened my life, I would have done, but they took me by surprise. I had time to draw my weapon, but I was outnumbered, and they had no time to spare for a fight in which my great-uncle would surely have supported me.

Vaedecker had not dismounted, and he was looking about him as he listened to Reinmar's reply, clearly uncertain as to what to do next. 'Damn their insolence!' he said. 'They're taunting us – but if we ride after them, we'll probably ride into a trap. Your great-uncle refused to go with them, you say?'

Reinmar had not said anything of the sort, but he had no objection to the sergeant leaping to that conclusion. 'He's an old man,' Reinmar said. 'He can't fight. He has no desire to do anything but wait at home for whatever transpires. He cannot see that anyone has any reason to hurt him.'

'I have not,' Vaedecker agreed. 'But the enemies we have to face are not the kind to need reasons. Beastmen would rip him apart and dine on his flesh whether they were hungry or not. The best of their allies are no better, and the worst are far worse. But it's not my job to defend him, or yours. You'd better come back to town with us. Von Spurzheim would not like me to leave you to walk unprotected. He thinks you might be useful to him – and the horses you've just lost weren't his to begin with, although we might have made good use of them tomorrow.'

'You think the battle will begin tomorrow?' Reinmar asked, as he came forward to join the troop, ready and willing to walk between their two ranks if Vaedecker would not let him ride two-a-back.

'It has already begun,' the sergeant said, reaching down after only a moment's hesitation to draw Reinmar up behind him.

'From now on, its fury will only increase. I doubt there'll be an all-out assault today, but our adversaries will be busy nonetheless, and so shall we.'

Once Reinmar was safely installed, though, and the drumming of four dozen hooves on the dry ground had set up a secure screen of privacy, Vaedecker changed his tune.

'What went on in there, Master Wieland?' he whispered over his shoulder. 'Why did they come to fetch her, when they could not have known that the sentries would be so ineffectual? Why didn't they take you with them?'

'I don't know,' Reinmar answered, knowing that it sounded weak, although it was only a little short of the whole truth. 'Perhaps they did know that the sentries would be off their guard. Perhaps the sorceress had power enough for that, even when she seemed older. As for me – they still think of me as a pawn in their game, fit for baiting traps and running errands. So do you, it seems.'

'Not I,' Vaedecker contradicted him, implying that there were others who might. 'I've seen you in action. Who is she, Master Wieland?'

'Her name is Valeria,' Reinmar told him. 'My great-uncle knew her in Marienburg.'

'Ah,' the sergeant said. 'We have heard of her. Von Spurzheim will probably be glad that she is here. He wants the battle to be conclusive as well as to win it. This has been a long and arduous campaign.'

'You don't seem to be in wholehearted agreement,' Reinmar observed.

'Life is a long and arduous campaign,' the soldier told him. 'I have always found it better to fight little battles, one at a time. Given that we never run out of enemies, it seems unnecessary and unwise to fight too many at a time. There's more pleasure and profit in an endless series of small victories than in a single costly blaze of glory, believe me.'

Reinmar did believe him, but knew that the choice that Vaedecker had outlined was not his to make, and might not be von Spurzheim's either.

CHAPTER TWENTY-EIGHT

WHEN MATTHIAS VAEDECKER helped Reinmar down from his horse on the edge of Eilhart's market square Reinmar found himself on the outskirts of a seething crowd. The anxiety in the air was palpable, but he did not see the cause of their consternation until he had pushed his way through the crowd to the focal point of its attention.

Laid out in open view on the steps of the corn exchange were six corpses. Not one was fully human. All of them had two arms and two legs, but in all cases but one of these limbs were brutishly thickened and shortened. Three of them had only one hand, the other being replaced by a claw, and two of these had feet like massive taloned paws. Their heads were the worst parts, not one of them being even approximately human. One had a head like a bull with heavy horns, another like a bison and a third like a monstrous cat. The fourth head was wolf-like, more hideous than that of the beastmen that he, Godrich, Sigurd and Vaedecker had fought; the remaining two were like snakes save for their awful compound eyes.

Reinmar had no need to ask why these bodies had been put on display, but his neighbours, seeing that he had only just arrived, were more than enthusiastic to tell him.

'Creatures like these are pressing forward from Holy Hill, west of the Schimel Farm,' Aloys Walther the baker's son informed him. 'They've attacked Vitway and Konigmuell. The town is cut off to the south and west, and at least two of the locks on the river have been smashed. Barges can no longer get to Eilhart Pool, and any rowboats that contest the river's faster flow are deluged with arrows at the Heiligergap. An army of monsters is massing, pressing forward all the while, and they say we'll get no more reinforcements for at least two days. It's too late for anyone else to flee, though – we all have to report for assignment to the defences.'

'We've strength enough,' Reinmar assured him. 'I've fought the beastmen once, and they're far less powerful than they are horrible.'

Long queues of men were already winding halfway around the square, waiting to be interrogated as to the weapons they possessed and the training they had had in their use. Although they were orderly they were far from silent; rumours were flying in every direction. Reinmar had only to walk back to the stable to which Vaedecker's men had taken their horses to hear half a dozen more reports like the one Aloys had poured into his ear. The place-names were sometimes different, but the import was always the same. The town was cut off, or would be within a matter of hours. The flow of military reinforcements had slowed to a trickle, and Eilhart was certain to be attacked before another contingent of the Reiksguard could be mobilised to reinforce its defenders.

All of this had seemed to be a relatively distant prospect when Reinmar and Albrecht had left the town, but it was palpably imminent now and it no longer seemed so odd that the enemy had come to Albrecht's house. Any outlying dwelling, it seemed, was ripe for invasion now. Thanks to the flood of refugees flocking into the town with tales of horror, and the similar flood whose northward routes would soon be cut off, there could be no one within twenty miles of Eilhart who did not know that the town was effectively under siege, and that it would soon have to be defended against a fierce and massive assault.

The town crier was busy in front of the tower that housed the market bell, but it was not his job to put out the call for conscription. Reinmar paused to listen to him, but only for a minute. The proclamations that he was repeating, probably for the tenth or fifteenth time, were to do with the conservation of water – the waters of the river had apparently been fouled and were unfit to drink even after boiling – and the powers of requisition that had been granted to the Reiksguard and the followers of Machar von Spurzheim for the building of barricades.

When Reinmar rejoined Matthias Vaedecker he asked the soldier whether he ought to join one of the queues to await the attention of a recruiting sergeant. He was told that he had already been assigned.

'To you?' Reinmar asked.

'Aye, but don't thank me for my generosity,' Vaedecker told him. 'We're at the upper neck of the river, commissioned to stop and sink anything that comes down.'

'The river above Eilhart is supposed to be unnavigable,' Reinmar observed, although he knew perfectly well that whatever the enemy cared to set upon the waters would float well enough. They would not come in heavily-laden barges but in skiffs and rafts – and they would be very difficult to stop. Vaedecker's men would undoubtedly cast nets and booms across the watercourse, but such barriers could be cut or broken, and while they were being hacked, sawed and smashed the enemy vessels would pile up, discharging missiles to either side. It was impossible to guess which of the many barricades placed across the roads into the town would be the most heavily beset, but one thing that was perfectly certain was that the neck of the river would see fierce and crucial fighting. Once that entry-way was breached, the enemy forces would have a vital artery to carry their assault deep into the town's heart.

'Don't be afraid, either,' Vaedecker added. 'You'll have some of the best infantrymen this side of Middenheim around you, and many of the townsfolk in the rank will be men who know their business. The crossbows and pikes will do the donkey-work at first. Your people will not be forced to go hand-to-hand unless and until they storm the shore, and we'll do everything in our power to make sure they can't outnumber us.'

'What time shall I report?' Reinmar asked.

'You've already reported,' Vaedecker told him. 'You're under my command now, though I'll have to trust you to go to von Spurzheim and tell him everything you can about what happened at the house. When he's satisfied, you must come back to me so that I can show you your position. After that, you can go home to eat and gossip – but the moment you hear the clamour of the bell you must come running, and if no clamour sounds you must listen for the hours. Even if all is quiet you must be at your post by six o'clock, and you must keep watch till two in the morning. If nothing has happened by then… well, we'll know that when it does, it'll be even worse than it would have been had they come more hurriedly.'

Reinmar nodded, then set off to look for the witch hunter while Vaedecker went to see to the organisation of his men.

Von Spurzheim was by no means hard to find, having stuck hard to his base in the town hall, but he was busy with his maps and surrounded by men, including four Reiksguard knights. Von Spurzheim's estimate of the likely time of the attack had been hastily revised, and everything was now being organised in haste. The knights and the witch hunter's lieutenants all seemed to be busy quarrelling, although Reinmar assumed that they would have preferred to describe their argument as a tactical discussion. He had to wait for an opportunity to signal his presence to the witch hunter, and then had to wait far longer for von Spurzheim to find an opportunity to break away. When he did manage to disengage himself, the witch hunter immediately took Reinmar into another room and closed the door behind him.

'If they only spent as much energy in fighting the enemy as they do in trying to secure and increase their own authority,' von Spurzheim said, 'the banks of the Reik would be a better and happier place. They all know full well what the situation is, and how urgent it has now become. They know that I have the warrant of the Grand Theogonist himself, but even if they were kneeling before the War Altar and the Staff of Command they would be bickering over trifles. When the fighting starts they will be heroes all, but they do not know how to be single-minded about anything but violence. Who injured the sentry I could ill afford to lose, Reinmar?'

'Two monks from the valley – the two who tried to sell me dark wine while I was there. They probably had others with them, but it was Brother Noel whose sword was red with blood.'

'Why did they come? Surely not for the housekeeper?'

'The woman in the house wasn't Albrecht's housekeeper,' Reinmar told him. 'She was a sorceress by the name of Valeria.'

Von Spurzheim looked up at the ceiling, annoyed that no one had been able to tell him that while he still had time to react. 'The lady scholar!' he exclaimed. 'I thought she'd be half way to Middenheim by now. What a thirst she must have to make her put her head into the lion's mouth! Did she exercise power of command over the monks?'

'It certainly seemed that she did,' Reinmar said. 'There might have been a fight had she not told them to leave me be. I doubt that was for mercy's sake. They brought her wine, and she grew young after drinking it – but she did say that the gathering army was nothing to do with her, and that her business was of another kind.'

'She doesn't care about Eilhart,' the witch hunter muttered. 'It's Marienburg that's uppermost in her mind. She may not mean to lend her power to the fight, but she'll use it in one way or another. I'm sorry, lad – I had no idea that I was sending you into a viper's nest. What did your great-uncle do?'

'Nothing,' Reinmar reported, economically. 'He refused to go with them, and they seemed to think him irrelevant to their present concerns.'

'And what did you do?'

'Nothing,' Reinmar said, again. 'I had no chance to draw my blade, and had no reason to think that help would come if I called.'

'But the monks must have recognised you, and they could hardly be of the opinion that you were irrelevant to their concerns,' the witch hunter observed, shrewdly. 'They did not know what you had done when they met you with Matthias as you made your escape from the valley, but they must know now. They let you alone, even so.'

'Because they had more pressing matters to attend to,' Reinmar insisted – but von Spurzheim knew that there had to be more, and Reinmar had to provide a further explanation. 'Albrecht and Valeria were lovers once, as you obviously know, and they had a child. Valeria asked Great-Uncle Albrecht if I were one of them. He implied that I might be, although it was a lie, and it was on that account that she told the monks to leave me alone.'

Von Spurzheim looked at him long and hard before saying: 'And what was the attitude of the monks?'

'They were bitterly angry,' Reinmar told him, uneasily. 'They told her what I had done in the underworld, offering it as proof that I am a dangerous enemy. She would not listen.'

Von Spurzheim might have interrogated him further had he not been in such a hurry, but he shrugged his shoulders then, as if dismissing the matter until a more convenient time. 'Your charmed life may be a more valuable asset than I imagined,' he said wryly. 'Do you know where to report to Sergeant Vaedecker?'

'Yes.'

'Then you had best go. By nightfall, every able-bodied man in town must be thoroughly certain of what his role is to be in the coming conflict. It seems to be coming sooner than I hoped, but we can still win it. We must.' Reinmar opened the door to go out, but von Spurzheim decided that he had not quite finished, adding: 'We are fighting for our lives, Reinmar. Every one of us. No one here can make a private arrangement with destiny. No one.'

'I think my Great-Uncle Albrecht knows that,' Reinmar said, deliberately misunderstanding the real implication of the witch hunter's warning – but the last darkly quizzical look von Spurzheim directed at him before the door closed told Reinmar that the witch hunter knew well enough that his threat had not fallen on deaf ears.

The streets through which Reinmar walked to the neck of the river were very crowded, and everyone he passed was urgently busy. Some were carrying provisions home, or bringing weapons out; others were boarding up windows or strengthening the slots that would hold the bars securing their doors. There were no children out of doors; those who had not been sent away were being kept inside, probably banished to cellars and attics.

Reinmar had never seen so many unsmiling people, or witnessed such a flush of collective anxiety overlaying the pallor of fear.

The docks and warehouses of Eilhart's port were clustered a furlong below the neck of the river, where the waters had been artificially broadened to form a deep pool. The 'neck' qualified as a neck because it had two huge storehouses to either side of a narrow gap, through which the water was forced to flow more rapidly, but there were no quays for unloading. Goods were sometimes lowered into boats from the wide and glassless windows of the storehouses, using block-and-tackle systems strung from jutting beams, but the traffic was one-way. The storehouses were used to stockpile grain, turnips and beets from the surrounding farms, almost all of it for local use. Each had three storeys, with holes cut in each floor through which long ramps extended, also equipped with hauling gear. By the time Reinmar arrived, there was at least one crossbowman at every window – and Reinmar had no difficulty in judging that those at the highest would be least likely to get hurt, always provided that the buildings were not fired. Although the shell of each storehouse was brick, the floors and ramps were wooden.

The windows on the ground were, unfortunately, low-silled and broad. They had been built for the convenience of moving goods out, not keeping invaders at bay. Grain-sacks filled with sand and earth had already been piled up to make the defences higher, and criss-crossed planks had been nailed in place to make the apertures less inviting, but these measures were makeshift at best.

Matthias Vaedecker showed Reinmar which of these openings was to be his station. It was the middle one of three, neither the furthest upriver nor the furthest down, but Reinmar could not see that its position would make much difference to the safety of his situation,

'Any boats moving through the narrows will be easy targets for the bowmen,' the sergeant said, addressing a gathering of all the men assigned to the ground floor of the westernmost storehouse, 'and they are highly unlikely to have as many bows as we have, or any great skill in using them – but they will have clubs and spears, which they will wield with very considerable strength if they get close enough. We have put our best net at the head of the gap and our strongest hawser just behind it, and I don't doubt that we shall wreak havoc among them until those defences are breached – but once the head of the passage is clear of obstruction we have only one more net and two more booms.

'The second net is placed two yards ahead of this middle window, so that those it interrupts will be vulnerable to fire without being able to make overmuch use of their weapons. We must make the most of that vulnerability, because the tide will turn their way if the second net is breached and the entire race fills up with crowded boats.

'Don't become too confident if the fight goes our way at first – the longer it goes on, the harder it will become. The first kills will be ours, but this is not an enemy much given to retreat and they will keep on coming. We must keep on killing, and killing, and killing, until there is nothing left to kill. Whatever happens, we may not retreat.

'The barricades across the roads are tactical positions that might be abandoned if necessity presses, but this gap and these two storehouses are vital to the defence of the town. We do not give way. Whatever happens, we hold our positions to the last man. We may hope for reinforcements if the attack is concentrated here to the exclusion of other vulnerable points, but if no reinforcements come we must fight until we die. Is that understood?'

Looking around, Reinmar could see that it was fully understood by the men wearing colours, who had been in such situations before, but that it had caused great consternation among the townsmen and the farmers who had been assigned to support them. Even so, there was not a man among them who did not want to put on a brave face. They had all heard tales of what had happened to the farms that had been attacked, and they had all seen the bodies in the market place. No one wasted time wondering about the possibility of negotiation or mass evacuation.

'Right,' the sergeant went on, as soon as he had left a decent pause. 'I want every man who has never used a pike or blade for fighting educated to the limit of what can be achieved. My corporals will sort you out into groups, according to your training, and they'll do everything in their power to advance your capability in the time that remains to us. No one is excused, except to take an hour's leave to eat, which we shall do in strict rotation. If any of you have been trained with sword or staff, you'll help with the education of the others.'

There was a deal of confusion then, while all of this was sorted out, but Vaedecker took Reinmar to one side so that he could speak to him confidentially.

'You can take your last leave soon,' the sergeant said, 'but I want you back by six, as I told you before. Pikes and half-pikes will be far more use than swords to begin with, but we haven't enough of them and it will come to swordplay sooner or later. I'll give you two or three willing lads now, while some time still remains to teach them something worthwhile – but whatever you fail to teach them, at least make sure that they don't hurt themselves or one another, and don't leave them exhausted.'

Reinmar promised to heed all this advice, and did so, although it was obvious to him the farmhands given to him for instruction had far more strength than skill. He judged that they would be able to do better with the scythes and pitchforks they had brought than with the rusty swords they had exhumed from long storage, but he tried to educate them anyway. If he accomplished nothing else he showed them how best to balance themselves while they thrust, and how to minimise the target they presented to an enemy.

As soon as he was given leave to go, Reinmar hurried off home. He was hungry and thirsty, but he was also anxious about what Albrecht had said to him before he went to meet the sergeant.

The shop was closed but the door had not been barred; Reinmar obtained entry readily enough. He called down to the cellars but obtained no reply; there was no sign of his father, or Godrich. That was not in the least strange, given that they must have been ordered to report for assignment exactly as he had. He ran upstairs and went immediately to Marcilla's room. He found her alone there, but she was as fast asleep as she had been before he left, and seemingly quite tranquil. He knelt beside her pallet and took her hand in his own, but he was gentle because he did not want to wake her. He made certain that there was fresh water by her pillow, and a piece of bread, before he tiptoed away.

It was possible, Reinmar supposed, that Ulick had gone with Godrich and his father to claim a role in the defence of the town, but he dared not make that assumption. He closed the gypsy's door as quietly as he could before making his way to his own room. He wanted to make sure that the phial he had stolen from the underworld was still where he had put it before he went to find something to eat.

He realised as soon as he opened the door that something had gone badly awry. The odour that filled the room struck him dumb and motionless.

Chapter Twenty-Nine

There was a stranger in Reinmar's bedroom, standing in front of the mirror on the wall and studying himself carefully. More remarkably still, the stranger had put on Reinmar's best suit of clothes. The man was taller and better-proportioned than Wirnt, although his features were not entirely dissimilar – but they were no more similar to Wirnt's than they were to Gottfried's, or even Reinmar's own. The stranger seemed much younger than Wirnt, though not as young as Reinmar, but the gleam in his eye was as bright and as startling as the luminosity that Reinmar had seen in the eyes of the aged priest in the underworld as he offered Marcilla's comatose body to the avid flower.

The hectic nature of that brightness did not reveal itself fully until the stranger turned to look Reinmar in the face. It was as if the intelligence behind the eyes had caught fire, burning out of control. This is a madman, Reinmar thought – which seemed to make it all the more remarkable that the man might have been mistaken for his father's younger brother, had his father had a brother.

It was not until the sweetly cloying odour that saturated the atmosphere of the room released its grip on his thoughts that

Reinmar realised that the resemblance might be less remarkable than it seemed.

'Damn you, child,' the stranger said. 'Have you nothing in your wardrobe that a man might wear with pride?'

'Grandfather?' Reinmar asked, falteringly.

He could not quite believe it, no matter how likely it had seemed as a matter of calculation. He was too accustomed to seeing Luther Wieland as a frail old man, as broken in spirit as he was in body. This man was not merely hale, but keen and poised in spite of the uncanny fervour in his eyes. He still seemed mad, but he also seemed a man of action, a man of real power.

'You're a liar as well as a fool,' Luther Wieland said, accusingly. 'Were you saving the draught for your pretty plaything? Was not your first loyalty to me? And why should you worry, when you had such a powerful potion? Did you not know what you had? You could have diluted it a hundred times and filled a rack in the cellar with the produce. Well, it's mine now. Did you really think that your hiding-place was safe, when you knew full well that this room belonged to me when I was a boy like you?'

The stranger stabbed a stern finger in the direction of the slit in the wall, from which the mortar had been snatched. The questions poured out of him, glorying in their own profusion; it was as if a rusted tap had finally been freed to turn. There was nothing loving in the stranger's expression. His eyes were darker as well as brighter than the old Luther Wieland's, and the darkness was not merely a matter of colour. Reinmar did not doubt that this man was as dangerous as his enfeebled grandfather had been harmless.

'Monsters are coming, grandfather,' Reinmar said, swiftly. 'An entire legion of them. There are men of a sort, albeit deformed, but there are half-men too, whose human flesh is mixed with animal. There will be worse, if Sergeant Vaedecker's judgement can be trusted. All Eilhart is panic-stricken. This is not a good time to make yourself manifest as a sorcerer.'

'Sorcerer!' the rejuvenated Luther's laugh was bitterly sarcastic. 'Is that what you think, child? I thought you had more sense than that ungrateful whelp of mine. I thought that you and I had an understanding. I am no magician, but I am a man. I am everything that a man is supposed to be – which is to say that I am not a wasted, helpless, fatuous cripple, victimised by cruel time. I am a man, Reinmar, alive and capable of feeling. All the pain is gone, and all the ignominy. Gods, what a fool I was! To consent to become what my vile son made of me! What a wreck of a man I was miserably content to be, when all that I needed to restore myself was an occasional goblet of wine. How could I be so stupid? I have always tried to give you better advice than that snake, Gottfried, but I was never capable of giving strength to it till now. Listen to me Reinmar, and listen well: time is the ultimate traitor, the worst of all curses. Today you have the gift of youth, but through all your tomorrows you will pay an extortionate price for that fleeting privilege. Fight, Reinmar – fight the tyranny of time with every last vestige of your strength and spirit. Never consent to be bound by its curses. Fight, with every magic that the world can offer!'

'Grandfather,' Reinmar said, feeling quite weak now that the odour of the nectar of dreams had vanished from the air, 'you do not understand how that liquor you have drunk is fed and formed. It is the produce of living human flesh.'

'Of course it is!' the restored man answered, throwing his arms up flamboyantly. 'And how is your own youth any different? Is its origin any more comfortable to contemplate, when seen with an analytical eye? All flesh is the product of flesh, all youth the product of youth. Our mothers are diminished by the childbirth that makes us, and we accept their willing sacrifice as the price of our own virility. What real difference is there between the sacrifice of maternal flesh and the one that you saw? We are men, child, and we must sustain our manhood against the vicious ravages of time by any means we find. If we must fight to do it, we must fight with all our strength – and we ought to love the battle with all the fury of our hearts.'

The leather belt that Luther had fastened about his waist was not Reinmar's, nor was the pouch attached to it. Those had come from his own trunk. Reinmar assumed that the phial he had stolen from the underworld was now in that pouch. He wondered how much Luther had drunk. Even a single sip might qualify as an overdose.

'You won't find it easy to leave the town, grandfather,' Reinmar said stubbornly, 'And if you stay, you'll be recognised soon enough as an enemy. Our neighbours are in a mood to turn on anyone they can blame for their plight.'

'How will I be recognised? Will you denounce me as a sorcerer, even though I swear to you that I am a man like any other? Is there any man in Eilhart who would recognise me, if I were in any room but this, regarded by any eye but yours? Why should you or anyone think me an enemy? Why did you bring me the dark wine, if you did not want to see me as a man?'

As before, there were far too many questions in this torrent for Reinmar to formulate any coherent reply to any one of them. They were well enough formed, and challenging, but they were too abundant and too inconsequential to form part of any rational conversation. Reinmar looked more closely at his grandfather's fine new features, and saw that they had something of the same reckless quality. Luther Wieland rejuvenated was a handsome man – considerably more handsome than his son, Gottfried – but there was a profoundly unnatural extravagance in the colour of his cheeks and the heat of his gaze. The life restored to Luther by the nectar of the underworld was too feverish, too assertive in its grip upon his soul – but how could he possibly have resisted the temptation to take too generous a dose of the concentrated essence, when he had been so weak and tremulous before?

'What will you do, grandfather?' Reinmar asked, struggling to keep his voice quiet and even. 'Will you fight for Eilhart, or against it?'

'Am I a man or a monster?' Luther retorted.

'At this moment, I am not entirely sure,' Reinmar told him. 'That is why I ask.'

'If I fight at all, I shall fight for glory,' the handsome man assured him. 'If I condescend to fight, I shall fight for love of conflict, because I am a man.'

'It seems to me,' Reinmar said, pensively, 'that a surfeit of humanity might be almost as dangerous and almost as daemonic, in its way, as a lack of it.'

'Then you're a fool and a coward, child,' Luther snapped back at him. 'Human life is sensation, and the best sensation is luxury. There is no higher end.' He moved away from the mirror at last, and made as if to push past Reinmar and leave the room.

Reinmar stood where he was, and would not be thrust aside. 'What will you do with the phial and its contents, grandfather?' he asked.

'Keep it and use it, what else?' the other informed him, scornfully. 'You matched your wits against mine and you lost. The girl can fend for herself, and you must let her go her own way. In the end, she'll heed the summons graved within her flesh, and there's nothing you can do to hold her back. Now stand aside – and never get in my way again. Never.'

Reinmar hesitated, but he could hardly draw his blade against his own grandfather, so he stood aside and let Luther stride from the room. As he listened to the retreating footsteps, as Luther bounded down the steps two at a time, he felt an odd thrill within his own limbs. It was as if some slight leakage of the rejuvenated man's joy in the recovery of his power had entered into him.

Reinmar found the stray piece of mortar on the floor, and replaced it in the slot in the wall. Perhaps it was a good thing, he thought, that the nectar had been taken out of his hands. Perhaps the responsibility had been too much to bear. But his hands were trembling when he heard footsteps ascending the stair again, in a much more sedate fashion.

When Gottfried Wieland appeared in the doorway of his son's room his expression seemed incredibly tired and drained by comparison with Luther's. It was also pained, and accusing.

'You brought him dark wine,' Gottfried said dully. 'In spite of everything you saw, you brought him the wine of dreams.'

'It's worse than that,' Reinmar confessed. 'I stole a little of the nectar from which the dark wine is made. I would not have given it to him, but he found it. I think he has taken too much.'

'The slightest sip would be too much for him,' Gottfried replied, acidly. 'He's been too long unhinged to gain anything from luxury but recklessness.'

'He seemed a little more clear-headed when he left,' Reinmar suggested. 'The madness was less intense than it was while the odour lingered.'

'Why didn't you give it to the witch hunter?' Gottfried demanded.

'I don't know,' Reinmar said, defensively. 'I don't even know why I took it in the first place.'

'Have you eaten?'

Reinmar, slightly startled by the change of subject, put his hand reflexively to his belly. 'No,' he admitted.

'You must. Everyone now seems certain that there'll be fighting tonight, even if the worst of it is some days off. Who's your commander and where's your station?'

'Vaedecker – I think he asked for me. The storehouse at the neck of the river.'

Reinmar saw Gottfried's eyes grow slightly wider. 'That's a compliment you might regret,' he said, 'but he demanded Sigurd too and I had to send him, not an hour ago. If that's where you are there's all the more need to fill your belly. You haven't much time, I suppose?'

'Less than half an hour now,' Reinmar admitted.

Gottfried was already drawing him out of the room and down the stair. 'All the servants have gone to their families,' the wine merchant said. 'Godrich asked for a station at the warehouse, and got it, but it would not have been diplomatic for me to do likewise. I'm on the western approach – difficult ground, but tenable. We'll eat what we can in the kitchen, and then make parcels of anything left over. We'll split a bottle of hock now, and we'll each take another with us – but you'll have to share what you eat and drink at your post.'

When they got to the kitchen they found that its supplies had already been severely depleted by the servants, but a man as careful as Gottfried always kept good reserves. There was no bread left, but there were various salted meats and pickled vegetables, a few bruised apples, a little butter and some sugar. Reinmar and his father ate while they packed up what they could.

'If there are no servants here,' Reinmar dared to ask, 'who will tend to Marcilla?'

'Marguerite might look in, if I leave a key with her father,' Gottfried said. 'If not, the gypsy will have to fend for herself if and when she wakes.'

'Where's Ulick?'

'I've no idea.'

Reinmar paused before saying: 'This impending battle really isn't my fault, father.'

Gottfried looked genuinely startled by that. 'Of course it's not.' he said. 'I told you before not to blame yourself. It was inevitable from the moment the witch hunter arrived. The monsters began massing before you left in the wagon – I was a fool to send you out, but I was afraid that we might all be thrown in jail if Luther or Albrecht said the wrong thing, or nothing at all. This is a settlement of debts that were contracted long before you and I were born, when Eilhart first became involved in the trade in dark wine. I always knew that I couldn't stop the trade, but I hoped to postpone the reckoning a while, and I did. None of this is your fault. None of it.'

'I tried to destroy the supplies of wine stored in the underworld – but I stole a measure of the nectar too. That, I fear, was twice a provocation.'

'These things need no provocation,' Gottfried assured him. 'Their only intent is harm and their subtler sorceries are worse, in the long run, than brute assault. They have raised an army to fight von Spurzheim, not to punish you. If they desire to do that too – and they might – they'll use subtler means than cold iron and brute force. Eilhart is under threat because the world is under threat, and the world is under threat because there is malice abroad, not because of anything that you or I, or even that old fool Luther, has done. Don't blame yourself for giving Luther what he wanted so desperately – the desire was his, after all, and the craving was all that was keeping him alive.'

Reinmar could not remember his father ever delivering such a calculated and uncritical speech. It scared him, for it let him know how desperate the situation was. If Gottfried Wieland had been intimidated into giving his generosity free rein, the world must indeed be on the brink of disaster.

'I'm glad Sigurd will be close by, when the battle starts,' Reinmar said, as he finished the dregs of wine from the jar that he and his father had been passing back and forth.

'So am I,' said Gottfried. 'If you have to stand back-to-back with anyone, choose him. If you have to slip past Vaedecker to seize the position, do it.'

'And who will you stand back-to-back with, if the fighting comes to that?' Reinmar asked.

'I'll make up my mind about that when I've seen how the fighting goes,' Gottfried told him, dourly. 'Some hardened infantryman, I suppose. Not one of my fellow tradesmen, if I can help it – and not one of von Spurzheim's zealots. With luck, all I'll have to do is stand and cheer while the Reiksguard cavalry charges from the marketplace and the bowmen let fly. You'd best go now. I have to make sure that the shop and the cellars are locked up as tightly as possible – there's something about a battle that loosens people's respect for their neighbours' property.'

'But you'll leave a key for Marguerite?' Reinmar said.

'If you insist. Go. Take an extra jar for Sigurd.'

Reinmar obediently picked up an extra jar of wine, although he was already more than amply burdened. Then he said goodbye, hoping as he said it that it would not be the last goodbye he ever had to offer, and that it would not be the last that his father ever had to receive.

CHAPTER THIRTY

REINMAR HAD TO trot through the streets in order to be back at his post before the market bell chimed six, but he took what comfort he could from the fact that the alarm had not yet been sounded.

As he neared the top of the slope, he could see plumes of smoke ascending into the sky from distant barns and houses that had been sacked and set alight, and the deepening blue of the evening sky was already tinged with purple and pink. He looked back toward the north, and saw the surly glow of airborne smoke particles there too. No one had thought that the beastmen and their allies could have moved so swiftly to surround the town – but the fact that they had must mean that their forces were spread thinner than they would have wished. So Reinmar told himself, at least.

Once he was inside the storehouse, he found Sigurd easily enough and gave him the wine. Sigurd was surprised to see him; Matthias Vaedecker had obviously not taken the trouble to share the news that Reinmar had been conscripted to his command. 'You should not be here, Master Wieland,' the giant said. 'You are too young to be thrust into the first line of defence. Far too young.'

'I'd rather be with the best soldiers than the worst,' Reinmar told him. 'There'll be no safety anywhere until the battle is won.'

'True enough,' Sigurd conceded. 'Stay close to me, sir. If we fall, we'll fall together – but there's no monster born that can bring us to that. If it were you and I against the world, we'd come through unscathed.'

'It certainly won't come to that,' Reinmar assured him. 'Von Spurzheim's come this far – he won't be beaten now. He'll crush the enemy, and then he'll march on the valley and the underworld beneath the monastery. He's irresistible.' He deliberately made no mention of magic, although he had taken leave to wonder privately whether von Spurzheim's close retinue included priests who might try to neutralise any spells that might be cast by the likes of the lady Valeria.

'That's the spirit, lad,' another voice broke in, eager to join the conversation. It was one of Vaedecker's infantrymen, who did not know either of them but obviously thought it worth the trouble to cultivate their acquaintance. 'From what I've seen, the things we have to fight are the dregs of the enemy's reserves – nasty but unskilled. They'll be tough, but by no means unbeatable. At the end of the day, even the best of them are little better than animals. We're men.'

Reinmar could not help but remember his grandfather's similarly insistent assurances of his own humanity. 'Do you think they'll come tonight?' he asked. 'Von Spurzheim said this morning that they probably would not come until tomorrow night.'

'Oh yes,' said the infantryman, sounding like a man who had learned much from experience. 'They'll come tonight, even though it's too soon to allow them proper preparation. They've already begun the work of slaughter, and once that kind begin, they can't be made to pause. They're animals: cunning, but not clever; vicious, but not artful. They're coming now – and as soon as they arrive, we'll be in the thick of it. But we'll win. As you say, we're irresistible.'

It was all too obvious that the soldier was trying hard to convince himself – and Reinmar recognised the wisdom of making that kind of effort, for his own and everyone else's benefit. He got up and went to find Matthias Vaedecker, who was still trying to drum some semblance of discipline into the dullest of the townsmen.

'They're ready, sergeant,' Reinmar said, quietly. Then he raised his voice in order to add: 'This is their home, after all. They'll defend it with every last vestige of their strength. Eilhart is the best town on the Schilder. Nobody who lives here will do anything less than his best to save it from the vermin that are determined to foul it.'

Matthias Vaedecker looked at him, and grinned. 'Master Wieland!' he said, raising his own voice rather more than was necessary. 'Another brave slayer of beastmen! I'll take your word for it – you know these people better than I.' But when he had dismissed the men, and told them to rest a while, he became much graver.

'It's going to be bad, Reinmar,' he said confidentially. 'You and I have seen what they've been summoned to defend. It's no mere patch of ground. News of its existence is already speeding northwards, so another army will certainly come if von Spurzheim fails, and another after that, but we've been on the road for a long time. No one else has von Spurzheim's knowledge, or his conviction. Whoever comes in his stead, if anyone has to, won't be half as determined to find the valley, let alone to prevent the supply-line from renewing itself. For a prize like this one, the enemy will likely send forth daemons as well as brutes, and this is the point they'll be most anxious to breach in order to strike at von Spurzheim himself. I don't know how insanely suicidal they're prepared to be, but I know that it's going to be bad.'

'But in the end, we're irresistible,' Reinmar said, wryly. 'We're men, after all, and they're monsters.'

'It's precisely because we're men that we're no more irresistible than they are,' the sergeant replied – but the reply was a whisper, spoken softly so that no one else would overhear it. Reinmar felt oddly privileged to be the chosen recipient of such a dangerous truth, but he soon went back to his station to sit down with Sigurd.

The time dragged on with such painful slowness that Reinmar almost began to wish that the enemy would appear and put an end to his suspense. Given that an attack was now inevitable, he thought, it might be best to get it over with. He was obviously not the only one who felt that way, but all that came down the river between six and midnight were two sharpened tree-trunks, neither of which broke through the nets that the defenders had strung across the flow.

'They can send as many of those as they wish,' Vaedecker called to his men. 'They're the ones who'll be fighting from the water, not us.'

When the market bell struck midnight a tangible ripple of tension passed through the crowd, but it was no alarm signal; the hour came and passed like its predecessors. Half an hour afterwards, though, a different missile came floating down the river: an oarless rowboat whose interior had been stuffed with oil-soaked chaff and kindling. The chaff had been set alight, and by the time the nets caught the boat it was ablaze like a giant candle. The nets, being beneath the surface, were not in the slightest danger of catching fire, but the light of the fire reflected from the faces of the waiting bowmen and the projecting heads of the pikes that had been laid down on the lowest floor.

'The light won't tell them anything they don't already know,' Vaedecker called out, as promptly as before. 'It's just a gesture, intended to unsettle us. When the time comes to fight, fire on the water will be our ally, not theirs.'

The fire in the boat died down to mere embers, and finally sputtered out. It was then that the enemy came, perhaps hoping to gain some tiny advantage from the afterglow that the flames had left in the defenders' eyes. The boats came swiftly, skimming the surface while their occupants lay flat, with blades ready to attack the nets.

The signal must have passed like lightning into the centre of the town, for the market bell immediately began to jangle wildly, sounding the call to arms.

'Bowmen ready!' Vaedecker shouted. 'Pikemen stand by!' It was the last order he was able to give so clearly, for heavier boats were making their way down the river behind the first few, and these were loaded with fighting-men. Some, no doubt, were beastmen with the voices of beasts, but even those which had human throats and tongues gave voice in a markedly bestial fashion as soon as the arrows began to fly.

Reinmar leaned forward to see what was happening, but Sigurd pulled him back from the lip of the opening at which he crouched, anxious that he might present a target to an enemy bowman. For this reason, he heard rather than saw the bolts fired by Vaedecker's crossbowmen as they rained down upon the boats, slapping into the wooden hulls and clicking into the water. He saw arrows hurtling into the warehouse, and immediately wished that the openings in its flanks could have been smaller, but the pikemen were crouching very low, waiting for their turn without exposing themselves. Vaedecker was still shouting, punctuating his commands with curses whenever they did not have the desired effect. The war-cries of the beastmen and their subhuman allies were mingled with screams, but as the noise grew it became increasingly difficult to tell the difference between howls of aggression and howls of pain.

The noise seemed to take hold of Reinmar's heart, almost as if it were a kind of magic, forcing the pace of its beating to increase. It seemed, too, that the beat became lurchingly unsteady. Reinmar hoped that that, at least, was only an illusion.

Reinmar never heard Vaedecker give the order, but the pikemen closest to the north side of the building and those at the middle aperture – including Sigurd – began to pick up their weapons. A full-length pike was so long, and its head so heavy, that no one but a giant could thrust repeatedly, especially at an awkward angle, so the weapons were not yet of much use, but the fact that they had been taken in hand at all testified to the fact that the heavier boats must have drawn in close to the warehouse walls, waiting only for the clearance of the nets and the boom that were preventing their further progress.

'What's happening?' Reinmar shouted at Sigurd.

The only authentically human voice he could hear for a few moments afterwards was Vaedecker's, as he urged his crossbowmen to fire and fire again and to make every bolt count, but Sigurd did eventually turn. 'Not long!' was what he shouted – which Reinmar took to mean that the nets had been cut to shreds, and that only the metal hawser forming the boom was offering significant resistance to the passage of the boats.

The logs had been sent down first in order to increase the load on the boom, and the boats were increasing that stress with every minute that passed, but Reinmar knew that the creatures within the boats must be paying a heavy price. Arrows and crossbow bolts would thin them out – and when the boom finally broke, the pikemen at his own station would seize their own opportunity.

Reinmar tried hard to force himself to be still, fearful that he might start trembling long before he was actually drawn into the action. His self-discipline seemed effective, and he felt the thump of his heartbeat ease a little. The boom was still holding, it seemed, and everything was going to plan.

And then, within the space of half a second, the plan went wrong.

All of a sudden there were two fronts and not one. The watchmen at the doors to the street set up a clamour of their own, and men wielding swords and half-pikes began to pour through into the interior of the storehouse. The lanterns set above the doorways reassured Reinmar that they were men, some wearing Reiksguard colours and others having faces that he knew, but he realised immediately that they were in retreat, and that the barricade they had been manning must already have been breached.

Matthias Vaedecker was shouting at the top of his voice, and Reinmar knew – even though he could not make out more than one word in three – that he had to come into the action now. He and the other swordsmen had to make sure that anyone or anything that was not one of the town's defenders would die as soon as he or it passed through either of the two broad doorways that opened on to the street. Alas, the feeble attempts that the watchmen made to close the doors once they had admitted their retreating allies were immediately cancelled out, for the pursuers already had battering-rams in play, having presumably used them to smash through the barricade at the north end of the street. Both doors were thrust back again and the battering rams kept on coming, their sharpened heads aimed at the backs and legs of the defenders.

Those among the fleeing men who knew what they were about tried to turn as soon as they were inside, but there were too many among them who did not know, whose further attempts to dodge and find positions of safety interfered with the rank of defenders that was forming to cover their retreat and carry the fight back to the enemy.

The squat figures who were carrying the head of the ram on their shoulders were ready targets, but they took a dozen cuts apiece before they went down, and there were more behind them to maintain the ram's momentum for a few precious seconds more. That was all the time required to clear the doorways and make a way in, and by the time Reinmar had joined something resembling a proper formation of spearmen and swordsmen the chance to seal the breach had gone.

As the rams bounced and rolled, knocking more defenders down, the enemy produced enough swords and spears of their own to make the fight seem almost even. It was, at any rate, even enough to be fierce.

There was light enough for Reinmar to see the faces of the creatures ranged against him. He was slightly surprised to see that only a few were significantly unhuman, but the rest made up for their lack of literal bestiality with as much sheer ugliness as he had ever seen packed into human features. Their eyebrows were huge, their chins jutting and their gritted teeth were yellow and overlarge. They were exceptionally hairy, and a few had so many warts as to seem toadlike, but they had hands and they had minds, and the manner in which they wielded their clubs and blades spoke of practised skill and malign intelligence. When they leapt forward they were undeniably reckless, but they were not by any means easy targets.

As soon as Reinmar had thrust forwards for the first time, and felt his blade connect with something hard, he knew that he was in terrible danger. The line of which he was a part had been too hastily-formed, and the men in it too lightly drilled. It was already ragged, and at dire risk of fragmentation – but it had to hold, or the entire space within the vast storehouse would become a chaotic battle-zone. If the men at the riverside were to continue doing their job they needed to be covered; they had to be able to devote their entire attention to the battle on the water, or it would be lost within an hour.

Fortunately, Reinmar was not the only man who knew that the line had to hold, and Vaedecker's men were not about to let the failings of farm-hands and shopkeepers ruin their formation. Those with half-pikes were already drawing a picket-line, with swordsmen between them – and their precision was so plainly manifest that even the most thick-headed townsmen could see what they were about and why. Reinmar inserted himself smoothly enough into a position between two men who knew exactly how to lay about them with the heads of their half-pikes, and as soon as they saw that he knew how to ply his sword they gave him room to do it. Their weapons were heavier than anything the enemy forces had, and it required considerable luck as well as skill for any enemy to get past the sharpened blades.

As soon as any enemy did, Reinmar was ready, the point of his sword licking out with confidence as well as alacrity, aiming for the throat if he could and the belly if he could not. His adversaries thrust back, of course, but the squat builds that had been to their advantage while they hoisted the rams were not nearly so useful in this kind of a fight, and even the one that thrust at him with a spear was too slow and too clumsy.

Reinmar twisted to let the head of the weapon pass his chest without cutting the cloth of his jerkin, and by the time the spearman tried to ram the shaft sideways into his ribs Reinmar's sword had run right through his adversary's eye into his brain. It would have been a bad stroke in a more open fight, because it took him several seconds to wrench the blade free again and bring it back into play, but with the blades of the half-pikes hovering nearby there was no chance that any enemy could take advantage of his pause.

By the time Reinmar had freed his blade he had to take a great stride forward, for the line was in motion. The battering rams lay still now, and even those 'spearmen' who had only pitchforks had seen how things were working out, and where they were required. The enemy was being harassed in the street as well as in the storehouse, and their numbers were being cut back too quickly; the fury of their assault had won them ground but it had cost too dear, and the townsmen were far better deployed to reinforce their compromised position.

Reinmar had expected the ugly folk to fight like wild things, but he remembered now that even the beastmen he had fought in the little wood had shown a certain tactical acumen. These squat subhumans were by no means undisciplined, and they understood strategy well enough to know that there was no point pressing forward once a cause was hopeless. It was their turn to make a solid formation as they fell back to the doorways, and they did it with almost as much efficiency as might have been expected of Vaedecker's infantrymen.

Are they soldiers after all, Reinmar wondered? Are they mercenaries, who know fighting as a business rather than a mania? Perhaps they are – and perhaps we shall see far worse very soon, when all the strategy has been worked out and the fight turns to madness. He did not cease thrusting with his sword while he took leave to wonder, but the bloody blade cleaved nothing but air now as the brutes fell back and exercised due wariness. The creatures blocked the thrusts of the half-pikes quite comfortably now that Vaedecker's men had aching arms.

Had the townsmen in the street managed to form up on the outside of the doorways they could have cut the retreating half-men to ribbons, but the battle in the street was still raging and the last dozen of the invaders slipped out easily. One of Vaedecker's corporals immediately began shouting to his men to secure the doorways and not to let anyone in or out. The corporal began grabbing townsmen one by one, thrusting them either in the direction of the doorways or back towards the unloading-platforms, where support was still required.

Reinmar moved towards the river without waiting for selection, intending to take back his position beside Sigurd.

Chapter Thirty-One

SIGURD WAS BUSY now and could not keep Reinmar from looking out on to the river's foaming surface.

The first boom had been breached, so the crowded company of boats had moved forty yards downriver, but its vanguard had been caught and held by the second barrier. The men and beastmen in the boats were able to shoot and thrust at the townsfolk defending the storehouses to either side of them, but by virtue of being trapped in crossfire – and directly beneath the crossbows positioned in the upper storeys – they were taking very heavy casualties indeed.

Reinmar immediately saw, and fully understood, that beastmen were in the majority here, and that this was no measured move of a kind that mercenaries might have calculated and executed. The creatures on the boats were hurling missiles in every direction, howling insanely as they did so, leaping at the ledges like mad dogs – but these were far less like dogs than the wolf-like beastmen surprised by Godrich's runaway wagon. These were even more nightmarish than the bodies that had been laid out in the marketplace, with horny heads and blazing eyes, and claws instead of hands.

The contrast between this fight and the one that Reinmar had just helped to win was so striking that a lump rose in his throat, making it impossible for him to swallow. There was nothing useful he could do, as yet, because the long-handled pikes were still doing more than adequate damage in the hands of men who had the strength and skill to wield them – and Sigurd was doing as much damage as any of Vaedecker's veterans, by virtue of his reach and power.

The crossbowmen had done the bulk of their work and they were now conserving their bolts, although they remained ready to pick off selected targets. Most of the pikemen, Reinmar saw, were using their weapons as much to push as to cut, tumbling the beastmen into the water rather than striking deep into their skulls and torsos. Sigurd was the only one who was using the blade of his pike almost as if it were an elongated battle-axe, slashing at faces and limbs.

Reinmar presumed that the regulars knew what they were doing, but he could not help feeling direly anxious when he saw that in spite of their crazy anatomy the beastmen were able to swim. Those which had been thrust into the water were in considerable danger of being crushed by the jostling boats, but those which could avoid being caught were able to tread water well enough. They were waiting impatiently, but they were waiting nevertheless for an opportunity to rejoin the fight to some effect, and in the meantime others of their kind were working away at the second barrier.

Reinmar could see that the nets had already been sliced up by the beastmen's curiously dextrous claws, and he judged that the boom could not last more than a few minutes. He gripped his sword tightly, in anticipation of its further employment.

'Ready, lad?' Sigurd shouted above the din, audible only because Reinmar was fast by his side.

By way of answer Reinmar raised the bloodstained tip of his sword. He was ready – and he knew that he had to be, because the fight was about to become much fiercer. Once the enemy was able to use the river as a way into the heart of the town another incursion like the one that had battered down the warehouse doors would not be as easily turned back, because there would be no reinforcements ready to rush forward. Once the river was open, every man in the town would be in the thick of the action. Then, and only then, would the relative strength of the two companies become clear. Then, and only then, would the defenders discover exactly what kind of monsters the enemy would employ to take advantage of the inroads made by its shock troops.

Reinmar rested the tip of his sword on the ground, conserving the muscles of his arm. He could see that even Sigurd's arms were beginning to falter now. Pikes were most useful when their hind ends could be embedded in soil and their heads directed forward like a wall of giant thorns at charging cavalry. They were not meant to be wielded like glorified spears, and Sigurd was paying the price of his unorthodoxy. Reinmar could not see another pikeman who did not have the butt of his weapon grounded, nor could he see a single one whose brow was not covered by the sweat of extended effort. Even so, the beastmen were fighting at closer quarters than they had been a few moments before. They were dying in considerable numbers, but they were still coming recklessly for more. Not only were they coming, but they were beginning to make good headway.

Two in three pikes had now been grasped by clawed arms stronger than the tired limbs of their owners. Beastmen were actually using the weapons deployed against them as levers and ladders. There were defenders in the water now as well as attackers, and the attackers had the advantage there – whether the swimmers were townsfolk or Vaedecker's regulars they had no expertise at all in fighting on the water, and the sheer animal fury of their adversaries would have been decisive even if they had not been so heavily outnumbered.

More and more beastmen were scrabbling at the ledges of the unloading-bays now, and there were too few blades available to thrust them all back. Sigurd was the last man to drop his pike, but drop it he did, then turned to snatch up his staff – the weapon to which he was most accustomed. 'Now! Now! Now!' he was shouting, at Reinmar and everyone else around him, although none of them could have been in the least doubt that the utmost effort was called for, and that the battle for the storehouse would be won or lost within a quarter of an hour.

Then the second boom broke, and the third almost immediately afterwards. Reinmar knew that the greater battle for the fate of Eilhart passed into its second and deadlier phase – but so had the lesser conflict which was his part in it. From now on, there would be no letup until the battle was decided.

Reinmar had to focus absolutely on the matter of survival.

Vaedecker's infantrymen were already trying to form a defensive line so that the enemy might be confronted with an uninterrupted series of blades, but they had taken casualties and some of their number were still out of place, having been sent to defend the doors on the other side of the building.

The earlier skirmish had been easily won, but it had taken its toll on the organisation, deployment and readiness of the trained soldiers. Now the townspeople had to show what they could do against creatures out of a nightmare. Reinmar and Sigurd placed themselves in the line, and were immediately engaged in furious action.

Reinmar stuck very fast to Sigurd's left-hand side, not merely for his own protection but because the giant needed a blade to assist the work of his staff. Because it had no heavy metal head Sigurd's weapon was less effective than it might have been at cracking skulls, but the advantage of its relative lightness meant that the big man could move it with lightning speed.

Tired though his arms were by their exertions with the pike, Sigurd's reflexes were unimpaired, and as the monsters clambered up out of the water he struck them hard, two or even three at a time. Some fell back into the river, while any that did not sprawled on the stone floor, wide open to the thrusts of Reinmar's blade. Reinmar thrust and thrust and thrust again, but the targets kept re-presenting themselves, and every target had arms and claws, and legs and claws, and a brutal head with horns that might be as long as a man's arm.

Swordplay had always seemed reasonably easy to Reinmar while in training, when thrusts were only intended to demonstrate the possibility of harm. He had thought then that he had an aptitude for this kind of work, but he realised now that an 'aptitude' was not much use in a real fight, where raw power and endurance were the most decisive factors. Reinmar had already discovered that actually doing harm was far more awkward and bruising than merely demonstrating a capacity, and the beastmen climbing out of the bloody water rammed that lesson home.

It had been bad enough trying to cut the squat subhumans or the wolfheads, but the kinds of beastmen that faced Reinmar now were far more difficult to hurt. Not one of them wore artificial armour, but that was because they did not seem to need it. Their clawed arms, in particular, were encased in impenetrable shells, and the horns atop their heads were not merely decorative, always moving this way and that to parry blows of every sort with stubborn solidity.

Reinmar tried at first to aim for the softer parts of the beastmen – their bellies and their throats – but such thrusts were too easily turned aside and ineffectual even when they drew blood. He realised that if he were to strike disabling blows he had to find a weakness that was more easily exploitable. When his sword had bounced off clawed limbs three or four times, though, he realised that there was a disadvantage in the kind of integral armour that the beastmen had. The limbs of such creatures were not nearly as clever as human limbs, because they were too rigidly articulated – and the joints were their most vulnerable points. No fatal wounds could be inflicted by thrusting at what the beastmen had instead of elbows and wrists, but once their claws became unusable they became dead weights, worse than useless.

Reinmar shouted this advice at the top of his voice to anyone who might be listening, but there was no way of knowing whether anyone could hear or understand him. For his own part, he continued thrusting, left then right, then left again, as Sigurd's busy staff set up targets for him and deflected any weapon aimed at his head or heart. Reinmar had to look out for his own feet, but he was a great deal nimbler than beastmen of these cumbersome kinds, and he felt fully entitled to consider himself an aggressor, in command of the manner and tempo of the fight.

That changed. By slow and gradual degrees their situation was transformed, and not to their advantage. He and Sigurd were driven back from the water's edge, one step at a time. As they were driven back they were parted from the swordsmen and spearmen who had tried to form a line with them, and who were also being driven back now that gaps had appeared where men had fallen.

Reinmar knew that he and Sigurd had to delay for as long as possible the eventuality that would force them to stand back to back, isolated from all other support and devoid of further choices. If that time came, he knew, their little fraction of the battle would be all but lost – but in trying to force exactly that situation, their enemies were taking substantial losses. The beastmen who were lunging at them refused to die, but now they seemed to have very little, save for their own awful mass, with which to threaten the defenders. Reinmar, Sigurd and their immediate companions had rendered too many claws completely useless with heavy blows and pricking wounds, and the bloated eyes of the foul creatures were becoming very vulnerable as their horns became less adept.

Had the bull-horned beastmen been the last wave of the enemy force that was attempting to storm the storehouse, the battle to defend it would probably have been won within a few more minutes – but they were only second-line forces, little more than human battering-rams intended to sow confusion and gain space. It was impossible to read expressions in their unhuman faces and horrid eyes, but they fought more like automata than men, with dour purpose but no real fervour.

The creatures that came after them were very different, far more frightening and vastly more dangerous.

Chapter Thirty-Two

Even when they had all contrived to clamber up from the boats that had brought them, the newcomers were no more than six in number, sent against a company of defenders that still numbered nearly a hundred, but these were monsters of a far more extravagant kind than any the defenders had seen before.

They were six-limbed, their hindquarters being reptilian, save for the fact that they had massive stings like scorpions. Their forequarters had the merest hint of humanity about the articulations of their arms, but these were clawed like those of the horned beastmen. Their heads were insectile, with large compound eyes, but their mouths were like circular sphincters from which huge tentacular tongues extended like writhing snakes. They were huge, longer and taller than horses.

These enemies, unlike their predecessors, were silent – which allowed Matthias Vaedecker the opportunity to be heard again.

'Blademen fall back!' he was screaming. 'Bowmen, shoot! Flood the fiends with arrows! Now! Now!'

Reinmar had hardly had time to take note of the multifarious stink that had permeated the storehouse during the earlier phases of the fight. His nose had been numbed by the sharp odour of the burning chaff, and while he had been panting with exertion he had been breathing through his mouth. The odour of the ichor shed by the horned beastmen was far less sweet and cloying than the scent of blood, and its malignity had undermined the disgust that normally attached to other odours typical of mortal combat. Reinmar became briefly aware of that obscene odiferous chorus now, though, because it was suddenly compounded and swiftly overwhelmed by something infinitely sweeter – something which immediately put him in mind of the shock he had experienced in the underworld when the riot of the spilled wine of dreams had assaulted his nostrils.

That shock had been further compounded when he had sniffed the nectar from which the wine of dreams was made – and so was this one. Reinmar felt as if he had been struck in the chest by an invisible blade, and that something had reached into his chest cavity to take a taloned grip upon his heart.

Vaedecker was still shouting at the men on the storehouse floor, commanding them to retreat from the things he had called fiends. It seemed to Reinmar that the order ought not to have been necessary, especially as the crossbowmen were already making rapid inroads into their reserves of bolts, but it quickly became obvious that not everyone was capable of obeying. The men who were closest to the monsters moved towards them, not away, and not with any obvious aggressive intent.

Reinmar realised, almost as if he were looking at himself with distant and alien eyes, that he was among the company that was moving forward instead of falling back. He understood well enough, as the cloying odour made his head swim, what must be happening. Here was an animal perfume that was related to the flowery nectar from which the wine of dreams was made: luxurious, entrancing, instantly addictive. Its effects were immediate, although they might well turn out to be transient, but anyone who breathed in enough of the scent would lose their mind to it long enough to rush towards the open arms of the monsters, there to await the ultimate untenderness.

As the captivated men moved helplessly forward, the six massive stings struck out again and again, not striking at them but at those who came to help them and drag them back. The clawed arms occasionally lashed out like skilful sabres, but the serpentine tongues seemed equally avid and almost as dangerous. The strokes administered by the fiends' tongues were by no means violent – indeed, they seemed lascivious in their delicacy – but they were effective nonetheless. Such lickings did not seem to strike their targets dead but anyone who was touched by the snaking tongues, however lightly, either fell unconscious or lurched stupidly aside, apparently incapable of further intelligent action.

Reinmar wanted to shout to the men behind them that they should let him be and save themselves, but it would have done no good. Sigurd was in service with the Wieland family, and nothing in the world could have persuaded him to retreat while Reinmar was in mortal danger. Sigurd grabbed Reinmar with one arm, while the other dropped the staff and picked up a discarded half-pike.

Reinmar could not help struggling against the restraining arm, and he felt his strength grow as he did so, as the strength of madmen was reputed to do – but Sigurd was a giant and he, when all was said and done, was still a boy. If the monster's magic was irresistible, so was Sigurd's resolve, and Sigurd was determined that the monster which had made Reinmar captive could not keep him. As the sting lashed out, so did the half-pike, and it was the exoskeleton supporting the sting that cracked and splintered.

The claws were already scything forward, and Sigurd had not time or space to avoid them. He had to bring both his hands into play then, but as it released Reinmar the giant's arm spun him round like a top, sending him spinning and sprawling to one side, unable to follow the imperative that had asserted itself upon his mind.

The awful perfume still filled Reinmar's head, refusing to let any impulse form in his brain but a determination to throw himself at the monster, but the fall jarred and bruised him, and knocked the breath out of his lungs, so that he had no alternative but to lie there like a puppet whose strings had been cut.

In the meantime, Sigurd attacked the monster with all the fury of which he was capable. One claw shattered, and the blade of the half-pike slashed through the creature's bulbous eye – but the remaining claw clamped itself upon Sigurd's neck like scissors, and squeezed with terrible force. A lesser man would have been beheaded in a trice, but Sigurd's neck was as sturdy as the rest of him, and he had a second or two to react. The blade of the half-pike cut again, at the monster's own neck.

It was the last stroke Sigurd made, but it had all the power of a conclusive blow. As the giant's windpipe was crushed and the arteries to either side of his neck fountained blood, the loathsome creature that had killed him died in its turn, its horrid head half-severed from its compound body. Reinmar had thought that his inability to move was the worst of his utter subjection to the power of the creature's vile musk, but now he found that it was not. What was worse, by far, was the alien emotion that exploded in his consciousness as he felt the rush of the fiend's exultation in the destruction of Sigurd – and, simultaneously, the searing flash of Sigurd's death-agony.

Like a cockroach deprived of its head the monster did not die immediately, but raced forward like a runaway carriage – but it no longer had the power to do any physical harm.

Alas, the power of its perfume was not so easily dissipated, and Reinmar felt as if the shock of its death was running through him from top to toe like a slow and turgid lightning bolt. The compulsion to hurl himself into the creature's gaping embrace was gone, but its absence only made his senses reel, and he had to fight with all his mental might simply to remain conscious and to take stock of what was happening within the storehouse.

Within two or three minutes, fifteen or twenty men had been killed or disabled, while only one other attacker had fallen under the hail of crossbow bolts. The bolts had momentum enough to pierce the creatures' natural armour, but whatever organs they struck within were not sufficiently vital to cause them to fall.

'Spears!' Vaedecker was shouting. 'Throw anything that comes to hand – but stand clear! Stand clear, if you value your lives!'

Reinmar judged that Vaedecker's own position was by no means remote enough, and as the monsters fanned out and rushed forward they moved swiftly enough to ensnare many of those who were trying to obey his order and move away from them. In their hurry to escape, men were bumping into one another and stumbling over fallen bodies. Some still tried to haul their victimised companions to safety, but for every one who succeeded another was captivated.

Still the arrows struck home, three and four at a time, but still the monsters did not fall.

Matthias Vaedecker picked up a spear, and hurled it with all his might at one creature that was heading straight for him. It seemed a do-or-die move, for he had to brace himself to do it, and the creature was scampering forward so swiftly that he had to leave himself within range of its deadly perfume – but the spear struck it squarely in what would have been its breast had that part of its anatomy been human, and the point passed clean through to jut out behind.

Reinmar's vision was blurring, but there was no mistaking the expression of sheer joy on Vaedecker's face. He had never seen a man so exultant. Remarkably, it called forth an echo in Reinmar's captive soul: a renewal of the sensation that had flooded him when his subjection to the first fiend had forced him to share in the ecstatic quality of its murderous delight.

Vaedecker's spear-thrust had done more damage than even a creature of that kind could take, and the monster collapsed – but it was not dead, and it continued to exude its seductive secretion.

Vaedecker should have moved back, but instead he moved forward, helplessly drawn. The exultation in his face collapsed into fear, with such astonishing alacrity that Reinmar could not help wondering whether exultation was anything more than terror in disguise. Reinmar wanted to get up, to race to the sergeant's aid no matter how foolish the move might be, but the moment he managed to shift his arm slightly he was overwhelmed by the flood of pure pleasure that drowned his mind all over again and made him helpless.

Had the monster not been hurt Vaedecker might have died immediately, for the sting could have stabbed him – but the muscles controlling the creature's sting seemed to have lost their power, and its claws were also flat on the ground, sabre-like no longer. All that remained to be faced was the writhing tongue, lashing reflexively back and forth. Reinmar contrived, in spite of his captivity, to fix his eyes on that tongue, and saw that Vaedecker would be drenched by its loathsome saliva within a matter of seconds.

Again, Reinmar struggled to rise, fighting the drug that had laid him low. He told himself that he had already tasted the wine of dreams, and had dreamed in consequence, but that he was not its slave, and that the resistance he had so far exerted against the wine must come to his aid now.

It did not.

It was left to one of Vaedecker's own men to race forward, hurriedly but purposefully. If his expression was any guide, he too felt a rush of pure joy as he struck at the lashing tongue with his sword, severing it from the dilated mouth and sending it writhing out of harm's way, like a worm cut by the plough.

That stroke should have saved Vaedecker's life. In a fairer world, it would have – but there was one more monster yet to be struck down, and its sting was still busy. The creature scrambled over the body of its fallen ally, and while Vaedecker was still falling, unable to take control of his limbs, the point of the sting hit him squarely in the face, slicing through his cheek and into his jaw.

This time, mercifully, there was no echo in Reinmar's own being; he was allowed the freedom to be anguished as he saw his friend die.

The monster was immediately hit by half a dozen spears and arrows, and it fell no more than ten seconds after its final victim, but Reinmar knew that Vaedecker was finished, and would never rise again. The battle for the storehouse might leave sixty or eighty survivors on Eilhart's side, who would surely reckon themselves heroes and victors, but neither Sigurd nor Vaedecker would be among them – and that, to Reinmar, was defeat.

The entrancing perfume did not disappear when the sixth and last fiend fell, but its subjective meaning underwent a sudden shift in Reinmar's fugitive consciousness, utter foulness replacing its seductive force so abruptly that he retched helplessly. He tried yet again to raise himself up, but yet again he failed. This time he lost his vision entirely, and with it any sense at all of time or space. He did not fall unconscious, but he could not locate himself, in the storehouse or within his own body. It was as if he had been snatched upwards to a great height, from which the whole world would surely seem tiny, if only he could see.

When sight of a sort came back, though, all he could see was Eilhart: Eilhart in flames, falling into charred ruins as the heat surrounded him; Eilhart with ogres and ghouls rampaging through its streets, the luckier fraction of its population put to the sword; Eilhart reclaimed by leprous vegetation and slimy vermin, naught but a scar on the land gathered about the stagnant marsh that had been the proud terminus of the Schilder's trade. It was mere illusion, of course, no more real than that dream-castle in the clouds to which he had climbed after first tasting the wine of dreams.

When he found his body again, it was staggering to its feet, with nothing in its nostrils but the reek of blood and the stink of shit. He shook his head, attempting to clear it, but his vision was still blurred and he could not see where he ought to go, or what it was from which he needed to withdraw. For several seconds he was quite helpless – and then he felt strong arms grab him and draw him away.

There was a voice shouting very close to his ear, but it did not seem to be shouting at him. It was demanding more arrows and more spears, but it had a desperate edge to it that suggested that there were no more crossbow bolts to be fired and too few spears to be hurled. Reinmar's body continued to resist the demands of his will, but not because he was any longer captivated by an odorous magic. He realised, somewhat to his surprise, that he had simply exhausted his strength. His limbs would not work properly, and his breathing was impossibly laboured. He needed to lie down, to be given a pause in which he could recover, but the battle was still going on, after a fashion. There were no more six-limbed horrors rampaging about the storehouse, scuttling this way and that, but a fair few beastmen still remained, lashing out with their claws and clubs.

'Come on!' the voice said, much clearer now that it was addressed to Reinmar alone. 'Got to get you out. We've men enough to mop up.'

He was unceremoniously dumped on a floor that seemed to have become incredibly hard, and lay there for several seconds while the man who had helped him – for a moment he wondered whether it might have been Vaedecker, impossible though that was – answered a more urgent need.

The storehouse had become much darker as lanterns had expired or been dashed to the ground, but there was still light enough, when his vision cleared, to see the face that loomed over him when he was shifted on to his back. At first, it seemed like the face of a lovely woman – but then the features shifted and it became the face of a moth like those he had seen in his dream, and in that form, for some perverse reason, it seemed more beautiful still. Then it changed again, abruptly, and became the face of the infantryman who had spoken to Reinmar and Sigurd before the battle began.

That was real, he decided. The other had been illusion.

He felt a pressure pushing against his left leg, and realised that the soldier had taken his blade from his hand and resheathed it for him.

'It's all right,' the man said, in a voice harsh with strain. 'It's over – here, at least. The corporal wants thirty to stand guard and thirty to go to the square to reinforce von Spurzheim's position, but you're in no shape to do either. Rest a while, and then go home, if you can.'

Reinmar struggled to focus his thoughts.

'Vaedecker?' he said, weakly.

'Dead,' the soldier told him. 'The giant too. In the morning, they'll say we won, but we didn't. We didn't stop them. No matter how many we killed, we didn't stop them. You played your part, though, and you've survived. Bruised, but not cut – that makes a big difference, when there's so much danger of infection. When you can walk, go home, but step carefully.'

All Reinmar could say was 'Sigurd?' – but the soldier had already answered that question, and it was not the kind of news he was eager to repeat. What he repeated instead was the advice to go home. He was being kind, although he was absolutely right in his estimation that Reinmar was incapable of further exertion.

When he was left alone, Reinmar lay where he was. It took several minutes to work out exactly where that was, but he managed it eventually, and began to measure the distance that extended between himself and the door to the street. There was a mournful hush in the storehouse now, and the odour of smoke in the air – but the smoke had drifted in from elsewhere; the building was not on fire.

Eventually, Reinmar managed to stand up. His limbs were aching and his lungs felt as if they were full of filthy vapour, but he was indeed uncut, and might have been unbruised had he not been dumped on the hard floor so many times.

When he made his way to the door the men to either side of it did not challenge his right to go through it. One of them, indeed, murmured: 'Well done, lad.'

The other said: 'Be careful. The street's secure again, but if you're heading into town you might run across a stray.'

Once he was out in the street the scent of smoke became stronger, but in comparison to what he had recently endured it did not seem foul or dangerous. He had only taken half a dozen steps when he had to pause and lean against a wall, but he could feel reserves of strength of which he had been previously unaware taking possession of his heart and legs.

'Go home,' whispered a voice that he could not recognise, but which seemed very sweet and loving. 'Go home and slake your thirst.'

There was no face to go with the voice, although something withdrew into the shadows when he looked around and he felt something that might have been fluttering wings brush his cheek. The strength that was flowing back into him continued to increase, but he became sharply aware of the dryness of his tongue and throat. He looked back along the street and then forward, taking stock of the bodies that lay about the doorway of the storehouse. Only one in four was a well-made human.

Here, as inside the warehouse, his own side had been victorious – but the victory had been costly. Had Reinmar been able to weep, he would have done so, because he felt he knew better than anyone exactly how costly it had been.

Chapter Thirty-Three

Reinmar had stood firm against swordsmen, against horned beastmen, and even against the transfigured scorpions, but he shivered now that he was alone with the dead. He was not alone for long, though. Other townsmen selected out by Vaedecker's regulars were stumbling after him. One or two were retching reflexively in reaction to the poisonous stink, but none had anything left in their stomachs to expel. They all needed better stuff to breathe, and they were as grateful as Reinmar for air that had nothing to foul it but smoke.

There were buildings burning in the centre of town, Reinmar realised, but only a few. The town would not be destroyed, unless matters became far worse, and the enemy forces seemed to have exhausted their efforts. They had attacked in a fast and furious manner and had paid the price.

Reinmar continued to support himself against a wall while he retched again, but he felt better for it. The loss of everything in his stomach had certainly left him with a raging thirst, and he felt that he would surely die if he could not find a cup of water soon, or a goblet of good Reikish hock, but he knew that he was only a few minutes from home once he could persuade himself to move again.

When he finally managed that, he was able to place one foot in front of the other with reasonable steadiness. Two of his neighbours walked with him, but he did not speak to them nor they to him.

There were no bloodthirsty beastmen running amok in the street, although he and his companions passed half a hundred men not much less wretched than themselves, and their condition was a telling commentary on the fierceness of the greater battle. As he passed from street to street, Reinmar saw that although the attackers had been forced to withdraw from the district soon enough, they had not gone without leaving their mark.

Whether by magic or mere violence, the enemies of Eilhart had reached far beyond the defensive barricades to spread their malice. They had left blood in every street, and broken glass. Reinmar knew that it would be much worse in the marketplace and on the docks, and did not doubt that morning would reveal scars on the houses of all the merchants and manufacturers who had built and kept the prosperity of Eilhart.

One of the sputtering fires, Reinmar saw when he came nearer, was burning in the immediate neighbourhood of the Wieland shop – but it was not the shop itself, and the neighbours who were chaining buckets of water from the nearest pump seemed to have it under control. He did not volunteer to help, but made instead for the door of his own home.

As he fumbled with the door-latch he looked down, and saw the condition of his clothing. He realised that he must be a frightening figure in the ruddy half-light, stained as he was by blood and ichor.

Why, he thought, I have become a monster of sorts myself.

The door was locked, and he knocked on it as loudly as he could, hoping that Marguerite was inside, and that she would not be too frightened to answer his summons.

He waited, but no one came.

He put his hand on the hilt of his sword, as if to feel the power that was within it now that it had drawn so much alien blood, but he did not draw it. His father would not like it if he forced the door, and he would have to put in enough work cleaning, sharpening and polishing his weapon without bending the blade by using it as a lever. He knew that he ought to climb up to the ledge of his window, as he had done so many times before, and slip in through the gap, but the thought of the effort and exertion that would be required made him hesitate. He hammered on the door for a second time, more loudly than before. The knock was not soon answered, and he eventually moved to turn away – but as he did so, he heard the sound of movement inside the shop, so he waited instead.

'Who is it?' asked a voice from within: Marguerite's.

'Reinmar,' he replied.

'Are you alone? Are you hurt?'

'Alone, yes. Hurt… perhaps a little. Not mortally.'

He heard the sound of the bar scraping against the door as it was removed. The door opened a crack, paused, and then swung wider – but Marguerite's face did not appear. Thinking that she had merely stepped back, using the door as a shield, Reinmar moved into the open space. The only light inside was a candle in a tray that had been set down upon the first stair in the flight leading up to the second storey.

The door crashed shut behind him and he whirled around.

Marguerite was there, but she was not alone, and the man behind her had a knife at her throat.

Reinmar felt a pang of bitter regret that he should ever have allowed his private way into the house to be seen and copied.

'Cousin Wirnt,' he said, hoarsely. 'Your friends and kinsmen have been asking after you.'

'I have had to be careful, cousin,' the stout man assured him. 'I had no sooner left your shop than von Spurzheim's men were snapping at my heels. What a pest that man is! I had no option but to hide, and by the time I tried to reach my father they had taken him away. I nearly returned to Holthusen, but that might have been more dangerous still, so I thought it best to wait for another opportunity to talk to my uncle. When I saw him leave, I nearly did not recognise him – but then I realised that you must have brought him wine, of the very highest quality. I am still willing to pay a fair price for the goods, of course – if a life can still be reckoned precious after tonight's pageant of destruction.'

'I'm sorry, Reinmar,' Marguerite said, in a voice almost as hoarse as his own.

Reinmar observed, anxiously, that the gleam in Wirnt's eye was not the glow of the wine of dreams but something more electric. The strength of his craving had obviously increased.

He was not mad, in the sense that Luther had been mad, but he was desperate and dangerous, and the steadiness of his hand was unlikely to be trustworthy.

'Let her go, Wirnt,' Reinmar said. 'Marguerite has nothing to do with any quarrel you might have with me. She came here to render a service of extraordinary kindness.'

'Should I be threatening the gypsy, then?' Wirnt countered, without moving the tip of his blade from Marguerite's windpipe. 'She's no use to you, I fear. The call that the source will send out after tonight's hectic work will be irresistible. You might even hear it yourself – but I must be gone by morning if I am to make the most of my opportunity, and I cannot go without a supply of the wine. You do have an abundant supply, do you not?'

'Actually, no,' Reinmar told him. 'My grandfather took it with him. There's none left in the house.'

'He had no bottle with him when I saw him,' Wirnt said, 'and he can't be such a fool as to march through the streets of Eilhart with a jug of dark wine when it is full of witch hunters. Where is it, cousin? In the cellars? No more lies, now.'

'It was pure nectar he had, not diluted wine,' Reinmar said. 'I'm not lying. If you hurt that girl, I'll kill you. Let her go.'

Wirnt's only answer to the threat and the demand was to press the point of his dagger into Marguerite's throat, drawing a trickle of blood. The fugitive candlelight reflected in her eyes acknowledged her terror, but she did not cry out. She was trying with all her might to be brave.

'Tell me one more lie, cousin,' Wirnt said, coldly, 'and I might press a little too hard.'

'You have already done that,' Reinmar retorted, with equal coldness. 'Now, you will have to earn enough regard to persuade me to let you out of here alive. You have no idea how much killing I have done this night, of not-quite-men and half-human chimeras and giant scorpions with entrancing scent.'

'You have killed such a fiend?' Wirnt retorted scornfully. 'I doubt that, unless you had an army at your back – and if you did, that army is not behind you now. I need the wine, cousin Reinmar, and I think you understand by now how powerful a need like that can be. You know full well that I'd fight you if I had to, and kill you if I must, and you do not seem to have strength enough to swat a fly, let alone engage a man like me in combat. I don't want to hurt anyone. I only want the wine you brought from the valley, and once I have it you can certainly trust me to take it far away from here. I'll take it all the way to Marienburg if I can.'

'And what makes you think that you can?' Reinmar countered, hoping that if he delayed long enough he might recover enough of his strength to make a fight of it. 'If even I might hear a call, for merely having sniffed a cork, what will keep you from the hidden valley and a niche in the stone floor, and a lovely flower sprouting from your flesh? Or has no one told you yet how the wine of dreams is made?'

'Reinmar, please.' The plea came from Marguerite, still terrified.

'Your little friend will not lightly forgive you for this unnecessary delay,' Wirnt said, smiling grimly. 'And when the cost of this night's work is counted, you'll need every friend you can find. You brought those monsters here, Reinmar – you. I am probably the only man for a hundred miles who does not bear you a grudge for that, because I know what your work has done to the price of dark wine, and I mean to have your secret supply for my own. I am young enough that I only need the merest sip for myself, and I know exactly what price to extract for the rest from those whose need and thirst is greater by far. Only let me have what I want, and the girl will be safe. I'll be gone in no time at all.'

'You'll have to find Luther,' Reinmar said, more desperately than before – but as he spoke he saw that Wirnt's eyes were no longer fixed on his. The stout man was looking past him, at someone on the stair, and there was a new uncertainty in his gaze.

Reinmar turned, hoping to see Luther, or Gottfried, or even Albrecht refreshed – but what he actually saw was Marcilla, perhaps awake but definitely dreaming.

The gypsy girl had her head slightly raised, as if she were listening intently or trying to catch a faint and fugitive odour. She was moving slowly but her body was quite poised, her eyes open but unseeing. When she reached the foot of the stair she moved towards the head of another – the stone flight that led down into the cellars.

'It seems that I do not need you after all, Master Wieland,' Wirnt observed, triumphantly. 'Your hiding place may be proof even against an educated palate like my own, but she belongs entirely to the wine, and has since the moment of her conception. You cannot hide it from her!'

Reinmar was not sure that this judgement could be accurate, given that Wirnt's mother appeared to be a sorceress, while Marcilla's had merely been a gypsy, but he had already been warned that the gypsy might find the nectar wherever it was hidden. He had brought her out of the valley, but it seemed that nothing he could do could free her from the call that she had heard.

He understood for the first time how hopeless his love had been, how small and impotent a thing any mere affection was against the kind of command that was incarnate in the perfume of the thing that Sigurd had slain, and which had slain Sigurd in its turn.

He understood, too, that perhaps Luther had not been fool enough to take the nectar with him when he left the house. Perhaps he had hidden it again, in some secret place of his own.

'Follow her!' Wirnt said, abruptly. 'I'll come along too – and remember that this pretty maid's safety is in your hands. If I get what I need, she'll be safe. If not – whatever might happen to you or me – she'll be dead.'

Reinmar did as he was told. He picked up the candle-tray from the bottom step of the wooden stair, and held it high enough to light Marcilla's way down the stone flight, although it did not seem that she was in any need of the guidance of mere light.

This is fortunate, Reinmar told himself, as he moved behind the ensorcelled girl. I would never have been able to convince Wirnt that my grandfather had the nectar, or that I could not find his hiding-place, but now I shall see where it is before he does. He has the dagger, but I have the candle.

He tried, desperately, to think of some way in which he could turn that discrepancy into a winning advantage without exposing Marguerite to any further risk of having her throat cut. He was still horribly conscious of his own enfeeblement.

Marcilla reached the bottom of the flight, and swiftly went on into the mazy corridors between the racks of wine.

There was little enough room here for people to pass in single file, and Wirnt had Marguerite to cope with as well as his own over-ample girth. Unfortunately, Wirnt knew only too well that there was a hazard in allowing Reinmar to move too far ahead of him and he quickly called an instruction to halt.

'Now, my dear,' Wirnt said to Marguerite, when Reinmar obeyed. 'I want you to move up behind your friend, and reach around him very carefully. I want you to remove his sword from its scabbard, very carefully, and drop it on the floor.'

It took longer than Wirnt must have hoped for Marguerite to do this, but she did it, and the sword clanged upon the stone floor.

'Good,' Wirnt said. 'Now, put your hands around him and clasp him tightly. From now on, the two of you must move as one – but I have the dagger at your back and I'll slip it through your ribs if I have the slightest cause. Now move on.'

Reinmar moved on. Marguerite's hands were clasped tight in front of his chest, and the pressure of her arms seemed a far greater restraint than it actually was – but he heard Wirnt pick up his sword as they pressed on, and knew that he was now at a very severe disadvantage indeed, even though he still had control of the light.

Marcilla had moved on swiftly ahead, but she came to a stop now, and moved her arms uncertainly, as if her fingertips were able to sense the direction of the missing phial. She moved off into a blind side-corridor, heading for a section of bare wall.

There was no more visual evidence of any loose mortar in this wall than there had been in Reinmar's bedroom, but Reinmar knew that Luther had lived in the house for a very long time, and that von Spurzheim could not have been the first warranted official to think that its cellars ought to be searched.

Wirnt, who had obviously reached the same conclusion, let out an audible sigh of anticipation.

Then there was an almighty crash, as something exploded upon the stout man's head.

Marguerite screamed as the sword or the dagger pricked her back, and clutched Reinmar so tightly that he dropped the candle-tray. The candle flickered, but its light did not fail, and the flame stabilised again when the tray came to rest right way up.

Reinmar turned, putting his own arms protectively around Marguerite's body and hoping fervently that she was not too badly hurt.

She was not. Wirnt had been felled far too abruptly to be able to carry out his threat. He had been struck from above, not from behind; he had had no chance to see or hear his assailant's approach.

That assailant was stretched out atop a rank of shelves, from which he had plucked the jar of wine that he had shattered on Wirnt's solid skull. Ulick, it appeared, had never left the house at all. He had merely hidden himself, in a place that was too narrow to accommodate anyone but a person of his slender configuration.

The gypsy boy's eyes were wide open, and must have been sufficiently capable of sight to guide his blow, but as soon as Reinmar looked into them he knew that Ulick's condition was exactly similar to Marcilla's. Reinmar deduced that he had been set here to stand guard over the phial that Luther Wieland had hidden in the wall, and keep it safe for his sister, perhaps also for himself.

Even so, Reinmar felt that he had to make an effort to talk sensibly to the boy.

'Ulick,' he said, quietly. 'You must not let Marcilla drink the nectar. If both of you will only consent to let it alone, there is still a chance that you might survive this dread affair. I understand now that I should never have brought it out of the valley, but I was confused by its perfume. It is evil through and through, and ought to be destroyed.'

While Reinmar was speaking, though, Ulick scrambled down the racks and picked up Wirnt's dagger.

Reinmar might have been able to make a grab for his sword had Marguerite not been in his way, but he could not bear to thrust her rudely backwards over Wirnt's fallen body, using her as a shield. It would have been too cruel even if it had not been too dangerous. It was Marcilla that he loved, still, but Marguerite was his friend, and she had already been frightened and cut for his sake.

'Is the nectar yours, Master Wieland?' Ulick asked, in a voice not quite his own. 'Do you claim it for yourself?'

'No,' Reinmar said. 'I do not. It is not the sort of thing that any mere man can or ought to possess – he who has it is himself possessed.'

He felt a hand upon his shoulder then, placed from behind, and felt Marcilla's fingers caressing the side of his neck. He felt her breath upon his cheek as she leaned forward to whisper in his ear – but the voice that spoke to him was not quite her own, and he knew that no matter how he had striven to deny the fact, she was already possessed.

Marcilla's voice, like Ulick's, was now the voice that had spoken to him out of nowhere while he was wide awake, and had spoken to him far more subtly in his wine-induced dream.

'Dearest Reinmar,' the voice said, 'we are all possessed, from the moment we first learn to see till the moment we must learn to die. We are possessed by our appetites and our lusts, and no matter how hard reason may fight for its empire, those claims of ownership can never be set aside. You are possessed, my darling, and the chit you hold in your hands is possessed too, securely and forever. You do not have the choice to be anything but a possession, and never will; the only freedom you will ever have is the freedom to be used in a better way than some few of your fellows. You might be mine, if you wished it, but if you will not be mine you will only be another's, or held in common by all my awesome kind, to be buffeted one way and then another, never knowing true rest or fair certainty or real pleasure. Far better to be mine, dear heart, knowingly and willingly. That way, at least, there is some slight reward in life, instead of endless worry and endless travail. Believe me, darling Reinmar, there is nothing you will desire more when you grow old than the opportunity to put the clock back and give yourself entirely to me. Seize that opportunity now, and save yourself a deal of pain.'

Reinmar's arms were still around Marguerite. She had relaxed into his grip and was pressing herself against him, breast to breast. He knew that she had heard every word, and that she was waiting with bated breath to hear his reply.

'I cannot,' he said. 'Marcilla, I cannot.'

He could not be sure that Marguerite would be prepared to believe that he was talking to Marcilla, and only to Marcilla, but he thought that it might be safer if she did.

'Corrupted by discipline,' said the voice, regretfully. 'If you could kill for me, you'd find so much more pleasure in killing. You glimpsed that, I think, in the instant before the fiend died. Can you not remember what killing ought to be, my love? Must you make it a matter of duty and discipline?'

'Take the nectar and go, Marcilla,' Reinmar said, his voice raw with thirst. 'Take it, I beg you, and go.'

The hand moved away from his shoulder, but it was not withdrawn. Instead the fingers reached up to put gentle pressure on his eyelids and deny him sight.

'Oh, my silly darling,' the voice said, 'I could have done that at any time since you stepped out of the underworld, but the game is not done yet. You do not understand me at all, for all your yearning dreams.'

And with that, Reinmar found himself falling slowly into unconsciousness. His throat was still desperately dry, but it proved in the end that he was even more tired than thirsty. He faded away into delicious, dreamless sleep.

Chapter Thirty-Four

Reinmar awoke when water splashed his face. When he raised his head the rim of a cup touched his lip and he drank avidly. He took the cup in his own hands and drained it completely before looking up into the candlelit face of the man who had given it to him.

'Godrich?' he said.

'That's right,' the steward agreed. 'What happened here, Master Wieland?'

For a moment, Reinmar did not even know where he was, but when his eyes had taken in the wine-racks he remembered. His first thought was to look for Marcilla, and it was not until he had registered the fact of her absence that he became aware of the significance of the fact that there were others missing too.

Wirnt had gone. So had Marguerite. Did that mean that she had been taken prisoner again?

Reinmar looked at the blank wall then, and saw a gap where a loose brick had been carefully removed. He stood up, silently cursing the discomfort that immediately afflicted his arms and legs. He looked into the hole, but there was nothing there. He put his hand into the space, extending groping fingers into every cranny. If the phial had been there he would have been able to touch it, but it was not. Had it ever been there, he wondered, or had the drama played out in the cellar been a mere charade from beginning to end? Had Marcilla led Wirnt to Ulick under false pretences, so that Ulick might smash the stone jar upon his head?

Godrich was still waiting politely for an answer.

'My cousin Wirnt was here,' Reinmar told him. 'He was looking for dark wine, but Luther had taken the phial I brought from the valley. If Luther really did hide what remained in here, I have no idea where it is now. What hour is it?'

'Three after noon,' Godrich told him. 'You should come upstairs, if you can walk. I've made a meal of sorts, though there's nothing at all to be bought in the market.'

'Three after noon! I must have slept the clock round, or very nearly.' Reinmar consented to be led away in the direction of the stair, but he looked for his sword first and was not at all pleased to find it gone.

'I dare say that you needed the sleep,' Godrich observed, as they began to climb the stair, unhurriedly. 'To judge by the state of your clothing, you were in the thick of it.'

'Is it over?'

'Not quite, but the Reiksguard have matters under firm control.'

'The Reiksguard. Not von Spurzheim?'

'He's dead. They suffered heavy losses reaching him, but reach him they did. Vaedecker too, I've heard – and Sigurd. Your father's safe, though.'

'What about your sons?'

'My family are all well,' Godrich said. His relief was obvious. 'We'll be safe now, I think.'

'I suppose so,' Reinmar said, as they moved into the kitchen. 'It was von Spurzheim they wanted dead. Vaedecker told me that he would be replaced, but that his replacement wouldn't have his knowledge, or his particular obsession. They'll search for the valley, but when they fail to find it, they'll go on to something else. The Reiksguard will maintain a presence in the town for a while, but they'll find better things to do soon enough. It's not over, by any means – but things will soon be back to normal, for those of us who survive.'

'The road to Holthusen is already open,' Godrich told him, as if it were proof. 'The river route will have to await the repair of the locks, I fear, and that will have to wait till the water runs a good deal cleaner than it does now, but more soldiers have already arrived to help with the clearing up. No one's taking tally of the enemy casualties, but ours – the town's, that is, not including soldiers – number a few hundred. Not as many as a thousand, thankfully. The soldiers lost hundreds too, of course, but the new forces will compensate for that. The fires were not quite as bad as they seemed, although the quays and the store-houses nearby were devastated and a dozen homes were gutted.'

By the time this speech was finished Godrich was filling Reinmar's cup again, from a pitcher. 'Take care, sir,' the steward added. 'Drinking water's in direly short supply.'

Reinmar felt a slight stab of guilt at the realisation that he had already emptied the cup. 'Where's my father?' he asked.

'Gone to look for your grandfather.'

Reinmar frowned at that. 'Gone where to look for my grand-father?'

'Albrecht's house. You should eat something, sir. It looks unappetising, I know, but you should eat.'

Reinmar looked at the 'meal' that Godrich had laid out. There was no bread and no meat, and the boiled vegetables were not in the least inviting, but he knew that Godrich was right. He ought to eat while he could. There would be such hunger in the days and weeks to come that even this would come to seem, in memory, an enviable feast – but there were more important things to worry about. 'Is the way to Albrecht's house safe?' Reinmar demanded, as he sat down and picked up a spoon. 'Is the house still standing, for that matter?'

'I don't know, sir,' Godrich told him. 'But Gottfried believes that if Luther is to be found at all, that is where he will be.'

'Wirnt will surely draw the same conclusion,' Reinmar murmured. 'That bastard stole my sword – and he may still have Marguerite. I ought to–'

'Eat first,' Godrich finished for him, nudging Reinmar's spoon in the direction of his mouth. 'I urged your father not to take the risk, but... well, sir, there is a matter between the two of them that has been unsettled for many years, as you probably know.'

'The matter of the dark wine,' Reinmar said.

'The matter of authority in the business,' Godrich countered. 'The matter of self-determination, and the power to achieve it.

Sometimes, sir, children are not as dutiful towards their parents as custom and morality demand.'

For a moment, Reinmar thought that he was being accused, but he realised that Godrich was referring to matters between Gottfried and Luther. He spared a thought too for Wirnt and Albrecht – and for Valeria. Whatever else the wine of dreams might give to its consumers, it was obviously very unhelpful to family feeling.

'Do you have any idea what happened to Marguerite?' Reinmar asked, as he continued forcing food into his mouth. There was turnip in the mess that had been piled on his trencher, and cabbage, but nothing that he could think of as pleasurable eating. Even so, he was hungry, and his stomach appreciated the bulk. 'She was with me in the cellar. Cousin Wirnt held a knife to her throat in order to compel me, but the gypsy boy knocked him out. Wirnt must have recovered consciousness while I was still asleep, and if Marguerite was still there, for whatever reason…'

'I haven't seen her,' Godrich said, 'but you should ask at her home before jumping to ominous conclusions. Change your clothes first, though – for your own sake as well as her mother's.'

'He has my sword,' Reinmar repeated, sullenly. 'Perhaps he has the nectar too – but if he did take Marguerite, he must think that there is still something to be won by bargaining, so I must assume that Marcilla took the phial.' He had finished as much of his meal as he was capable of putting down his throat, and he rose to his feet again.

Godrich obviously did not think he had eaten enough, but made no move to stop him.

'You're right about the clothes,' Reinmar said, as he turned to go to his own room – but he paused on the threshold and said: 'Did I do wrong, Godrich? Was it my foolishness that spoiled Eilhart?'

'I do not know what you did, sir,' Godrich pointed out, with a politeness so scrupulous as to be almost insulting. 'You did not confide in me.'

'I wasn't supposed to find my way into the underworld beneath the monastery,' Reinmar told him, flatly. 'The fact that I discovered the secret of the dark wine's manufacture was of no particular importance – but I spilled their vintages and I stole a vital ingredient that might have been used to make more. I robbed a dark god of a small fraction of his power to do evil. Should I have let that power alone, to continue in its subtle work of evil?'

'I cannot tell,' Godrich said. 'I wonder, though, why you did not tell anyone else about the nectar you removed.'

'I was angry and outraged,' Reinmar confessed, 'and I wanted to make my mark. I wanted to make my wrath felt, but I also wanted a secret to keep, a power of my own. I did not know who to trust, but that was not the reason for my refusal to trust anyone. I wanted to be a player in the game, not a pawn. Because of that, Eilhart was nearly destroyed.'

'Not because of that,' Godrich said. 'Those things which came last night have no other reason for being than to maim and destroy. Had they not fallen on Eilhart they'd have done the same work elsewhere. Eilhart is fortunate in having such passionate defenders. The world is the world, Master Reinmar. It is not your fault, or mine, that there is evil in it. We fight it as best we can. That is what you did.'

Reinmar nodded. 'Thank you,' he said, before ascending the stair to his bedroom.

Once there he went immediately to his closet and his trunk. He had spoiled so many clothes of late that he was lucky to have any left at all, especially since Luther had stolen his best suit, but it was Reinmar's good fortune to be the scion of an unusually prosperous family. The outfit he decided to put on was a little too small as well as inelegant, but it had to do.

The water left by his bedside for washing had not been changed for two days, and he did not suppose that it would be changed for another fortnight, so he was more careful than usual in trying to clean the worst of the muck from his hands and face. He succeeded well enough, although he still seemed a slightly sorry sight when he looked at himself in the mirror.

When he turned away from the mirror he intended to go to the door, but some unaccountable impulse made him hesitate on the threshold. He waited for a moment, trying to figure out what it was that had made him stop. Then, still without being certain, he turned back.

He went to his favourite hiding-place, in which he had secreted the phial of nectar before it was stolen by Luther. It had not been there when he had replaced the strip of mortar, but as soon as he removed the fragment again he saw that the hidey-hole was no longer empty.

Someone had replaced the phial, from which no more than a couple of drops had been removed.

'Marcilla,' he muttered. But he knew now that Marcilla was not wholly Marcilla, and that it was the other part of her – her possessor – that had put the phial back where Wirnt had already looked for it and failed to find it.

Everyone in the world, it seemed – and perhaps one beyond it – was determined that he should be a wine merchant, no matter how hard he might try to avoid that fate.

He took the phial, and put it in his pouch. Then he went back to Godrich and asked him for the loan of a sword.

Godrich told him that there was no weapon of any kind in the house, all of them having been requisitioned by von Spurzheim. 'I suspect, however,' the faithful servant said, 'that if you care to use your eyes as you cross the town boundary, you might well find something you can use.'

This prophecy proved correct, although Reinmar was careful to visit Marguerite's house before putting it to the test. Her mother had not seen her, and was extremely displeased to discover that she was no longer safe in Gottfried Wieland's house. There was nothing Reinmar could say in reply but that he was sorry, and to swear on his life that he would bring her safely home.

Chapter Thirty-Five

The soldiers and the townsmen had been busy all morning gathering everything that might be of further use, but there were far too many stinking corpses lying outside the barricades to have been properly examined. The blade that Reinmar eventually appropriated was crude, blunt and rusted, but he needed the reassurance of its weight far more than the keenness of its blade. He kept it in his hand while he marched steadfastly over the ridge and into the fir wood surrounding Albrecht Wieland's house.

There was smoke above the wood, but it was coming from the chimney of the house, not the embers of its timbers. The enemy that had fallen upon the town with such reckless fury had not been here, and no remnants of the hideous army seemed to be lurking in the wood, even though von Spurzheim's sentries had been withdrawn more than a day before. Reinmar never ceased to look about him as he went along the path, continually glancing over his shoulder to make sure that no one was sneaking up behind him, but the fir wood seemed utterly lifeless. No birds sang, no wind rattled the leaves, and the greenery seemed oddly faded.

When he came in sight of the door of the house, though, he saw that it stood open. That seemed to him to be a bad sign, and he gripped the hilt of his stolen sword more tightly. He approached stealthily, making sure that his boots made no sound as they trod on the soft leaf-litter beside the crudely-laid path that led to the door. When he came to the threshold he paused, listening intently, but he could not hear voices.

He slipped in quietly, and saw soon enough why no voices had been raised. For the time being, at least, the fighting was over.

If Albrecht's sitting room had been a mess before, it was pure chaos now. The table had been overturned and the chairs flung aside. Wherever there had been a pile there was now a mere scattering of individual objects, some crushed and some shattered.

The five combatants in the struggle had separated now that its fury was done, seemingly to count its cost – although one was so still that he was more likely to be numbered among the counted than the counters, and one so well-confined that she probably ought not to have been reckoned a combatant at all.

Marguerite would probably have cried out when she saw Reinmar, had she not been gagged. She was trussed too, her hands tied behind her and her ankles roped together. She had been set in a corner, probably upright to begin with, but had sunk into a crouch. Albrecht, the apparent corpse, was lying to the left of her, not four feet away.

The man was huddled into an almost-foetal position, his hands having clutched at his belly when he was cut and his knees having been drawn up in agony, so that his hands and thighs shared the work of trying to confine his entrails to their proper place. His brother, Luther, still seemingly young and still seemingly mad – though perhaps no madder, now, than Wirnt – knelt beside him, displaying his empty hands as if appalled by their helplessness.

Reinmar had no doubt at all that the sword that had slit Albrecht's abdomen was his own, wielded by Wirnt. Wirnt still held it, and still seemed ready to use it, but for the moment he had taken a defensive stance, setting his back against the other wall that extended from the corner where Marguerite crouched. He did not appear to have been injured, but he was panting hard. In his left hand he was holding a flask, which Reinmar recognised as the one that the monks had given to Valeria, and which Valeria had left behind half-full. It was not half-full now, but if Reinmar read the expression of Wirnt's face correctly, the rest had been spilled rather than drunk.

Until Reinmar came in, Wirnt's eyes had been fixed on Gottfried Wieland, who was supporting himself against the opposite wall, still upright but hurt by a long cut extending from his left shoulder almost to his midriff, which had leaked so much blood that Gottfried's shirt and trousers were soaked. Reinmar judged that the cut had scored half a dozen ribs, and must be very painful, but even though the blood-loss seemed massive, it was probably not life-threatening in itself. If infection set in, then Gottfried would certainly have to fight for his life, but for now he was very much alive and fully conscious. Had he a weapon in his hand, he might have made a formidable opponent for Wirnt, who was smaller and less athletic, but he had been forced to drop his sword in the course of the brawl, and it lay beneath Wirnt's foot. For that reason, if for no other, Gottfried was content to keep his back to the wall, offering no obvious threat to his mad nephew.

Marguerite and Gottfried both looked imploringly at Reinmar when they saw him, but neither spoke. Marguerite was silent because she had no option; Gottfried, presumably, because he did not know what to say.

Wirnt did.

'It was not my fault,' was what he said first, and he was quick to amplify his claim. 'I had no intention of causing injury to anyone, my father least of all – but he would not give me the wine. It was a purely private dispute, between father and son, that would never have turned to bloodshed if those who had no right to interfere had not thrown themselves into the quarrel. First this maniac arrives, calling my father brother, insisting that my father should take the draught himself. He was the one who forced me, in the end, to draw my sword, precisely because he had none of his own, and required a show of force to be controlled – except, of course, that he was too furious to be controlled, even by the sight of a naked blade. In time, I dare say, he would have seen sense – but then this perfect fool arrives, no sooner seeing my blade than he draws his own, and his opinion is that no one should touch the wine. Even then, we might have settled the argument as civilised men, if he would only have consented to sheath his blade while we talked – all the more so given that the real object of his ire was this creature that he called father – but he insisted on keeping the weapon handy.

'As soon as I realised the full truth of the situation I became conciliatory – a peacemaker, through and through – but my attempts to calm the situation were fruitless. There was a point, I assure you, when I almost ceased to care whether my father let me have the little measure of wine he had, because I realised how negligible it was by comparison with the other supply – the one that my Uncle Luther swore that he had hidden in the cellar. Far better, I told them, that we should all join forces in order that one or two of us could move to intercept the gypsy girl before she could make much headway southwards, while someone waited here for your arrival, in case you had managed to retain the prize. It was all so very simple... so very simple... except that your father and his father could not be quiet, and Albrecht simply would not surrender that trivial draught. And so it came to blows, with the result that you see. I wounded them both, I will confess, but it was not my fault.'

Reinmar listened until Wirnt had finished, because he knew that he had to understand what had happened, but as soon as the torrent of words sputtered and dried up, he addressed his grandfather. 'Is he dead?' he asked, meaning Albrecht.

'Not yet,' Luther replied, dolefully, meaning that it would take a miracle to save him.

'Father?' was Reinmar's next enquiry.

'It's a shallow cut for all the gore,' Gottfried reported, grimly. 'I won't die, but I can't deny that I'm weak and all-but-useless. If anyone kills him, it will have to be you. If you weren't my son, I'd say have at him and the best of luck, but if you have what he wants, it might save a deal of trouble if you gave it to him and let him go.'

'Do you have what I need?' Wirnt wanted to know.

'Yes I have,' Reinmar said, seeing no need at all to prove it. 'Perhaps you should try to take it, if you dare.'

Luther smiled at that, but the smile was humourless.

'This is the family business, after all,' Wirnt said. 'Even now, there is no reason for us to be enemies. I did not mean to hurt him. Even now, what I want is reconciliation, and harmony. I need the nectar, but once I have it, I am more than willing to make treaties and contracts. Von Spurzheim is dead, and half his entourage. There will be soldiers in Eilhart for years to come, and witch hunters in the hills, but nothing fundamental has changed. There are other battles to be fought, other crusades to be mounted, and the soldiers and witch hunters will see soon enough that they will be more profitably employed elsewhere. We are businessmen, are we not? Let us behave like honest tradesmen.'

'If you can kill him,' Gottfried Wieland said to his son, 'I'd be obliged if you'd do it soon.'

'I believe that I can,' Reinmar said – but his opportunity to try had already vanished. It had been easy enough for him to enter the house unheard even while its occupants were temporarily silent. It was even easier for those who had come after him. He had not the slightest idea that anyone was behind him until he felt an arm slide over his shoulder like a snake and the edge of a dagger laid upon his windpipe.

It was not the man who held the knife to his throat who spoke, though; it was the woman who had come in behind him and now stepped past him.

'My son is right in what he says,' she said, 'no matter how far his actions have put him in the wrong. No matter what disasters have caught us up or how badly we are hurt, we are a civilised family. Those of us who are scholars have been long estranged from those of us who are tradesmen, but that was always petty foolishness. Our aim now should be reconciliation.'

Valeria did what no one else had dared to do, placing herself casually at the very centre of the room, so that she could look regally around at all its other occupants, drawn back against its various walls.

All Reinmar could see of the man behind him was the sleeve of his robe, but he guessed that it was Brother Noel before he heard the murmured instruction to drop his weapon. He had no choice but to obey.

Valeria did not seem quite as young as she had when Reinmar had last seen her, although she was still more vibrant than she had been when he first caught sight of her.

'I thought you had gone to the secret valley,' Reinmar said bitterly. 'The attack on Eilhart was supposedly not your concern.'

'I had a dream,' was the lady's reply. She seemed to think it adequate.

Luther stood up and turned his back on his unconscious brother. 'Did you come for me?' he asked.

'She came for me,' Wirnt was quick to say. 'I am her son.'

'I think you will find that she came for the nectar,' Reinmar said quietly.

'I did not come to hear you play guessing games,' Valeria informed them, impatiently. 'I am the only one here who knows what this is all about, and the only one who knows how matters should proceed. I am the trusted one – the only trusted one.'

Reinmar was surprised, but only slightly, by the distinct note of anxiety in her voice. She had been in control of the situation when she had last visited the house, but she knew that things were different now. 'None of you is trusted, or ever was, or ever shall be,' he said, boldly. 'Yours is a game in which trust has no part, and lust is everything.'

The dagger was drawn more insistently against his throat, but the edge did not break the skin.

'Now the whelp knows everything!' Valeria exclaimed, raising her hand in a languid gesture of contempt. 'He is his father's son, it seems. What a fool you were, Luther, to subject yourself to such as these.'

'Give them what they want, Reinmar,' Gottfried said. 'They have all the advantages now. Give them what they want and take Marguerite back to Eilhart. I can walk behind you, while they all find their own road to Hell. My father has had his last chance. From now on, we are our own masters, without obligation.' Reinmar knew that he was speaking hopefully, trying to persuade himself that all might yet be well.

Reinmar knew, however, that all was not well.

'I don't understand,' he said. 'Why didn't you bring the nectar when you had the chance, grandfather? And why did Marcilla put it back where you found it? Why does it keep coming back to me?'

'You stole it,' Noel murmured in his ear, jut loud enough for the others to hear. 'Thieves must be careful what they steal, lest the objects of their desire should steal them in return. You are ours now, Master Wieland, whether you know it or not.'

'That's a lie!' Gottfried was quick to say. 'All of these are slaves already, but you are not. You should have smashed the phial when you found it, or spilled the liquor into the town sewer to mingle with all the blood it has spilled. Even now, it is not too late.'

'But it is,' Brother Noel insisted.

'Be quiet,' Valeria said, to Gottfried as well as the monk. 'I say again, we should not be quarrelling over this. This is a family affair, after all – I include the girl, of course, since she seems so enthusiastic to join our little clan. What you have in your pouch, Reinmar, is what has brought us together after so long apart, and may keep us together in spite of our cuts and bruises. It can make us strong again, after far too many years of weakness.'

'I fought last night to defend the town against monsters out of a nightmare,' Reinmar told her. 'I saw my friends killed, and barely escaped death myself. Do you think I am ready now to become part of that nightmare?'

'What better time could there be?' Valeria countered. 'But that is not what anyone asks of you, Reinmar. No one here was fighting on the other side last night. We had better things to do with our time, and with our youth. The young do not know the value of youth, Reinmar, but I can assure you that I know it as well as anyone else alive. You might think I use it recklessly, but you will understand one day – as Albrecht understood, though he tried so hard to forget, and as Luther understands again, though he could not always remember it. We all know that it is best to stand aside from the battle that is mundane existence, let alone the kind of battle that you fought last night. Perhaps it is good that you did that, because you need to learn – but there is so much more that you might learn, if you would only seize the opportunity.'

'This is nonsense,' Wirnt said, impatiently. 'You may play whatever games you want, mother, but I came here to get the wine of dreams for myself, and I still mean to have it. I can take it, if I must.' He stepped forward, raising his arm slightly, to remind everyone that he still held Reinmar's sword, and that it was by far the best weapon on display.

The forward step was a mistake, because it brought him close enough to his mother to allow her to reach out and take his wrist – the right wrist – in her own delicate hand. The casual act could have been mistaken for a gesture of affection and reassurance, but it was not.

Wirnt immediately tried to break free, but he could not, and while he struggled, his face grew somewhat older and the grey in his hair increased its dominion over the black. Flesh seemed to melt away from his overgenerous belly, leaving him almost as thin as his father had been. In the meantime, Valeria recovered the tiny fraction of her renewed youth that she had lost since she drank from the flask that Wirnt still held in his left hand.

'Don't be silly, Wirnt,' Valeria said. Then, to Reinmar, she said: 'Sons can be so unruly, but their mothers always have the measure of them, even when their fathers retain no authority at all.'

Reinmar heard Marguerite's muffled gasp of astonishment, but no one else seemed even faintly surprised by what had happened. As she had openly declared, Valeria was the one who best understood what this was all about, and how it should go – but there was audible anxiety in every sentence that she spoke, no matter how contemptuous the words might be. She knew how the confrontation ought to go, but she was far from certain that it would.

'I will not be your apprentice, lady,' he said.

'Nor I yours,' she replied. 'But there is a business to be run and a trade to be organised, and it requires a trusted man. You are a trusted man, now, in every sense of the word.'

'My father runs the business,' Reinmar said. 'I have no ambition to replace him before he is ready to be replaced.'

'Take out the nectar, Reinmar,' Valeria said. 'Let us all see what this is about.'

'Don't,' Gottfried said – but Reinmar knew that there was no point in leaving it where it was. He took out the phial, and held it up.

'There is more than enough for all of us to take a sip,' Valeria observed. 'The girl too, if she will. It will calm us all, and smooth our negotiations. It will revive those who need reviving – it may even have power enough to save Albrecht's life.'

It occurred to Reinmar when the sorceress spoke of taking 'a sip' that even she had no idea how powerful the nectar was. Luther knew, if he still had enough self-possession to know anything at all, and Noel presumably knew, but Wirnt and his mother did not.

'The last thing I need is medicine of that kind,' Gottfried growled. 'I shall not drink, and nor shall my son. Nor will Marguerite.'

'I'll gladly take your share,' Luther told his son roughly. 'Gladly.'

Wirnt opened his mouth as if to advance his own claim, but nothing came out but a croak. He seemed astonished by his sudden weakness, appalled by the consciousness that he had tried to speak to some effect but had only been able to utter a wordless sound that might have been the dying breath of a carrion crow.

Reinmar was still certain that he had never been meant to find his way into the underworld, but he understood now that not everything that he had done there had been his own move in the continuing game. When he had taken up the phial he had yielded to temptation, and had never been free of it since. Even this was not an opportunity to free himself from that temptation, but only to postpone the conflict until another time. He was marked now, and the wine of dreams would follow him wherever he went, because he had penetrated its most precious secret. The events of the previous night might only be a sample of things to come, if he would not join Valeria's conspiracy.

Valeria was smiling now, but her smile was uneasy. 'This is a great day,' she said, although the falseness of her confidence was obvious. 'The reunion of a family; the healing of wounds old and new; the beginning of a new enterprise.'

'I will not be part of it,' Gottfried insisted. 'Reinmar–'

'Don't be a fool, Gottfried,' Luther interrupted. 'You were young and stubborn when you set your face against this trade – as young as Reinmar is now – but you're not so young now. You need the wine more than any of us, else you'll die screaming when that wound turns septic.'

'I will not die screaming,' Gottfried told his father, blending rage and outrage in his tone. 'All flesh must wither and die, and all spirit too. Nothing can set that inevitability aside. There is nothing in that phial but delusion, and brief delusion at that. I have seen its promises, and I have seen them fail. I am an honest trader, and I intend to remain one for many years to come. You must make your own choice, Reinmar, but you've seen what life has made of me and you've seen what life has made of your grandfather.'

'I've seen far more than that, father,' Reinmar said. 'I've seen the source of the wine, both the flower and the root of its temptations.'

'You could not save the gypsy,' Valeria told him, although he already knew it, 'because she never had the least desire to be saved. She was made to be a dreamer, and nothing could have kept her long awake once she had been called to her dream. Nothing. What could any mere man offer her, when she already had the love of a god?'

'Let me go,' Reinmar said to Brother Noel. 'Take the knife away, and I'll open the phial.'

The monk hesitated, but he had to look to Valeria for instruction.

She nodded, and Noel removed his arm. He even took a step backwards, fully convinced that if things went awry he would have every opportunity to stab Reinmar in the back.

Reinmar transferred the phial from his right hand to his left, but he made no move to open the seal. Instead, he looked at Wirnt. 'I believe that you have my sword,' he said.

Wirnt hesitated, and Reinmar saw a sharp glint enter the eyes that gleamed within his cousin's suddenly-aged face. Wirnt freed his right hand from Valeria's grip, and made a show of reaching out towards Reinmar – but it was the point that he extended, not the hilt.

'Don't be silly, Wirnt,' Valeria said, again – but it seemed that Wirnt had heard that particular injunction once too often. He slashed sideways with the blade, seemingly with all the force he could muster – not at Reinmar, but at his mother. The blade sliced into her throat, severing her windpipe and causing blood to fountain from her arteries at either side of her neck.

The expression on her face was one of the utmost astonishment.

As Valeria crumpled to the litter-strewn floor, Wirnt freed the blade again with a sudden wrench, and moved the tip in a slow arc, threatening to cut anyone else who moved.

'Sons can be so unruly,' he said, mockingly, 'but mothers must learn to let go. Do you not agree, Cousin Reinmar? Will you not agree with me that I had no choice? She really shouldn't have tried to favour you over her own son, should she? That wasn't right. You don't really want that phial, do you? I shan't be robbing you by taking it off your hands.'

Reinmar smiled, as if to agree, and held out the object of the other's fierce desire as if to surrender it.

That was when Brother Noel – who had come late to his vocation – hurled his dagger with all the force he could muster. The blade buried itself to the hilt in Wirnt's chest, cutting deep into his heart. While Wirnt was falling, Reinmar stepped forward, using his left hand to pluck the sword from the dead man's nerveless fingers.

The compound stink of blood and shit filled the room, but Reinmar was used to that by now and did not feel the need of a stronger perfume to cloak its vileness. He was now a man to whom the sight and nearness of death came naturally: a man who could anticipate the malice of others and make them pay the price of folly. And why should he not extract such prices in full, given that he was not merely a man who had fought and killed beastmen, and matched wits with fiends, but an honest tradesman?

'The Lady Valeria should have known, if anyone did, how weak the bonds of family affection become, when they are strained by the wine of dreams,' he observed. 'You must go away now, grandfather. There is no safety for you here. If you manage to reach Marienburg, tell anyone who asks that there will be no dark wine to be had for a year and more, and none to be had in Eilhart at any future time – not, at least, from the Wieland shop.'

Having said that, he suddenly felt quite tired, but he knew that it was not a decision he would regret within the next few years, so long as he was awake and free of dreams.

'One day, Reinmar,' Luther said, in a low voice, 'you will understand. You are too young now, but you will never have Gottfried's gift of utter insensitivity, no matter how you may try to cultivate it. One day, you will understand.'

Reinmar turned briefly to look for Brother Noel, but the monk had seen Reinmar take back his sword, and he knew the havoc that blade had already wreaked among his brethren. He was running away as fast as his legs would carry him. Reinmar did not expect to see him again. Luther had not moved to follow him as yet, and his attitude suggested that he was in no hurry, but his awkward stance betrayed his deep anxiety.

Reinmar looked down at the fallen bodies of Wirnt and Valeria – which seemed older now than they had before they suffered the fatal blows – before looking up at his grandfather.

'Don't ask me to give you the nectar, grandfather,' he said. 'Don't try to take it, either. You've had your share. Just go.'

Luther seemed to be on the point of arguing, but he was not as mad now as he had been. Recent events had overlaid a new sobriety upon his hard-won youth. He looked hard at his son, but Gottfried was deliberately looking the other way, refusing to see him.

In the end, Luther took one more look at the condition of the flesh on his once-wrinkled hands, and decided that Reinmar was right. He darted a glance in Albrecht's direction before he left, but did not take the trouble to check whether there was any life remaining in the fallen man.

It was left to Gottfried to haul himself painfully to his feet and make his way to where his uncle lay. His verdict was succinct. 'Dead. We can only hope that he lived long enough to know that he was properly avenged.'

When Reinmar looked down again, he saw that Valeria's corpse was still mutating, although Wirnt's had settled. Her flesh had shrivelled considerably, so that the skin lay upon her bones like parchment. The blood that had spilled from her gaping wound was now as black as ancient ink, and every bit as dry.

Valeria must have hoped that she was invulnerable, Reinmar supposed, because she knew some petty sorceries. In fact, she had been as vulnerable as anything alive to the whim of the mysterious creature that she worshipped: the dark and playful god whose name he had not yet contrived to discover and probably never would. She had died anxious, perhaps because she understood how capriciously vindictive that whim had become.

Reinmar remembered something that Matthias Vaedecker had said to him. The greatest power our enemies have is not that they can release daemons upon the world, but that they can twist their knives inside the hearts of those we know and love, turning cousin against cousin, brother against brother.

Foremost in his mind, however, was one of the slogans that his father had been so enthusiastic to teach him.

Good wine matures.

'We have to go back now, father,' he said to Gottfried, as he went to free Marguerite and help her to her feet. 'The battle is finished, but the war goes on. Eilhart will not be rebuilt in a year – and from now until we all die, there will be people in the town who shudder every time they hear tales of monsters in the hills.'

'There will always be monsters in the hills,' Gottfried said weakly. 'We must all learn to live honestly and carefully with our fears, as we must all learn to live honestly and carefully with our lusts and appetites.'

'And with our dreams,' Reinmar said, as he replaced the phial in his pouch, taking great care to ensure that the stopper was secure and that the glass was in no danger of breaking.

He knew exactly where he would hide it, once he was home.

ABOUT THE AUTHOR

When asked why he dresses entirely in black, Brian Craig claims to be in mourning for H.P. Lovecraft, but the real reason is too dreadful to reveal. The rumour that he joined the British Antarctic Survey in 1993 'to get away from it all' is false; he failed the medical and had to join the French Foreign Legion under a pseudonym instead. He is not allowed to discuss the reasons for his dishonourable discharge therefrom in 1999, but he is glad that he will now have more time to write and play cricket.

Brian Craig was the author of *Zaragoz, Plague Daemon* and *Storm Warriors* in an earlier range of Warhammer novels, and has contributed short stories to a range of anthologies, including *The Dedalus Book of Femmes Fatales,* edited by Brian Stableford. He is 28 and only looks older because his troubles have aged him.

Also from the Black Library

TROLLSLAYER

A Gotrek & Felix novel
by William King

HIGH ON THE HILL the scorched walled castle stood, a stone spider clutching the hilltop with blasted stone feet. Before the gaping maw of its broken gate hanged men dangled on gibbets, flies caught in its single-strand web.

'Time for some bloodletting,' Gotrek said. He ran his left hand through the massive red crest of hair that rose above his shaven tattooed skull. His nose chain tinkled gently, a strange counterpoint to his mad rumbling laughter.

'I am a slayer, manling. Born to die in battle. Fear has no place in my life.'

TROLLSLAYER IS THE first part of the death saga of Gotrek Gurnisson, as retold by his travelling companion Felix Jaeger. Set in the darkly gothic world of Warhammer, Trollslayer is an episodic novel featuring some of the most extraordinary adventures of this deadly pair of heroes. Monsters, daemons, sorcerers, mutants, orcs, beastmen and worse are to be found as Gotrek strives to achieve a noble death in battle. Felix, of course, only has to survive to tell the tale.

Also from the Black Library

SKAVENSLAYER

A Gotrek & Felix novel
by William King

'BEWARE! SKAVEN!' Felix shouted and saw them all reach for their weapons. In moments, swords glittered in the half-light of the burning city. From inside the tavern a number of armoured figures spilled out into the gloom. Felix was relieved to see the massive squat figure of Gotrek among them. There was something enormously reassuring about the immense axe clutched in the dwarf's hands.

'I see you found our scuttling little friends, manling,' Gotrek said, running his thumb along the blade of his axe until a bright red bead of blood appeared.

'Yes,' Felix gasped, struggling to get his breath back before the combat began.

'Good. Let's get killing then!'

SET IN THE MIGHTY city of Nuln, Gotrek and Felix are back in SKAVENSLAYER, the second novel in this epic saga. Seeking to undermine the very fabric of the Empire with their arcane warp-sorcery, the skaven, twisted Chaos rat-men, are at large in the reeking sewers beneath the ancient city. Led by Grey Seer Thanquol, the servants of the Horned Rat are determined to overthrow this bastion of humanity. Against such forces, what possible threat can just two hard-bitten adventurers pose?

Also from the Black Library

DAEMONSLAYER

A Gotrek & Felix novel
by William King

THE ROAR WAS so loud and so terrifying that Felix almost dropped his blade. He looked up and fought the urge to soil his britches. The most frightening thing he had ever seen had entered the hall and behind it he could see the leering heads of beastmen.

As he gazed on the creature in wonder and terror, Felix thought: this is the incarnate nightmare which has bedevilled my people since time began.

'Just remember,' Gotrek said from beside him, 'the daemon is mine!'

FRESH FROM THEIR adventures battling the foul servants of the rat-god in Nuln, Gotrek and Felix are now ready to join an expedition northwards in search of the long-lost dwarf hall of Karag Dum. Setting forth for the hideous Realms of Chaos in an experimental dwarf airship, Gotrek and Felix are sworn to succeed or die in the attempt. But greater and more sinister energies are coming into play, as a daemonic power is awoken to fulfil its ancient, deadly promise.

Also from the Black Library

REALM OF CHAOS

An anthology of Warhammer stories edited by Marc Gascoigne & Andy Jones

'Markus was confused; the stranger's words were baffling his pain-numbed mind. "Just who are you, foul spawned deviant?"

The warrior laughed again, slapping his hands on his knees. "I am called Estebar. My followers know me as the Master of Slaughter. And I have come for your soul."'
– **The Faithful Servant,** *by Gav Thorpe*

'The wolves are running again. I can hear them panting in the darkness. I race through the forest, trying to outpace them. Behind the wolves I sense another presence, something evil. I am in the place of blood again.' – **Dark Heart,** *by Jonathan Green*

IN THE DARK and gothic world of Warhammer, the ravaging armies of the Ruinous Powers sweep down from the savage north to assail the lands of men. REALM OF CHAOS is a searing collection of a dozen all-action fantasy short stories set in these desperate times.

Also from the Black Library

SPACE WOLF

A Warhammer 40,000 novel
by William King

Ragnar leapt up from his hiding place, bolt pistol spitting death. The nightgangers could not help but notice where he was, and with a mighty roar of frenzied rage they raced towards him. Ragnar answered their war cry with a wolfish howl of his own, and was reassured to hear it echoed back from the throats of the surrounding Blood Claws. He pulled the trigger again and again as the frenzied mass of mutants approached, sending bolter shell after bolter shell rocketing into his targets. Ragnar laughed aloud, feeling the full battle rage come upon him. The beast roared within his soul, demanding to be unleashed.

In the grim future of Warhammer 40,000, the Space Marines of the Adeptus Astartes are humanity's last hope. On the planet Fenris, young Ragnar is chosen to be inducted into the noble yet savage Space Wolves chapter. But with his ancient primal instincts unleashed by the implanting of the sacred Canis Helix, Ragnar must learn to control the beast within and fight for the greater good of the wolf pack.

Also from the Black Library

RAGNAR'S CLAW

A Warhammer 40,000 novel
by William King

One of the enemy oficers, wearing the peaked cap and greatcoat of a lieutenant, dared to stick his head above the parapet. Without breaking stride, Ragnar raised his bolt pistol and put a shell through the man's head. It exploded like a melon hit with a sledgehammer. Shouts of confusion echoed from behind the wall of sandbags, then a few heretics, braver and more experienced than the rest, stuck their heads up in order to take a shot at their attackers. Another mistake: a wave of withering fire from the Space Marines behind Ragnar scythed through them, sending their corpses tumbling back amongst their comrades.

FROM THE DEATH-WORLD of Fenris come the Space Wolves, the most savage of the Emperor's Space Marines. Ragnar's Claw explores the bloody beginnings of Space Wolf Ragnar's first mission as a young Blood Claw warrior. From the jungle hell of Galt to the polluted cities of Hive World Venam, Ragnar's mission takes him on an epic trek across the galaxy to face the very heart of Evil itself.

Also from the Black Library

FIRST & ONLY

A Gaunt's Ghosts novel
by Dan Abnett

'THE TANITH ARE strong fighters, general, so I have heard.' The scar tissue of his cheek pinched and twitched slightly, as it often did when he was tense. 'Gaunt is said to be a resourceful leader.'

'You know him?' The general looked up, questioningly.

'I know *of* him, sir. In the main by reputation.'

GAUNT GOT TO his feet, wet with blood and Chaos pus. His Ghosts were moving up the ramp to secure the position. Above them, at the top of the elevator shaft, were over a million Shriven, secure in their bunker batteries. Gaunt's expeditionary force was inside, right at the heart of the enemy stronghold. Commissar Ibram Gaunt smiled.

IT IS THE nightmare future of Warhammer 40,000, and mankind teeters on the brink of extinction. The galaxy-spanning Imperium is riven with dangers, and in the Chaos-infested Sabbat system, Imperial Commissar Gaunt must lead his men through as much in-fighting amongst rival regiments as against the forces of Chaos. FIRST AND ONLY is an epic saga of planetary conquest, grand ambition, treachery and honour.

Also from the Black Library

GHOSTMAKER

A Gaunt's Ghosts novel
by Dan Abnett

THEY WERE A good two hours into the dark, black-trunked forests, tracks churning the filthy ooze and the roar of their engines resonating from the sickly canopy of leaves above, when Colonel Ortiz saw death.

It wore red, and stood in the trees to the right of the track, in plain sight, unmoving, watching his column of Basilisks as they passed along the trackway. It was the lack of movement that chilled Ortiz.

Almost twice a man's height, frighteningly broad, armour the colour of rusty blood, crested by recurve brass antlers. The face was a graven death's head. Daemon. Chaos Warrior. *World Eater!*

IN THE NIGHTMARE future of Warhammer 40,000, mankind teeters on the brink of extinction. The Imperial Guard are humanity's first line of defence against the remorseless assaults of the enemy. For the men of the Tanith First-and-Only and their fearless commander, Commissar Ibram Gaunt, it is a war in which they must be prepared to lay down, not just their bodies, but their very souls.

Also from the Black Library

INTO THE MAELSTROM

An anthology of Warhammer 40,000 stories, edited by Marc Gascoigne & Andy Jones

'THE CHAOS ARMY had travelled from every continent, every shattered city, every ruined sector of Illium to gather on this patch of desert that had once been the control centre of the Imperial Garrison. The sand beneath their feet had been scorched, melted and fused by a final, futile act of suicidal defiance: the detonation of the garrison's remaining nuclear stockpile.' – **Hell in a Bottle** *by Simon Jowett*

'HOARSE SCREAMS and the screech of tortured hot metal filled the air. Massive laser blasts were punching into the spaceship. They superheated the air that men breathed, set fire to everything that could burn and sent fireballs exploding through the crowded passageways.' – **Children of the Emperor** *by Barrington J. Bayley*

IN THE GRIM and gothic nightmare future of Warhammer 40,000, mankind teeters on the brink of extinction. INTO THE MAELSTROM is a storming collection of a dozen action-packed science fiction short stories set in this dark and brooding universe.

Also from the Black Library

STATUS: DEADZONE

An anthology of Necromunda stories, edited by Marc Gascoigne & Andy Jones

'Knife-Edge Liz closed on Terrak Ran'Lo. The old man was moving for cover, crouching behind a side-table. She fell upon him, dragging him to the ground. His breath was wine-rancid, his eyes glazed with age. He looked at the woman, her face sprayed with the blood of the inquisitor, and his eyes span.

"A message from the Underhive," Liz spat and pulled the trigger.' – **Rat in the Walls** *by Alex Hammond*

'Outside the Last Gasp Saloon, Nathan Creed examined the scrap of parchment. If the map was genuine, Toxic Sump's dome was built directly on top of another, much older settlement. Who knew what ancient treasures lay buried beneath the ash? Creed took the cheroot from his mouth and spat into the dust. The prospector had known. Now he was dead.' – **Bad Spirits** *by Jonathan Green*

ON THE SAVAGE factory world of Necromunda, renegade gangs struggle for survival in the shattered tunnels and domes beneath the teeming hive-cities. STATUS: DEADZONE is an awesome anthology of dark science fiction short stories from the devastated urban hell of Necromunda.